The Next Big Thing

Also by Sadie Hayes

The Social Code

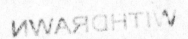

The Next Big Thing

A Social Code Novel

Sadie Hayes

St. Martin's Griffin ❧ New York

THE NEXT BIG THING. Copyright © 2013 by Palindrome, LLC. All rights reserved. Printed in the United States of America. For information, address St. Martin's Press, 175 Fifth Avenue, New York, N.Y. 10010.

www.stmartins.com

Design by Anna Gorovoy

Library of Congress Cataloging-in-Publication Data

Hayes, Sadie.
  The next big thing / Sadie Hayes.
      p. cm.
  ISBN 978-1-250-03568-4 (trade paperback)
  ISBN 978-1-250-03569-1 (e-book)
  1. Universities and colleges—Fiction.   2. New business enterprises—Fiction.
3. Brothers and sisters—Fiction.   4. Twins—Fiction.   5. Social classes—
Fiction.   6. Orphans—Fiction.   I. Title.
  PZ7.H3148727Nex 2013
  [Fic]—dc23

                                                                2013018115

St. Martin's Griffin books may be purchased for educational, business, or promotional use. For information on bulk purchases, please contact Macmillan Corporate and Premium Sales Department at 1-800-221-7945, extension 5442, or write specialmarkets@macmillan.com.

First Edition: November 2013

10 9 8 7 6 5 4 3 2 1

Ron Conway, John Doerr, Heidi Roizen, Roger McNamee, Guy Kawasaki, Mary Meeker, Jack Dorsey, Tina Seelig, Tim Draper, Michael Dearing, Bill Gurley, and Brendan Fitzgerald Wallace.

Thanks to all for being an inspiration. And thanks especially for having a combined four million Twitter followers. #SocialCode @DigitalSadie

Acknowledgments

As a writer, I feel infinitely privileged to have had a piece in the Social Code project, which was the culmination of so much vision and energy and work. Dan Kessler and Panio Gianopolous: there are no words to capture my respect and appreciation—your talent is so real and inspiring, and your trust in me has been nothing short of transformative. Thank you also to Carey Albertine, whose support and vision are a constant source of energy and wisdom. And of course, a special thanks to Jennifer Weis and the St. Martin's Press team, and to our evangelist Susie Finesman for bringing it all together.

Part I

Reverse Engineering

All Hands on Pitch Deck

Adam Dory felt the impending doom of his own suffocation as the walls closed in on each other and the air left the room. He could feel T.J. and Amelia on either side, oblivious to what was happening to them. The two just sat there, trapping him as if they enjoyed watching his potential slowly peter out.

"I'm not going to sugarcoat this: I don't believe in your team."

Adam concentrated his eyes on the venture capitalist, Ross Brown, who sat at the table before which the three Doreye cofounders stood, delivering this news.

He wished T.J. and Amelia would go away. Especially Amelia. People didn't treat her like a prima donna because she wasn't girly, but she had lately become the worst kind of high maintenance. Worse than any of the sorority girls Adam knew. She took every opportunity to blabber on about Internet freedom, and insisted they not charge users for any of Doreye's services. She acted like her programming was the only thing in this company that mattered, despite seeing how hard Adam—whose job it was to make money—worked.

"Your product is one of the best I've ever seen. The design is flawless, the user experience unmatched. And your business model is really provocative," Ross Brown went on, referring to the

PowerPoint presentation Adam had just delivered, a fifty-page deck of slides articulating the business plan he'd slaved over for the past three weeks in preparation for this meeting. It was because of Adam's hard work that they were now asking Pingree Kort Collins, one of the world's most prestigious venture capital firms, for a ten-million-dollar investment. That they were sitting across from Ross Brown, the firm's most prolific partner, was a testament to their success.

"Unfortunately, plans and products aren't the only pieces of a company: The team is critical, and I'm concerned about you three."

"Do you mind if I ask why?" T.J. piped up, his voice shaking in an effort to control his frustration. Adam clenched his jaw. He knew T.J. was going to try to blame this on him, and it made him furious. If the team wasn't doing well, it was because T.J. was too busy working out and schmoozing with investors to do any actual work. What did he care? Unlike Adam, who had no money and two-and-a-half more years of college to get through, T.J. had graduated and was already rich. For him, Doreye was just another toy, like his BMW, to show off to girls.

Ross Brown lifted his eyebrows and tilted his head, studying T.J. as if to discern whether he really wanted to know. The two junior partners at the table smiled surreptitiously at their boss, like hyenas eager to witness a mauling.

He undid the buttons at his wrists and rolled up the sleeves of his crisp white shirt, showing off his tanned and muscular forearms.

"For starters, none of you has any experience." T.J. started to protest, but Ross cut him off. "And no, T.J., watching your father invest in start-ups does not count. In addition, you've got competing male egos in T.J. and Adam and competing sibling egos in Adam and Amelia." Ross paused. "Which might lead you to believe Adam is the problem, were it not for the fact that eliminating Adam would leave just T.J. and Amelia, who would never get any actual work done since T.J.'s too distracted by girls and Amelia would rather write code than make money."

The hyenas smiled, their eyes darting across the three victims before them.

Adam looked at T.J., whose face was red, either from blushing or with rage. "So what do you suggest we do?" T.J. asked firmly.

Ross Brown shrugged and sat back in his chair. "For starters, define your roles."

"What do you mean?"

"None of you has a title. If you want to make this work, you need to be very clear. Who is responsible for what? Amelia should obviously be chief technology officer, responsible purely for the product and its development. Take her out of the business side of things entirely. She gets no say in how you make money."

Adam watched his sister drop her head as she toyed with the zipper on her hoodie. Finally, Ross was saying something that made sense.

"T.J. should be CEO, obviously, given his connections, his age and experience, and his ability to talk confidently when presenting."

Adam's jaw fell open. T.J.? CEO? Adam should be CEO. He'd just delivered a twenty-minute speech about Doreye; was he not "talking confidently when presenting"?

"What am I then?" he heard himself blurt.

Ross smiled, pleased with himself for predicting exactly how Adam would react. "You're chief operating officer, in charge of execution."

"Execution?"

"Yes. You're the only one hungry enough to make this thing work. Amelia builds the product and T.J. is out talking about it. You make sure the company functions and that the right people are in the right positions."

"I'm human resources? HR?" Adam choked. Was Ross Brown seriously suggesting that Adam's value was hiring and firing people and making sure they remembered to submit their expenses on time?

"COO may not be the most glamorous role, but it's critical. And human resources is *the* most critical of all. If you'd been listening to me three minutes ago you might have noticed that the whole reason I'm passing on this investment is because I don't believe in your team." Ross's voice was irritated. "That's your human resources," he said sardonically, glaring at Adam for a moment before standing up from the table, the hyenas following his lead. Adam felt his face flush.

"On that note, I've got another meeting. Keep me informed of progress. If you're able to address some of the issues we've talked about, I'd be happy to give Doreye another look. As I said, it's one of the most promising products I've seen in quite some time, but you've got a lot of work to do."

Ross and the hyenas let the door of the conference room fall shut behind them. The tension in the room was thick, and Amelia could feel her heart pounding, afraid to look up at T.J. or her brother. Things hadn't been very organized since they'd gotten back from Maui—Amelia would sometimes go days without seeing either of them—but she was embarrassed to know outsiders like Ross were talking about it.

"I think he's right," T.J. said, finally breaking the silence.

"Of course you do," Adam jumped in angrily. "You want to be in charge."

"Someone needs to be," T.J. snapped. "And clearly neither of you is capable of it."

"I'm sorry?"

"Amelia doesn't even want us to make money, and you're too afraid of her to insist we do." T.J. was talking only to Adam, as if she weren't even there. She looked up defensively.

"I—" she tried to interject softly.

"What?" T.J. turned to her, irritated. "You don't."

"I just think—" Amelia's desire to keep Doreye free for users and open-source for developers had been a hot button, and she was struggling to articulate to T.J. and Adam why nothing on the Internet should be about making money.

"I know what you think," T.J. said, cutting her off, "and it doesn't make any sense. At least not if you want an actual company—which I think you do, don't you?"

She nodded and looked at the floor. She missed the version of T.J. who used to defend her, like he did when that reporter in Maui cornered her about the juvenile detention center. What had happened to that T.J.?

"Wouldn't you rather be off the hook for any of these conversations? Haven't you always been saying you just want to go back to coding?" T.J. pressed. It was true.

"Yes." Amelia didn't look up. She thought, *And I want the nice you back.*

"Good. Then you're CTO. That's all you do now: no more on the business side."

"I'm not being COO," Adam said, bringing the attention back to him. "It's demeaning."

"It's your only choice."

"Since when do you get to decide?" Adam was fuming.

"I don't," T.J. said. His whole body was taut, focused on what he wanted. "The three of us make decisions by majority vote. So it's up to Amelia."

Her head jolted up at the sound of her name. T.J.'s blue eyes were piercing into her, as though he could see her whole heart exposed. He took a step forward and placed his hand on her shoulder, close to her neck, so that his hot fingers rested on the skin near her collar. "What do you think, Amelia?" he asked softly, kindly. That was it; that was the T.J. she missed.

"I think you should be CEO," she said softly, looking into his eyes.

"Oh, this is such bullshit." Adam threw up his arms.

His voice made Amelia snap out of her T.J. trance. "What, Adam? T.J. makes more sense as CEO, you know that."

"No, I don't."

"He's older and more . . . polished," Amelia tried.

T.J. smiled at the support and let it make him generous. "And here's the thing, Adam. If I don't do a good job, you can fire me."

"What?"

"As head of HR, you can fire me if I don't do a good job."

"Why don't I just fire you right now, then?" Adam said, and snarled.

"Because you need me," T.J. said with equal intensity. "And you know that."

Amelia's eyes darted between the two men, their eyes locked on each other. Ross was right: They were competing, but Amelia wasn't sure over what. She didn't know a lot about these things, but felt like if they could just work together they'd actually get a lot done.

"Fine," Adam spat. "I don't even care anymore."

"I hope that's not true; we need you," T.J. said in his newly adopted CEO tone.

"Oh, screw you," Adam said, rolling his eyes as he picked up his backpack and headed for the door. "I have to go to a meeting. I hope you're happy," he flung at Amelia before letting the door slam behind him.

Amelia let her eyelids flutter up to look at T.J., but he was packing his presentation materials into his messenger bag and not looking at her.

"I think that was the right thing to do," she told him.

"I know it was," he answered without looking up.

She let her incisor pinch the inside of her lip until it went numb.

"You've got to let me handle the business side of things now, okay, Amelia?" He finally looked up.

She swallowed and nodded.

"This is really serious." His face said as much. He lowered his voice and glanced around as if checking for hidden cameras in the conference room. "We have enough money to last us for six more weeks, then we're done, okay? Like, *done,* done. We've got to raise money or all of this"—he gestured around the room—"all of this goes away."

"I understand," she said softly.

"Good."

2

My Milk Shake Brings All the Boys to the Yard

"Could I have some whipped cream, please?" Patty Hawkins asked the waitress at Peninsula Creamery as she reached for the syrup to smother her Belgian waffle. It was Saturday just before noon, she was ravenous from a late-night party at SAE, and her boyfriend (if she could really call him that; they hadn't exactly DTR'ed yet) had left their booth to take a call just as they sat down fifteen minutes ago.

The waitress returned with a dish of whipped cream, and Patty dolloped it generously onto the oversize waffle, sticking the covered spoon into her mouth as she glared at Alex through the window, pacing back and forth on the sidewalk while speaking excitedly into his phone and using lots of hand gestures as if to better get across his point to the person on the other end of the call.

She was seated at a red vinyl booth in the corner, the one they always sat in on Saturdays. Well, always meaning the previous five Saturdays, not counting the first Saturday, when they sat at the counter of the diner. Although Patty loved this Palo Alto institution, she hated sitting at the counter and only did it that one time because the hostess on duty was new and didn't recognize Patty or realize who her family was. The hostess had since been corrected, and so, every Saturday, Patty and Alex sat in the corner booth and were provided a complimentary bag of homemade white chocolate macadamia-nut cookies with their check, which Patty always accepted graciously and with her best attempt at surprise.

Patty put one piece of waffle in her mouth after the other, hardly swallowing in between, and studied the family at a table in the center of the restaurant. The mother—a blond woman with a Bar Method physique—leaned across the table to cut her eldest child's pancakes while pulling a ketchup bottle out of reach of a toddler in a high chair while thanking the waitress for bringing a towel to clean up the milk shake that the latter had just knocked over. Her husband, a clean-cut blond man in khakis and a polo, was giving her a thumbs-up from the hostess stand, where he was apparently receiving good news through the cell phone pressed to his ear, but she failed to notice.

Is this where I'm headed? she thought to herself as she chewed another gooey bite. Without looking down, she speared a strawberry from Alex's plate and stuffed it between her lips to join the bread and syrup and cream already there. *And would things have been different with Chad?*

She had to stop thinking about him. But she couldn't. She kept thinking about the ice cream on her leg, about the car, about the waterfall and her heart beating with equal parts competition and sexual attraction.

She hadn't heard from him since Hawaii—none of them had. Or maybe Shandi had, but clearly she'd never know that. They'd all just pretended like none of it ever happened, and now Shandi was reengaged, to a guy named Sean, and Mr. Hawkins was happy because Sean was a great golfer. Mrs. Hawkins was happy, too, because Sean's mother was not nearly as attractive as Chad's mother had been, so she'd have the advantage in all the wedding photos and those that followed after.

And so maybe love and marriage really were that fickle. Maybe it was just about finding the person who fit your hobbies and your income and your respective level of attractiveness. So that when you were cleaning up milk shakes for kids who wouldn't sit still, you didn't mind that your husband was on the phone because you knew you'd go play golf together later and whatever he was doing on the phone would ensure you had enough money to pay for Bar Method classes and a babysitter to watch the kids while you went to them.

Kind of like how they'd had enough money to pay someone to return all the wedding gifts and to send Shandi to study under a grand master at the Sorbonne so that they could make up a believable story that Shandi had gotten a call the night of her rehearsal dinner offering her the highly coveted position. So that narratives of heartbreaking postponement of true love in the service of once-in-a-lifetime tutelage and contribution to the Academy could emerge and triumph in Atherton. Oh yes, they all ate it up: That diligent, brilliant Shandi Hawkins, foregoing an easy path with a hot young husband to support her, chose instead to pursue a passionate interest in art that would take her around the globe studying old relics, consequently unable to begin a life with a man who was probably unworthy of her to begin with.

"Shandi Hawkins the free spirit," they'd say with envious admiration. "Shandi Hawkins, who chose life over love," they'd tell one another before and after their Pilates class. Shandi Hawkins, who avoided their own fate by freeing herself from the shackles of suburban life. It was a triumph for the kind of lives they wished they'd had the courage to lead.

Never mind that the Sorbonne opportunity had in fact come about after several calls made upon the family's return from Hawaii. Never mind that the real reason Shandi stood Chad up at the altar was because she'd run into her old fling, Sean, on the beach at the Four Seasons, where he was attending the Tech-Crunch conference. Never mind that T. J. Bristol was the one who walked in on Shandi embracing her new lover while still wearing her wedding dress. Never mind that Shandi pleaded with T.J. to break the news to Chad, who was standing on the altar waiting for her to appear.

And never mind that Shandi and Sean were engaged one month later, Shandi having apparently decided she could maintain all-consuming commitment to her work while planning a new wedding and life with him.

Chad deserved better anyway. Chad deserved Patty.

"You won't believe what just happened!" Alex returned to the table, wide-eyed and grinning. "TechCrunch just tweeted about us!"

"That's great," Patty said, forcing an enthusiastic smile as she reached her fork across the table to his strawberry-covered waffle, her own plate now clean. He didn't seem to notice.

"Seriously, Patty, can you believe it? I mean, we've only been going for two months. We're hardly off the ground, and here TechCrunch already wants to feature us!"

"They're not really *featuring* you, are they?" Patty grimaced.

"Feature, tweet, whatever. They've already picked us up, Patty! That's such a good sign of what a great idea this is. And this'll totally help us get an engineer."

Alex, a fifth-year senior at Stanford, had signed up for a class at the design school because, thanks to having spent his first four years majoring in football, he still needed twelve units to graduate and heard it was an easy three. Two months ago, he and his friend from the team, Bo, had come up with an idea for an iPhone app that facilitated the late-night delivery of fast food to drunken college kids. As seniors on the football team, Alex and Bo had routinely hazed freshmen teammates by making them drive to In-N-Out at 2:00 A.M. and bring them back burgers when they got the munchies.

"Don't you see, Patty? We're solving a major pain point for people. First of all, people get their drunk snacks. Second, underclassmen can make a little money. Third and finally, we're preventing drunk driving, so the university should be really supportive. TechCrunch totally gets that, and that's why they're writing about us."

Patty took a sip of her Diet Coke. "No offense, Alex, but Tech-Crunch tweets like a thousand times a day—are you sure you're not getting ahead of yourself? You don't even have an engineer to program the app."

Alex's grin faded. "Jesus, Patty. All due respect, but you don't understand how this works, okay? I get that your dad's a venture capitalist, but you've never started a company before. You have no idea what an accomplishment this is."

Patty glanced at the mother of two, her food untouched as she handled her children, her husband still on the phone.

"You're right," she offered softly.

"You have no idea how emotionally volatile the past two months have been. I know we've been hanging out all that time, but you seriously have only seen like this much of what I've been going through." He pinched his fingers to indicate how little anguish, frustration, and stress she'd seen. "I mean, this could be my destiny, you know? I could be, like, the next Zuckerberg."

Patty couldn't help but laugh, and immediately choked on her Diet Coke, but Alex was so caught up in his vision that he didn't notice.

"Crap—what if it's too early? What if someone steals our idea now?" Alex's excitement suddenly turned to dismay. "You know we had a focus group the other day—I bet that's how it happened. I bet someone in the focus group leaked it to the press."

She reached across to eat more of his waffle, which he still had not touched.

"I bet it was that Mormon kid. Frank or Franklyn or Frick or something. Honestly, I don't mean to sound racist or anything, but I don't trust those guys at all. They're too nice and too smart and too blond, all of them."

"Why don't you target Mormons?" Patty asked.

"What?" Alex snapped. "What are you talking about?"

"For your company. Why don't you target the Mormon students? They don't drink. They're incredibly responsible. They could be your drivers."

"I can't think about that right now, Patty; I have to figure out how to make sure our IP's protected." Alex's head was really swimming now. "Babe, I gotta go call Bo. I think we need to get an attorney. Do you mind?"

Patty inhaled deeply and shook her head. "Go for it; I'll get the check," she said, but he was already out the door.

3

300 Words or Less

"You have two weeks to finish whatever assignment you owe Marsh or this *U* on your transcript is going to become an *F*, and you'll have to retake your social science requirement." Adam's academic advisor, Professor Johns, a chubby historian who wore thick black glasses and combed his thinning brown hair over in a heavy side part, peered at him from across the wide desk.

"And unlike some teachers at this school who might let you withdraw, Marsh *will* fail you and it *will* affect your GPA in a serious way." Johns put his finger up to Adam as his chest puffed and puffed and he let out a gigantic sneeze. "Excuse me," he said as he pulled out a handkerchief to wipe his snotty nose.

Adam focused on his upper lip to keep it from grimacing and giving away his disgust. He had spent the entire morning thinking about how he was going to confront T.J. about the investor meeting the other day. Adam had changed his mind: He should be CEO and he was ready to fight for it.

"What do you have left to do for him, anyway?" the advisor asked Adam, bringing him back to the room.

Adam shrugged at how unimportant this was compared to the other issues on his mind and said stubbornly, "It was almost a year ago. I was called on and perfectly described the prisoner's dilemma, but Professor Marsh found it . . . disrespectful. So he asked me to write some stupid paper about what I'd rather be doing than sitting in his lecture hall. It doesn't even have anything to do with political science. I aced every single test we had—like, *aced* them. If it weren't for this, I would have had the highest grade in the entire class. It's bullshit."

"No language, son," Johns snapped. "Professors have their right to make requirements of their students, and Marsh is not an unreasonable man. I'm sure whatever he asked you to do is perfectly in line. Now, if you'll excuse me, I've got to run to teach a group of imbecile freshmen the significance of the French Revolution whilst they disregard Napoleon Bonaparte in favor of their Facebook newsfeeds," Johns said, and snorted as he pushed his heavy body up from his chair.

"You're a smart kid, Adam. Don't waste your moral indignation on Marsh."

Adam conceded that this wasn't a battle he had time to fight. He collected his bag and plodded down the worn carpeted stairs into the main quad, where a large group of Asian tourists in sunhats took photographs and listened eagerly to a chipper tour guide lecturing them on the tough admissions requirements for undergraduates these days. Adam recognized the tour guide— Lindy Shorenstein—from the frat house. She was an SAE groupie: one of the girls who constantly got enormously drunk and hung out in the lounge, inevitably ending up in bed with one of the six or seven guys in the house who would have her. Adam had run into her this morning wearing a tight, short skirt from the night before and stealing a Pop-Tart from the kitchen as she walked, barefoot, back to her sorority house. He wondered what the smiling-and-nodding Asian tourists would think if they'd known.

Adam snickered to himself, but Lindy's eye caught him as he walked past. She waved enthusiastically and belted to the group, loud enough for him to hear, "And that"—she pointed—"is Adam Dory! Adam is one of our famed en-tre-pre-neurs. Lots of

Stanford students start companies, but only a few of them succeed." She paused for effect. "And if you ask me," she said, turning
to Adam and winking, "Adam Dory might just be the next Steve
Jobs."

The crowd oohed and aahed and Adam, helpless, blushed.

He waved and smiled, politely at the tourists and genuinely
at Lindy, ducked his head, and hurried to Green Library. He
swiped his ID card at the turnstile and climbed the stairs, scan-
ning the room for the most uncomfortable chair available, and
found it at a metal desk in the corner of the medieval history
section facing a blank, windowless wall.

He sat down at the desk, unfolded his laptop, and opened a
blank Word document.

What I Would Rather Be Doing Than This
By Adam Dory

Adam typed, then watched his cursor flash on the screen,
waiting for inspiration.

I would rather be:

Working out.
Drinking beer.
Hooking up with Lindy.

He paused. Then typed rapidly.

Cuddling with Lisa.
Smelling her hair.
Kissing her neck.

He sat up and jabbed at the "Delete" key angrily. As he was
doing so, a Skype message popped up in the corner. The message
was from Ted Bristol.

Ted_Bristol:
Heard about the investor meeting. U OK?

Adam sighed and responded: *Sucks*. He paused before continuing:

DoryAdam:
Sometimes I wonder why I bother working so hard if I'm just going to keep getting put down. No offense to your son, but I'm going to tell T.J. I'm CEO or I'm done.

Adam had quite fortuitously met Ted Bristol at a beachside bar in Hawaii. At the time, Ted didn't know that this young, ambitious entrepreneur was Amelia Dory's brother, and Adam didn't know that this kind, thoughtful Scotch drinker was his girlfriend Lisa and coworker T.J.'s father. But Ted had sent Adam an e-mail following the meeting, and slowly became a mentor. Adam had never really thought about why Ted had taken such an interest in him, but he was glad he had. It was nice having someone in his corner, someone to take his side. After all, the great venture capitalist Roger Fenway—who had discovered Amelia—always took her side. It was nice having someone who understood the impulsiveness of T.J. and Amelia and the constant challenges Adam faced working with them.

Ted had asked Adam to keep their business relationship a secret, which bothered Adam a little bit. He wanted the world to know that someone as smart as Ted Bristol recognized that Adam was the real deal. But on the other hand, Adam had kept his relationship with Lisa a secret from Ted, so he owed it to him to respect his privacy wishes, whatever the reason.

Ted_Bristol:
Don't do that. You've got to be in this for the long term.
DoryAdam:
Long term? It's been almost a year.

Ted_Bristol:
A year is nothing. Be smart about this and your time will come.
DoryAdam:
But COO's a bullshit role.
Ted_Bristol:
Every role is what you make it. Good entrepreneurs make every situation work to their advantage.
DoryAdam:
I'm not seeing it.
Ted_Bristol:
COO lets you set things up the way you want them when you take over.
DoryAdam:
When do I take over?
Ted_Bristol:
You'll know.
DoryAdam:
But T.J.'s going to get all the credit no matter what I do.
Ted_Bristol:
Do you want credit or power?

The cursor blinked in front of him but Adam didn't know how to answer. He finally typed.

DoryAdam:
Both
? Is that wrong?
Ted_Bristol:
Ha no. But you have to be patient. Your moment will come. And in the meantime you can't let your emotions get in the way.

Adam thought back on how the investors had responded to him in the meeting the other day. They hung on his every word. When Ross criticized the team, he wasn't talking about Adam: He was talking about the other two. Ted was right; he just had to be patient, to sort out the issues with T.J. and Amelia in a way that appeased Ross, and at the same time work hard to prove to everyone that he should be in charge when the company got big.

DoryAdam:
You're totally right
Ted_Bristol:
I know. This ain't my first rodeo, Adam.
DoryAdam:
Where are you Skyping from?
Ted_Bristol:
London.
DoryAdam:
Whoa!
Ted_Bristol:
Just here for quick business. Listen, though: keep your head up. You're almost there. You'll be on top soon enough. Got 2 go.

With that, Ted was gone, but Adam felt differently as he moved back to his Word document.

He took a deep breath, smiled, and felt his fingers start moving.

I would rather be creating, building, and running a company.

I'm sick of being a nobody. I'm sick of not being as smart as my sister or as confident as guys in the fraternity or as privileged as snobs from Atherton.

I'm sick of doing the classwork, getting the highest marks for it, and then getting a U because, for once, I behaved like a normal college kid and got distracted by normal college kid things. I'm sick of having to be the responsible one. Of having to work and go to school and start a company and watch out for my sister and do it all with no parents and no money and no girlfriend.

I want to start a company because I want something that's

mine. That I can point to and say, "I'm not as rich or as good-looking or as smart, I don't have everything, but I've got something. And it's mine. And it matters."

I want to show the people who doubted me and ignored me that they shouldn't have: I knew what I was doing. I had a plan. And look at me! Just look at how GOOD I am at this. Because I may be good at acing Political Science tests but I'm DAMN good at running Doreye. Better than T. J. Bristol, even if he gets the credit at first, and better than Amelia, even if she is a genius.

And having those eyes on me—the investors' and Lindy's and the Asian tourists'—that makes me feel . . . alive.

I'm sorry for not paying attention, but I'm not sorry for having something more important that I need to do. Because this—Doreye—is more important than the prisoner's dilemma. It's bigger. And I'm going to show the world.

Word Count: 301

Adam's hands lifted from the keyboard, where he'd been typing furiously. He stared at the words on the page before him as if in disbelief. Where had all that come from? Those words? That ferocity of feeling?

Adam looked up at the cement wall. A spider crawled across a crack in the paint toward its web on the ceiling. He knew what he had to do.

4

Sharp as Nails

"Downtown? Mani-pedis at Simply Be?" Patty texted her mother.

She knew it didn't matter whether she was downtown or not; ever since the wedding, Chloe Hawkins had been on a mother-daughter bonding kick. She was convinced that Shandi's wedding debacle had been her fault—that she hadn't provided sound and sufficient womanly advice. And that was *Shandi,* with whom she spoke regularly and had a close relationship. *Patty* was an enigma to her, the daughter she'd never fully been "in touch with," which put her in even greater danger of ill-advised decisions that carried power to tarnish the family name.

Patty, naturally, milked this: Whenever she wanted a shopping trip or lunch at Evvia, she'd text her mother suggesting they get together, and Mrs. Hawkins would be right there.

But this afternoon it wasn't just the sudden horror that it was February and her toes were still painted for Malibu a summery Strawberry Margarita shade that made her reach out for a mom date at the Simply Be nail salon (though the new purple shade Susie Barrett was wearing in class the other day was a significant catalyst). Patty's head was still spinning from yesterday's brunch with Alex, and she wasn't sure where to turn.

"Just got off tennis court. Can b there in 20—pick u up?" her mother replied.

"No I'll meet you there," Patty texted back.

"Perf!"

Her iPhone vibrated with the message. Patty rolled her eyes at her mother's attempts to be cool with text abbreviations. This whole mother-daughter thing was going to take some getting used to.

"Thank you, ChaiLai," Patty said, handing her regular manicurist the bottle of Midnight Plum she'd selected as the appropriately close-but-not-copying-Susie shade. ChaiLai, a true artist with a nail file, approved the color before ushering Patty into the massage chair.

"Cute color!" Chloe Hawkins exclaimed. "I'll take that, too!"

Patty gave her mother a look.

"What? A woman can't take fashion advice from her hip daughter?" She grinned at Patty, and then at ChaiLai for support, her face still flushed from tennis.

Patty sighed. "Whatever, Mom."

Mother and daughter sat in silence as the women at their feet chattered away in their native Thai.

Mrs. Hawkins finally broke the silence. "Something on your mind?"

The moment she'd seen her mother, decked out in a short white tennis skirt and matching spandex top, an outfit far too tight for any mother of two to justifiably wear, even if she did have a body any normal mother of two would envy, Patty realized that she'd made a mistake.

"No," Patty said, reaching for a magazine in her purse. "Why?"

Mrs. Hawkins lifted an eyebrow. "You texted me for a thirty-dollar pedicure. You never text me when the bill's under three hundred dollars."

Patty felt her face flush as she looked at the magazine—it had never occurred to her that her mother had realized her scheme.

Chloe went on: "So I figured something must be up that you

can't talk to one of your girlfriends about. And I fully understand if you've changed your mind and don't want to talk to me about it, but I know you've already read that issue of *Vogue*, so if you get bored, I'm here."

Patty turned her head skeptically. "How do you know I've already read this issue?"

"Because it's the January issue. And you've read every issue of *Vogue* on the day it arrived since you were fifteen years old."

It was true: Patty knew the day the magazine arrived in the mail (the seventh, or the soonest weekday after) and always planned two hours to cuddle up with a cup of Earl Grey and peruse its pages, a once-a-month ritual she treasured.

She folded the magazine in her lap. "Okay, fine."

"Don't feel pressured," her mother said, laughing. "I'm just saying I'm here."

"It's Alex."

Her mother took a deep breath.

Patty sighed and went on. "Yesterday we were at the Creamery and he was on his cell phone the whole time for his stupid company. And I'm happy for him—I really am—I mean, I always knew he was more than a dumb jock, and I think this is really showing him that he is, too. I mean, that he has more potential than just playing sports. But, Mom, the company is . . ."

She stopped, afraid to say it.

Mrs. Hawkins pressed her. "The company is . . . ?"

She sat up, changing her mind about what she was going to say. "Well, it's doing great. I mean, TechCrunch just tweeted about it. And Alex thinks that really means it's going places, and maybe—I mean, he's probably right." She looked up at her mother. "And that's great, right?"

"It is," her mother agreed.

"So why am I not happy for him?"

Mrs. Hawkins rolled her lips into each other and searched her daughter's face before responding. "That's a brave thing to admit. What does your gut tell you?"

"What do you mean?"

"When you're listening to him talk about the company, what are you feeling, if not happiness?"

Patty looked over to the window and thought back on yesterday. "Annoyance," she finally answered, turning back to face her mother. "I felt really annoyed."

"What was annoying about it?"

"It's a stupid idea," Patty said. "It's not a business. It's a one-off college kid app that about twelve people will use and nobody will pay for, and he's treating it like it's the next frickin' Google."

Mrs. Hawkins let out an understanding chuckle. Which made Patty laugh, too, at how ridiculous it sounded when she said it out loud.

"And I'm sitting there, Mom, trying to be supportive, but I just can't stop thinking about how *stupid* this is, and how he's not even doing it right. I mean, he doesn't even have an engineer. And he thinks all these freshmen—who by the way don't have cars—are just going to sign up to drive around to deliver food to drunk upperclassmen late at night. At least I suggested he use the upperclass Mormon students as drivers."

"That's a clever idea, actually," Mrs. Hawkins inserted.

"Right? I thought so," Patty agreed. "But anyway, I think I was annoyed because . . . well, because I just feel like he's acting like it's such a huge deal, and honestly, Mom, anyone could do it. Does that make me a bad girlfriend?"

Mrs. Hawkins took another deep breath. "Can I tell you a story?"

"Yes," Patty said, feeling surprisingly affectionate toward her mother all of a sudden and open to a good lecture.

"Around fifteen years ago, when your father and I had just moved you and Shandi to California, he comes home talking about these two engineers he met at Stanford and this computer thing they're building in a garage in Menlo Park. The Internet is a totally new concept, but these guys have figured out a way to sort all of this information on 'the Net' and rank which Web sites were more important than others. And your dad, bless him, can't stop thinking about this company and how interesting the technology is. He keeps going on and on with algorithm this and algorithm that. And he wants to put all of our money—we didn't have much then—into these two guys named Larry and Sergey."

The pumice stone was making Chloe lose her train of thought. "Kim Cuc, do you mind going a little easier on me?" she asked the pedicurist, turning back to her daughter.

"Anyway, we go have dinner with these two engineers and a group of investors, and they're all going on and on about the programming and the code and this and that. And finally I ask, 'How are you going to make any money off of this algorithm?' And they all just look at me like I'm crazy. They launch into this hubbub about how 'People will pay for it if it's good enough' and 'On the Internet it's more important to acquire customers than make money' before dismissing my question entirely and going back to their code discussion. It goes on like that and they're getting each other riled up about how this math equation—or algorithm, whatever—is going to be worth billions of dollars. Meanwhile, I'm in the corner, seething with anger because, evidently, I'm just there to eat the soup."

Mrs. Hawkins was getting worked up just remembering this dinner, despite the lavender lotion being massaged onto her feet.

"Patty, at that point I didn't give a damn what they thought of me or why I was invited along. So I turn to these guys and tell them what I think anyway. 'You should sell ads.' All ten of them stop talking and look at me. Your father tries to settle me down with a 'What do you mean, dear?' And I say, 'No one is going to pay to use an algorithm they don't understand. But they are going to use your little search engine to find things they want, like a restaurant's address, or a newspaper article, or something they might want to buy on the Net. I bet companies would pay good money to have their Web site show up on the first page—hell, I bet they'd compete to pay the most money to show up as the number one search result. But,' I told them, 'you make the ads look like every other search result. And I bet you two geniuses'—and, Patty, I swear to God I pointed my finger right at Larry Page and Sergey Brin—'I bet you two geniuses could figure out a way to use all this data and math to choose which ads matter to each user.'"

"Mom." Patty's jaw dropped. "Google ads were your idea?"

Mrs. Hawkins winked at her daughter.

"This is crazy. Without ads Google wouldn't have gone anywhere. I mean, if they'd charged, people would have kept using Yahoo! or something. And if they hadn't done either, they wouldn't have made any money."

"And there would be no Google. No Gmail, no Google Maps, no self-driving cars . . ."

"But," Patty continued, "but why haven't you ever said anything to me?"

"Business isn't rocket science, Patty. Don't get me wrong, people like your father and your boyfriend Alex work really hard. And it takes a lot more than just a good idea at a dinner party to build Google. But don't let anyone make you feel like you're stupid. Just because they speak in jargon and are quick to cut you off doesn't mean they're smarter than you. All that jargon is like a secret language. And they say crazy stuff in this secret language, like how their *algorithm* will use *crowdsourcing* to *disrupt* the *disruptors* or else they'll *pivot* their *go-to-market strategy*. . . . But just because you don't speak their language doesn't mean you can't communicate. Just because you don't know their jargon doesn't mean you don't understand."

"Doesn't it drive you crazy that you didn't get any credit?"

"For Google? I didn't need it, Patty. I wanted to stay at home and raise a family and play tennis during the day. And I got that, and really appreciated your father for going to the office every day so that I could do it."

She paused and studied her daughter. "But that was what *I* wanted. And you're not like me, Patty."

Patty felt her heart clench.

"And you're not like your sister. And I don't mean that one is better than the other, but you're never going to be happy on the sidelines. So don't waste your time there."

Patty felt the tightness in her chest well up into her throat and tears start to form in her eyes. She couldn't describe it, but that was the nicest thing her mother had ever said to her.

"So what do I do?" Patty whispered.

"About Alex? Oh, I don't know—I'm just so glad you're not pregnant!" Mrs. Hawkins laughed.

"About me, Mom," Patty said.

Her mother smiled, more seriously this time, and said, "Go get in the game, Patty. It's where you belong."

5

Star Power

"You want Amelia Dory on our list?"

Brandon Carrington lifted his eyebrows skeptically over his thick hipster glasses as he took a sip of his martini.

"Why not?" T.J. asked as he watched a hot blonde's spandex-clad butt cross the bar to a plush sofa, where she placed it next to an older man.

"Don't play dumb, T."

T.J. looked back at Brandon, who'd been a junior when he was a freshman fraternity pledge. Despite all the hazing Brandon had bestowed on T.J., or maybe because of it, the two had stayed close after Brandon graduated and joined *Forbes* magazine as a staff writer. Now, Brandon was in charge of compiling the "Thirty Under Thirty" list for the magazine, which showcased the most promising young entrepreneurs in the world.

T.J. had called Brandon last week to cash in a favor: In his first move as official CEO of Doreye, he was determined to get Amelia Dory on that list.

Now they were sitting at the bar in the Rosewood hotel just off Sand Hill Road, and T.J. was determined not to leave until he had his way. And he knew just how to get it.

"You can't pretend like Doreye isn't a thousand times better than most of the companies you put in the magazine. Remember last year? That bespoke dog-clothing company you featured? Where'd that gem of an idea end up?"

"It's on hold."

"Exactly."

"But only until after the wedding."

"What wedding?"

Brandon chuckled to himself, drinking more of his martini. Despite his edgy Warby Parker glasses, he was pure blue blood: white skin and blue eyes and strong bones that indicated Viking heritage. "The founder's wedding," he said. "Remember her? Most perfect rack I've ever seen." He closed his eyes to reflect on her cup size for a moment. "Get this: The week after we publish the list, she gets about a thousand calls, one of which is from a forty-five-year-old billionaire angel investor 'interested in the dog-clothing space.' And was he ever. Five months later she's his fiancée. Now the company's on hold until after the wedding because she wants to"—he made air quotes—"'really be able to enjoy the wedding planning process,' and the dog clothes were taking too much time."

"And that's an accomplishment that you and *Forbes* magazine are proud of?"

"You're missing the point, T. We're not selling the bespoke dog-clothing company, we're selling the girl *running* the bespoke dog-clothing company. And honestly, we're not even really selling her; she's selling *us*. I mean, our magazines. A hot blond University of North Carolina cheerleader starting a company? Who gives a shit what that company actually does; our readership likes seeing pictures of people like her."

Brandon finished his martini and lifted his hand to the waiter to indicate another round. T.J. grimaced at him.

"What?" Brandon caught his stare and shrugged. "Don't shoot the messenger, T. I don't make up the rules. Who am I to judge what readers like? All I know is no one wants to look at pictures of a not-very-cute Stanford kid who thinks the Internet is an exercise in sharing and caring."

T.J. took a long, slow sip of his Scotch and winced at Brandon's reality. A year ago, he would have agreed with Brandon, but now that he'd gotten to know Amelia, he saw past her geeky exterior. She was legitimately impressive, not like so many other people who made the news. If people didn't care about her, they should.

The Rosewood bar opened onto a terrace that looked westward, where the orange sun was setting over the Santa Cruz Mountains. It was Thursday night, and the bar was packed with Silicon Valley dealmakers and the women who followed them. The Rosewood was the after-five place to be seen in Silicon Valley. The investors and entrepreneurs who held meetings at University Café by day came here for cocktail hour; only here they drank martinis instead of coffee and met with women instead of engineers. He peered at the sun setting beyond the crowd as if for inspiration, or perhaps approval, then turned back to Brandon.

"What if I make her hot?"

Brandon almost choked on his martini. "What?"

He couldn't change the game, but he wasn't going to let it stop him. "She's pretty," T.J. insisted. "With a little primping, I know she could take a photo that would more than meet your standards."

"Oh, God. Don't tell me you're trying to pull a *She's All That?*" Brandon rolled his eyes.

"What? You know you've hooked up with less attractive girls."

"When I was blacked out, maybe," Brandon said, smirking.

"I can make her attractive," T.J. insisted, "which will be an addition to the fact that she's actually talented and worth reading about."

Brandon looked carefully at his friend. "Did your ex-girlfriend really screw you up so badly? That you're going for nineteen-year-old engineers now?"

"I didn't say I was attracted to her; I said I could make her attractive." T.J. glared at his fraternity brother, daring him to push him further.

"Speaking of your ex-girlfriend, I saw her in L.A. Hate to say it, bro, but she's gotten really hot."

"Do we really have to talk about this?"

"I mean, it's not just her ass, it's like her confidence or something. Maybe it's because she's older."

"Please don't," T.J. said, meaning it. The thought of her dumping him still made him cringe.

Brandon opened his mouth to say something, but stopped himself, looking to the bartender for another drink instead.

"So what do you say?" T.J. pressed.

Brandon sucked in a deep breath. "Listen: I'll cut you a deal. We'll put Amelia on the list for the photo shoot and see how the pictures turn out. There's one company on the list that might fold before publication anyway, so if that happens we'll need something to fill in."

T.J. smiled and sipped his drink, satisfied. Just what he needed to prove he was the right CEO to get Doreye back on track. "So it's a deal? Amelia on Thirty Under Thirty."

Brandon rolled his eyes. "If you and the photographer can make her passably good-looking, then yes, it's a deal."

The two men clinked glasses again as they drank to their dealmaking. "Shall we conquer this bar?" T.J. asked.

"But of course," Brandon agreed. "Just one question."

"Shoot."

"Why feature Amelia instead of you? You know we'd slap that pretty face of yours on the list in a heartbeat."

T.J. thought about it for a second. "Nah. I think I'm better suited to be the chess master, not the pawn."

Brandon shook his head, laughing, and toasted T.J. again. "You always were a prick."

T.J. smiled at the compliment, locked eyes with a doe-eyed brunette in the corner of the bar, and stood up to go talk her into bed.

Out of Focus

Patty hadn't slept in two days. She'd only left her room in the sorority house to work out and get food, which she'd brought back to her desk to eat. She'd even foregone the Sigma Chi party last night to work on her new business plan, finding that instead of being sad to miss it, she was actually thrilled to have several hours of quiet in the house while all the girls were at the party.

She glanced around her room, a small rectangle on the second floor whose walls she'd painted a light pink to complement the deep plum comforter set she'd special-ordered for sophomore year. The floor was littered with empty coffee cups and discarded Post-it notes. She'd stripped the bulletin board above her desk of the photos and concert tickets and other memorabilia she used to display and replaced it with ideas for the new company: whom she would sell to, whom she would hire, how she would charge the former and pay the latter, what the marketing materials would look like, and where she would advertise.

She took a deep breath and looked at it one last time for motivation before she headed downstairs to test the hypothesis. She couldn't help feeling nervous, even though, looking at the bulletin board and her two days of work, the plan seemed so obvious, so flawless in its need and execution that she didn't see how it could *not* work.

The idea had come to her in a brief moment of inspiration. After her brunch at Peninsula with Alex and her pedicure date with her mom, Patty had spent hours thinking about and fine-tuning what she could do that was valuable to other people. What did she have that others didn't? What could she do that others couldn't? What was she able to see that others couldn't see? Figuring that out, she was sure, was the key to figuring out her way of getting in the start-up game.

It was at the campus gym that inspiration struck. As usual, she'd brought her *Us Weekly* and set up on an elliptical under a television hanging from the ceiling that the staff kept tuned to *E!*.

She started with the people around her: One elliptical over, a pudgy Asian guy in tattered sweatpants was huffing and puffing, sweat pockets thick on his gray t-shirt. On the other side, a slim redhead wearing nondescript cotton shorts and shirt sat on a stationary bike, her legs hardly moving the pedals, engrossed in a thick biochemistry textbook. In front of her, a buff Latino guy in high-school-gym-issued basketball shorts and t-shirt studied his biceps in the mirror as he did endless reps with a thirty-pound weight.

Next she considered the noise in the room: On the television above her, a L'Oréal ad was running, selling extrahydrating shampoo. Her magazine was opened to a CoverGirl ad pitching new extralength mascara. She took out her earbuds to hear what was on the gym speakers: The radio had cut to a Macy's winter merchandise arrival sale. She looked at her latest e-mails on her iPhone: Bloomingdale's shoe sale, Groupon for Shellac mani-cures, Lacoste semi-annual sale at Stanford Shopping Center.

She had suddenly felt the acute awareness that she was surrounded by ads, and they weren't trying to reach these other people in the gym; they were trying to sell to *her*.

Patty Hawkins, in her Lululemon shorts, American Apparel sorority t-shirt, custom Nike tennis shoes, high performance

Nike Dri-Fit socks; Patty Hawkins, with her two-hundred-dollar haircut and four-hundred-dollars-every-twelve-weeks highlights, her makeup bag full of Bobbi Brown foundation, Trish McEvoy eye shadow, Smashbox eyeliner, and NARS blush, all of which she'd carefully researched as the best product offered by its respective brand; Patty Hawkins, who matched her Natori bras to their partner panties; Patty Hawkins, who read *Vogue* and *Us Weekly* and ate Fage Greek yogurt and drank Diet Coke and took class notes in Moleskine notebooks with purple La Pen pens: *She* was an advertiser's *DREAM*.

And for the first time, on that elliptical, Patty saw herself for what she was to an advertiser: an image-conscious big spender whom they desperately wanted to purchase their products. And far from feeling exposed or exploited, this made Patty feel empowered: They wanted *her* to like *them*. She, and girls like her, could make or break their brands. She was incredibly important as a consumer, and that made her incredibly powerful.

Since that moment Patty had developed a full-blown business plan wherein she got girls like her together to talk to advertisers. She'd start, naturally, with local businesses and girls in her sorority. But then she could move on to other college campuses and reach out to national brands. She could leverage the sorority for more girls to participate. She'd do local in-person meetings, or one-on-ones, or online surveys. Brands would pay her and she'd pay part of it out to participants, or they could pay her cash and the participants in free products. She looked at her Facebook friends list and counted the number of girls who'd qualify: 348. And if it caught on, all of them had networks of their own they'd tell about it.

She'd make a Web site where girls could keep a profile and be contacted directly by marketers. Maybe she'd even give it a social angle, like Toms shoes, and donate part of her profits to women's shelters.

But the question remained: What to call it? "Girl Talk"? Too hipster band. "Female Insight Network"? Good acronym, but it sounded too corporate. "What are we?" Patty said to herself. "We're like . . . a female . . . focus group. I'm organizing focus groups for advertisers targeting cool girls."

"Focus Girls." That was it. She smiled and nodded to the bulletin board. It was the last piece, but now she was ready.

That was a week ago, and today Patty was ready to get started. She grabbed a notebook and headed down the stairs to meet T.J. and her first trial group.

She'd called T.J. when she'd had the idea to get his opinion on the company—mainly to make sure she wasn't crazy—and he'd suggested she do a test run pronto. They'd agreed that Franklin Whittaker, a successful investor in retail companies whose kids she used to babysit, would have a good product to test, and he readily agreed to have one of his marketing officers come run a focus group for a new makeup brand. It hadn't been hard to convince eight of her sorority sisters to give an hour to the group, especially when she guaranteed free makeup samples and a potential job lead for a cool new company.

"Nervous?" T.J. stood up from the bench in the Delta Gamma entryway as Patty skipped down the stairs.

"A little," she admitted.

T.J. reached out a hand and massaged her shoulder. "Don't worry," he said, smiling. "You're going to do great."

"Thank you so much for being here," she said honestly, her heart beating fast with helpless flattery at T. J. Bristol's attention. Even though she never really had a thing for T.J., it was impossible to avoid his charisma when he aimed right at you.

"Girls ready?"

"Let's go see."

They went into the lounge, where her eight volunteers were already sitting around the fireplace chatting. Richard, the marketing officer for Tinsley cosmetics, arrived shortly thereafter. He was tall and handsome, a fortysomething metrosexual who oozed fashion sense and sex appeal. The girls were putty in his hands as he asked them questions about their preferences for foundation and what bothered them about their current mascara.

In the end, he gave everyone a bag of sample goodies and passed his card to Sarah, a senior who was looking for a job in marketing after graduation.

"That was *amazing*," Sarah squealed after Richard left. "Like, I would *pay* to do that all the time, Patty."

The other girls agreed, and Patty felt her face flush and her heart swell. It worked! She'd created a company girls wanted to be a part of. She'd uncovered a need that mattered.

She heard a pop and turned around. T.J. had opened a bottle of champagne and was pouring glasses for the girls.

"To Patty!" they chimed, clinking glasses.

Patty sipped her champagne and looked thankfully at T.J., who was flirting with Sarah. Her mind flashed involuntarily back to the definition of his chest muscles when she'd been on the treadmill next to him at the gym in Hawaii and she imagined them beneath the navy polo he was wearing now. He was so much cooler than Alex . . . and maybe now that she had a company of her own, he was the kind of guy she should be going for instead of dumb jocks. She shook the thought from her head, joining the chatter about how hot Richard was and what-was-everyone-wearing-tonight-to-the-party-at-SAE.

7

Having a High Time

"Are you okay?" Roger asked gently, looking over at Amelia as the pair walked the three-mile path that led to and from campus to the Dish, a towering old satellite dish Stanford University once used for space research that now, its technology long since replaced by better science, served as a recreational haven for the community.

Their weekly walks had become increasingly important to Amelia as Adam had become more and more distant.

She swallowed and said, "I guess I'm just confused."

"There's a lot to be confused about," Roger offered. She'd filled him in on the meeting at PKC, on their new role designations, and on T.J.'s latest request that she do a photo shoot for *Forbes* magazine.

"Do you trust T.J.?" he asked.

"Absolutely. He's loyal and smart and . . ." She blushed, conscious of how such admiration would come across.

"And Adam?"

Amelia was quiet. Then she said quickly, "Of course I trust Adam. Adam's my brother."

"I didn't ask whether you *love* Adam, I asked whether you trust him."

Amelia felt a lump forming in her throat. She turned to Roger, looking very seriously at him. "Adam is the only person I've ever had in my life; he is everything to me."

Roger lifted his eyebrow and met her sternness with his own. "That's not what I asked."

"I'm just worried he's susceptible to pressure."

Roger shrugged a shoulder. "Most of us are."

"T.J.'s a really great leader," she said to change the subject.

He sighed and said, "Speaking of susceptible . . ."

"What?" Amelia looked up, blushing.

He grinned back at her. "Be careful, Amelia."

She rolled her eyes in annoyance. "Can we please talk about something else? I'm sick of thinking about Doreye for the moment."

"As a matter of fact, there is something I want to talk to you about." He cleared his throat. "I'm going away for a while—a few months, maybe; I'm not quite sure of the dates."

Amelia felt her stomach drop, her brain jumping to spring break and how she'd been secretly hoping he'd invite her to spend it at his house in Santa Cruz. Now she'd have to figure out something else to do to distract herself from the loneliness of the empty campus. "Where are you going?" she asked, trying not to sound disappointed.

"I haven't yet decided. I'm overdue for a sabbatical and I want to find somewhere I can be disconnected."

"Oh," she mustered.

"You're angry with me," he observed.

"No, I understand."

"I'm calling your bluff. Spill it."

"Well," she started, "I just find it a little . . . selfish . . . that you would want to just drop off the face of the earth and leave people you care about hanging like that." She blushed at the forcefulness of her comment. "I mean, I'm not saying you care so much about me, or that you should . . ."

This time Roger stopped, grabbing Amelia by the shoulders

and staring down at her with an intensity that surprised her. "Amelia . . ." He paused. "Listen to me very carefully: I care about you, okay? I care about you more than I can say."

She looked at his watery eyes and felt puddles form in her own. She swallowed hard to keep the tears back.

"And not just as a mentee, okay? Or as an investment. You are one of the most special people I've ever come across, and the more this"—he stopped and corrected himself—"I mean, the older I get, the more I realize how lucky I am to have people like you in my life to pass things on to, and to carry on my vision."

"I just wish your timing were better. Adam's been so distant, and I don't have anyone else," Amelia sputtered, no longer trying to hold back the tears.

Roger pulled her into a hug. "You've got to be strong, my dear. Just focus on what your heart is telling you to do and you'll discover you've got all the strength you need to do it."

She let the tears flow into his shirt until she didn't have any more left.

"Come on," he said, "that'll do you for a while." She nodded in agreement. She wasn't sure where all that emotion had come from, but she felt better now that it was out.

"Just make me a promise while I'm gone?"

"Okay."

"Leave those tears up here. Don't let them"—he gestured with his chin down to Silicon Valley below—"don't give them the privilege of seeing you cry."

She swallowed and looked out at Stanford's campus and the valley around it. "I won't. Never."

"Because, Amelia," Roger said, and took a deep breath, "people think Silicon Valley is all friendly innovation, but there are sharks out there. You can't always see them, but they'll attack the minute they smell blood in the water."

8

Small Favors

"I just don't understand why you can't say thank you." Adam's voice cracked in his effort to control it.

"Because I don't understand what I'm thanking you for," Amelia stubbornly insisted from the passenger seat.

"Are you freaking kidding me?" Adam clenched the steering wheel and turned to face his sister. "I skip my classes to drive you to this Thirty Under Thirty extravaganza, give up my whole evening to wait around so I can drive you back to Palo Alto, and not only do you show up late, you actually have the nerve to complain to me about having to be here?"

A car honked and he noticed the light had changed. "Chill out!" he screamed at the car as he moved his foot to the gas.

"I'm sorry I was late, and I'm sorry you had to give up your day," Amelia said as diplomatically as she could, "but *A*, I didn't ask you to do those things, and *B*, I don't understand why I can't talk to you anymore about the things that make me nervous."

Adam's blood was boiling. Amelia could be so mind-blowingly clueless. "*A*," he said, "you didn't ask—you *never* ask—you just assume. You always assume that I'll just be there to do whatever you need." As he said it, he realized how true it was. "And *B*, you don't get to talk to me about this because you know *I* want it. I *want* to do the press and the photo shoots and the stories, and it's so . . ."—he searched for the words through his anger—"it's so unfair that you get all of this when you don't even want it."

Amelia was silent. She stared straight ahead and kept her jaw locked. "This is it," she finally said.

"What?" He jumped.

"This is the hotel," she said in calm irritation.

He rolled his eyes in annoyance as he pulled into the driveway. "You go on and I'll go park," he said, but Amelia was already out of the car. She slammed the door behind her.

Adam parked the car and took deep breaths as he walked from the lot up to the St. Regis Hotel, where *Forbes* was holding their Thirty Under Thirty photo shoot. By the time he got there his anger felt suppressed and his heartbeat had returned to normal.

"I'm Adam Dory," he said to a woman with a clipboard who guarded the entrance to the banquet room where the event was taking place.

"You're not on the list," she said simply.

"No," he explained, "I am. I'm Adam Dory, with Doreye. It's D-O-R—"

"I know how to spell it; you're not on the list," she said flatly, unwilling to negotiate. "Each company got two names and yours is not one of them."

"But I'm the COO of the company," Adam explained, still getting used to the sound of his new title.

"The what?"

"Never mind," Adam scoffed, his angry heartbeat returning. "Who's on the list besides Amelia, then?" He knew T.J. was back in Palo Alto.

"Patty Hawkins."

"What? Why is she on the list?"

The woman shrugged and looked past Adam to the next person in line. "Can you please step aside?"

Adam's patience snapped and he felt like his head would explode. He clenched his jaw and glared at the woman, feeling his nostrils flare as he took four deep breaths and tried not to think about how much he hated T.J. for not talking to him about this and hated Amelia for being too oblivious to care.

He stormed out the glass doors, narrowly avoiding a cab as he pounded across the street onto Union Square, not sure where he was going but certain he needed to get somewhere quickly.

"Adam!" He faintly heard his name but didn't turn. "Adam!" He registered the voice and finally squinted across the street to see Ted Bristol waving from the entrance of Saks and coming toward him followed by . . . Lisa.

Before he could process it, or the shocked paleness of Lisa's face, Ted and his daughter—Adam's ex-girlfriend—were right in front of him. It had been weeks since Adam had seen or spoken to Lisa, and as much as he had tried to get her out of his mind, he felt relieved to see her, looking as perfect in person as she had in his dreams.

"Adam! What are you doing in the city?" Ted shook his mentee's hand firmly and patted his shoulder. "How's everything going? Have you met my daughter, Lisa?" He presented his daughter, whose face was sheet white.

Adam swallowed. "You look very familiar," he said, and offered his hand to shake hers.

She took it. "Yes, you too. From around campus, I guess?" Lisa looked long and hard at Adam. "Dad? How do you know Adam Dory?"

"Adam's become a mentee of mine. He's COO of the company your brother's working for at Roger's incubator—Doreye."

"COO?" Lisa asked, emphasizing the O, as she searched her former lover's face for his reaction to that title. Adam's anger burned in his throat. She had no right to look at him like that anymore, as if she knew him.

"Yes," Adam said firmly. He turned his attention to Ted. "What are you doing here?"

"I had to come up to the city for an event tonight and promised Lisa a shopping trip for her birthday." Ted gestured toward the oversize Saks shopping bag he was carrying. "Don't have girls, Adam, they'll wipe your bank account clean."

Lisa's birthday. Adam had completely forgotten. He wondered what she'd done to celebrate and felt a pang of jealousy knowing he hadn't been invited to the party.

Ted looked at his watch. "Hey, listen, Adam, did you drive up here?"

"Yeah." Adam snapped back to face Ted. "I just . . . had some COO duties."

"Do you think you could give Lisa a lift back? Like I said, I've got this event, and that way she won't have to take the train."

"Oh, that's okay, Dad," Lisa jumped in, her face blushing furiously. "I don't want to put Adam out."

Ted looked at her and said, "Don't be ridiculous. I'm sure he doesn't mind," then turned back to Adam. "Do you, Adam?"

Adam swallowed, glancing between father and daughter, and finally mustered, "No, no, of course not."

Ted clapped his hands. "Great! We're all settled, then." He kissed his daughter on the forehead and handed her the shopping bag. "Happy birthday, my dear." He turned to shake Adam's hand and gave him a hundred-dollar bill. "You two have dinner on me. And thanks, buddy. I owe you one."

Ted hailed a cab before Adam could put his dropped jaw back in place. He turned to face Lisa, who looked to be in equal shock.

"I need a drink," Adam said. He turned to find the nearest bar, not caring whether Lisa followed or not, but hoping she would.

9

Dress for Success

It took Amelia several minutes to calm down after Adam dropped her off to go park. He'd driven like a maniac the whole way here; she'd known he was angry, but then when she tried to talk about it he just attacked her. She had to be so guarded now: It felt like everything she did lately made him mad. She checked in with a woman at the front desk and went straight to the bathroom, where she locked herself into a stall, closed the toilet seat lid, and slumped herself on it. She hugged her knees into her chest and buried her face into them, trying to press the tears back into her eye sockets as she counted out ten deep breaths, then another ten, and another. She kept replaying Roger's words: "Don't let them see you cry." It had hardly been two weeks since he'd given her that lesson, and here she was, already about to blow it.

Why had she agreed to do this event? She *hated* stuff like this, hated the attention. And Adam was right: This was the part he wanted to do. Why hadn't she just let him? Instead, she'd accepted T.J.'s suggestion unhesitatingly and made the whole thing with Adam worse.

Whether Adam had a right to be upset or not, she felt like she was losing her brother and best friend and couldn't do anything to stop it.

Her iPhone vibrated and she pulled it out of her pocket. It was a text message from T.J.: *"Thinking about you. Smile pretty. Know you'll be great!!"*

Amelia wiped the wetness from her eyes. At least she had T.J. She didn't want to do this at all, but he'd seemed so anxious when he asked her to do it—"for me," he'd said—she knew she couldn't say no. She took one last deep breath. She had to just do it without thinking about it, and once it was over she could go home and be alone. Yes. *Just get through this, Amelia, and you can go home and turn on your computer and shut everyone else out.*

She walked through a ballroom where photographers were directing confidently smiling young entrepreneurs beneath lighting umbrellas. The room was buzzing with makeup artists and photographers and people with clipboards.

"Amelia!" a familiar voice called out, and Amelia turned to find it. "Amelia, over here!"

Patty! Patty Hawkins was skipping toward her.

Patty grabbed her by the shoulders and pulled her into a hug. "Amelia! Where have you been? I was so worried. Come on." Patty grabbed her by the hand and swept her away without explaining why she was here, and Amelia felt her heart lift. She wasn't sure she'd ever been so happy to see her freshman roommate.

Patty pulled Amelia into an empty conference room and plopped her into a hairdresser chair that sat before a makeup table littered with beauty tools and a large tri-fold mirror. Patty put her hands on Amelia's shoulders and took stock of her face. "Now, where do we start?" she said warmly.

Amelia was afraid speaking might make her cry again, but she whispered, "What are you doing here?"

Patty smiled broadly. "T.J. asked me to come. He said you might need some girl support . . ." She paused. "And, Amelia, I was so proud that you were on *Forbes*'s Thirty Under Thirty I could hardly stand it. I don't know that I've ever been so proud of anyone ever. And I want you to freakin' nail this photo shoot and show them all how cool you are."

Amelia could have hugged her. She took back every critical thought she'd ever had of her freshman roommate: She was an angel, and that was all there was to it.

"That said," Patty said, and sighed, "you're going to have to trust me here."

"Do whatever you have to do," Amelia said. "I'm in your hands."

Patty nodded. "Okay. Let's go, then."

She slathered a thick cream onto Amelia's face and neck and produced tweezers she used to pluck out half of Amelia's eyebrows. Tears streamed down Amelia's cheeks with the pain.

"Do you seriously endure this pain every day?" Amelia cry-laughed.

"It gets better, I promise. It's like bikini waxing: You get used to it and it doesn't hurt so bad."

"Do you know how screwed-up that sounds?"

"I guess I'd never thought about it until now, but, yes, you have a point." Patty stopped her plucking for a moment to consider. "But you know what? I also have a point, which is that you do not want to be the entrepreneur known for bushy eyebrows."

Amelia laughed and conceded.

Patty pulled Amelia's hair out of its ponytail and grimaced at its tangles as she went to work with a hair dryer and curling iron.

"So what have you been up to?" Amelia asked when she'd regained her composure post-tweezing.

"Honestly?" Patty said excitedly. "I've been working on a company of my own."

Amelia tilted her head and looked at Patty in the mirror. "Really?"

"Yes! And I don't want to jinx it, but it's going really well."

"What is it?"

"It's called Focus Girls. Basically, I put girls I know who are big shoppers and trendsetters in touch with companies. There are so many companies in the Valley who want to have sorority-girl types as customers, but they don't know how to reach them or adapt their products to our tastes. So I put the two groups together."

Amelia turned in the chair. "Patty, that's a great idea!"

Patty smiled, genuinely pleased by Amelia's compliment. "Thank you!"

Amelia turned back around, her mouth still agape at her friend's accomplishment.

"And it's going well, you said?"

"Totally. I mean, I'm not in *Forbes* or anything, but I've got a hundred girls signed up, and we've had like twenty-five clients express interest already. They pay me *five hundred dollars* per session, and I pay the girls half, so I'm actually making a lot of pocket money. At first I was targeting big companies—you know, marketing departments at the Gap and that sort of thing. But now I'm more gearing toward start-up and VC types in Silicon Valley. Mostly men who don't have a clue about women."

"Patty, that's so cool."

"Thank you," she said, smiling. "Now let's do your makeup."

Patty came around the chair to face Amelia and opened a makeup bag.

"How's the sorority?"

"Shush," Patty reprimanded. "Be still while I do your mascara."

"Sorry."

"Sorority's good but I'm not really doing much this quarter. Honestly, Focus Girls is taking a lot of my time. But I don't really even notice—I just love it so much, you know? Like I even try not to get that drunk when I go out in case a client calls with an emergency."

Amelia wanted to ask what kinds of clients had emergency focus-group needs, but Patty was wielding a liquid eyeliner pen perilously close to her eyeball, so she kept quiet.

"Okay, no looking in the mirror yet. I want to get you dressed first and then do a big reveal."

"Oh, God, Patty, I am not wearing your clothes." Hair and makeup was one thing, but Amelia was not prepared for skimpy skirts and stilettos.

"Don't worry," Patty said as she reached into a Neiman Marcus bag, "I went shopping for you. T.J. told me to put you in a dress, but I said, 'Amelia Dory in a dress? Never.'"

"Thanks, but why never?"

"Beauty is only beautiful if it's authentic. You wearing heels is not authentic."

Patty handed Amelia a stack of clothes folded in tissue paper. Amelia unwrapped the paper to find a slim pair of faded jeans, a loose white t-shirt, and a tailored navy hoodie that was the softest she had ever touched.

"It's cashmere," Patty said, handing her a slightly padded lace bra. "Men are going to look at your boobs whether you want them to or not, so you might as well make them pretty. You can't wear that training bra of yours forever."

Amelia blushed, comparing the bra she held in her hands to the stained-from-wear one currently on her body.

She caught a glimpse of the price tag on the cashmere hoodie and almost fell out of her chair: $320.00! "Oh my God!" she blurted. Patty reached for it and ripped off the tags. "You weren't supposed to see that."

"I can't take this," Amelia said, pulling her hands from the package in her lap as if afraid to touch it.

"You can and you will," Patty said. "It's Focus Girls profit. And I owe you: I never would have started this company if it hadn't been for your example. So really I owe you a lot more."

Patty looked at her watch. "Now go get dressed before we miss your shoot."

Amelia jumped from the chair and went behind a curtain in the corner to change. The jeans fit tight around her hips and the t-shirt felt like butter on her skin. The bra was visible through the t-shirt but Patty insisted that it was the style before handing her a pair of leather ankle boots with gold buckles. "Boots go over jeans," Patty instructed.

Amelia took a deep breath and emerged. Patty sat in the chair, arms crossed, and smiled. "Perfect."

She led Amelia to the mirror. "I don't need to see," Amelia said, but as she opened her eyes on herself, Amelia felt her heart jump. She couldn't remember the last time she intentionally looked in a mirror; in fact, she went out of her way to avoid them.

But it wasn't so bad looking when the reflection looked like this. She turned her face and touched her cheek as if to prove it was really her. She noticed with surprise the length of her legs, the roundness of her butt. She touched her hair, which fell in full curls past her shoulders. She felt like someone else, but felt happy knowing that she wasn't someone else. This was her: The reflection was what she had become.

She turned to Patty, still sitting satisfied in her seat, and whispered a silent "Thank you."

"Amelia Dory?" The door swung open and a gruff woman dressed in black with a headset and clipboard barged into the room. "Amelia Dory, we needed you out here ten minutes ago." The woman looked up from her clipboard and stopped, tilting her head at Amelia, then lifted her eyebrows at Patty as if to say, "Nice work."

The woman led Amelia and Patty to a platform draped in a sheet against an expansive black backdrop where a photographer waited, flipping through photos on her camera.

"Riley, Miss Dory is ready whenever you are," the gruff woman said to the photographer, who lifted her eyes and offered Amelia a warm smile.

Amelia wasn't sure what it was about Riley, but she instinctively liked her. Her dirty-blond hair was thick and long, pulled into a sloppy ponytail; she was tall and athletic-looking; and her smile was warm. She was wearing a black t-shirt and jeans tucked into boots. "Nice look," she said, acknowledging Amelia's jeans-in-boots and Amelia blushed as she realized they were wearing the same shoes.

Patty's phone rang and she looked down at it. "Amelia, I've got a client. I gotta run, okay?"

Amelia turned and replied, "Yeah, sure."

Patty squeezed her hand. "You are beautiful, Amelia. In so many ways."

"I don't know how I'll ever thank you."

"By keeping your eyebrows plucked. That's all I ask." Then she answered the phone and ran out the door.

"Shall we get going?" Riley led Amelia to sit in the center of the platform. "Tilt your head this way," Riley instructed. "Perfect, just like that. Your chin toward me, please. Now hold it."

Amelia tried to keep the head position and smile, but ended up giggling and breaking the pose. Riley snapped away, laughing along with her and coaxing, "Good. These are really good shots."

Amelia tried to think back to the last time she had her photo taken. Of course there were candid pictures taken on iPhones, but she never posed for those, and they, at best, showed up on Instagram, not in *Forbes* magazine.

Click. Click.

"So you're the next big thing?" Riley asked as she clicked away.

Amelia blushed and shook her head. "No. I just like programming. And I guess I'm good at it."

"Please. Clearly you're good at it. And you enjoy it, which is the important part."

"Is that how you ended up working for *Forbes*?" Amelia asked.

"You could say so." She paused and pushed a piece of hair off Amelia's forehead, snapping another shot as Amelia smiled for the camera. "After I graduated from college—I went to Stanford, too—I moved down to Los Angeles to be a freelance photographer. I ran into Brandon a few weeks ago—he was an old buddy from college—and he got me the gig at *Forbes*."

She sat Amelia on a stool and gently turned her head so that she was looking back over her shoulder. "Here, don't smile for this one. Look a little serious, like you're looking back on your past."

"Who's Brandon?"

"You haven't met Brandon? He's the one who wrote your piece." She snapped the camera. "Perfect. That's it. Maybe open your lips just a little. Yep. Great."

Click. Click. Click.

"I figured he'd interviewed you for it."

"No. T.J. handled the whole thing. I just showed up for the pictures."

Click. Click. "Who's T.J.?"

"T. J. Bristol—our CEO."

Riley dropped the camera. "T. J. Bristol?"

"Yeah. Do you know him?"

Riley's face lost all of its color. "We—" she started. "We went to college together," she said hurriedly, biting her lip, and, just as quickly, resumed the photos.

10

When Text Becomes Subtext

Lisa was almost running to keep up with Adam's quick pace as she followed him into a dive bar on Market Street. He walked straight to the bar without acknowledging her.

"Jack and Coke," he demanded, "double."

"ID, please?" the bartender retorted.

Without missing a beat, Adam pulled out his fake and plopped it on the counter, as if insulted he should be asked.

"Listen, Adam." She touched his arm to get his attention, and he felt his heart race. "I'm going to take the train."

"No," he said too quickly. "I mean, do what you want."

"I just want to know why you're talking to my father."

"It's got nothing to do with you."

"Does he know . . . ?" She scrunched up her forehead. "About us?"

Adam scoffed, "Of course not. We only talk about business."

"Okay, because I'd really appreciate it if you—"

"I'll never tell him," he cut her off, rolling his eyes. "Not like I want him to know, either." He thought about whether this was true and decided it was.

Adam rapped his fingers on the bar as he waited for the server to return, pretending to ignore Lisa but fiercely conscious of her breath at his side.

Lisa stood for a second glaring at him, and finally said firmly, "I'm going to get a table and order dinner. Join if you want."

He felt his control deflate as he picked up his drink from the bartender and handed him fifteen dollars. He took a long sip and followed Lisa's path to the table, where she didn't look up from the menu as he sat down.

A waitress approached the pair. "I'll have the chicken club, with avocado, no mayonnaise, and extra mustard," Lisa announced.

"For you?" the waitress asked, turning to Adam.

"I haven't had a chance to—" Adam started, then stopped himself. "Just bring me a burger. Everything. Medium rare. And another of these." He pointed to his drink.

"So I take it you're still mad at me?"

Adam rolled his head back in disbelief. "Yeah. I'd say so."

"I told you I was sorry."

"Sorry isn't enough."

"What is?"

"I told you I loved you."

"It was complicated."

"You're a liar."

"I'm worried about you."

"Stop being such a snob."

"How does that make me a snob?"

"Being 'worried about me'? It's putting yourself back in your little better-than-me bucket, looking down on poor Adam with pity, like I'm some child you have to feel sorry for. I don't need your pity."

"I don't pity you, Adam; I'm worried about you. There's a difference."

"Like there's a difference between cheating and being in a 'complicated' relationship you haven't gotten around to getting out of?"

"Are you ever going to let it go?"

Adam stopped and took a sip of his drink, then kept drinking until it was gone. "Where is the waitress?" he snapped.

Lisa was silent. "Listen," she tried, "maybe it was delusional, but I guess I convinced myself I was doing the right thing. Even when I talked to Amelia about it she—"

"What?" Adam's face snapped toward her. "What did you say?"

Lisa's eyes darted, trying to think of what she'd said to elicit such a reaction.

"What do you mean 'when you talked to Amelia about it'—about what?"

"She caught me and Sundeep on a date when you and I first got together, and I explained the whole situation."

Adam felt like someone had punched him in the gut. "Why?" he whispered, unable to find any other word.

"I needed to talk to someone. And Amelia knew both of you, so she had context, and she agreed that I needed to tell Sundeep I wasn't in love with him in my own time. And she's such a good person, I really value her opinion, I guess."

Adam couldn't breathe. Amelia knew? The whole time? When they were in Maui . . . she knew Lisa was dating Sundeep? She knew and never told him? *No,* he thought, *Amelia is not a good person.*

The waitress arrived with their food. Adam took his cocktail and asked for another. The waitress glanced worriedly at Lisa, who shrugged. "It's all a moot point now, though, I guess. I broke up with Sundeep right after Maui and haven't seen him since."

Adam didn't hear her; his head was spinning as he sucked the booze through the straw, his anger shifting from Lisa back to Amelia. *I do everything for her,* he seethed. *I make sure she doesn't get in trouble when she hacks into things, I figured out how that knockoff RemoteX was sabotaging us in Maui, I saved the company during her meltdown, I drove her to freaking San Francisco for an event I couldn't even attend. And this is how she repays me? By letting some spoiled cheater lead me on?*

Lisa cut into her sandwich and kept her eyes on her food. Watching her calmly bite her chicken further infuriated Adam.

"You are unbelievable, you know? Your nerve?"

"I'm sorry?"

"How dare you call my sister."

"How dare you buddy up with my father."

"It's such a waste you got him as a dad. I'll trade you him for Amelia—you two deserve each other."

"What is that supposed to mean?"

"I meeaan"—he was starting to slur his words—"What a screwed-up world that we're both orphans and I get no parents in Indiana and you get Ted *Fricking* Bristol and a mansion in Atherton! And you and T.J. don't even appreciate him."

Lisa tensed. "What do you know about my relationship with my father? You have no right to judge."

"Your father would rather have someone like me as a son than your brother, I know that much."

"You're drunk."

"Why else would he be my mentor?" Adam asked proudly. "What do you think of that? He's coaching me through Doreye. Through all the annoying crap your brother and my sister are putting me through. Your father's the only one who sees what I am capable of."

Lisa pushed the food on her plate with her fork, clearly upset.

Adam picked up his third drink and stared Lisa in the eye. "He's going to help me fulfill my potential. Then you'll be sorry you chose Sundeep over me. When I'm running some big company and don't even remember your name."

"You shouldn't get close to my father," Lisa said, and returned his cold stare.

Adam laughed. "You're just jealous. Daddy's little girl has to compete with a new favorite. Imagine what he'd think if I told him what a whore you are."

Lisa pushed her plate at him and stood up. "You're an ass." She pulled her coat off the chair and started to storm out of the bar.

Through his alcoholic haze, Adam panicked and stood up. "Wait, Lisa, wait—I didn't mean it. How are you going to get home?"

"I'll take the train."

"But I—" He grabbed her arm but she pulled away violently.

"I don't need you, Adam. I thought I did, once, but I don't, okay?"

The bar door slammed behind her and Adam looked sheepishly around him as people's eyes turned back to their meals. He waved to the bartender and said, "Another Jack and Coke, please."

11

Things That Go Beep in the Night

"Roll onto your side . . . that's it . . . all the way over . . . there . . . now just stay still," said the nurse, a rotund woman in pink polka-dot scrubs, coaching Roger from his backside, where she was administering a shot into his butt cheek.

Roger lifted an eyebrow and gave T.J. a knowing glance.

"Almost done," she said cheerily.

Roger offered a closed-lipped smile to her broad grin and said, "But you didn't buy me dinner first."

T.J. burst into laughter. Which made Roger burst into laughter. Which made the nurse yell at Roger for moving too much while she had a needle in his butt cheek.

Once she departed, Roger readjusted his hospital gown. "Enjoy the women while you can, T.J. One day the only attention you'll get is a polka-dotted nurse injecting *your* ass with hormones."

T.J. smiled at Roger, who was handling his illness with characteristic dry humor. "You're looking better this week; how are you feeling?"

"Comes and goes," Roger answered honestly. He paused for a moment. "It's already spread to my bones."

T.J. could feel goose bumps across his skin. He didn't know a lot about cancer, but he knew by the gravity in Roger's voice that this wasn't good. "Do you feel okay?" he asked, his voice just beyond a whisper.

"They've got stuff to manage the pain. Apparently there's a club in Berkeley for guys with prostate cancer to do LSD," Roger offered positively.

"LSD? That's allowed?"

"Hallucinogens are a pain management technique in many cultures. The Huichol people use peyote. Other tribes use magic mushrooms. I plan to appeal any legal charges on cultural grounds."

"Which culture is that, Roger?"

"Who cares? These cases never actually get through the courts because the defendants all die before the appeals process is finished. We infirmed are a prosecutor's worst nightmare!"

T.J. couldn't share his laughter at that morbid reality.

Roger was nonplussed. "Did you know that a million years ago at Xerox PARC, when we came up with the Internet, we were all tripping on LSD? Maybe this time I'll come up with something even crazier."

T.J. wasn't encouraged by this. "Have you told Amelia yet?"

"No," Roger admitted. "I told her I was going away for a while to give me cover, but I didn't tell her the reason. I wasn't sure she could handle it. Have you heard how the photo shoot went?"

"Yeah," T.J. said as he grinned and pulled his iPhone proudly out of his pocket, "Brandon sent me the photos. Patty did an awesome job cleaning her up."

Roger took the phone, but as he flipped through the photos his face went white.

"What are you doing, T.J.?" he said softly but firmly.

T.J. looked up at him innocently. "What do you mean?"

"You sent someone to 'clean her up'?"

"Brandon wouldn't put her on the list unless she looked hot. And she does. She *is*."

Roger carefully studied T.J.'s face.

"What?" T.J. asked defensively. "I got her on the list, didn't I?"
The older man sniffled.

Now T.J. was annoyed. "Honestly, Roger. If I hadn't sent Patty they wouldn't have put Amelia in. And if *Forbes* had photographed Amelia in her normal state—with food on her shirt and all that—people would have made a total mockery of her. I'm not saying she has to be hot, I'm saying it's my duty not to let her invite humiliation. I didn't make the rules."

"I guess I'm just a little surprised Amelia went for it."

"Maybe she's starting to get it."

"Or maybe she's doing it for someone else."

"What are you implying?"

"Be careful, T.J. She's not one of your sorority girls."

T.J.'s jaw clenched and he looked Roger straight in the eyes and said firmly, "I know that."

The two men held the glare for a moment, searching each other's eyes for deceit. As close as Doreye had brought them, T.J. knew Roger had never let go of the early hesitations he'd expressed during their first meeting at University Café.

"She's come to mean a lot to me," Roger said. "I don't want to see her hurt."

"Neither do I," T.J. said, and meant it. "But sheltering her from reality isn't doing her any favors. And the reality is that the press likes women better when they're pretty. Lucky for us, Amelia has it, she just needs help showing it."

"I think you overestimate that 'reality.'"

"You can't protect her forever, you know."

"I know," Roger conceded. "I just don't think she's ready."

"She isn't, or you aren't?"

"I'm dying, T.J. How is one ever ready for that? She's my last mentee, my last chance at having a legacy that lasts beyond me. Please don't let her lose it."

12

Miss Taken Identities

Adam paid the bill and moved to a seat at the bar, his emotions flipping between shame and rage.

He was embarrassed by his behavior—at how unwilling he'd been to even give her a chance and how humiliating it was that she'd called him on it in front of the entire bar. But then he remembered what an unacceptable thing she'd done and felt his jaw pulse with anger at the way she thought she could toy with him and lie to him like his feelings didn't matter. But then he thought about her hair and about how he used to have permission to touch it, and he felt his heart break all over again.

He took a swig of his drink. Enough about Lisa. That was over. That was done. He'd moved on to bigger things—to big-deal mentors and . . . and a pathetic post managing human resources for his sister's company. How could his current reality—demoted position, no girlfriend—be so disconnected from the version of himself he'd thought he'd become?

His brain was fuzzy from the booze and he looked around as if noticing he was in a bar for the first time. A basketball game was playing on the television screen behind the bartender, and he tried to focus his eyes on the ball, but couldn't quite make it out. Where had he gone wrong? The game cut to an ad for the

local news, where a broadcaster offered a sneak peek at tonight's big story. Adam squinted to see the shot, which looked
like it was at . . . Oh my God—was that Amelia? The shot cut to a
banner for *Forbes*'s Thirty Under Thirty.

Adam stood up, grabbing on to the bar to steady himself, and
pulled his face closer to the television. *Who are they interview-
ing?* Adam squinted again. *Oh my God. It's Amelia.*

His chest instinctively filled with pride: His sister was on
television! And she looked beautiful! But then his brain clicked
and he lost his smile. His sister was being praised as a genius,
his sister who betrayed him and made him look like an idiot in
front of the only girl he'd ever loved. His sister was laughing on
television and he was alone at a bar. How could she leave him
like this?

Adam shook his head in a desperate attempt to sift out all
the anger and pain and self-doubt. He could follow Ted's advice
about being patient as COO all day long, but that didn't mean he
couldn't give Amelia a piece of his mind.

He snorted with anger, downed his drink, put a twenty-dollar
bill on the bar, and headed for the St. Francis.

This time there was no security to stop him.

He tried to focus his vision as he found his way up to the
event and into a huge conference room scattered with remnants
of the day's activities. He peered around the room for Amelia,
letting his eyes adjust to the darkness and the fact that the booze
was causing his brain to take just a little longer than usual to
process everything he saw.

"Is that the famous Mr. Dory?" a woman's accented voice called
from behind him. He turned to find a gorgeous blonde in a short
black dress with piercing eyes smile at him. Adam was caught off
guard as the woman reached out to touch his arm. "It is! Adam
Dory, what a pleasure to see you again. Why aren't you in the
Doreye photos?"

Adam swayed on his feet, his eyebrows furrowed. He recognized this woman, but couldn't figure out from where.

"I mean, you're the real brains in the operation. I never did understand why Amelia always got all the credit."

"Not anymore. Not for long. No more *Mister Nice Adam*. It's time for her to share," Adam blurted.

The woman smiled, satisfied she'd struck a chord.

Where was she *from*? "Have you seen my sister?" he asked bluntly.

"Sure"—she smiled and pointed—"she's right over there. I hardly recognized her."

Adam walked away, then realized he'd just abandoned a gorgeous woman who was complimenting him, and turned back around. "Wait there," he said, lifting a finger to indicate he'd only be a minute. "I'll be right back. I have to talk to my sister, but I'm not done with you."

The woman smiled and said, giggling, "I'm not going anywhere, Adam."

Adam spotted Amelia laughing with a reporter, her hair curled in pretty perfection that made him even more annoyed.

"Amelia!" he called out as he walked toward them. "Amelia, we need to talk."

"Adam!" She didn't look pleased. "Where the hell have you been?"

"They wouldn't let me in," he said, swaying on his heels. "Only you and Patty were on the list." He spat the words at her, then demanded: "We need to talk."

"Adam, have you been drinking?"

He ignored her. "You pretend like you're innocent, and so people let you have everything—the photo shoot and all that—but you're not innocent. You know *exactly* what you're doing."

Amelia jumped up from the stool and tried to pull him to a corner. "Adam, let's go over here."

But he batted her away. "No! You can't hold me back!"

"How am I holding you back, Adam?" Amelia said in a quiet, deliberate voice.

"You're a liar!"

"What did I lie about, Adam?" Amelia was quiet and patient, as if trying to calm down a child, which only made Adam angrier. He wasn't a child.

"You knew about Lisa!" Adam bellowed. "You knew about Lisa and Sundeep the whole time and you never told me!" He felt his heart break all over again as he said the words out loud.

Amelia moved toward him, her arms wide to embrace him in a hug, but he moved back.

"Oh, Adam," she said, her face wracked with guilt. "Adam, I'm so sorry. It killed me. Every single day it killed me. But I didn't know what to do, Adam, I swear. I swear I didn't know what to do."

"Just tell me," Adam pleaded. "All you had to do was *tell* me."

"I didn't think you'd listen."

"How would I not listen?" Adam's voice was cracking. "You're my sister. My twin sister. And my best friend."

"Adam, I'm so, so sorry." Tears were forming in Amelia's eyes in reaction to her brother's pain.

Adam snorted, his pride reemerging as his brain reminded him why he'd come here in the first place.

"Adam," Amelia said, her soft-but-stern voice returning, "Adam, I think you need to sit down. Let me get you some water."

"No!" Adam belted. "No! No! No!" He shook his head violently.

"Adam can come with me," a woman's British-accented voice interrupted. The blond girl-woman from earlier appeared next to Adam. "It's probably not a good idea for you two to be together right now. I can take care of him," she said, turning to Amelia. "I owe you one after Maui."

Adam still couldn't figure out who this woman was, but he liked having her here, by his side, facing off against Amelia. She was like his sidekick.

"Violet? What are you doing here?" Amelia took on a very serious tone as she addressed the woman.

Violet, Adam thought. *What a beautiful name*. He turned to look at her. Gosh, she was pretty.

"I'm just trying to help your brother, Amelia."

"Trying to help?" Amelia scoffed. "Please leave us alone."

"No!" Adam jumped to Violet's defense. *Maybe I will go with her after all,* he thought. She'd said such nice things about him, and she was really pretty.

"Adam, don't you realize who this is? This is the woman from RemoteX. Our *competitor*? This is the woman who sabotaged our demo in Hawaii. This is the woman who posed as a reporter and grilled me on our past."

"So I was working for a competitor; can you blame me for trying to win?" Violet explained innocently. "Things are different now. RemoteX is done and we have no reason to be on bad terms. Let me make it up to you both."

"How can you possibly expect us to be friends after that?" Amelia's jaw jutted forward. She was dumbfounded.

"You can't blame her for being good at her job," Adam said matter-of-factly.

"I assure you," Violet soothed, "RemoteX is a thing of the past; you and Doreye can have the whole market. I'm on to bigger and better things." Adam felt Violet's soft, delicate fingers grasp his arm, which made the skin on his neck shiver.

"Yeah, Amelia. Don't get so sensitive."

"Adam, you're drunk. You're in no state—"

The accusation infuriated Adam and he cut his sister off. "What do you know about me and my state? I'm going with Violet. Figure out your own way home."

Adam heard Amelia's voice plead behind him as he turned to the door, but wasn't sure what she said. Violet was by his side, and he was going wherever she wanted to take him. From now on, Adam was putting himself first.

13

Detour

Amelia could feel her stunned pulse slowly beating as Adam stormed out with a victoriously smiling Violet. The few people left in the room slowly dropped their stares and went quietly back to what they'd been doing.

"Do you need a ride?" Riley's soft voice startled Amelia. "I'm heading back down to the Peninsula; I could drop you on campus."

Amelia looked up; Riley was holding her coat in one hand and Amelia's backpack in the other. "Yes. I could use a ride," Amelia admitted, too worn out to insist on not being an inconvenience.

"Come on," Riley said, tilting her head toward the door, "let's get out of here."

Amelia walked in silence next to Riley, who politely smiled and said good-bye and thank you to all the *Forbes* people and St. Francis staff and even the valet who pulled a red Saab convertible around and ushered Amelia into the passenger seat.

Riley turned the heat on in the car and plugged her iPhone in to connect to the car's stereo. "Do you like the xx?" she asked, as the band started streaming through her phone to the speakers.

"Sure," Amelia said meekly.

"My dad was a musician, so I'm kind of a music junkie," she said kindly.

Amelia knew Riley was trying to make her feel better with the small talk, and she appreciated it.

Riley guided the car out into the street and asked, "Are you hungry at all?"

Amelia thought about food for the first time all day and realized she hadn't eaten anything since a bowl of cereal that morning and was, in fact, starving. "Yeah, actually I am really hungry."

"Good. Meatball subs okay? There's this little spot in North Beach I'm craving. It's a little out of the way, but totally worth it."

Amelia blushed at Riley asking her permission. "Yes, of course," she said, and smiled genuinely. "That sounds great."

"Good!" Riley said. "Because I honestly was going to make you go regardless."

The two women smiled at each other. Amelia was feeling better.

North Beach was the notoriously seedy part of San Francisco, a hodgepodge of tourists and strip clubs and old-world Italian cafés. Riley parked the car in front of Hungry I, a strip club whose massive fluorescent sign boasted "the prettiest ladies in San Francisco." Riley was similarly unfazed by the men who catcalled as they walked across the street to an old-looking Italian deli.

"Don't pay attention to them," Riley instructed Amelia, who suddenly realized they were looking at *her*. Riley led Amelia through the gritty glass door of the deli and up to the counter, where a fat man with a waft of greasy black hair smiled broadly. "Miss Riley!" he announced in a thick Italian accent, wiping his hands on his white apron as he came from behind the counter to kiss her on either cheek.

"Giovanni!" Riley returned his warm greeting. "This is my friend Amelia."

Giovanni embraced Amelia. "A friend of Riley's is a friend of mine. What can I get you?"

"Meatball sub for me," Riley told him, "extra provolone and extra marinara."

"Coming right up," Giovanni said. "And for you, Miss Amelia?"

Amelia blushed and looked at the menu. "Um . . . I'll have the same?"

"Good choice."

Riley glanced at her watch and then led Amelia to a table with a checkered tablecloth. Another man came out with two wineglasses and a bottle. "Special treat for an old friend and a new one," he said, smiling warmly at Riley as he poured wine into the two glasses. "Sangiovese," he announced.

Riley stood up and gave him a warm hug. "You all still spoil me."

"It's been a long time, my dear," he said.

Riley sighed. "Too long! I assure you, they have nothing like this in Los Angeles." She smiled as Giovanni brought the sandwiches out to the table.

"*Saluté!*" the men said.

"How do you know them?" Amelia asked as she took a bite of her hot meatball sub, which was, as promised, the best she'd ever had.

"Oh, God." Riley laughed. "When I was in college, my boyfriend and I stumbled upon this place and loved it so much that it became our bimonthly date spot. We'd come into the city every other Friday and take that table over there and eat meatball subs. His parents kept an apartment here, so we'd steal their wine and sneak it in." Riley chuckled, thinking back on being under twenty-one. "After a while, Giovanni thought we were so cute he'd give us wine instead of making us hide it. He knew we were underage but didn't care." Her smile indicated it was a favorite memory. "Seriously, we must have come here thirty times."

Amelia also smiled at the story. She could imagine Riley coming here with some handsome musician boyfriend.

Riley clenched her teeth as if wondering whether she should

say it, but finally conceded to herself. "I guess I should mention that my college boyfriend was T. J. Bristol."

Amelia almost choked on her meatball. "*T. J. Bristol*? Was your boyfriend?"

Riley laughed. "Yeah, I know."

"But you're so . . ."

"Don't say ugly."

"No, no, not at all." How could she even joke about that? "You're just so . . . mature."

"I was two grades ahead of him. I hope he's doing well; I literally haven't spoken to him since we broke up. Needless to say, I was a little taken aback when you said he was your CEO."

Amelia's mind was spinning, mostly thinking about T.J. having cute bimonthly dates in an Italian deli. In a million years she'd never have guessed he had that side to him. It made her skin tingle: Maybe he wasn't just attracted to dumb sorority girls after all.

"Anyway!" Riley exclaimed, hoping to change the subject. "These subs are delicious, right?"

"So good," Amelia agreed. She looked at the wine, which she hadn't yet touched, and boldly took a sip. It was bitter, but after a second in her mouth turned a little sweeter and tasted good. She had another sip, trying not to blush at the thought of college T.J. and Riley.

"Thank you," Amelia finally said, looking from her food up to Riley.

Riley smiled her warm, genuine smile. "You're welcome, Amelia."

They finished their subs and said good-bye to the Italians, who insisted Amelia come back anytime. Between the wine and the meatballs, Amelia was feeling warm, like she could deal with Adam tomorrow.

They got back in the car and headed up the 101.

"So what kind of musician was your dad?"

"He played guitar and was lead vocals in this Grateful Dead cover band. With my godfather, Roger."

"Roger Fenway?"

"Yeah! Do you know him?"

Amelia laughed. It was like she and Riley were meant to know each other. "Yeah, he's my mentor. I mean, he's the reason Doreye even exists. And honestly, he's like a dad to me. I mean, I didn't have a dad, and Roger's like the closest thing I've ever had."

Riley smiled. "Of course. That's just like him."

She fell silent and the air in the car suddenly felt heavy.

"Are you okay?" Amelia asked.

"It's just so sad," Riley said, and shook her head as if trying to shake tears out of her eyes.

Amelia wasn't sure what Riley was referring to. "That I didn't have a real dad? That's okay," she consoled.

"I mean what's happening to Roger. First his wife, now he's got stage four? It's just not fair."

Amelia's heart imploded with a pain different from any other pain she'd ever felt. "Stage-four what?"

"Did you not know? Roger has cancer."

14

The Waiting Game

T.J.'s body felt heavy as he left Stanford Hospital. He'd never really had to deal with death before—all four of his grandparents were still alive, and the only funeral he'd ever been to was for a great-uncle he'd never met. His golden retriever had died when he was eighteen and he had been unspeakably sad for more than a month, but it didn't really feel fair to draw a comparison between Roger and Flash.

As he climbed into his car, T.J.'s phone rang from his pocket. His iPhone announced it was "Lisa Sister" (he'd added the "sister" piece so as not to confuse her with "Lisa Hookup," a girl of the same name he frequently sexted).

"Hey, Sis," T.J. said, trying to sound cheery, "what's up?"

T.J. heard his sister sniffle on the other end. "T.J. . . . . T.J., I . . ." She was sobbing and couldn't get a sentence out.

T.J. sat forward, instinctively launching into protective-big-brother mode. "Lisa, what's wrong? Where are you?"

"I'm on the train," she stammered, "back from San Francisco."

"How close are you? Are you okay? Did someone hurt you? Lisa, tell me you're okay."

"I'm okay," she sniffled, "I just really need someone to talk to and I—"

"I'm coming to get you. Get off at the Menlo Park station, okay? We'll go back to my apartment and we can sort everything out."

"Okay," she said quietly. "Thank you, T.J."

"I'll be waiting when you get off. And I'll beat the living crap out of whoever did this to you."

T.J. was waiting when Lisa got off the train, and together they sped back to his apartment, the modest penthouse of one of the few upscale apartment complexes in downtown Palo Alto. He made hot chocolate while she changed into a pair of his sweats.

"Thank you," she said, and sighed as she took the mug from him and curled her legs up under her on the couch. Her face was stained with tears, but she'd regained her composure.

T.J. took the chair opposite the couch. "Do you want to talk about it?"

She sighed and said, "Yeah," but that was it. She took a long sip of her hot chocolate and sighed again.

"It's okay," he probed gently. "Whatever happened isn't your fault, and whoever hurt you"—he laughed gently—"will seriously die, okay?"

She smiled at his attempt to make her feel better and swallowed to gather her courage. "It's Adam," she said.

"Who's Adam?" he asked.

She lifted her eyes. "Adam Dory?"

T.J.'s jaw dropped. "Adam *Dory*?" he repeated.

"Yes, Adam Dory."

T.J. couldn't hide his speechlessness, and Lisa turned her eyes to the floor to avoid his shocked expression as she went on.

"Adam and I were . . . hooking up." She glanced up—yes, he was still in shock. "Well, it was more than just hooking up. We were together, and I was going to break up with Sundeep so I could be with Adam, but then Sundeep's family disowned him. I just couldn't, you know? I couldn't break up with Sundeep no matter how much I cared about Adam. And Sundeep and I . . . well, we'd become so platonic, we might as well have just been friends anyway."

She paused. T.J. closed his jaw, but his eyes were still wide.

"And then over Christmas, when we were in Maui, Adam saw Sundeep and me together and figured it out before I could tell him myself. Now Adam hates me, which I *totally* understand, but he, like, won't even give me a chance to explain. I know it was my fault, but he's just being a total asshole."

"So you saw him in San Francisco?"

"Yes. I was with Dad at Saks and we ran into him." Lisa started to tell him about what she'd learned about Ted mentoring Adam, but she caught herself. Knowing that the father who had never given T.J. the attention he wanted was now doting on someone else would crush her brother. Better stick to her own plight. "So Dad asks Adam if he can give me a ride back to campus because he's got that party—but then as soon as he left Adam got really drunk and—" Lisa paused, her eyes refilling with tears.

T.J.'s head was spinning. His little sister had been hooking up with *Adam Dory*? Dweeby Adam Dory had been secretly dating his sister for months while sitting across from him discussing business strategy? His first instinct was to rip Adam's head off, but the situation kind of made him respect Adam; she may be his sister, but Lisa was a hot item. And keeping cool with T.J. while he was secretly banging his sister was pretty slick.

T.J. got up from the chair and moved next to his sister, putting his arm around her and pulling her head in to his shoulder, trying not to worry about the mascara smearing onto his favorite Façonnable button-down. "It's okay, Lisa," he said, stroking her head. "Everything's going to be okay."

"You're not mad?" she sniffled into his shoulder.

"Of course I'm not mad. You're my little sister. You know I'll always be here for you." He gently pushed her up so he could look at her and smiled jokingly. "Even if you do have terrible taste in men. I mean, seriously . . . Adam Dory?"

She laugh-cried with him for a moment before reburying her face and letting out a heaving sigh. "But there's another thing, T.J."

"What is it?"

"I haven't told anyone at all, T.J. I think I'm afraid to."

"You can tell me anything, Lisa. You know that."

"The last time Adam and I were together was in Hawaii, and that was about two months ago, and . . ." She started but couldn't finish. She pushed herself up and looked T.J. straight in the eyes. No need to think or feel, just deliver the facts: "I haven't gotten my period since."

15

Duping Delight

"Where are we going?" Adam asked Violet. Not that it mattered. She was hot and she was leading him away from the St. Francis and he would follow her anywhere, but he felt like he should ask.

"There's a party I want to crash," she answered without more detail. She then caught herself, saying, "I mean, if that's okay with you?"

"Oh, of course," Adam said casually, watching her hail a taxi. *Crashing a party in the city? How cool.*

Adam admired the view of the San Francisco Bay as the car sped along the Embarcadero. Violet was texting furiously on her iPhone. "Sorry, just have to do something quickly for work." She smiled at him from her side of the car. "You know, the day is about to start in London."

"It's no problem," he said, smiling as he rolled down the window. She was so pretty.

"Thirteen twenty," the cabdriver said as he turned off the meter and pulled up to an old warehouse on the water. Violet quickly swiped a credit card, carefully hiding the name on the card from Adam.

Adam wasn't paying attention, though, and got out of the car to wait for her. The warehouse was an unlit cement block with industrial doors. Thick painted block letters read PIER 24 on the wall facing the street, and graffiti tags littered the side. Just behind the building was an old wooden deck where the violent waves of the San Francisco Bay lapped its rotting wooden posts.

Adam jumped as a homeless man stumbled toward him, pushing a rickety shopping cart overloaded with God-knows-what. The man was singing to himself and not paying attention to Adam, but Adam nevertheless ducked his head and got out of the way, instinctively covering his nose at the man's stench as they walked by. Where *were* they?

"You're not scared, are you?" Violet teased. Adam watched the cab speed off behind her and felt his heart momentarily clinch in fear that he'd done something very, very stupid.

But he let that thought go and instead tried to focus on the way her tight dress pulled across her hips.

"Stop staring at my legs." She smiled and grabbed his hand, saying, "Let's go."

If I'm going to die a horrible death, Adam thought, *at least I'll go having held the hand of a gorgeous woman.*

Violet's high heels clicked on the sidewalk and she fearlessly led him to the run-down warehouse. She approached a side door and lifted the grimy cover of a keypad, where she entered a code with her purple-polished finger. Adam heard a buzz and Violet pushed the door open onto a dark corridor, stepping carefully to avoid spiderwebs and exposed electrical wires.

Adam stopped short, an image from *The Godfather* suddenly whizzing into his brain, causing him to feel alertly sober and afraid. "Where are you taking me?" he snapped, glancing behind him and calculating the distance to the door.

Violet howled with pure enjoyment as she pressed her body against his, placing her hand on his pecs. "I know it looks sketchy, but this is San Francisco: Sketchy is the new chic."

"Who are you?" His whole body was on fire with fear and excitement.

"Think of me as a friend," she said determinedly, her eyes peeking from below her blond bangs as her hand slid down his abs until her fingers toyed with his belt buckle, "and I hope that we can begin to be more than friends."

He could smell her skin and feel her breath on his own, and this made the rest of his body pulse, the speed of his heartbeat not subsiding, but shifting to a different cause.

"I'd like that, too," he whispered.

"Good." She grinned, letting go of his body and firmly intertwining her fingers with his. "I think we're going to have a lot of fun together, Adam Dory."

He could still smell her breath on him and feel her hands on his body as he followed her down the remainder of the corridor and through another door, this one opening onto a large room with the highest ceilings he'd ever seen. Although a moment ago there was silence, suddenly music blasted from a DJ booth and at least a hundred chicly dressed people milled about with drinks in hand. Two walls of the room were entirely glass, looking out on the Bay at Alcatraz and toward the Bay Bridge, perfectly framed by the deep purple of the night sky. The walls made it feel like there was no divide between the inner and the outer world—like you could step into the water and reach out to touch the bridge's lights. Adam had never seen San Francisco like this.

She laughed, saying, "See? Told you I wasn't taking you somewhere to kill you." She pulled him toward the bar. "Let's get a drink."

At the bar, Violet struck up a conversation with a couple who greeted them kindly. "This is Adam Dory," Violet said, "the mastermind behind Doreye." The man lifted his eyebrows and clicked his glass to Adam's, clearly impressed.

"Well done. I've heard a lot about the app—really looking forward to the big launch."

Violet handed Adam a Jack and Coke, which she had ordered without even asking him what he wanted. He quickly downed it and ordered another. He was feeling alive and exuberant, like this was the missing element that he'd been searching to find.

Violet kept blindly talking to people she didn't know, always making a point to introduce Adam as the expert at the helm of Doreye. They all accepted it as absolute truth; no one said, "Oh, I thought there was a girl running it," and no one ever asked, "Isn't that T. J. Bristol's thing?" He was perfectly credible as its leader, and Violet was beginning to show him it could be his.

After a while people started dancing and Violet led Adam to join in. She stepped back and forth and rocked her hips just so; she shook her head to the music, letting her blond hair move sexily back and forth over her bare shoulders. Adam had the unbelievable urge to cradle her head in his hands and feel her hair through his fingers and pull her mouth onto his and pull those hips toward his own. He forgot all about Lisa.

He was about to get up the nerve to do so when the DJ stopped the music and said, "Ladies and gentlemen, thank you all for coming tonight to celebrate. Ted Bristol is here to share a few words."

Adam felt his face go white with panic as he recognized Ted walking onto the stage. He was supposed to have given Lisa a ride back to campus. What if Ted saw him—what if he already had? Violet had just spent the last hour introducing Adam to half the room: Surely he was caught.

He looked at Violet, who was looking straight at Ted Bristol. Ted turned his gaze in their direction and Adam ducked his head and shuffled to the bathroom.

Violet caught his arm and followed. "Where are you going?"

"Why is Ted Bristol here?" he whispered to Violet.

"Gibly was his company."

"This is a Gibly party? I thought Gibly was shut down."

"No. They just sold to a British company. Sale closed like two weeks ago. This is the celebration party. Poor Ted," Violet went on. Did she know him?

"Why?"

"He got totally screwed in the deal. After that hacker, there was such a massive PR debacle, the company barely sold for anything."

Adam's heart sank hearing her words. Had Amelia really caused all that? Once again, Amelia's pretend innocent do-goodery had hurt someone. And his mentor, no less.

Of course, Ted wasn't going to be his mentor much longer if he found out Adam was at the Gibly party with Violet instead of driving his daughter Lisa home.

Violet looked at him. "Are you okay?"

"I gotta go. Now," Adam said. "How far is it to the St. Francis? My car's still there."

"Adam," she reprimanded, "chill out. You're way too drunk to drive. Just have fun and crash at my place tonight." She bit her lip and smiled.

Adam's instinctive defensiveness at being called out as a drunk was immediately offset by the epic victory of getting to sleep at Violet's apartment.

"Okay, but I think we should head out of here. Now."

She smiled at his assertiveness. "Whatever you want, Mr. Dory."

And just like that, Adam, the mastermind behind Doreye, was off to spend the night in the city with a beautiful woman. Maybe things were finally turning around after all.

16

Smooth Boolean Operator

Amelia tiptoed into the hospital room, where she had ridden her bike as soon as Riley dropped her off at her dorm, oblivious to the fact that it was nearing midnight and the streets were pitch-dark. "How could you not tell me?"

Roger's eyes were closed in half-sleep and his face was long and pale. An IV was feeding clear liquid into his arm, which was half the size it used to be, and plastic tubes exhaled oxygen into his nostrils.

"Amelia Dory the magazine star," he said, and smiled weakly without opening his eyes.

Amelia's anger melted into concern. She moved closer to Roger and whispered, "Why didn't you tell me?"

Roger opened his eyes. "I should have. But I didn't know how."

Amelia thought about how she'd said the same thing to Adam.

"Are you angry?"

"No."

"How did you find out?" He coughed. He still hadn't opened his eyes, as if conserving all the energy he had.

"Riley. She was the photographer for the *Forbes* thing."

Roger's eyes brightened into a smile. "That sneaky girl. You stay close to her, okay? She's special. Like you."

A nurse came in to check Roger's vitals.

"I can come back," Amelia said, hoping he'd say no.

"I'm sorry I'm not much company," he said, his voice weak. "I'm just so tired." His breathing grew steady and Amelia stayed— she didn't know how long—watching his fragile chest rise and fall until the nurse asked her to leave.

Amelia left the hospital and got on her bike, her brain spinning. It was all too much: Roger and Riley and Adam and T.J. She didn't know what to do, but knew she couldn't sleep and found her bike pointed to Gates.

She got to her old computer terminal and said hello to her fellow night programmers, wondering why they were staring. But then she remembered she was wearing her new clothes and makeup and blushed helplessly.

She pulled on headphones and opened Spotify, typing "The xx" into the radio playlist and letting the beat of the music flood her ears as she inserted a thumb drive and opened her Ubuntu box to continue working on the nested conditionals she'd started last week. She was solving for a negative feedback loop in the Doreye app that caused the program to hog the mobile device's RAM and waste all of the battery.

Amelia didn't lift her eyes from the screen until five hours later, when she noticed that the sky had an orange glow from the rising sun. She sat back and watched it, breathing deeply and feeling calm, or perhaps delirious from working for so long.

"Good morning, stranger." T-Bag, her old flamboyant friend from ZOSTRA parties, was suddenly beside her.

"T-Bag!" Amelia smiled and jumped from her chair to give him a hug. "What are you doing here? I thought you were going abroad this quarter?"

"I considered it, but why leave all this?" He gestured around him. "I decided instead to start pursuing my master's degree, as one does," he said, nodding in humble recognition of having taken the stereotypical path of engineers pursuing as many degrees as possible so as not to have to face the real world.

He looked at his watch. "And now I am charged with TAing the eight A.M. section of Computer Science 101." He let his eyes get wide and silently mouthed, *Oh my God.*

Amelia chuckled imagining T-Bag, one of the university's smartest programmers, tutoring the Intro to CS crowd. "Will you walk me to class?" T-Bag suggested.

"Would love to," Amelia said, grinning. "I'm so happy to see you."

Now that Adam and Roger weren't around, maybe T-Bag could be her support.

As they walked down the stairs to T-Bag's lecture hall Amelia saw the building doors open, and a flushed T. J. Bristol rushed through. Her heart froze. What was he doing here? She blushed and brushed her face, trying to wipe away the sleepless night as he spotted her and waved.

"Amelia!" He was walking over, and she shifted anxiously on her heels. T-Bag lifted a silent eyebrow in her direction as if to say, "Who is this frat boy and why is he talking to you?"

"Hi, T.J.," Amelia said, aware of T-Bag watching and evaluating. "What are you doing here?"

T.J. reached out his hand to T-Bag. "I'm T.J.," he offered.

"Theodore." T-Bag took his hand and nodded.

T.J. turned back to Amelia, reaching out to rest his hand lightly on her arm. "You caught me! I'm taking the Intro to Computer Science class." He lifted his hand and shrugged. "I thought since I'm working in tech I ought to at least try to understand the basics."

Amelia smiled and her cheeks burned at the same time: Was it really possible a guy like T.J. could care that much what geeks thought? *Stop,* she told herself. She didn't know what had been going on lately, but it felt like she couldn't stop rushing to T.J.'s defense. Not necessarily to other people, but to herself. It was making her nervous around him, too, nervous about what he was thinking . . . especially what he was thinking about her.

"That's great, T.J." She covered up the thought just in time for another to creep in: *Oh my God, is T-Bag going to be T.J.'s TA?* Her head was freaking out but she said as coolly as she could, "Let me know if you, you know, need any help or anything."

"No offense, but there's absolutely no way I'd be able to ask you for help. You'd lose all respect for me!" T.J. said. "I mean, assuming you've got some respect for me now."

Amelia blushed furiously. Was he trying to make her self-conscious? The threesome stood for a moment in awkward silence until T-Bag broke it. "Are you in room G-107? I believe I'm your TA."

"Yes, I noticed you as the guy who sits in the front looking exasperated and annoyed at my questions." T.J. smiled. "We should probably head inside?"

"Indeed," T-Bag agreed. "Miss Amelia, such a pleasure to run into you. Were I at all interested in women I'd tell you that you look absolutely stunning today." He leaned down to kiss her cheek.

T-Bag's gesture left T.J. not sure how to say good-bye, and so he leaned forward and gave Amelia a kiss on the cheek, too. "Yes, you really do," he whispered in her ear.

The two men headed for G-107. Amelia stood in the hall watching them go, her face on fire from where T.J. had kissed her.

17

"Another for my little little!" Sally slurred, motioning to the bartender to bring Patty another tequila shot.

Aside from being the daughter of a billionaire hedge fund manager in New York, Sally was Patty's big sis's big sis in Delta Gamma, and was tonight being very generous with her alcohol intake, her affection, and her credit card.

She leaned over the bar to the man pouring the tequila shots; he was tall and angular, with slicked black hair and olive skin. "My friend Patty here," she said drunkenly, "started a comp-a-ny."

He smiled flirtatiously at Sally, leaning in to her tequila breath. "And what kind of company did she start?"

Sally grinned and blushed. "You are C-U-T-E!"

He returned the grin and she put a twenty on the bar and told him to keep the change, even though their shots were four dollars apiece.

"Cheers," she said, and clicked glasses with Patty and shot back the tequila, sucking on a piece of lime to chase the taste.

Patty did the same, squinting at the sourness, but Sally had moved on to another conversation before Patty could thank her.

She sat the empty shot glass on the bar and thanked the cute bartender. Patty hadn't been out at all since she'd started Focus

Girls, and the alcohol felt good and familiar as it hit her bloodstream.

"What kind of company did you start?" the man sitting at the bar to her left asked. His hair was graying, but he had a young vibe, dressed stylishly in a purple checkered shirt, dark-wash jeans, and Gucci loafers.

She studied him for a moment, not used to talking to strangers in bars, then decided he was okay and turned her shoulders toward him.

"You really want to know?"

"I do." He took a sip of his drink. "I'm a VC. Give me your elevator pitch."

"Well," she said, and took a deep breath, "Focus Girls is dedicated to connecting companies with their most valuable consumer: young women. We provide a platform for connecting marketing departments with the college-age female influencers they want to be advocates of their brands."

"You're a Focus Girl?" the man asked.

"Have you heard of us?" she asked eagerly.

The man let out a laugh. "Uh, yeah. All the guys on Sand Hill are talking about it."

"Really?" Patty surged with pride.

"I know a couple guys who are pretty excited about it. Don't kid with me here: You seriously do it?"

"I don't just *do* Focus Girls," Patty said, smiling, "I *started* Focus Girls."

"Exciting." The man lifted his eyebrows and took a sip of his beer, turning his eyes away from her as if he needed to process what he'd heard. "You don't seem so"—he caught himself—"you just don't seem like the type."

"What is that supposed to mean?" Her delight gave way to offense. Who did this guy think he was, saying she couldn't start a company? She was just as capable—no, *more* capable—than half the "entrepreneurs" she knew at Stanford.

"You're just not what I expected, that's all," he said. "Pretty girls like you don't—"

"Don't what?" She set her jaw angrily and turned to the bartender. "Could I have a glass of water, please?" she said steadily, intentionally disacknowledging the man.

"What?" he asked.

She took a long sip of her water and finally turned back to him. "'What?'" she parroted. "I'll tell you what: Just because I'm a girl and just because I'm young and just because I have one iota of fashion sense doesn't mean I can't start a company just as well as some loser engineer or douche-bag MBA, okay?"

"That's not what I meant—" the man started.

Patty downed her water and glared at him. "Whatever," she said as she turned away.

"No, wait. You totally misunderstood what I said. What I meant was—" But she didn't hear the rest.

How dare some guy in a bar tell her what she could or couldn't do? How dare he make judgments about what she was capable of? She shook her head angrily, as if trying to scrape the memory of the incident from her brain, and went to find Sally.

18

Making the Grade

"I don't often follow up with students on their work." Professor Marsh took a handkerchief from his pocket as he flagged a waiter. "Another Syrah for me, please, dear," he said to the waitress, and then to Adam, "especially after nine months and especially when those students nearly fail my class for insubordination."

The waitress waited to take Adam's order. "Anything for you?"

"I'll have a Coke, please," he answered.

"Suit yourself," Marsh responded as he sniffed and wiped his nose with the handkerchief. "One of the perks of being a grumpy old man is that you can drink whenever you please." He sat back and considered, "On the other hand, I suppose that's one of the perks of being a college student these days as well."

Adam laughed nervously. It was his first time in the Faculty Club, the esteemed faculty-and-their-guests-only members club whose old-school décor and secretive allure seemed out of sync with the rest of Stanford University.

Marsh had invited Adam here in response to his makeup essay assignment, which he'd sent in an e-mail with the subject line "What I would have rather been doing than sitting in your class, one year later."

Now, they sat in a dark dining room with high ceilings, next to an imposing stone fireplace. The table was covered in a white cloth that matched the napkin Adam had been proud of himself for remembering to unfold and put in his lap.

"So," Adam began hesitantly, "are we cool with the class? I mean, did I pass now?"

"Oh, sure," Marsh replied slowly. "I suppose I wouldn't actually have failed you, but I was curious whether you'd come through with something."

Adam felt momentarily betrayed: Why had he made him write that essay if he'd never actually have failed him?

But Marsh anticipated the question. "You see, as a professor, you're made to teach these imbecile classes to groups of students who will do nothing with them. It's aggravating beyond belief, but occasionally you find a student who seems to actually get it. Of those who get it, however, maybe one in ten actually does something with his or her talent. Whilst unconventional, in class that day you proved something. Your off-the-cuff description of the prisoner's dilemma showed that you have a natural intuition for the subject, as well as an ability to apply it in unique ways. The essay assignment was my wanting to see whether you're the one in ten who takes it somewhere."

Adam was trying to let this all sink in: No one had ever complimented him on his academic performance; all the praise had always gone to Amelia.

"That's not why I brought you here, though." Marsh scratched his nose. "I wanted to find out more about this company of yours everyone keeps talking about."

Adam sat up in his chair. "People are talking about it?" Everyone always said professors hated when Stanford kids started companies because it distracted them from studying. Why would Marsh have heard—or care—about Doreye?

"Yes. It sounds like it's a very nice . . . app." He sounded awkward saying the word. "I'm curious what you're doing with it. The . . . app, I mean."

The waitress returned with their drinks. "Thank you," Marsh said, and nodded at her.

"Well, Doreye is an application that enables your iPhone to see other devices; it basically turns your iPhone into a central remote control or radar."

"And is this one of those companies that collects user data?"

"Well, sure. Utilizing personal data is necessary for the app to function."

"The usual for me, Mary," Marsh said, transitioning his attention casually to the back-again waitress. "Have you had a chance to decide?" he asked Adam, who quickly glanced at the menu before him.

"I'll have the ravioli, please." Adam chose the first thing he saw.

"And do you have any qualms about that?"

"About ravioli?"

"No, about collecting user data?"

"It's what we need to make the app work. Don't worry, we scramble everything; it's not like we save it."

"Has anyone ever approached you about doing anything with it?"

"No." Adam felt himself prickle. What was this man getting at? "Why?"

"Just personal curiosity. The legal issues surrounding privacy and technology interest me. What's your view on it? I mean, if someone asked you to sell user data?"

"We'd never do it. I don't know if you know my sister, but she'd totally flip out. She doesn't even want us to charge users to download the app."

Marsh chuckled. "Is that so?"

"It's annoying."

Mary returned with their food and Adam inelegantly shoveled an entire ravioli in his mouth.

"Do you ever feel your sister's moral compass is holding you back?"

Adam almost choked. "How did you know?"

Marsh stopped chewing and looked carefully at Adam. "How do you mean?"

"Oh, she just doesn't see the bigger picture sometimes," he said honestly. "Like she gets so set in her ways, she can't rationalize how sometimes you have to do certain things you don't like in order to get the outcome that's best for the company."

Marsh looked back down at his food and began eating again. "Interesting," he said. "And you're fund-raising right now? Are you looking at VCs in the Bay Area or talking to any European firms?"

"No, we're just focused on Sand Hill Road right now."

"That's very exciting,"

Marsh went quiet. Adam looked at him, wondering what to say.

"So do you have any advice?"

Marsh looked surprised by the question. He shrugged. "Be careful."

"What do you mean?"

"You're very politically astute, Adam. Your articulation of the prisoner's dilemma indicated a natural understanding of group theory few can grasp. But that power has responsibility."

Adam blushed at the compliment. "So you're saying . . . ?"

"Be careful. Surround yourself with good people lest you rationalize behaviors you'll later regret."

Mary came back to clear their plates.

"Dessert?" Marsh smiled.

As Adam left the Faculty Club, he found a text from Violet, whom he'd seen almost every day since they got acquainted in San Francisco. Unlike Amelia and Lisa, Violet encouraged Adam. She was impressed with his intelligence and ability and wasn't afraid to say so. Plus she was totally sexy: She was older and from England and had a real job. He didn't know exactly what it was, but she had to travel a lot and it seemed exotic, and being around her made him feel important.

"How'd lunch go?"

He tapped a response:

"Good. Really good. He said I'm one of the most politically astute students he's ever had."

"Impressive."

"He had a bunch of questions about Doreye though."

"Like what?"

"Nothing major. Wanted 2 know abt user info. Told him Amelia crazy abt it staying secure."

"Ugh, she's so naïve."

"U think so?"

"Of course. It's not like ur collecting hard core data. U have to do what's best for the co. who knows what that will be?"

"Ur right. Abt the bigger picture. That's what I told him."

"Can't let her stand in the way if it comes to that."

"Totally. CU tonight?"

"U bet."

19

Snapshots

T.J. pulled into the driveway of his parents' house, his skin still damp from his workout despite the fact that his t-shirt was high-quality Dri-Fit. He had planned to only go to the gym for a quick round of chest tri-delts, but he spotted a hot Persian girl in spandex short shorts going into spinning class and decided he could spare the hour to watch her sweat; he followed her into the studio and snagged the bike next to her, along with her phone number.

Totally worth it, even if it meant he would be late to have dinner with some old college buddies at the Rosewood. They'd understand. First, though, he had to grab his golf clubs from his parents' attic, where he still stored all his sports equipment, for an early-morning tee time.

He was disappointed to see his father's car along with another he didn't recognize in the drive.

He opened the back gate and followed the brick path toward the kitchen door, but as he got closer he heard voices on the patio. He started to backtrack and go through the front of the house instead, but then it seemed foolish to go to so much trouble to avoid his father, and he was kind of curious what was going on.

His father's laughter drifted toward him and then a woman's voice said, "For what it's worth, you haven't aged a bit."

T.J. felt his heart clench. He knew that voice.

"You have." His father. "That is, you've blossomed into a beautiful woman from a pretty college girl."

She laughed, and her laughter turned T.J.'s legs to cement at the same time it awakened all his other senses. Was it possible?

The flash of a camera illuminated the backyard. Then another. The voices bantered but T.J. could no longer make out what they were saying.

Riley was here—here in his yard, just around the corner, not twenty feet away. T.J. was heaving, his mind whirring with what to do. *Just one look,* he thought. Or maybe just grab her from behind, like he used to do, and kiss her neck and feel her melt in his arms. Or maybe . . . No. No. No. Her eyes came rushing back into his mind, the vision of their seriousness when she dumped him and said, "I can't do this anymore. I'm done," forever emblazoned on his brain. He had to get out.

T.J. willed his legs into action and headed back toward the gate. He'd forgotten all about the golf clubs. He just knew he had to get back to his car and drive away as quickly as humanly possible. He beelined toward the driveway, cutting through his mother's carefully manicured flowerbed. He couldn't care less about the roses; he just needed to get out.

As he pushed past the hydrangeas, his foot tripped the automatic lights that wrapped around the house's eave. He heard the laughter around the corner stop as the white lights came on, but he didn't stop. *Must get back to car.*

"Who's there?" his father's voice called. "Hello? Lori?"

T.J. fumbled out of the hydrangea bush and jogged toward the gate, his hands shaking as he struggled with the latch. Why would the damn thing not open? Why was Riley laughing with his father in his backyard? Screw it. He gripped the top of the fence and hopped over, just as he heard his father's footsteps on the path behind him. "Hello? Who is that?"

He raced around to the driver's seat and climbed into his car just as his father opened the gate. "Who is that?" his father's voice tried again.

T.J. was maniacally focused on getting his key into the ignition but his hands were shaking. "T.J.?"

Caught. He couldn't drive off now. But how could he face Riley, having just run from her like a coward? And sweaty from the gym to boot? This is not how he'd imagined their reunion.

T.J. swallowed hard, staring at the steering wheel as if for inspiration.

"T.J., what are you doing home? You'll never guess who's here!"

He took a deep breath, killed the engine, and climbed halfway out of the car, leaving one foot inside as he waved over the top of the vehicle. "Hi! Sorry—just realized I left my wallet at the gym—gotta run back and get it before they close. Hope I didn't interrupt!"

That was good, he thought, as he started to duck back into the car. But right at that moment, *she* appeared next to his father, the house lights silhouetting her lean curves in the purple dusk. She waved and pushed past Ted, coming straight toward him.

He got in the car, but she caught the door before he could pull it open, placing herself between the car and the ajar door, her thin waist close enough to reach out and touch. "Hi," she said, the syllable lingering for a moment before he responded.

"Hi, Riley." She smelled just like he remembered, like she hadn't changed perfumes since college. Was it lavender or rose?

She raised her eyebrow and he felt her eyes studying him as he looked ahead at the dash.

After a moment she let out a quick guffaw and shook her head in false disbelief. "Are you really not going to say anything?"

He didn't look at her—he couldn't. "What would you like me to say?" he asked the dash.

"I don't know?" she started, but it took her a moment to figure out what to say next. "You could say hello. You could ask how I am or say that it's good to see me. You could even ask why I'm here."

Maybe she was here to apologize, to tell him it had all been a big mistake. The worst decision she'd ever made in her life.

"Why are you here?" T.J. asked pointedly.

"I'm doing freelance work for a magazine that's running an article on your father. Seriously, T.J.," she continued, "we haven't seen each other in over two years, and all of a sudden I'm in your backyard and your reaction is to run?"

He felt his anger well at her presumptuousness. She was in *his* yard; how dare she talk to *him* about what was appropriate. And how dare she assume he was *running away*.

"I was not running from you, Riley." He finally turned to look up at her as he said her name. Her hair was pulled back in a ponytail, accentuating her cheekbones, which seemed to have become more pronounced since he used to stare at them while they were making out in his frat house, holding that face in his hands and kissing her over and over and everywhere. "I have to go, because believe it or not, I have a life. I'm sorry I don't have time to stay and catch up," he said spitefully.

Her lips split open in . . . hurt? Disbelief? Their eyes were locked, hers searching his for some indication, and his stubbornly not conceding, glaring at her with as much resolve as he'd ever had to not be made vulnerable.

She shook her head and dropped the stare. "Fine," she said.

"Great," he answered, turning his attention back to the ignition and starting the engine. She didn't move, though, and he didn't attempt to force her.

"Really?" Her voice was frustrated. "You're *really* going to drive off," she said meanly.

"Yes, Riley. I'm really going to drive off."

"I wish you wouldn't, T.J."

The sound of her voice saying his name made his heart stop again, bringing up all the emotions linked to memories of all the times she'd said it before. "I have to go," he said quietly, reaching for the door.

She slid her hips to get out of his way and he slammed the door. She didn't move as he turned the car around and drove away.

London Fog

Violet extended her crossed leg and admired the new red-with-a-pink-bow-on-the-heel stiletto pump on her right foot, half listening to the conference call about some new company acquisition that was playing through her phone's headset. Her boss had asked her to join the call. Technically, he wasn't really her boss, just one of the people who paid her retainer and gave her assignments.

She'd picked the shoes up at the Ted Baker near Oxford Circus yesterday. They were a statement, but she liked them. Yes, definitely a good purchase.

She put the phone on mute and let out a vocal sigh, staring out her window at the London skyline, framed by a drizzling gray sky and pierced by the modern skyscraper nicknamed the Gherkin.

These calls bored Violet, as did being back in London. It was full of stuffy old men, and she had no influence; she preferred the can-do-it-ness of Silicon Valley and the eternal optimism (or was it naïveté?) of the Americans.

She heard a *blurp* and turned to her computer screen. A Skype message popped up in the corner from Adam Dory: "*You free?*"

She looked at her clock: It was almost noon here, meaning it was almost 4:00 A.M. in California. What was Adam doing up so late?

She keyed "*Sure*," and clicked into Skype.

"You're up late," she said into her headset.

"What are you wearing?"

"New red stilettos. They match my underwear."

"You are so hot," he slurred. She smiled. Yes, she preferred the Americans.

"Are you drunk?"

"No," he answered quickly. "Maybe a little." He paused. "I did what you said."

She sat up in her chair. "You got another meeting with Ross Brown? When are you meeting him?"

"Tomorrow," Adam said, "at noon."

Crap, Violet thought, no way she could get back in time. "Does Amelia know?"

"I thought you said I shouldn't tell her about it," he whined.

"No," Violet said quickly, "of course you shouldn't. She's not supposed to be part of the business conversations anymore."

"I wish you were here."

"Is T.J. coming?"

"I told him about it and told him I was talking to them about COO stuff. Honestly, he was being super weird on the phone. I don't even know if he heard."

"What's going on with T.J.?"

"Don't know. He said something about a girl. I'm kind of glad he's not going to be there. I don't want him interfering."

"Good for you."

"Do you think I'm doing the right thing?"

"You know I think you are," she said carefully.

"Ted does, too."

"You talked to him about it?"

"Yeah."

"Good. I mean, it's good to get advice from your mentor."

"I wish you were here."

"You're drunk."

"I know."

"Go get some sleep. You have a big day tomorrow."

"Okay."

"I'll be thinking about you, okay? Let me know how it goes."

She clicked out of the Skype window and took a deep breath, as if saying a silent prayer for tomorrow's meeting, before turning back to the call just in time to hear a question addressed to her. "I'm sorry," she said into the receiver, "can you repeat the question?"

"We just wanted an update," the voice replied. "You've been in Silicon Valley for a few months, now, Violet, and our partners are quite eager. Do you have any new leads?"

"Patience is a virtue in this business, gentlemen," she coaxed. "But I do have one company in mind. It's better than Gibly and has access to just the kind of user data the Aleister Corporation wants; I don't want to jinx it, but things are looking quite good."

Alarms and False Alarms

Amelia felt the vibration in her pocket before her sleeping ears registered the sound and she awoke to her iPhone ringing. She shook her head and readjusted her glasses, which were twisted from where they'd been pressed against her arm on the table at the library where she had, evidently, fallen asleep studying for an upcoming history test.

She didn't recognize the number on the iPhone screen, and said sleepily, "Hello?"

"Amelia?" She slowly registered the frantic female voice as Riley's. "Amelia, are you on campus?"

Amelia unnecessarily peered around at the library stacks before answering, "Yeah, I'm at the library, what's up?"

She spoke in short breaths, intentionally keeping her statements factual. "I'm heading to the hospital. I think you should, too. Roger's not doing very well. I just got the call. If you're close I can pick you up."

Amelia's brain clicked to alert and she started closing up her books and packing her bag. "No, it'll be faster if I bike. I'll meet you there."

She ran down the library steps and got on her bike, focusing all her attention on getting to the hospital so that she wouldn't think about why she might be doing so, or what it would mean for Roger.

"His cancer is progressing much more quickly than we expected," the nurse whispered to the two girls. She'd closed the curtain that separated Roger's bed from the other beds, but Amelia could hear him retching behind it.

"Why? How?" Riley's eyes were glassy.

The nurse shrugged her shoulders. "He refused the chemotherapy. I can't say I blame him, but it means nature's going to take its course on whatever timeline it wants."

Riley stretched her fingers and clenched them into a fist at her side over and over, a nervous habit Amelia hadn't noticed before.

"So what do we do?"

The nurse's eyebrows lifted in the center and she pursed her mouth empathetically. "You wait."

Riley nodded silently.

Another nurse stuck her head out from the curtain and said, "He heard your voices. Do you want to come in?"

"If I'd known a seizure's all it took to see my two favorite women, I'd have had one a lot sooner." Roger smiled weakly from his bed without opening his eyes.

"Keep saying stuff like that and we're never coming back," Riley said as she pulled a chair to the side of Roger's bed and leaned forward to drop her head on his shoulder, gently stroking the arm that lay above the covers by his side. He turned his head to kiss the top of hers and Riley said softly, "I'm not ready yet."

Amelia watched the pair and realized, suddenly, that Riley had called her not to see Roger, but because Riley needed someone there to support *her*. And rather than being annoyed, the thought that she had the capacity to be that person for someone other than Adam made her feel happy despite the circumstances.

Roger opened his eyes and turned his attention to Amelia.

"My Amelia," he said, and the effort it took to speak was evident. "I hope this isn't distracting you from prepping for your meeting." He closed his eyes again as if to save energy. "I'm so proud of you."

She lifted an eyebrow and looked down at him. "What meeting?"

"Your PKC meeting," he said, swallowing painfully. "Ross Brown stopped by yesterday and he mentioned he was having lunch with Doreye today."

Amelia felt her heart sink into her stomach. She wanted to think Roger was delusional, that the meds had messed up his brain, but something told her he wasn't.

"Did he mention where?" she asked casually.

"Imagine it's at PKC," he said, his voice drifting. "My dear, you really must get better at details."

Amelia glanced at her watch: It was 11:54. PKC was on Sand Hill Road, a ten-minute drive from the hospital. She looked up at Riley, panicked.

Riley took her keys from her coat pocket, looking down at Roger to confirm he'd fallen asleep, and handed them across the bed to Amelia. "Go!" she whispered. "I'll stay here, you've got to hurry!"

Amelia took the keys, wondering whether she should tell Riley she'd never made it through driver's ed. No, couldn't think about that right now. She nodded hurriedly and scrambled out of the room toward the parking lot.

Syntax Error

Adam cracked his knuckles and wiggled his jaw to loosen his throat. He peered out onto Sand Hill Road and imagined for the hundredth time what it was going to feel like when Ross Brown decided he was ready to give him ten million dollars.

Visualization was a technique Ted Bristol had taught him during one of their prep sessions for this meeting. He'd told him it was a common tool for athletes: Imagine what it would feel like to catch that ball, to make that pass, to see the scoreboard show your victory, and its likelihood was statistically more probable. So Adam had spent the last few days thinking about what Ross's handshakes would feel like and practicing saying, "Thank you, Mr. Brown. I know you won't regret this, and I look forward to making Doreye the next big thing."

Adam did not, looking out at the Porsches and BMWs in the parking lot, think about Amelia. Or, at least, he didn't acknowledge that the back of his mind was thinking about her. "Focus on the goal," Ted had told him, and that's what he intended to do.

The path to the goal was incredibly clear. He'd tossed and turned about how to save Doreye, how to get what was best for the company and for himself. And then, the day after the photo shoot fiasco in San Francisco, the solution dawned on him. It came out of nowhere, but then felt so obvious he didn't know how he had missed it. There was one thing holding Doreye back from the next stage of growth, and Adam was the only one capable of eliminating it.

"Welcome, Adam," Ross Brown said from the doorway as he entered, followed by the hyenas and an attractive Asian girl in a low-cut blouse.

"Just you today?"

"Yes," Adam said clearly. "Just me."

Ross caught him staring at the girl's cleavage. "This is Lucy, our intern," he said, presenting her. "I hope you don't mind if she joins us?"

"No, no." Adam blushed. "Not at all." He smiled helplessly. She smiled back. Adam's blood heated.

The investors took their seats as an assistant brought a tray of gourmet sandwiches in and put them at the center of the table.

"I want to start by thanking you for meeting with me on such short notice," he started. Ross and the hyenas stared silently, waiting. Adam could hear his heart pounding in his ears. He hadn't factored a hot girl into his visualization. *Calm down,* he told himself, *just calm down.*

"Last time we met you expressed a lot of concerns. And I'll be honest, I was incredibly defensive at first. In fact, I really thought you were wrong. But we implemented the division of responsibility you suggested and we've all gotten comfortable now with the roles that are ours."

Ross reached for a sandwich and gestured with his hand to go on.

"And we've taken it a step further." He paused. "We've been thinking more about what's required for our long-term strategy— what is required beyond the launch."

Ross didn't say anything so Adam continued, "You see, our product, as you said, is top-notch. It's flawless, in fact. Ready to go. What's important now is monetization. Our focus needs to be on selling our flawless product and making money—a lot of money—off of it. And that requires—"

"Adam." The conference room door swung open and Amelia, her face flushed from running, burst in. "Adam, we have to talk."

Adam's mouth opened in surprise as he looked at her, then back at Ross, then at Lucy, who was licking mustard off her bright red lip. Adam shook the image out of his head. This was definitely not part of his visualization. "Can you excuse us for one second?" Adam asked Ross.

Ross sighed audibly. "Do what you need to do."

"Thanks," Adam said as he moved quickly around the table, picking up a folder as he went. He pulled Amelia out of the room and wondered how he was going to recover with Ross.

He knew what she wanted to say to him: that the app was supposed to be free and open-source, that charging was against her philosophy, and countless other tech-age platitudes that were based in her naïveté. *No, she isn't going to ruin this for me, not again.*

"What are you doing here?" he snapped as he closed the door to an empty conference room.

"What am *I* doing here?" Her eyes got wide. "What are *you* doing, meeting with investors without telling me?"

"I'm getting Doreye funding," Adam said emotionally, the words invigorating his conviction in what he was about to do. "I'm going to walk out of here with ten million dollars to grow the company. I'm going to become something, Amelia."

"But we haven't talked about this."

"We haven't talked about it because you don't want to think about it. You've been too busy promoting yourself in magazines."

"Is that what this is about?" Her voice was angry. "About my being in the *Forbes* article and not you?"

"I'm not jealous of you, if that's what you're saying. Don't flatter yourself." Adam had convinced himself he'd moved past the *Forbes* article.

"Why didn't you tell me you were doing this?" she asked.

"Why didn't you tell me about Lisa and Sundeep?" he came back.

"So *that's* what it's about!" She let out a laugh and touched her hand to her temple. "Geez."

Adam felt his nostrils flare. How could she treat something so serious so lightly?

"No, Amelia. It's about the fact that I can't trust you. And that you're getting so self-focused that you're missing what we need to do for this company."

She crossed her arms and sat back on one hip, looking at him with a half-smile, like he was a child doing something entertaining. Adam's blood was boiling. This was the moment he had been planning for weeks, the single move that would at once save the company, convince Ross to invest, and prove to everyone that he was a great leader willing to take action.

"Which is why, Amelia, you're fired."

She rolled her eyes and tilted her head, lifting her eyebrows. "Oh, am I?" she asked sarcastically.

"Yes." He swallowed and started speaking in a measured tone, reciting the words he'd been practicing but hadn't been sure until this moment he had the courage to deliver. "Check the papers on titles you and T.J. were so happy for me to sign. As COO I'm in charge of personnel. I make the operating decisions necessary for this company to succeed, and it is my decision that it's best for the company if you move on." He kept his voice level.

"What are you talking about, Adam?" She moved her weight forward, finally starting to take him seriously.

He felt all the emotions he'd suppressed since Maui overwhelm him: the jealousy and the anger and the heartache that had made him feel so powerless for so long.

"I'm talking about *you're fired*. You've run your course with Doreye. It's time for us to monetize and to make this a big business, and you're standing in the way."

"You can't unilaterally make a decision like that."

"Yes, I can."

"No, you—"

"You're the one who gave me this authority." He'd gone through all the documents a dozen times and knew he was right. "You're fired. It's what's best for the company."

Adam watched his sister's face drain. She suddenly looked incredibly frail, like if you breathed too hard she'd topple over. She'd always been thin, but confrontation usually made her seem stronger, like when they'd arrested her in Indiana and she'd faced the officer with fierce determination in her jaw and in her eyes, or when she confidently fended off the reporters' attacks in Maui.

He couldn't look at her. He could think about it later: Right now he needed to go get that check. He shifted his weight to move past her to the door.

"How could you do this to me?" Amelia's voice hissed from behind him.

"It's not about you. It's about Doreye."

"No, it's not about me, and it's not about Doreye, it's about you." She paused. "And what you've become."

"Don't be dramatic, Ameel. It doesn't suit you."

"Those aren't your words. This isn't Adam Dory," Amelia pleaded, her voice cracking.

"This is exactly who I am," Adam snapped at his sister as he handed her the folder he had carried out of the conference room. "These are your signed termination papers."

Amelia opened the folder, the reality of what was going on hitting her.

"You planned this?"

"It's over, Amelia. Good leaders don't solve problems, they prevent problems. And who knows what problems were coming between us."

"But you can't do this without me." Amelia's mouth was dry, her spirit broken.

"Yes, we can. The technology's ready and now it's time to monetize. And you were a hindrance to that, not a help. It's my turn to steer this ship."

Amelia, paralyzed by surprise and fear and loss, dropped the folder to the ground. Adam walked out the door without turning around.

Adam shut down the part of his brain that wanted to think about where Amelia was going next and whether she was okay. He shut down the part of his legs that wanted to run after her and take it all back. Walking into the conference room, Adam refocused on his purpose for being here. "Where were we?" he said, smiling at Ross.

"You were saying I'd been right, and that you'd been thinking about the long-term strategy," Ross said. He seemed curious more than annoyed, and Adam relaxed.

"Oh yes," he said, and settled back into his groove. "The long-term strategy requires different skills than those that have gotten us to here. And given the truth of your own critique, we've decided to change the team."

"Who's out?" Ross asked, as if it was nothing.

Adam paused, surprised by his casual tone. Adam swallowed. "Well, Amelia," he answered.

Ross nodded. "Okay."

"Okay, what?" Adam asked, his heart in his throat.

"Okay, I think it makes sense," Ross said, nodding. The hyenas grinned. "I have to admit, I'd written you off as a bit of a coward, but this is an incredibly bold action. It says a lot about your character."

Adam winced—him, a coward?—and leaned forward on his toes to hear Ross's next words.

Ross flipped through the business plan Adam had sent him last time. "And frankly, if you've got the guts to fire your own sister, I think you've got the guts to do what this company needs to do to make a lot of money off of your product."

"Does that mean . . . ?"

"No." Ross shook his head. "I'm not going to give you ten million dollars."

Adam's heart sank. Lucy sat back in her chair, no longer interested in him. *Shit*, Adam thought, the panic sinking in. All of this was for nothing. And Amelia had the papers, so he couldn't even pretend he hadn't done it.

"I'm not going to give you ten million dollars," Ross continued, "because I don't think that's the right number. If you actually pursue this strategy, particularly the one around monetizing user data, I think Doreye is worth a lot more than your forecasts indicate."

"What?" Adam choked, his mouth dry. Lucy's red mouth opened and she leaned forward again.

"And we've recently gotten some more funds of our own to deploy. I want to work on the numbers, but I think you can count us in for twenty million."

Adam's chest collapsed in shock and his face went white before folding into an enormous smile. "Twenty . . . ?" he breathed.

"Yes. That's the right number. But as I said, we'll need to go through some more analyses, and be sure this is okay with the other investors, but this is exactly what we've been looking for." Ross stood up and came around to shake Adam's hand. "Good work, Adam; we'll follow up tomorrow."

Adam's face felt like it was going to crack, he was smiling so big as he took Ross's hand. It worked! He'd actually done it!

The hyenas shook his hand, too, and then it was Lucy's turn. "Mind if I take your photo?" she asked, pulling out her iPhone.

Adam beamed as the flash went off. "Thanks," she said, and smiled.

"Thank you." He returned her grin, following her swaying hips as she left the room and already enjoying his new life.

Adam's heart was light as he packed up his things. It almost felt empty it was so light, like all the stresses that had been weighing it down—money and Amelia and what to do—were suddenly just gone. He felt his phone vibrating and reached into his pocket to take it out. It was a text message from Violet: *"Twenty million???"* Adam smiled helplessly and texted back: *"How'd you know??"* Violet didn't miss a beat: *"TechCrunch is tweeting about it!! Congratulations!!!"*

He grinned helplessly. More buzzes came as he headed to the parking lot. Everyone was learning about it courtesy of a real-time tweeting mole inside PKC. *Lucy,* he thought. The fact that she was a social-media spy made her that much hotter. He accepted the adulation from Ted and ignored the concerned, frantic texts from T.J. and Arjun, their lead engineer who had always idolized Amelia.

They'd come around. He was one day away from getting a term sheet for twenty million dollars; how difficult would it be to convince them he'd done the right thing? For the first time in his life Adam felt like he could do anything; like he was in control—both of Doreye and of his own destiny. He told himself he deserved a moment to enjoy that sensation.

If only he'd known how short-lived his liberation would be, he might have tried to store some of it, to tuck it away so he could draw some courage when everything started, shortly, to unravel.

Part II

Parallel Circuits

23

That Path Is for Your Steps Alone

Amelia Dory barely noticed that her black dress was soaking wet. She was lost in thought and emotion, not able to shake the feeling that her life was turning out differently than she had planned.

California was not like in the advertisements. When Amelia had moved to Palo Alto from Indiana, she expected beaches and palm trees; nobody mentioned that it would rain four months a year. Similarly, when she started college nobody told her about all the stresses—the expectations and the deadlines and the social pressures. And nobody ever told her that opening yourself to care about and trust a person was just a way of setting yourself up for emptiness when one day they disappeared forever.

And so Amelia stared numbly as Roger Fenway's casket disappeared underneath one shovelful of dirt after the other. And she listened to the rain fall on the tarp that covered some of the guests. And she thought about the Math 51 problem set that was due tomorrow, and then she berated her brain for drifting to something so insignificant at a moment like this.

Roger's sister had flown in from Seattle to settle his estate and oversee the services. She'd asked Amelia to join the dozen or so close friends and family at the burial before the full service at Stanford's Memorial Church. "Roger would have wanted you there," she'd told Amelia heroically. "He talked about you a lot."

A preacher in a long black robe read the twenty-third psalm and someone involuntarily wailed in grief. Amelia's wet eyes stayed focused on the dirt filling in the hole that now held her mentor.

The Lord is my shepherd, I shall not want.
He maketh me to lie down in green pastures . . .

The reading of a psalm seemed too formal for a person like Roger Fenway, and she wondered what he would say if he were listening to the service.

She let her mind wander to when she'd become comfortable with Roger, when she'd first felt like she could trust and learn from him. It was just after her first TechCrunch interview when Roger drove her back to the incubator. "Do you like the Grateful Dead?" he'd asked. She'd gone to the car expecting to talk about the interview; to hear his critique and his plan for next steps. But instead of being serious about it, instead of focusing on work at all, he'd talked about music. It was that moment when she knew he had perspective, he knew how to live. She'd felt the light electric vibrations of his Tesla Roadster beat along with "Ripple" and the other songs he played for her, and felt for the first time unafraid of being part of a business.

The priest's lips kept moving, but Amelia listened to Roger's voice singing the lyrics "ripple in still water . . ." Yes, Roger would be singing if he were here.

When the last of the psalms had been read and the coffin fully covered with dirt, Riley squeezed Amelia's hand and gently ushered her to the parking lot.

Riley didn't say anything as she drove them to campus, until she pulled into a reserved space behind the church and shut off the engine. "You have to be brave," she told Amelia, and Amelia felt herself nod.

Riley held an umbrella over Amelia, who had blow-dried her hair and put on makeup the way Patty had taught her at the *Forbes* event, not because she wanted to look pretty, but because she needed something to do this morning while she waited for the four o'clock service to begin.

Amelia was startled as they entered the main quad: It was crowded with people dressed in black, filtering in two long lines from Memorial Church's grand entrance. A camera flashed and Amelia realized the photographer was aiming his camera at her. Riley shooed him away and guided Amelia inside.

The church was a California take on a grand European cathedral: Mosaics on the wall and stained glass in the windows shimmered in the light of candles lining the altar. There were easily a thousand people in the sanctuary—friends, employees, entrepreneurs, and admirers. Riley and Amelia walked with Roger's family and close friends down the center aisle. Adam, who was seated in a pew halfway down, caught Amelia's eye with a sympathetic stare. Amelia looked away.

Amelia tried to listen to the preacher's remarks. She wanted to feel some significance. She studied the flickering light of the candles and Roger's smile in the photo his sister had placed next to the pulpit, looking for a sign. But she found nothing. Her brother was gone, her company was taken away, her mentor was dead. She'd opened herself up to the world, and for what?

"The Bristols are having some people over for dinner," Riley offered. "Will you come?"

They were standing in the church's alcove after the processional following the service.

"I don't really feel like it," Amelia said, and shrugged.

"Okay," Riley replied understandingly. "Can I at least give you a ride back to your dorm?"

"I think I'd like to walk, actually."

"I get that, too." Riley tried a smile. Riley was taking it as hard as Amelia; she had known Roger her entire life, not just a year. Amelia realized she was so lost in her own thoughts that she hadn't even noticed Riley's own suffering today.

"I'm sorry," Amelia offered, "I know today's been awful for you."

"Helping you helps me," Riley said, and gave her a hug. "Call me if you need anything."

"I will."

Riley got into her car and drove away as Amelia stepped out into the dark drizzle.

"Amelia," she heard Adam's familiar voice calling from a distance, but didn't turn to find it.

"Amelia, stop!" He was beside her now. She kept walking, and he matched her pace.

"I don't want to talk, Adam," she said quietly but firmly.

"I know you don't, but you need to—*we* need to."

She stopped and turned to him and snapped, "Since when do you give a shit about what I need?" Amelia was surprised by the force of her own words. She'd never cursed at someone before, and it felt good.

Adam paused in surprise at her forcefulness. "You know I didn't mean for it to happen like this."

"How did you mean for it to happen?"

"I wanted us to be partners, but it wasn't working. Someone had to do something or there wouldn't have been anything for us to be partners *of*."

"Don't make your actions heroic, Adam. You got greedy. Greedy for power and for money and for fame. And you were jealous of me for having what you wanted."

"You didn't want the responsibilities that came with the position. You hated that photo shoot, and you know it. Why should you get to have something you didn't even want when it was exactly what I did want? You were the greedy one, Amelia."

"Quit deluding yourself. You pushed me out because you were angry I hadn't told you about Lisa and Sundeep."

"I had every right to be angry. How am I supposed to trust you anymore?" Adam fought back.

"Yet you could trust the woman who tried to sabotage our entire company."

"Violet isn't what you think."

"I don't know what to think anymore, about her or you."

"Can we please start over?"

"What, do you want to go back to Indiana?" Amelia spat back at him, secretly wishing they could. "Look around you. Things have changed. *You've* changed. There's no going back to the way things were."

"Amelia, you're my sister. You're all that I ever had before we got here. I don't want to lose you."

"You should have thought of that before you got rid of me."

They were a foot apart from each other and even in the dusk Amelia could see Adam's face go red with shame and anger. She glared at him, jaw tensed, not letting go.

"Fine," he spat angrily. "Your pride is going to get you."

He turned on his heel and Amelia watched him walk past the church and join Violet at her car.

She wanted to shout out: "What are you doing? She's the bad guy." But her world was in such disarray that Amelia wasn't sure she could trust her own instincts. No matter how right she'd thought she'd been, the Sundeep secret had destroyed Adam's trust in her, and look where that got them. Maybe Violet wasn't as bad as she thought; and even if she was, Adam wouldn't listen to Amelia. And why should she save him from trouble anyway? Let him work out his own problems this time.

Amelia gave the church one final glance and for the first time noticed the rain dripping from her hair and felt the sadness— and the freedom—of being entirely alone.

24

Bullish

"Everything okay?" Violet offered, the way women do when they know everything is not okay.

"Fine," Adam said firmly. "I don't want to talk about it."

"Then we won't," Violet agreed as they got into her car and drove downtown for dinner. "I think we should go to the Old Pro," she suggested, wiping her wet bangs from her forehead, "drink beer and ride the mechanical bull. Can you imagine the sight of it? The two of us fresh from a funeral, wearing all black and riding the mechanical bull? I didn't know Roger well, but I have a feeling it's what he would have wanted."

Adam smiled at her. He'd secretly been hoping they could go somewhere quiet, have a bottle of wine, and call it a night. But Violet's spontaneity—her total disregard for convention—was what he loved most about her, and if that meant chugging beer tonight, so be it. "Sure," he said. "Sounds great."

Violet's phone started to ring as they reached University Avenue. She glanced at the caller ID and pulled over, answering, "Can you hold for a second?" Then, muting the phone, she turned to Adam. "I'm so sorry, Adam, but this is a super important and confidential call—could you give me just five minutes?"

This had been happening a lot lately; Adam obediently got

out of the car. He went into the Walgreens on the corner to dodge the rain and wait for Violet to finish.

He wandered the gum aisle and thought about whether he'd prefer cinnamon or mint. Just as he was settling on a three-pack of wintergreen, he saw a blond ponytail walk up to the register. It was Lisa.

Adam instinctively ducked behind a candy display and watched her hesitantly put her purchase on the countertop.

The cashier glanced at the two boxes Lisa had placed before him and gave her a look before picking one up to scan.

Adam peered to see what she was buying.

"Such a cliché, isn't it?" Violet suddenly appeared beside him. "Sorority girl stocking up on pregnancy tests." She smirked and turned her attention to the Raisinets on sale.

Pregnancy tests? Lisa was pregnant?

Jealousy pulsed through Adam's veins. She was having sex with someone else. And that someone else had knocked her up. His brain was hazy with rage and it took every ounce of self-control not to run out from behind the display and confront her.

He watched Lisa cram the tests into her bag and pull the hood of her sweatshirt over her ponytail as she headed out into the rain.

"You ready?" Violet said, startling him. "Sorry about the call; was a false alarm. But I needed gum anyway."

He followed her absentmindedly to the counter, his brain weighing whether it was Sundeep or someone else, but too foggy with envy to make sense of any of it.

"Hun, give him the gum," Violet said, and jabbed her elbow into his side and indicated the cashier.

He finally settled on a thought: *That slut,* and slammed his wintergreen three-pack onto the counter, swallowing hard to fight back his overwhelming grief.

"Why are you being so incredibly dull?"

Violet looked at Adam with bored eyes as she lifted an overly ketchuped garlic fry with her bright red fingernails to her equally bright lips. She took special care to chew it in the side of her mouth in order to maintain her grimace.

"Violet, we did just come from a funeral," Adam defended himself, thankful to Roger for giving him an excuse for his disinterest, even if it wasn't the real one.

Violet kept chewing as she stared at him with an eyebrow lifted, finally saying, "Please."

Her tone offended him; she knew how he'd felt about Roger. She knew he'd sat in the service today listening to all the stories of Roger's endlessly generous encouragement of young entrepreneurs and resenting the man in the coffin for never extending the same loving kindness to him.

But Adam thought he'd done a good job hiding these feelings and was, therefore, irritated that Violet knew.

"I'm going to get more beer," Violet announced, polishing off her glass and standing up from the table, brushing past Adam and grazing his arm with her soft fingers so that all of his hairs stood up, wanting more.

The Old Pro, a two-story sports bar with a mechanical bull, was the raucous Palo Alto hot spot for after-work revelers, drunk college kids, and scantily clad girls. Adam watched Violet push her way through the crowd. She had a way of leading with her hip, turning more than necessary to make the slimness of her waist and perfect curve of her ass appreciably obvious to the men she brushed past. Adam took a sip of his beer, unsure whether that made him like her more or less.

He stared out the window at people passing with their umbrellas, unable to get Lisa out of his mind. *Pregnancy tests.* How was it possible?

Adam found it difficult not to think about their own failed attempt at sex. He'd been a virgin, of course, and Lisa had been, too—or at least that's what she'd told him. But then again, she'd also failed to tell him that she was secretly dating Sundeep. Adam had wanted so badly for Lisa to be his first; not just because at nineteen years old he thought he was past the point of waiting, but because he . . . well . . . he loved her. And he wanted to be the one that made it special for *her* first time, too.

And so they'd talked about it and she'd said she wasn't ready and he'd said, "That's fine, just let me know when you are."

But then one night right before Hawaii they'd both gotten very drunk at a Secret Snowflake holiday party and ended up in his room in the frat house and one thing led to another and then it was happening, just like that, and then it was over, just as quickly. And they laughed and apologized and made humor out of embarrassment, with Adam wishing he could say it's never happened before and Lisa wishing she could say it was perfect. The whole thing felt anticlimactic and wrong and so not the way either of them had planned that when they woke up the next morning they'd decided it really shouldn't count. Adam immediately started planning a romantic redo with candles and music and had even let himself fantasize about it happening in Maui.

But then everything had, obviously, fallen apart. And now, almost three months later, some other guy got that moment, and Lisa was probably comparing that guy to Adam and losing any respect or affection she'd had for him in the process.

Adam caught his breath at the thought and he pushed out a sharp exhale, turning his attention back to Violet, who was at the bar, flanked by two older guys, her head thrown back in a laugh. Who cared about Lisa anyway? He had Violet now. That woman at the bar whom those two guys wanted was with *him*. And even though they hadn't had sex yet, they surely would soon, and Violet was certain to be amazing in bed and teach Adam how to be spectacular and the sex would make *Lisa* look bad. And once that was done he wouldn't have to think about Lisa at all and that whole chapter of his life would be closed.

He took a sip of his beer and closed his eyes, trying to imagine Violet naked.

But then his brain drifted and his eyes snapped open as his heart started to pound: What if the baby was his?

Suddenly it was crystal clear. Like a movie montage, he saw that night with Lisa and then he saw sex ed class in Indiana and then he heard Lisa's desperate voice cry out "I don't need you" in San Francisco two weeks ago. Was it possible? Would God really be so cruel?

No, he told himself. That was December, and now it was the end of February: In three months she would have realized. But maybe she didn't realize she missed her period the first month, given that their encounter didn't count and she still thought herself a virgin. But then maybe when she'd missed her second period it dawned on her that something was wrong.

And if it had been two months . . . his brain scrambled . . . what happens after two months? It's too late to take the morning-after pill; was it also too late to get an abortion? Adam thought back to the memorial service in the church with the stained-glass windows of Jesus—ws Lisa religious? Adam then thought about his own ethics—was he religious? What were his own beliefs on abortion? Could he ask her to do it? Did he even want her to do it?

Adam's pulse was pounding. He gripped the table to steady himself, his eyes starting to lose focus as he searched for breath. He needed fresh air. Now. He practically fell off the chair in his rush to get outside just in time to keel over and vomit into the gutter.

The bouncer, a three-hundred-pound, heavily tattooed, bearded man who looked like he collected Harleys, scoffed and came over to make him move, assuming he was drunk.

"Dude. Can't do that here. Move on," he said, and pulled Adam up by the elbow.

"No, I'm . . ." Adam started, but opening his mouth made him get sick again, this time all over the sidewalk and the bouncer's shoes.

"Aw, gross, man. Stanford nerds can't hold their beer."

"No, I'm not drunk, it's just—" Adam looked up at the bouncer with pleading eyes. "I really messed up, man. I really, *really* messed up."

There must have been something particularly pathetic about Adam's appearance, because the bouncer took a deep breath and walked him to a bench on the corner, where he gave him a shopping bag and told him to take it easy.

Half an hour later Adam pulled his head up from between his knees to see Violet standing in front of him with an annoyed look on her face. They left the Old Pro and headed back to Adam's frat house, where Adam collapsed on his bed, unsure what to do.

25

Who Can You Trust?

"I know I shouldn't, but I just love Swedish meatballs. I wish they didn't always have them at funerals, though." A platinum blonde with chipmunk cheeks in a tight black dress and four-inch heels chattered to T.J. as she plucked another Swedish meatball off a passing hors d'oeuvres tray and put it into her pink-glossed mouth. "Like, I remember when my grandmother died everyone brought Swedish meatballs and we were stuck with them, eating them for, like, a week, and I felt so guilty because I felt like I shouldn't be eating. You know? I should be one of those people who loses ten pounds when they're grieving, but I just love these little meatballs so much I kept sneaking into the kitchen to get more. I probably *gained* like ten pounds."

T.J. responded with a close-lipped smile, looking past her and through the doorway into the living room at Riley. Riley's face was pale and her eyes moist. She wasn't wearing any makeup. She sat in a wooden chair, bending over her long crossed legs and resting her chin in her palm. She was watching a little boy—Roger's nephew, he thought—color in a book on the floor, occasionally offering her crayon suggestion when he looked up to her for approval. She looked like a painting, and it infuriated T.J.; Roger dead or not, she had no right to be in his house acting so nonchalant.

"So what do you do?" the girl asked.

"I'm sorry, what?" T.J. looked at her. She was pretty but trying too hard.

"What do you do? Are you still in school or what?" She pushed her hair behind her ear.

"I run a start-up," T.J. answered shortly.

"Oh, that's so cool! I'm thinking of starting a company after I graduate in June. Harvard's got a really great entrepreneurship program, and I've been taking a lot of their classes." Her chatter clung to his nerves.

T.J. took a sip of the Scotch he was drinking and moved around to her other side so that his back was to the living room. She smiled, apparently interpreting this as a suggestive move.

What is wrong with girls? T.J. thought. *Who flirts at a funeral?* But then he felt guilty, knowing he'd probably flirted at funerals before, too. "What did you say?" he asked the girl again.

"I *said*"—she dragged the syllable—"I'm thinking of starting a company, too, after I finish college. I'm at Harvard."

"That's great," T.J. said absentmindedly.

"Don't you want to know my idea?" She batted her lashes and smiled coyly.

Not in the slightest, T.J. thought. "I definitely do," he said instead, "but first I'm going to get you some more wine." He gestured to her empty glass.

"Oh! Thank you!" she said brightly.

"Be right back."

T.J. took the glass and turned to go through the living room, to tell Riley something—he wasn't sure yet what—but when he arrived she was gone. He closed his eyes and swallowed. *Get a grip,* he told himself as he poured a glass of wine in order to give his trip to the living room a purpose.

"Excuse me, sir," said a member of the waitstaff as he tapped T.J.'s shoulder. "Your mother asked if you'd please meet with her and your father in the study."

"Yes, of course," T.J. said as he turned around, giving one final glance to the living room to see if he'd somehow missed Riley, wondering in a moment of panic if she had left.

"Back already?" the blonde asked cheerily.

"Just a sec," T.J. answered, ducking across the kitchen, pretending as though he'd forgotten something, before heading back to the study.

He stumbled into Riley, their bodies briefly colliding in the doorway. She lifted her head and looked at him, searching his eyes. T.J. opened his mouth but nothing came out.

"Sorry," she mumbled, and gently pushed past him to the back door, closing it softly behind her so as not to make a sound. It reminded him of how she used to do that in college when she snuck in late at night, always so careful not to let the door slam.

"Dammit." T.J. shook his head angrily at himself.

T.J. stepped into the study to find his mother chastising his father. "Who's Nina, Ted?"

"I don't know what you're talking about."

T.J.'s ears perked up and his eyes darted from mother to father and back to mother again.

"She said she was following up on an inquiry about Nantucket? That someone had called asking for a broker?"

"Oh, of course. Phil recommended her. I'm doing some research for a company I'm considering investing in; needed some information on the summer home rental market."

Lori studied Ted, not yet convinced. "So you're not selling our house in Nantucket?" She emphasized her point: "The one we built together and where we've spent every summer with the kids?"

Ted leaned over and kissed his wife's forehead. "Of course not, dear."

Her body relaxed and she let her arms drop from where they were crossed over her chest. "I'm sorry," she said. She had a habit of apologizing whenever she stepped out of neutral. "I guess I'm just emotional from all this funeral business. And I've always dreamed of Lisa getting married in that house and I just got nervous because I know the Gibly deal didn't go like you wanted it to and I didn't know if—"

"It's okay," Ted cut her off, pulling his wife into a hug so she couldn't see his face as he rolled his eyes.

"You wanted to speak with me?" T.J. interrupted, annoyed at his mother's weakness and his father's dismissal.

"Yes," Ted answered, quickly dropping his embrace and heading behind his desk. Lori sat quietly in a chair.

T.J. had a love-hate relationship with his father's study. On the one hand, he admired and someday wanted for himself the always-polished mahogany desk, the rugged leather chairs, and the floor-to-ceiling bookshelves filled with silver awards. On the other hand, he associated the study with his father's voluntary absence, and with the fact that he only came here when he was being reprimanded or lectured.

"Roger's death has made us think more seriously about what happens to you and your sister if something happens to us," Ted said matter-of-factly. "The last thing I want is for you and Lisa to be burdened with a complicated inheritance. Or, worse, for all the wealth I've built to get tied up in court."

Ted removed a stack of folders from the desk's inner drawer. "The past few days I've been on the phone with Johan to make sure that your and your sister's trust funds are in order."

T.J. nodded at the reference to the family's attorney. He didn't actually know how much money he was going to inherit from his father, and the thought of his trust fund gave him a strange mix of excitement and dread. On the one hand, he'd always been adamant about making it on his own; on the other hand, it was nice knowing there was a big chunk of change waiting for him when he turned forty.

"Are you sure we shouldn't wait for Lisa?" Lori asked, obviously disturbed by her husband's lack of emotion around such a sensitive subject. "Have a family conversation about it?"

"I think it's best we handle it separately." Ted's voice didn't open the door for disagreement. "Lisa will have more questions, and she seems so stressed with school right now I don't want to add something else to her plate."

T.J. winced at the mention of his sister. She was stressed, but school was the least of Lisa's worries. She'd told their parents she had a school project and couldn't make the funeral, but she'd told T.J. she'd text him tonight after she took a pregnancy test, which she'd finally worked up the courage to go buy.

"In that case, I'm going to leave you boys to it," Lori announced, slapping her hands to her knees and pushing herself out of the chair. "T.J., come find me before you leave." She kissed her son on the cheek.

As soon as she left the room Ted handed T.J. a thick document titled "The Terrence John Bristol Irrevocable Trust."

"We're going to make some amendments to the documents, but I wanted to get your signature on this as soon as possible. The suddenness of all this"—Ted gestured out to the funeral guests and spoke with urgency—"has made me realize I shouldn't put off until tomorrow what could be done today."

T.J. looked at his father; maybe he was right, but it felt wrong to be talking about inheritance at a funeral. He wondered if Riley was still here.

"So you know, your current trust is partly cash and partly equity in some of the investments I've made. You'll receive a modest allowance from the cash until your fortieth birthday, at which point you have access to the full sum, which is currently valued at twenty-two point six million." Ted smiled at the amount, pleased with himself.

T.J. was surprised by his own numbness to the number—maybe because he knew he couldn't have it until he was forty, maybe because he knew he'd want to make far more on his own regardless, but the amount didn't make any of it feel more real.

"So what's changing? Why do I need to sign?"

"We're adding a few more caveats," Ted replied in a measured tone. "As you know, the fund is activated early if you get married."

"Are you and Mom afraid your grandkids would otherwise starve?" T.J. bristled.

"But after this week," Ted ignored his son's jab, "and after what happened to Roger, we wanted to add a clause that says if something happens to your mother and me the trust becomes immediately available: You don't have to wait. Also, I opened it so that you can make contributions of your own. If, for example, you wanted to put your Doreye shares into the trust."

T.J. didn't want to hear his father talk about Doreye. He blamed himself for what happened to Amelia and was having trouble motivating himself to care about the company without her.

"Why would I do that?"

"To avoid taxes."

"That's legal?"

"Totally."

"So what do I need to do?"

"Just sign here," his father said, pointing. "That moves your Doreye shares. And here"—he pointed to another paper—"That makes your trust available immediately if something happens to us."

"Okay, sure," T.J. said, deciding that it was harmless, and that the tax thing made sense if Doreye ever did go anywhere.

T.J. signed the papers and got up to leave.

"Is there anything else?"

"That's it. Just know I'm trusting you not to kill your mother and me to get to that money early," his father joked.

T.J. stared at his father. How could he joke about such a thing? He left the room silently to go find Riley.

26

Super Cheesy

Amelia was lying on her bed looking at the ceiling, where a stain shaped like Florida was growing out of the corner. She was on the top floor of the dorm and imagined the rain pooling above the plaster, then imagined the plaster giving way and the water rushing in to flood her room.

She'd moved into Alondra, a freshman dorm that gave her free room and board in exchange for being on call to help residents when they had computer problems. She missed her old dorm, but she hadn't had any other options. Fenway Ventures paid for housing for Doreye employees; now that she wasn't an employee, and Roger wasn't there to amend the contract, she had to do something. She knew Adam would have found a way to cover her if she'd asked—he wasn't *that* heartless—but she couldn't bear the thought of asking him for anything right now.

Someone knocked on her door but she decided not to hear. She knew she should take her job seriously, but right now the prospect of resolving an RSS feed error and teaching a freshman the importance of installing updates felt a lot less important than tracing a crack in the ceiling to its origin.

"I know you're in there!" a voice called from outside.

It took her a moment to register it through the door as T-Bag's.

She continued to silently ignore. Was it just her or was the Florida stain expanding? Maybe the roof's gutters were clogged? She should call maintenance.

Amelia heard a key in the door and sat up, startled as T-Bag opened the door and thanked Raj, the RA downstairs who had a master key to access all the rooms. "What are you . . . Raj, why'd you let him in?"

"Because he's required to in cases of emergency, and this is an emergency," T-Bag answered. Raj stood in the doorway and gave Amelia an it-was-you-he-was-going-to-bother-or-me shrug before leaving to tend to other RA duties.

It had been three days since Roger's funeral and Amelia had only left the dorm once to go to a history class that she'd left as soon as she'd arrived, realizing she still couldn't handle being around people. It wasn't just Roger she was grieving for, it was everything.

T-Bag sat a shopping bag down on Amelia's desk and started emptying its contents. He'd diligently checked in on Amelia each evening since the funeral, leaving notes and texts each time she didn't answer.

"You know I'm usually much too prideful to chase after someone who ignores my text messages," he said, pushing his tortoiseshell glasses up on his nose. "But for you I make an exception. Now," he said, and pulled the foil off the top of a bottle that looked like champagne and massaged the cork out of the bottle as he spoke, "I assume you haven't eaten in days and anorexic-thin is *so* 1996, and I refuse to let you lose your fashion sense just as you're acquiring it." The cork popped and let out a stream of white air. He poured two glasses, real ones that he'd brought, and handed one to Amelia.

She accepted and took a long sip. It was delicious. "What is this?"

"It's girl beer. Lambic ale. From Belgium. They make it with fruit so it tastes like delicious fizzy apples instead of pee."

Amelia smiled; snobbery around the cheap-beer-drinking habits of American college students was one of T-Bag's favorite soapboxes.

"Now that drinks are settled . . ." T-Bag looked around the room and found the large monitor Amelia and Adam used to use for movie nights. It was stowed on the floor next to her desk and covered in textbooks. He pulled it out and positioned it across from the bed, tossing four DVDs at Amelia.

"You're in charge of the movie; I'll get the fondue started."

"Fondue?" Amelia asked as she looked at the movie titles, all foreign names she'd never heard of. One had a picture of a dark-haired girl smiling slyly at the camera under the title *Amélie*. "What's this one?" she asked T-Bag, who was plugging a pot into her surge protector and clearing her desk for his culinary feat.

Even in his kindness T-Bag couldn't hide his disappointment. "Seriously? You of all people. It's the one we're watching. End of story. Get your glasses on, though—it's got subtitles."

T-Bag emptied a bag of cheese into the pot, and it simmered noisily as it hit the heat. He produced a tray of neatly chopped vegetables, breads, and cured meats. "Not sure how the meat'll hold up in melted fontina, but a meal's just not complete without a good sausage, don't you think?"

Amelia wasn't sure if this was innuendo or thesis but she smiled either way. She was about to ask why he was here but then reconsidered: Whatever the reason, she was glad, and didn't want him to leave.

Noticing her empty glass, T-Bag poured another. "Don't hold back—I brought three."

Amelia let out a laugh.

"Ahh! A full laugh! I'm winning!"

When the cheese was satisfactorily hot, T-Bag handed her a skewer and they devoured the fondue, she sitting on her bed and he on her desk chair.

T-Bag chatted incessantly, filling Amelia in on all the drama she'd missed in the Comp Sci department. Raul had turned down his offer from Google to go work at Microsoft, which was devastating to Vlad, who had wanted the Google position and now had to accept one at Cisco.

"Dessert?"

Amelia nodded as she poured herself another glass of Lambic ale.

"I'll cut the cake; you get the movie started."

The two watched *Amélie*, which made Amelia feel warm and good for the first time in as long as she could remember. The beer did, too, as did T-Bag's presence in the room. At the end of the movie, she declared it her new favorite, and T-Bag proclaimed he'd adopt the French pronunciation of her name going forward in recognition of this fact.

"Go wash your face," he said, and tapped her leg, recognizing her increasing yawning. "No going to bed with clogged pores."

She was tired, but she didn't want him to leave. She was already dreading waking up tomorrow, alone, back in her misery.

She went to the bathroom and brushed her teeth. When she came back, T-Bag was inflating an air mattress on the floor.

"What are you doing?"

"I'm staying. It's raining and I live on the other side of campus. Don't make me go out there, Amélie." He smiled. She knew this wasn't the real reason, and appreciated his lie. "Don't worry, I only snore a little bit."

She smiled wordlessly at him as she crawled into bed. "Thank you," she whispered, to him, and to whoever else was listening.

The next morning, Amelia woke up to a text message from Adam. She ignored it and rolled over, happy to find T-Bag softly snoring on her floor.

She climbed quietly out of bed and crept over to her computer. Her head was a little foggy from the beer last night, but her heart felt as light as it had in a very long time.

She logged into her computer and opened her terminal to a block of code she'd been working on before Roger died. It greeted her with a compiler error, which felt like a metaphor for pretty much everything.

Before she could get started, a g-chat message popped up in the corner of her screen. It was from T.J.

Hi, he'd typed. She hadn't talked to him since the PKC meeting, and her throat burned wondering whether he agreed with Adam.

Hi, she wrote back.

T. J. Bristol: How R U?
me: Fine
T. J. Bristol: Really?

She looked at the question: Was he talking about Roger? Doreye? *I'm fine,* she decided to repeat. Then, finally, *How are you?*

T. J. Bristol: I'm failing CS 101.
But I bet you could have guessed that (-;

She smiled at the computer screen. Yes, she did expect T.J. would be an awful programmer, even if it was super basic.

Do you need help? She was feeling generous after last night, and she missed T.J., even though their relationship was starting to feel weird lately—or maybe *because* their relationship was starting to feel weird lately.

T. J. Bristol: Desperately. Are you being
serious?
me: Sure.

She hesitated before finally keying in: *Not like I have a lot else going on these days.*

T. J. Bristol: :-/
   When is good?
me: Now?
T. J. Bristol: That's great. I'm just doing some
   work but can be on campus in 20 mins.
   Pick u up?
me: Sure.
T. J. Bristol: Awesome.
me: Just one thing.
T. J. Bristol: Anything.
me: No talking about Doreye.
T. J. Bristol: Deal.

"You little flirt!" Amelia was startled by T-Bag, who suddenly appeared reading over her shoulder. "You saucy girl, tutoring one of my pupils."

"I'm just going to help him with his homework." Amelia avoided his eyes so he didn't see her blushing.

"Where is he taking you? Somewhere fancy?"

"Gates, I imagine." She rolled her eyes at him.

"Is he picking you up?" T-Bag asked coyly, dipping his chin and smiling.

"As a matter of fact, he is."

"Date."

"No: homework."

"Can I get a lift, then?"

She hesitated. "Yes. Just to prove it to you."

T-Bag got up and started refolding the air mattress. "Are you going to wear your nice hoodie?"

"As a matter of fact, I am," Amelia said, and pulled the hoodie from the photo shoot around her shoulders. It had become her daily wardrobe.

"I can't believe you've got the attention of T. J. Bristol. He is so dreamy."

"We're just friends," she said, ending the conversation and turning her attention to carefully applying mascara.

"Thanks again for coming over last night," Amelia finally said. "I didn't realize how much I needed . . . a friend."

"Don't worry about it. Was fun for me, too." He smiled warmly, then added, "Miss Amélie."

27

My Sister's Keeper

Adam rolled over and picked up his phone, hoping for a text from Lisa, or Amelia, or Violet, but finding none. He took a deep breath and lifted himself out of bed.

He grabbed a bagel in the kitchen and rode his bike to the new Doreye headquarters, a spacious old house in downtown Palo Alto that they'd converted into a funhouse workspace. They painted the walls bright blue and brought in two foosball tables and lined one wall with vending machines that accepted fake quarters so you didn't actually have to pay. There was a cotton candy machine and a Red Bull fountain and a keg that was always tapped. Adam even interviewed chefs and picked the one who made the best beef burrito.

Adam entered the front door and went upstairs to his office without saying hello to the two engineers hard at work in the living room–turned–programming room. After Amelia left, they promoted Arjun to team lead and hired six new engineers and a designer specializing in user interface.

Adam sat down at his desk and stared at the furniture catalogs in front of him. The furniture downstairs was from the old incubator and desperately needed a refresh. He'd been working for the past week trying to figure out what desks to order to keep the right aesthetic without blowing their budget, not that they were too constrained after the last deposit from PKC.

A knock on the door interrupted him. Arjun peeked his head in. "Do you have a minute?" he asked.

"I'm kind of in the middle of something," Adam said, irritated. "Is it important?"

"It kind of is," Arjun said.

"Okay, come in." Adam sighed dramatically, putting the catalog to one side and motioning for Arjun to sit down. "What's going on?"

"Well, we're running into some problems with the algorithm."

"What kind of problems?" Adam lifted an eyebrow judgmentally. The technical stuff bored him.

"Amelia's design is . . . advanced. She built it so the Doreye app could do a lot of things at once. For example, I can use the radar feature to find my keys while changing the channel on my television and turning on my Wii—"

"Arjun. What's the problem?" Adam was particularly annoyed at any mention of his sister or her accomplishments.

"She developed an artificial intelligence that would sort this out on the fly, except that whenever we test it, the device we test it on crashes."

"What do you mean?"

"I mean that there is no device that can run Doreye. No device has nearly fast enough processors or enough RAM. Doreye . . . doesn't work on an iPhone."

"What about Droid?"

"Nope."

"That's not possible," Adam said, certain the engineers missed something.

"It is, though," Arjun insisted, hesitating as if there was more.

"What is it, Arjun?" Adam asked, exasperated.

"You have to bring Amelia back. We need her."

"We don't."

"We're at a standstill."

"Then work harder."

"But—"

"Listen," Adam interrupted, "if no one on the team is seriously smart enough to figure this out, then we'll hire someone else, okay? It's been three weeks since Amelia left; at least give it a try."

Arjun's chest puffed at the implication that he wasn't smart. "Yeah, of course. Sorry to bother you." He stood and left, shutting the door a bit too forcefully.

Adam had barely had time to recover from the affront before his door opened again.

"Hey," T.J. said, entering the office.

"Hey." Things had been tense between T.J. and Adam ever since the PKC meeting. Adam suspected T.J. wasn't talking to him out of fear that Adam would use the same authority to fire T.J. It was a power Adam secretly relished.

"Arjun told me he told you about the problem."

"Yeah, we've got it sorted," Adam lied.

T.J. looked at him, unconvinced.

"What?" Adam shrugged defensively.

"How'd you 'get it sorted'?"

"I told him to do his job and figure it out."

"Good, so you gave him permission to call Amelia?" T.J. said bluntly.

"Amelia doesn't work here."

"She'll know how to fix it. She had it figured out before you fired her."

"He can't call Amelia."

"Then figure out another solution, Adam," T.J. said firmly.

"Is that my job, T.J.? I can't remember. I'm just chief operating officer, didn't you know that?" he said passive-aggressively.

"Unfortunately, everyone at the company is afraid you'll fire them if they don't agree with you. If you're not going to let Arjun call Amelia, then use that HR power of yours to hire someone who can help."

Adam looked spitefully at T.J. and put his head on his desk.

"And while you're out solving problems," T.J. continued coldly, "have some respect and call my sister."

Adam was speechless. T.J. knew about him and Lisa? What else did he know?

28

No Talking in the Library

T.J. pulled up outside the dorm and found T-Bag waiting with Amelia. He stopped when he saw her and double-checked: He expected her to look sad, but she somehow seemed rejuvenated. Something was different about her, but he couldn't put his finger on it. He got out of the car and gave her a warm hug. It made him feel strong, the way her whole body fit into his arms. "It's good to see you," he whispered in her ear.

"You, too," she said, smiling.

It was a bright, crisp day, and the sun felt good after three days of rain. T-Bag pushed forward the front seat of T.J.'s BMW and climbed in the back. "I'm hitching a ride with you if it's okay."

"You don't think I'd piss off the guy grading my problem sets, do you?"

"God, I love having power over a man like you," T-Bag said, and flirtatiously pinched T.J.'s cheek from the backseat.

"Easy," T.J. said, trying his best to counterparry with his trademark charm, but was still wary of the whole gay-guy-with-a-crush-on-him thing.

Inside Gates, Amelia led T.J. to a computer while she went to check her CS department mailbox. T.J. watched her walk away—What had changed? His attention was distracted by the sound of Amelia's phone buzzing and he instinctively looked at the text message on her screen: *"You doing okay, love? Let me know if you need anything. xo."*

T.J. felt a sudden chill as he read the sender: Riley. *His* Riley? How did Amelia know Riley?

When he saw Amelia come back through the door, he quickly put her phone back down. "Anything good in your box?" he asked in polite fake interest.

"Just some graded papers," Amelia said, seeing the message on her phone, smiling, and typing a response. T.J. burned with curiosity. What were they talking about? Did either woman know about the other's relationship to him?

Amelia turned back. "Ready?" She pulled open the problem set T.J. had failed, and grimaced. "Here," she said, reaching across him to control the mouse. Her leg pressed against his as she scooted to reach, and he felt the heat of her body in front of his chest. She pulled the mouse over to her side and he leaned forward to focus.

"See these arrays?" she asked. "You need to highlight them— like this." She showed him. Without thinking, he put his hand on top of hers on the mouse. She pulled it away and let him take control.

"I think my problem is I can't concentrate," T.J. mumbled.

He could see her chest rise and fall. "It's hard," she said. "I mean, it can be really boring, but you have to pay attention to the little things or the program won't work."

She pushed the keyboard toward him. He keyed in the code as she'd instructed.

"There," he said when he was finished.

She pulled the keyboard back to her, careful to avoid his touch this time. "Let's try it." She hit a few strokes to run and they watched the screen.

```
def fib():
    x = [1, 1, 2]
    sum = 4
```

```python
    while True:
        x.append(x[1] + x[2])
        del x[0]
        if x[2] >= limit:
            break
        else:
            sum += x[2]
            pass
    return sum

def main():
    limit = 1000
    print fib()
```

```
TJ@ubuntu:~$ python fib.py
Traceback (most recent call last):
  File "ex2.py", line 18, in <module>
    main()
  File "ex2.py", line 16, in main
    print fib()
  File "ex2.py", line 7, in fib
    if x[2] >= limit:
NameError: global name 'limit' is not defined
```

"Dammit." T.J. put his hand to his forehead. "What'd I do wrong?"

"You probably just mistyped something. Sometimes one tiny missing variable can screw up the whole thing. Believe it or not, this one is a relatively easy fix." Amelia took hold of the keyboard again, but her eye caught something and she paused briefly. He followed her eye path: What was she looking at? He glanced at his arm muscles underneath his t-shirt. Was she admiring him? He flexed his bicep, just in case.

"So how are things at Doreye?" She changed the subject, her gaze now fully on the computer screen, fixing his bad code on the monitor in front of him.

"I miss you," T.J. said honestly, trying to follow her corrections but more interested in talking. Then, more cautiously: "I mean, we miss you. Really."

Amelia cocked her head. "Is everything okay?"

"I promised you I wouldn't talk about it."

"Yeah, but then I asked."

"It's not good," T.J. conceded. "Arjun's smart, but he's in over his head. If we don't figure out this battery issue, I think we're toast."

Amelia sat up in her chair. "What do you mean?" she asked.

"Investors want Doreye to go to market within a few weeks, but every time we run the app in the wild the phone gets hot and loses all of its battery, or crashes," T.J. said, and sighed, looking forlornly down at the keyboard.

"But it should efficiently use the native processor if the code is correct. The last iteration I wrote was incredibly smooth. Each string should have a minimal description that follows Kolmogorov complexity. It should be fine." Amelia's voice was getting heated.

T.J. laughed and said, "Are you listening to yourself? You don't realize how smart you are. Kind of like how you don't recognize how pretty you are." He was thinking about Brandon and how wrong his friend had been in his dismissal of Amelia.

Amelia opened her mouth but very little sound came out. "I—" she started, but a voice cut her off from across the room.

"You two about done here?" T-Bag called from the door.

T.J. tried to hide his annoyance. "Just about!"

"We're about to play a game of ZOSTRA if you'd like to join."

The spell was broken and Amelia resumed her previous calm. "Great! I'll be right there." She turned to T.J. "So I hope that helped?"

He looked back at the computer, remembering he'd asked her to help him with his problem set. "Oh, yeah, super helpful. I think I understand it now," he lied, then he threw in, "You're a really good teacher." He felt like he used to after playing a really hard soccer game and losing.

"Sure. Was totally happy to do it."

T.J. remained seated for a moment, hoping they'd return to the previous conversation. But instead Amelia started putting her pen and notebook into her bag.

"What's ZOSTRA?" T.J. asked, giving up and following her lead to put his own stuff away.

Amelia blushed. "It's just a computer game."

"Oh, that's cool," T.J. said. "Like Dungeons & Dragons?"

"It's not quite that dorky," Amelia assured him unconfidently. "But probably not your thing."

"Believe it or not, I was pretty good at D&D as a kid," T.J. told her, something he hadn't admitted to anyone since he'd decided he was too cool for the game back in tenth grade.

"Really?" Amelia asked, shocked. Her eyes glowed hopefully through her glasses.

"Dungeon Master extraordinaire." T.J. clicked his tongue proudly. He never thought that tidbit would pay off.

"Well, ZOSTRA is kind of like an expanded version, but everyone has his or her own avatar, it uses Google Maps for the geography, and there aren't too many rules around how you create your avatar."

"Sounds fun. Can I join you?"

Amelia blushed furiously at the thought, but knew she couldn't say no. "I mean, I'm sure you've got more important things to do, like run my company."

T.J. looked around. "Not much to run without you," he said, smiling weakly. "Besides, I need the mental vacation, and maybe playing ZOSTRA will get me some extra credit with T-Bag, which I clearly need."

Amelia hesitated. "Okay," she finally conceded, and they moved to the room next door.

"We're doing a mission today," T-Bag explained to the group. "Everyone has been assigned one character type from the graph here." He projected a matrix onto the screen that showed different character types. "One dimension is morality, where a character can be Good or Evil or Neutral, and the other dimension is ethics, where a character can be Lawful or Chaotic or Neutral."

"So," T.J. cut in, "I can be Evil and Lawful or Good and Lawful?"

"Exactly. There are nine alignments. For today's exercise, no one knows who is who, and the point is to play the game and, through each other's actions, figure out everyone's alignment. Remember, we all will interact differently to accomplish different goals." He looked around seriously. "A description of your player is being e-mailed to you."

"Excuse me." Amelia, adorably, wanted to get it right. "Can we go through a few alignments?"

"Of course, Amélie," T-Bag said, smiling, "I thought you'd never ask. Let's start with Lawful Good. These are the righteous crusaders or knights. They stand for a purpose and often die martyrs. Unlike Lawful Neutral, who are disciplined . . . like Jedi knights."

"I'm more interested in the villains," T.J. said, and gave Amelia a wink. She smiled. Which made him smile.

"So," T-Bag said, growing animated, "the Lawful Evil characters are the diabolical ones. Think of a comic book villain or a dictator or a white-collar criminal: They exploit the system to their own advantage. This is very different from the Chaotic Evil characters: the demons and terrorists. They care about nothing but their own desires, violating the freedom of others. They have no regard for honor and no scruples."

"So they are the ones to watch out for?" Amelia asked.

T-Bag sat down and, with dramatic flair, leaned in close to T.J. and Amelia. "No, my children. The Evil are not the ones to be afraid of. Instead you must watch out for Chaotic Neutral: Without moral code these characters are completely unpredictable. They are the wild cards. The free spirits. They change their appearance or disrupt order just for the sake of chaos. They change teams and allegiances on a whim. You cannot trust them."

"So we should always avoid Chaotic Neutral?" Amelia was trying to figure out the rules.

"They can be useful, Amelia," T-Bag said, leaning back and smiling, "because with the right incentives they can be quite powerful. If you ally with them, make sure you do so briefly and always have the upper hand."

The players broke apart with their character assignments. T.J. was assigned Lawful Neutral, the Judge archetype, and hastily created an avatar named Teranimus. *This should be easy,* he thought.

T.J. proceeded to spend the rest of the afternoon in the darkness of the Gates computer science building, fully engrossed in a fantastical mission that evolved into a quest across Northern Africa. The game was all online and provided access to perfectly pixelated images of the places they went. At first he had some difficulty navigating the tools and information but gradually got the hang of it. In the end, he, as Lawful Neutral, allied with an avatar named Hyperios, who was Neutral Evil, to prevent an avatar named Rollox, who happened to be Lawful Evil, from destroying a community he and Amelia (Lawful Good) were trying to build on an abandoned island.

By the end of the game, when all the characters were revealed, T.J. was mentally exhausted but strangely satisfied. He felt a weird bond with these geeks and a sense of accomplishment for having defeated a bad guy and built an island, even if it was totally fake. And he felt a connection to Amelia he couldn't quite describe. It wasn't what he felt with other girls, but it was something.

"Want to join us for dinner?" T-Bag asked.

"Dinner?" he said quizzically. "What time is it?" He glanced at his watch and almost choked: 7:28 P.M. Had he seriously just spent six hours playing this game? He was supposed to pick up a friend for drinks at the Rosewood at 8:00.

"Sorry—I gotta run meet a friend now. But this was really fun, guys, thanks for letting me play!" T.J. picked up his jacket and scurried out the door quickly, not noticing Amelia trying to work up the courage to ask him to wait.

29

What Light Through Yonder Window Breaks Down

Adam spent the rest of the day being wholly unproductive in his office. He would start writing an e-mail and then find himself opening a new tab and going straight to Facebook to look up Lisa and peruse her photos. Once or twice he almost put her name into his status update instead of the search bar, but caught himself just before pressing "Enter."

When the day was over and he mustered enough courage, Adam went to the Delta Gamma sorority. He followed the garden path around to the back right corner of the house, where the girls left a playing card in the latch of a side door to keep it from locking without making it obvious to passersby. The card trick was a secret the girls only told house boyfriends after swearing them to secrecy.

Adam opened the door and gently pulled it shut behind him so the card stayed in its place.

He heard music in the kitchen and made his way through the house's courtyard, which in the fall and spring was neatly occupied with lounge chairs where girls and their male followers skipped class to tan, but was for now barren, a dreary reminder of the winter rain.

Adam entered the foyer and shook his head to repel the

raindrops. He pushed open the swinging doors that led into the dining room and found a group of two dozen guys and girls drinking from red cups and talking loudly over the pop music coming from the speakers above.

He scanned the room quickly for familiar faces and found Lisa sitting on one of the dining tables, leaning her weight back on her hands and propping her feet up on a chair. She was surrounded by three guys he recognized from Sigma Chi, all grinning broadly at whatever she was saying as she let her head fall back in a laugh. She was wearing short shorts and Ugg boots, rocking her knees back and forth flirtatiously as she talked to them. Adam's face burned with jealousy.

He beelined for her, pushing his way between two of the guys.

"Lisa, we need to talk," he blurted out.

Lisa took a slow look at him and sipped her drink before responding, "No, Adam, we don't."

"Yes. We. Do," he said, pausing after each syllable and nodding his head toward the door to indicate he'd prefer to do it alone.

"Dude, if she doesn't want to talk, she doesn't want to talk," one of the guys said dramatically.

Adam ignored him. "Lisa, come on."

"I've got nothing to say to you, Adam," Lisa said, then added, insistently, "Really, I don't."

"But—" Adam started searching for something to say to get her to listen. The room's attention was quietly turning in their direction.

"But I saw you the other day," he finally blurted, "in the drugstore."

Lisa's legs stopped rocking and she stared straight into his eyes, daring him to say more. "That's great, Adam. I do from time to time go to the drugstore. Great place to buy shampoo, don't you think?"

"Ouch!" one of the other guys said, snapping his fingers, clearly drunk.

"Who is this guy, Lisa?" another asked, pointing to Adam.

"I know him," replied the third, "this is the dickwad that works at that app company and fired his genius sister."

A groan of jeers erupted from the crowd. Adam was undeterred.

"You were at the drugstore, Lisa, and you were buying—" He stopped himself.

Lisa had one eyebrow lifted and her left dimple smirked.

"I just think we ought to talk." Adam decided to go back to his original plan and tried to look kind.

"There's no need, Adam," she said with a calm he found alarming. "We have nothing to talk about. I don't need you for anything. You have nothing to worry about."

She turned her attention back to her suitors and continued a story she'd been telling before Adam arrived. Her long, smooth legs turned away from him. What he would do to touch them, just once.

Adam swallowed and looked around as if searching for what to do. He felt like he was caught in a bad romantic comedy and wanted the ending to come, for everything to work out and her to come back to him *with those legs*.

"Lisa," Adam tried again, "I know—"

Lisa didn't even turn her head to acknowledge his existence.

"I know you're pregnant, Lisa," he blurted out helplessly. The guys turned to look at Adam, then turned back to Lisa to see her reaction.

Her eyes drilled into him. "You don't know anything, Adam. Nothing. At all." She said it sharply, with no room for protest or error.

"But at the drugstore—I saw you—"

"Jesus." Lisa rolled her eyes and stood up, asking the guys to hold on for a minute while she dragged Adam to the next room.

"I don't know what you think you saw," Lisa snapped, "but how dare you come in here and say such things in public?"

"Well, I tried to talk about it in private, but you wouldn't—"

"If there was anything to talk about, I would have spoken to you in private. But there wasn't, so I didn't."

"Is it mine?" he pleaded. "If it is, we—"

"We," she interrupted, "are absolutely, one thousand percent finished."

"But I—"

"You are an even worse person than I thought." Now she was really going. "I don't know who you've become, Adam, but it's intolerable. Your sister doesn't know how lucky she is to get away from you, but I'm really starting to figure it out."

"I'm the same person—"

"Leave, Adam," Lisa said sternly.

"I will take care of it. If it's mine."

"Leave!" she screeched.

Adam turned on his heel and stomped back out into the rain.

When he got back to his room at SAE, he took off his wet clothes and fell in bed, annoyed by the pumping music of partiers outside.

He stared at his phone, hoping it would ring. Lisa or Amelia or Violet, though she wasn't really the consoling type. Nothing. He turned the volume up and positioned the phone next to his pillow just in case and went to sleep.

30

Board of Detractors

"I think it's time for us to take this company public," Ted Bristol announced firmly to the others at the table.

He was seated in the conference room of Berlin Partners, a venture capital firm with whom he'd done several co-investments.

The company in question was Jamify, a social network for sharing music. It started as an avatar-based social game where users had access to free music tracks they could then spin into new compilations. Due to a clever social engagement loop it quickly grew, and the founders leveraged their audience's enthusiasm to transform it into a music-sharing portal. Within a year, certain demographics were using the Jamify iPhone app more than iTunes. Ted currently owned a tenth of Berlin Partners' 51 percent ownership in the company.

"We've been sitting on the filing docs for months, but timing is never going to be better. The bank's already told us we can get twenty dollars a share, but I think, given the market, we could push that number closer to twenty-three."

"Ted." Susan Rawlings, a firm partner who perpetually looked pissed off, tilted her head. "The point still stands that the company *doesn't need the money*. The cash would just sit there, and the Street would eventually react negatively."

Ted sighed in irritation. "There's always something to be done with more money. Why not expand globally? Why not pay for celebrity sponsorships? The point is not to miss the opportunity to make Jamify bigger and maximize our gains."

"The company's gains, or our own?" Susan spat back. She'd always been a martyr for putting companies' interests before investors'.

Michael Berlin, the firm's founding partner, stepped in. "I think we're all smart enough to see each other's points. Ted's is a reasonable one for us to consider. Why don't we have the management team pull together a list of potential uses for the cash and plan to regroup with them on this next week?"

"Fine," Susan said as she closed her notebook.

Michael looked around the table. "If no one else has anything, Mandy'll circulate minutes and calendar a follow-up with the Jamify team."

The six other partners followed Susan's lead out of the conference room. "Hang on for a sec, Ted," Michael called after him.

Ted kept his seat and rubbed his neck as he looked out the window onto Sand Hill Road. He was glad he'd left his old firm to go out on his own, but he did sometimes miss this view and the power of knowing it was yours.

"We go back a long way," Michael started. "So I hope you won't mind me asking: What's going on?"

"What do you mean?"

"Pardon if I'm overstepping, but it feels like you're a bit desperate for cash."

Ted felt his face flush. He didn't immediately answer.

Michael pressed, "I'm not trying to pry into your personal finances, I just need to know what's influencing your suggestions for Jamify."

This made Ted's neck prickle. "I don't need to tell you," he said firmly, "that Gibly did not provide the windfall I expected." He paused. "But I resent the implication that my suggestions for a company's growth would be marred by my own self-interests. I am a professional."

"I know that," Michael said without changing his tone, "and I know that this is a volatile business. And I just want to remind you, as a partner and a friend, that in the long term things will sort themselves out, but you cannot rush things."

Ted concentrated on his breath and tried not to think about how impatient he truly was for the millions he'd make if Jamify went public at its current valuation. Six months ago he would have insisted the company hold out for more, but today, as he considered his balance sheet, devastated by the loss from Gibly's failed sale, he just didn't want to lose what they had.

"That TechCrunch article really screwed you over, huh?"

Ted nodded.

"You ever find out who it was?"

"Sure. I met the hacker before the article was published. I offered a hundred thousand dollars to keep quiet after our systems were hacked," Ted confessed for the first time.

Michael raised an eyebrow. "Who wouldn't take that?"

"Should've offered a million. Would've saved me two billion."

"What's he doing now?"

"Suffering." Ted didn't correct Michael; it was somehow more shameful to admit that a teenage *girl* had dismantled his entire career and legacy.

"Suffering?" Michael laughed. "Hell hath no fury like Ted Bristol's scorn. Are you filing a lawsuit?"

Ted had, of course, talked to his accountant about filing a lawsuit. What no one except Ted and his accountant knew, however, was that Ted Bristol had invested all of his personal assets into Gibly the day of the sale. It was a secret transaction, the kind that was only illegal if you were caught. The outcome was supposed to give Ted Bristol ten times the profit from the deal, which, until Amelia Dory's e-mail to TechCrunch, had been a certainty. So when the sale didn't go through, Ted didn't just lose the payout, he lost every penny and every stock he'd accumulated up until that point. The only money left was in his property, his cars, and in his kids' trusts. Suing Amelia would expose his own infraction. In the meantime, though, he had about six months of cash left to figure out what to do.

"No, I'm not suing. I want it to hurt worse than that," he said calmly.

31

Newest Profession, Oldest Profession

Lisa shut off the engine and checked her reflection in the rear-view mirror one last time. She looked herself in the eye and breathed "Okay" before handing her keys to the valet and heading down the stairs to the Rosewood's private dining room.

Lisa was typically nervous before starting new things, and tonight was her first session as a "Focus Girl." Despite Lisa's trepidations, Patty assured her friend there was nothing to be nervous about, and her sorority sisters who had become regular Focus Girls insisted it was "just what she needed" after the Adam incident last week.

Reflecting on it, Lisa was proud of how she handled it—she had, in retrospect, said exactly what she wanted to say given the circumstances and Adam's erratic behavior. Despite her best face, the whole incident rattled her, and the what-ifs made her heart race with anxiety.

The pregnancy scare had been a nonissue in the end. In retrospect it seemed silly. Her encounter with Adam was the only time she'd had sex; it was forgettably, drunkenly brief, and they'd used a condom and it had been more than two months ago. The tests had come back negative and, as though the universe was telling her to just be patient, she'd woken up with her period the next morning, giving her double affirmation that it had all been an ugly false alarm.

Her doctor told her that her missed periods were probably her body's reaction to the stress of so many changes. And there had been a lot of changes. She walked carefully in her heels down the stairs to the Rosewood basement. As if starting college wasn't enough, she'd gone from two boyfriends to none. And now she was starting her first paid job: being a Focus Girl for Patty Hawkins's new and increasingly talked-about company.

She checked the nameplate on the door of the Sequoia Room before entering to join four girls her age and five older men, all in their thirties, all dressed in nice suits and with slick hair. Everyone had a cocktail in hand.

One of the men approached and reached out his hand. "Lisa?"

"Yes," she said, and let his thick fingers enclose her slender ones. "I'm so sorry I'm late."

"Not a problem at all," the man said. "I'm Mark." Then, turning to the others, "Everyone, please welcome Lisa."

The group tilted their heads in acknowledgment and turned back to their conversations.

"Can I get you a drink?"

Lisa's eyes darted to the other girls, noting they all had wineglasses in hand despite also being underage. "Sure," she said, hoping her voice didn't betray her surprise.

"Pinot Grigio okay?" Mark asked. His hair was thick and dark and carefully combed on the sides. His suit was expensive looking and there was a polka-dotted pocket square in the front pocket. He wasn't fat, but he was broad. And he was at least ten years older than her brother.

"That's great," Lisa said, taking the glass he'd already poured.

"So which sorority are you in?" Mark asked.

"Delta Gamma," she answered. "Well, I hope so. I'm a pledge."

"DG . . . let's see . . . do you know Tiffany Jacobsen?"

"Sure! She's our vice president of communications."

"She'd be great for that," Mark said, sipping his drink. "I like her and her friends a lot. You're joining a great group."

Mark had a large brown mole on the left side of his jaw that moved with his chin when he spoke, and Lisa concentrated on his eyes when he spoke so that she didn't stare at the mole.

"What is your major?"

"I haven't decided yet," she said, not sure if there was a correct answer she was supposed to give. Patty had told her she'd matched the criteria for this Focus Girls session, but she was still unclear what those criteria had been. "What do you do?" she asked in exchange.

"I'm an angel investor," Mark said proudly. "I made some money off a company I started a few years ago and now I'm helping other aspiring entrepreneurs achieve their visions."

"That's great," Lisa said.

"You know," Mark continued, "it really is, Lisa." He reached out his hand and squeezed her shoulder. "I never thought anything could be so wonderful as succeeding myself, but turns out helping young people is even more rewarding."

Lisa took another sip of her wine and offered a polite smile. Something about this guy creeped her out.

"Do you want to sit down?" He moved his hand to indicate the table where the other girls were starting to sit down in every other chair, the men filling in between them.

"Sure." Lisa followed him to the seat he pulled out for her and sat down, adjusting the pashmina around her neck to fully cover her chest, which had a tendency to show a bit too much in the V-neck dress she was wearing.

Once everyone was seated, a waitress arrived with salad plates, which she presented before each diner, ladies first.

"Oh, I didn't realize dinner was involved," Lisa said to Mark.

"Of course!" He laughed, his mole shaking. "You didn't think we'd let you go hungry, did you?"

"I wasn't sure what to think," Lisa admitted.

"And what do you think?" Mark asked, leaning in a bit too close.

Lisa instinctively pulled her face back a few inches and turned her eyes down as she reached for a fork. "I guess I'm wondering what product you're testing," she said honestly.

"Oh, we're just looking for your perspective," Mark said calmly, reaching for the butter at the center of the table to dress his roll. "We're interested in finding out what interests you, you know?"

Lisa took a sharp breath in and concentrated on her salad.

Mark reached his arm around the back of her chair and reached beneath her pashmina to squeeze her shoulder. "Just relax," he said, "I promise we're not going to hurt you."

She couldn't stand the feeling of his thick fingers on her skin but she forced another polite smile. She looked at the other girls: She vaguely recognized one of them as a junior in Pi Phi. The other men were leaning in to their conversations and the girls were laughing merrily as the waitress filled up their glasses.

"So what are you investing in?" Lisa asked, leaning forward for the butter so as to move from beneath his arm.

He reached quickly to get it for her. "Allow me," he said importantly as he buttered her roll for her. She took the roll, which she didn't really want, and bit into it, nodding in false appreciation.

"I invest in all sorts of things," he said, wiping a hand alongside his slick hair. "I look for technologies that are really disrupting the industries they're in. And for superdynamic founders. That's the key, you know? The founder."

Lisa nodded in agreement. "Yeah, definitely."

"So what do you do for fun?" Mark leaned in again. She could smell his breath when he spoke. It smelled like peppermint-sprayed onions.

"Well, right now I'm focused on school, and trying to figure out the whole college thing," she answered honestly, "but I used to do theater, so I'm thinking of getting reinvolved in that, or maybe auditioning for one of the a cappella groups on campus."

"That's neat," Mark said disinterestedly, his body turned in his seat to face her. "Do you have a boyfriend?"

Lisa blushed and looked down at her frisée, a lock of hair falling down across her shoulder. "No, not anymore."

Mark reached his finger over to brush the hair back behind her shoulder, letting his finger linger on her skin. She shifted uncomfortably in her chair.

"Is everything all right?" he asked gently but in a way that made Lisa nervous.

"Yes, of course," she lied.

"I mean, with your ex-boyfriend. You said 'not anymore' as if there was a lot behind it."

How did he know that?

"Is there anything I can do to make it better?" He leaned in again with his peppermint-onion breath.

"I'm so sorry," Lisa said, "I have really got to use the restroom. Do you know where it is?"

"Sure, let me show you," Mark said, standing up from his chair.

"Oh, that's okay," Lisa insisted, "you don't have to get up. I'm fine. Really."

She stood up and walked toward the door, praying that Mark wouldn't follow her. When she got to the bathroom, she leaned over and gripped the counter. Her head was spinning and she felt like she had had the wind knocked out of her.

Nausea overcame Lisa. All she could see was Mark's mole moving up and down as he spoke, and it made her queasy. She splashed her face with water in the sink. She wasn't sure what was wrong with him, but she couldn't go back in there.

She shook her face, trying to regain her presence, took a long look in the mirror, picked up her purse, and headed out to the parking lot, holding her breath until she was in her car with the doors locked.

32

Cruise, Control

Jim poured Adam another Jack and Coke and he sipped it absentmindedly.

"You okay, Adam?" Jim was the bartender at Rudy's, a dive bar on University Avenue. Ever since Adam had moved the Doreye headquarters a few blocks away he had become the bar's youngest regular and Jim's biggest consumer of Jack Daniels.

"Fine," he said, which was a lie but one he didn't care to explore.

Like all good bartenders, Jim picked up on this and moved away with a simple "This one's on me."

Adam's hunched shoulders pulled his line of vision below the bar, rather than straight ahead at the bottle-lined mirror. Adam studied the fluorescent lights of the refrigerators that held row after row of Bud Light, all of which would be consumed tonight by customers eager to pay.

Maybe he should have gone into a product business, Adam thought. Maybe if there were a physical, tangible something he could sell he'd do better than having this ambiguous software no one—especially not him—really understood.

But the product wasn't the issue and he knew that. The issue was him. He wasn't as smart as his sister, plain and simple. He wasn't hot and rich like the other guys in the frat whom Lisa dated. He wasn't as adventurous and exciting as Violet, and he also felt increasingly uncertain her attentions would last. Insult to injury: Even Arjun, their pudgy technical lead who walked funny and had a constantly dripping nose, had a girlfriend and a measurable skill.

Adam finished the rest of his drink and gestured for another. It was his third? Fourth? He couldn't remember. It didn't matter: What else was he going to do tonight? Go back to the office and solve problems he couldn't solve? Go back to campus and hook up with Lisa? All the pipe dreams he'd had six months ago were shot and he knew it.

He thought back on the lunch with Professor Marsh. He'd had such unconquerable confidence then; what had happened? He didn't want to, but the drinks let him into the part of his brain that knew exactly what had happened: He'd fired Amelia. He'd offended Lisa. He'd had a chance to elevate his social status via the frat, but he'd prioritized the company and now he was the same poor loser from Indiana he'd been on day one at Stanford, except now he didn't have anyone to commiserate with.

Adam's palms started sweating and the sweat seemed to hang on his skin, making him suddenly feel claustrophobic sitting in this empty bar. *I've thrown it all away*, he thought. He had to get out of here. He stood up from the bar and rushed for the door and the fresh air it promised.

"I'll put it on your tab," Jim called from behind the bar, but Adam didn't respond as he pushed out onto the sidewalk and swallowed the damp air. It was drizzling lightly and he made no attempt to shield himself as he walked the two blocks to his car.

That was one thing he had that he didn't have before: a car. He kicked the front tire angrily. He thought back on how excited he'd been when he'd realized they had enough money saved from Roger Fenway's incubator income to buy it. Adam Dory, buying his own set of wheels! At age nineteen! Now he looked at it in disgust: a 2003 Honda Civic with a hundred thousand miles. He didn't know which was more pathetic, the car or the excitement he'd had for it.

Adam pulled onto University Avenue and followed it to Palm Drive. The majestic palm trees that lined the road were framed by the gray clouds of winter rains; it looked like they were mocking Adam for believing life could have been as picture-perfect as they'd promised the first time he saw them. Adam felt encouraged to press his foot on the gas and pulled left onto Campus Drive before turning right onto Galvez, just past the Alumni Center.

"Fuck!" Adam gasped as he noticed blue lights in his rearview mirror. Was the cop car following him? How long had it been there? He hadn't been paying attention.

Focus! Adam told himself, his heart pounding as he pulled over to the side of the road and put his car in park.

The cop knocked on the window and Adam rolled it down.

"Evening, son," he said. "License and registration, please."

Adam pulled out his wallet for the former and reached into the glove compartment, praying the registration was in the stack of papers stored there.

"Know why I pulled you over?" The cop leaned down so they were face-to-face. He was Hispanic, somewhere in his forties, with a thick neck and a wide face. He had a dark mustache that was carefully trimmed and turned down precisely at the corners of his lips. Adam thought it looked foolishly stereotypical for a Hispanic cop and despite his panic couldn't suppress a slight laugh. "No, sir, I don't know why you pulled me over," he said.

"What's funny?" the cop asked.

"Nothing," Adam retorted, but something about how comical the mustache was, curled down as if this man spent extra time at the mirror each day to get it *just right* gave Adam more confidence. "Why did you pull me over?" he asked.

"You didn't stop at the last stop sign. There is a four-way stop at Campus and Galvez."

"I did stop," Adam retorted, remembering now that he had specifically moved his foot from the gas to the brake pedal.

"Not fully."

"Are you serious?" Adam asked.

"Yes," the cop said, not acknowledging Adam's tone. He began writing something on his ticket.

"What are you writing?" Adam persisted.

"A ticket. Failing to stop at a stop sign is a four-hundred-dollar violation."

"Are you kidding?" Adam's voice was less controlled now. "But I stopped!"

"Not fully."

"But enough to know everything was clear! Isn't that the point? To make sure everything's clear?" Adam could tell his words were coming out at an abnormal cadence but he didn't care.

"No, the point is to stop. That's why it's called a stop sign." The cop smiled from beneath his mustache, a genuine smile, not a mocking one, which irritated Adam all the more.

"Yeah, thanks," he snapped. "I can read. I go to Stanford, you know. Maybe you've heard of it. It's a college? Like, a really, really good one?"

"How much have you had to drink tonight, son?"

"Are you fucking serious?" Adam felt his blood start to boil.

"Yes. How much have you had to drink?"

"Oh, fuck you!" he exclaimed. "Just because I go to Stanford and you probably didn't even graduate from high school you're going to try to bring me down by insinuating I've been drinking?"

"How much have you had to drink?" the cop said calmly.

"A Jack and Coke," Adam snapped. "At Rudy's."

"At Rudy's?" The cop raised an eyebrow.

"Yeah," Adam snapped. "It's a bar?"

"According to your ID, you're nineteen."

"Yeah, well, I used—" Adam stopped himself. "I went to Rudy's after I had my drink at the office."

"Can you step out of the car, please?"

Adam got out of the car and followed the cop's instructions to walk in a straight line, which he failed; to touch his nose, which he failed; to follow the cop's fingers with his eyes, which he also apparently failed.

"Get in the car," the cop told him, indicating the police car.

Adam guffawed: "I'm sorry?"

"You can't drive," the cop said simply. "You have to spend the night with me."

"What!" Adam exclaimed.

"In jail," the cop assured him, "not with me and my wife."

"And your seven children?" Adam said under his breath. "Don't you all have like dozens of children?"

"I suggest you not add racial slurs to your line of offenses."

"Offenses?" Adam argued as he got into the cop car. "I haven't done anything wrong. I've just got more important things to be doing than this shit. I run a company, you know? In addition to going to the best college in the country. And you're going to interrupt my whole night and prevent me from building my company and doing my schoolwork because I didn't fully brake at a stop sign? It's bullshit!"

Adam punched his fist against the glass and fell back onto the seat with his arms crossed.

He protested the whole way to the police station on campus, where the cop led him into a holding cell, handed him a blanket, and slammed the bars closed.

33

Little Boy Blue

T.J. had tears in his eyes he was laughing so hard.

"And so then we're all standing in the street watching Jake, who by this point is *completely* naked, holding his laptop over his head like he's John Cusack in *Say Anything*. All the while he's yelling to this sorority chick that they're soul mates. All of her friends are freaking out, but she's laughing hysterically because, I mean, look at him." His buddy Robert was red with laughter as he punched Jake's shoulder, the latter blushing madly with a smile as he sipped his cocktail.

The three girls the trio of buddies had picked up were clearly not sure what to think, but played along and laughed flirtatiously as Robert recounted last year's "guys' week" at the New Orleans Jazz Fest.

"Honestly, he's exaggerating," Jake defended himself, putting his hand reassuringly on one of the girl's knees. "I never thought that girl was my soul mate."

The girl, who said her name was Betsy, sipped through her straw and peered at him with doe eyes. "Is that so?"

"Of course it's so, baby. I've never had a soul mate. At least not until an hour ago when I met you."

Now she blushed furiously. T.J. and Robert exchanged a look: Jake was definitely getting laid tonight.

T.J. rolled his eyes merrily. It had been a week, but he was still surprisingly jovial from his ZOSTRA win and the time he spent with Amelia—hanging out with her again relaxed him more than anything else. Since then, he and Amelia g-chatted regularly, and it felt nice to have someone *real* to talk to. On autopilot with his friends, T.J. turned his attention to Stacey, the girl who, by process of elimination, had fallen to him. "Have you been to New Orleans?" he asked.

Stacey had dark straight hair, cut short at an angle that followed the line of her exaggerated jaw. Her eyes were watery and reminded T.J. of a fish's. Not the best face, but her body had perfectly proportioned curves, and it took all the energy he could muster to keep his focus on her fish eyes instead of the cleavage spilling out of her tight black V-neck top.

"I have not," she said in a raspy voice. "It's been on my list for a while. I love jazz."

"Oh, yeah?" T.J. asked. "Well, we'll have to go together sometime." He clinked her glass, and she blushed. She was definitely the least attractive one of her friends, and he got the impression she didn't get compliments from guys like him very much.

"Anyone need a refill?" a cocktail waitress in a tight black dress asked as she picked up Betsy's empty glass.

"Round of tequila shots, I think?" Robert glanced around the group, who all nodded approvingly.

T.J. finished off his drink and handed his empty glass to the waitress, gesturing for another. As he turned his attention back toward Stacey, though, his eye caught a familiar face in the distance. T.J. squinted, trying to see who it was. His mind shut out the raspy-voiced Stacey and he felt his muscles tense as he recognized his ex-girlfriend Riley, in tight jeans and heels, walk up to the bar with a tall, athletic older man in a navy sports coat.

T.J.'s breath deepened and his jaw tightened as he turned his attention to Stacey. *Ignore it,* he told himself. *Pretend she isn't there.*

"Do you like jazz?" Stacey continued the thread from before.

"I do," T.J. said, "I love Coltrane."

"Me too," she said, her voice even raspier.

There was a moment of silence that Stacey took a sip of her drink to fill.

Who was she with? Who was that guy? He had to be at least forty. Was she really dating a *forty*-year-old? Had she actually gotten that desperate?

The tequila shots arrived and T.J. took his without waiting for the group.

"Dude," Robert said, punching him, "you didn't even toast."

"Sorry." T.J. picked up his Scotch glass, which the waitress had replenished, and joined it in the group's clinking glasses, neatly polishing it off in three deep chugs.

Stacey's fish eyes widened at his aggressive drinking. "What'd you do to him, Stacey?" Jake teased, and she furrowed her brow in concern.

T.J. clapped his hands together. "Nothing at all. Stacey is excellent company. We were just discussing her affinity for jazz."

T.J. felt the booze take hold and he closed his eyes with a deep breath before opening them again on Riley, now seated at a barstool, her knees facing her male companion. She'd taken off her chic suede jacket to reveal a sleeveless beige silk top that made her skin look white as milk from across the room.

"She likes Coltrane," T.J. announced to the group, turning his head back to them but unable to keep his eyes from flicking back to Riley, who he could see lean in seriously to her date as if saying something significant.

"I think we should do another," T.J. said, feeling antsy. He stood up from the couch. "Where's the waitress?" he said to the air before him, peering around.

Robert looked at Jake and Jake shrugged as if to say, "Your guess is as good as mine."

"Miss? Miss!" T.J. heard himself yell across the room. People turned to stare. "Miss, another round of tequila shots, please," he announced to the entire Rosewood bar. The waitress gave him a thumbs-up and he sat down, glancing back toward Riley and finding her eyes on him. She pursed her lips and tilted her head upward in acknowledgment of him as her glossed lips opened and she continued whatever she was saying to her companion.

T.J. clapped his hands together again. She'd seen him: Now he had to show her how good of a time he was having. "So, what do we think?"

"About what?" Robert asked, wondering why his friend was now on overdrive.

"What do we think about a little round of two truths and a lie? I want to know more about Stacey here." He put his arm around her waist and tickled her side as he squeezed her toward him.

Robert caught T.J.'s glance and followed it to Riley, then, realizing who it was, let out an "Oy vey" under his breath, finally understanding what was going on. "Epic idea, T," he said in support. "I'll start: I'm a certified scuba instructor, I sold a mobile app to Facebook last year for four hundred thousand dollars, and I have a third nipple."

"No way you sold an app to Facebook," Betsy blurted, tilting her head skeptically.

"Wrong. That one's true."

"For four hundred thousand dollars?" Betsy smiled more broadly.

"Then you don't have a third nipple," Stacey insisted, unintentionally cuing Robert to take off his shirt, revealing an enviable chest. He pointed proudly to a small red nub on the far side of his right pec, flexing as he did so. "Wrong again!" he said proudly. "The lie was scuba diving. That is scary as hell, all those sharks and crazy deep-sea creatures? No thank you."

The girls all laughed. Jake and T.J. joined in, even though

they'd seen Robert pull this same spiel dozens of times before. It always worked.

The entire bar was now staring at the table with the shirt-less guy, but Robert gave no sign of redressing as he leaned forward to eat an olive. That third nipple was the best thing that ever happened to him, providing such a neat excuse to constantly take off his shirt.

T.J. laughed again in exaggerated happiness before glancing back toward the bar—proud of himself for having waited a good thirty seconds since the last time. This time, he found an empty seat next to Riley's companion, who was studying his iPhone. His eyes darted to the door, where he caught her walking out toward the restroom.

"Excuse me," he abruptly announced to the table as he got up. He wasn't going to repeat last time.

"Careful," Robert cautioned quietly, but T.J. didn't pay any attention.

The men's and women's restrooms flanked a floor-to-ceiling mirror. T.J. caught his reflection in it as he waited for Riley to come out, and it revamped his confidence. He was attractive in college, but he'd gotten more so since; his eyes had lost their boyishness and his skin had grown more rugged.

Riley opened the restroom door and was startled to find him there. She'd reapplied her lip gloss in the bathroom, he noticed with jealousy.

"Oh," she said. "Hi, T.J."

"Really? Hi?" he blurted, wishing he'd thought harder about how he was going to start this.

She slunk her weight back onto one hip and tilted her head with annoyed patience. "What is it, T.J.?"

"What are you doing here?"

"I'm having a drink. As, it seems, are you."

"Who is that man?"

"That's none of your business."

"Are you sleeping with him?"

She didn't flinch. "Also none of your business."

"What I mean is . . ." He wished he hadn't brought up her date so quickly. He did want to know, but that wasn't the point. "Why are you back here?"

"I came up because Roger was sick, T.J.," she said gravely, as if talking to a child too self-absorbed to remember the last time they'd seen each other was at a funeral.

"Roger's dead," he said too bluntly. "Why are you still here?"

She glared at him, unsure whether to criticize his insensitivity or answer his question. "I've been doing some freelance work that went well, so I'm taking on another assignment. And the vibe is exciting up here, it's nice to be back in it."

"You. Can't. Stay. Here," he said, emphasizing each word, getting to the point.

She laughed, unfazed. "And why is that, T.J.?"

"Because it's mine."

"What's yours?"

"This." He swept his arm around them, noticing the mirror starting to sway and wishing he hadn't had that last tequila shot. "It's my . . . territory."

"I'm not having this conversation, T.J." She moved to walk away.

"No, stop," he said. He couldn't let her leave without her understanding.

"You're not allowed to come back here."

"Listen, T.J.," she said sharply, "you've made it excessively clear that you have no interest in being around me, okay? I get it. And while I do wish we could learn to be civil, you've convinced me not to expect it anymore. And I assure you, from the very bottom of my soul, that nothing about my coming back has anything to do with you."

The words landed like skewers. He realized for the first time how much he'd wanted her to be back for him, and how honestly she was just back for Roger.

He wasn't going to lose this one, though. "Doesn't matter. You come back, you play by my rules. Rosewood is mine, Atherton Country Club is mine, any alumni party where SAE is represented is mine."

Riley laughed and pushed her hand through her hair in frustration. "Jesus, T.J., you really have changed."

"What is that supposed to mean?"

She shook her head in disbelief. "You didn't want any of *this*, remember?"

He swallowed and waited.

"Remember those forever-long talks about how much you didn't want to be in Silicon Valley? How you didn't want to be in your father's shadow? How much you wanted to break out and do something big? You hated it here."

It was true. When they were dating, T.J. confided in Riley his fears and vulnerabilities. He would ask her what his purpose should be, and she would ask him the same. T.J. knew that when they were together he had envisioned a future that was very different from the life he now claimed.

"I was young."

"You were real. You wanted to break out and make a name for yourself. You wanted to be different from what you'd grown up with."

"I am," he said deliberately.

"No you're not. Look at you. You're becoming the same self-ish, controlling jerk you hated in your father."

T.J. didn't move. He stared at her with hate and admiration and attraction and disgust. Mostly he really wanted to pull her toward him and press her glossed lips to his own.

Riley saw that she struck a chord and backed off, her voice softening. "Country clubs? The Rosewood? Trashy girls? You're better than this, T.J." She turned to walk away.

"You're a real bitch, you know?" he yelled after her. "You just dig and dig and dig. It's disgusting."

She didn't even turn around.

He looked around for something to kick or throw and, finding nothing, slammed his fist into the wall. He felt the sting in his knuckles and it made him even more frustrated. He shook his hand in the air and caught his reflection in the mirror, which re-assured him. He was hot and successful and didn't need to waste any energy on some girl who didn't recognize it. But he also didn't need to waste it on the less-attractive wingman friend of the girl Robert wanted to sleep with.

T.J. turned back to the bar and scanned the room for the most attractive woman he could find. In the middle of the bar, perched on a stool with a pink-drink-filled martini glass in hand was a perfectly proportioned blonde in a short, tight black dress that showcased massive cleavage, flirtatiously giggling with two fat and balding men his father's age. She was definitely older, which was exciting, and he was definitely better than either of her other options.

Done, T.J. thought, beelining for the bar. He intentionally ac-cidentally brushed her arm as he walked past, then propped his elbow next to hers, just close enough that he could feel the warmth of her arm on his own.

"Macallan twenty-five, neat," T.J. told the bartender, loud enough for her to overhear. Which she did, and presently excused herself from her previous conversation, shifting her shoulders square to him.

"Aren't you a little young to be drinking Scotch?"

"What I lack in years I make up for in experience," he said, and grinned slyly. Her skin was Botoxed to flawless perfec-tion, her makeup applied with such skill it was hard to tell whether she was wearing it or if her eyelids were naturally purple-shaded.

She gave him a practiced laugh. She wore a necklace with a drop diamond that sank between her breasts, which were clearly fake in their round perch, but were so delectable and desirable as to silence any thought that the world shouldn't unhesitatingly encourage plastic surgery for all women everywhere.

"So who is my competition?" T.J. leaned in and said quietly, as though he cared whether the other men heard.

"Well," she said, nodding her head, "they work on Wall Street. In New York."

T.J. scoffed, "Please. You look like the kind of woman who can handle more adventurous men."

"What's unadventurous about Wall Street?" The woman pursed her deep pink lips.

"No risk-taking. Rich, maybe, but you have to take risks if you want to have adventure."

"Like you?"

"Yes." T.J. smiled and took a sip of his cocktail. "Like me."

She studied his face for a moment before taking a long sip of her own, letting her eyes look up to the ceiling as if she was thinking about something. T.J. waited patiently, thinking about what kind of underwear she was wearing. *Black lace thong,* he thought. *Maybe red.*

"Should we have an adventure?" she said, finally turning back to him.

"Can you handle it?" T.J. had been waiting to deliver this line and it came off just like he wanted.

She laughed her bosom-moving laugh again. "Oh, honey, I think so"—she downed her drink—"but don't let that keep you from trying to surprise me." She turned to the bartender and indicated he ought to put the two drinks on the investment bankers' tab and led T.J. out of the bar.

The pair got into a black town car that T.J. ordered via an app called Uber. He directed the driver to his parents' address in Atherton—they were out of town, and he couldn't take her back to his apartment, which, though awesome, was littered with Bud Light cans and young-single-dude-living-alone filth.

Once in the car, T.J. pushed himself over to the woman, who softened her neck and closed her eyes. He slowly brought his mouth to hers as his right hand gently cradled her head, her hair sifting between his fingers.

Her lips were strong and intentional, not slobbery and subservient like so many of the girls he made out with. He felt his excitement escalate as his fingers fell to her lap, making tiny circles against the bare skin of her thighs before slowly toying with the hem of her skirt.

The car pulled up to the house and T.J. quickly handed the driver two twenties as he followed the woman out of the car, where she was confidently walking to the front door, her hips swaying precisely in the tight black dress.

He approached her from behind and grabbed her hips, turning her around and slamming her back against the door as he pressed his lips against hers once more. She put a finger to his lips, though, to stop him, and whispered, "Ssshh . . . not here. You don't want the neighbors to hear."

"Are you loud?" T.J. grinned.

"I can be," she said, smiling back.

T.J.'s head was focused on the singular purpose of getting this woman naked as quickly as possible, but he managed to find the key and unlock the front door as she toyed with his belt buckle, softly teasing him. T.J. practically carried her through to the pool house. His room was clearly off limits, and the thought of having sex in his parents' bed was creepy.

When they pushed through French doors that faced the infinity pool she stopped him. "Wait," she said, looking around.

"What is it?" T.J. panicked, then got sly again. "You want to do it in the pool?" He smiled as he pressed his hips against hers and started to unzip her dress.

"No—I mean—just give me a second." She was staring around, studying the pool house. "What did you say your name was?"

"I don't think I did—I'm T.J."

"What's your last name?" She squinted, putting something together.

"Who cares?" He wanted her to stop talking, and he put a finger on her lips.

"I've been here before," she said.

"Not possible," T.J. said, looking at her breasts now and dropping his head to kiss them. "My family has lived here since I was born."

She pulled his chin up with a firm finger and looked him straight in the eyes. "I know you," she said, laughing. "You're Ted Bristol's son."

T.J.'s head was suddenly cleared of all the lust and imagery and anticipation he had as he heard his father's name. "How do you know my father?" he snapped, not wanting to piece together what she already had.

She laughed. "He picked me up in a bar and brought me back once, too." She rolled her eyes. "Jesus, I was young then—am I so old?" She was laughing at all this and T.J. felt his mouth go dry. "I guess it's true what they say: Like father, like son, eh?"

T.J. pushed her shoulders with unintentional force, and she stumbled back on her heels.

"What the hell?" she snapped.

"Don't say that," T.J. growled, turning and putting a hand to his brow. "Are you saying you slept with my father?"

"Yeah." She nodded, pissed off now. "Over there"—she pointed to a lounge chair by the pool—"and in there"—she pointed into the house—"and once in the hot tub." She was saying it matter-of-factly to rub it in, and it was working.

"And he was spectacular," she added, pulling her dress down and turning back toward the main house.

T.J.'s head was spinning. "You couldn't have—he loves my mother."

"Love?" She laughed. "Love has nothing to do with anything, T.J. Grow up."

T.J. fell, stunned, into a pool chair and watched her leave, unable to move or to speak, his pride empty and his brain spinning with all the ramifications of realizing his father had had sex with another woman in the same pool house T.J. himself played in as a child.

And underneath all that turmoil and fallout was an even more serious thought: The woman was right, and Riley was right—he was on the same exact path as the father he despised.

34

Adam Dory: Drunk, Racist Asshole

Adam opened his eyes onto a concrete wall and slowly rolled onto his back, to see a yellow fluorescent light buzzing from a damp ceiling. He lifted his hand to his temple, then reached behind his head to feel a concrete slab serving as a pillow. The sensation of the cold stone made him jolt upright, which brought the bars back into view, along with the slow recollection of what had happened last night. He remembered the bars slamming on him, he remembered yelling some more at the cop, he remembered an angry conversation with another drunk about a girl, and another guy in the cell pacing around bitching about some new cloud technology Hewlett-Packard was trying to steal from him.

But now he was alone in the cell: just him, the concrete wall, and the looming fate before him.

"Morning, soldier," a voice called from outside the cell.

Adam turned his head to see the cop from last night flipping through paperwork at his desk. He didn't look up as he addressed his ward.

Adam shook his head and let out a low groan. Finally he said in a croaky voice, "I'm in big trouble, huh?"

Now the cop looked up and shrugged sarcastically. "What

for? Running a stop sign? Driving drunk? Resisting arrest? Making racial slurs to a cop? Or being a spoiled, stuck-up idiot?"

Adam swallowed. His head hurt, as much from sleeping on the concrete bench as from the apparently too many Jack and Cokes.

The cop sighed as he paused in his paperwork and finally turned to Adam. "I gotta say, you did not do or say anything to be proud of last night."

Adam nodded silently, feeling genuine remorse.

"You Stanford kids," the cop said, shaking his head, "you get in this mind-set that the rules don't apply to you. Like breaking the rules is always okay because that's what Steve Jobs did or Mark Zuckerberg did or whatever. But get it together, man: You could have killed somebody last night driving as drunk as you were. Could have killed yourself. Some rules—some rules ain't meant to be broken."

Adam nodded more rapidly, twisting his hands in his lap and calculating just how much his life was now over with a DUI on his record. What would happen when his investors found out? It seemed inevitable that this would make headlines and spur the fame for which he'd so desperately longed, but that it would be all wrong. Instead of "ADAM DORY: MASTER ENTREPRENEUR," the headlines would read, "ADAM DORY DESTROYS DOREYE, INC. AND IS A DRUNK, RACIST ASSHOLE ON TOP OF IT ALL."

The cop stood up and put his key in the cell's lock, pulling the door open. He handed Adam his keys. "Your car's still on Galvez. There's a bus stop three blocks down from here, or you can walk."

Adam continued to nod and look at the floor, too ashamed to look the cop in the eye. "What"—he stumbled—"what happens next?"

"You'll get a ticket in the mail."

"Then what?"

"Then you'll pay it, presumably."

Adam lifted his head. "What about court?"

The cop shook his head.

Adam studied him, and he shrugged. "You're letting me off?"

He lifted his eyebrows. "Appears that way, don't it?"

"But I—" Adam protested helplessly. "But I was drunk. And then I insulted you. *Horribly.* I was racist and pretentious. And the irony of it all is that I'm a totally poor homeless kid who hates that crap. And here I was telling you that—"

"No need to repeat it," the cop calmly interrupted.

"How can you just let me off?"

"I took this job because I wanted to make this world safer and better. Last night, I wanted to punch the living daylights out of you, believe you me," the cop said, shaking his head, "but that wouldn't have made things any better. And neither will putting a permanent mark on your record that forever brands you as a drunk, racist loser."

"Loser?"

"Drinking alone on a Monday night? What the hell is a good-looking kid like you doing drinking alone on a Monday night?" The cop smiled under his mustache.

"But how do you know I won't do it again?"

"Eh," the cop said, and turned back to his desk, "I seen your type before. Good kids that just got off track. People think that bad things only happen in the ghetto. But it's just as common at your fancy Ivy League schools. You won't do it again."

Adam felt his heart tense and release and then tense up again, half expecting the cop to start laughing and lock him in jail forever. "So I can go?"

"You better go, man. I got paperwork to do and I been up all night listening to your drunk ass snore."

"And that's it? Nothing else?"

"You got a four-hundred-dollar ticket coming in the mail."

"Yeah, yeah, that's fine." Adam was so relieved to pay four hundred dollars, he wanted to write the check right now.

He turned and walked toward the door, then came back and reached out his hand. "Thank you, Officer—" He paused, realizing he didn't know his benefactor's name.

"Rodrigues. Anthony Rodrigues," the cop said, and accepted his hand.

"Thank you." Adam shook it gratefully and turned to go.

As he pushed out the door into the open sunlight, he heard Anthony's voice giving him some parting advice. "Hey, Adam? You get one more chance. Don't screw it up."

Adam swallowed and nodded, knowing—now—that he wouldn't.

35

Paying for It

"Oh, I just love this—try it on?" Mrs. Hawkins pulled a short navy sweaterdress off the rack and held it up for Patty to see.

Patty tilted her head and squinted in consideration. It was a cable-knit cashmere blend that would look darling with the new brown suede Stuart Weitzman boots she'd just bought, a seven-hundred-dollar splurge from this month's record Focus Girls profits. "Sure," she answered.

"Size eight?"

"Size six." Patty glared at her mother's implication. She'd put on a few pounds since she ended things with Alex, but she didn't need her mother's passive-aggressive reminders.

"I'll have her take both just in case," Mrs. Hawkins said, handing the dresses to the Neiman Marcus clerk to hang in the dressing room.

Patty decided to let it roll off—she was in a great mood despite her extra three pounds. Focus Girls business was humming, and clients and girls alike couldn't stop singing her praises. Every day brought new accolades from happy customers or happier employees, and she felt pride knowing that she'd created something that resonated with people.

"So have you been out with anyone since Alex?" her mother pried.

"No," Patty said nonchalantly, studying a chartreuse silk blouse. "No time."

She could feel her mother's disapproving glare from three feet away.

"Men my age, Mom, they're just so dull. I mean, admit it: Alex was way—well, he wasn't smart enough, don't you think?" She looked up with an honest expression.

Mrs. Hawkins moved around the table of sweaters that separated them and put her hand on her daughter's cheek, then laughed. "No, no—I supposed he really wasn't."

Patty laughed, too.

"Whatever happened to that ridiculous app company he was starting?"

"Oh, it folded." Patty rolled her eyes. "Obviously." She wrapped a silk scarf around her neck and studied its appearance in a nearby mirror. "Of course, he said it was because he didn't have the time to commit to it and it couldn't survive without his leadership, but in reality I think enough investors turned him down that he finally realized it was a stupid idea."

"I'm just not used to looking at you as a big-time entrepreneur." Mrs. Hawkins stood behind her and met her eyes in the mirror. "But I am so, so proud."

Patty returned her mother's smile. One of the best side effects of this whole experience was that it gave her and her mother something other than boys and clothes to talk about, and that made Patty see her mom in a new light, almost like a really supportive peer, not a nagging older woman.

But this moment was shortly interrupted by a phone call. Patty didn't recognize the number, and she excused herself from her mother as she picked up. "Focus Girls, this is Patty?"

"Patty, it's Marvin Fetzer; we spoke last week when I scheduled an appointment with four of your girls?"

"Yes, of course." Patty stumbled over her words, trying to recollect which one this was—there were so many now. "How was everything?"

"It was eighty percent perfect and twenty percent abhorrent."

"I'm sorry?"

"One of the girls was terrible. She was an absolute wet mop and left the evening early without even excusing herself."

"Which one?"

"She said her name was Lisa."

Patty remembered Marvin now: This was the event at Rosewood for the men researching young women's fashions. She'd sent Lisa Bristol for her first Focus Girls assignment.

"You're joking!" Patty gripped the phone closer to her ear as if it would help to convey her concern. "But Lisa's one of our very best," she lied. Although it had been Lisa's first assignment, it was Lisa Bristol for God's sake—she had to be good. "Something must have happened."

"Are you accusing—" Marvin's voice started to rise.

"No, no, no—I'm not accusing you of anything," Patty said, trying to recover. "I mean, she must have gotten sick or something. This is totally unlike her. I'll look into it immediately and get back to you with an explanation, but in the meantime we'll obviously give you a refund."

"I fully expect it."

"Of course, Marvin, of course. You get a full refund and my guarantee that this will never happen again."

"Thank you, Patty. As I said, your girls are usually top-notch. Otherwise I wouldn't have called. You can count on us continuing to be customers," he said matter-of-factly, and hung up the phone.

Patty stared at her iPhone. What could possibly have happened to Lisa?

Lisa sat forward with her elbows on the table, cupping her chin in her hands, her purple-polished fingers stretched alongside her thinly mascaraed eyes.

"Oh, Patty." She shook her head in her hands. "I'm so sorry. I totally failed you."

"I just want to understand what happened," Patty said honestly, unable to be angry at a friend who looked so shell-shocked.

They were at a back corner table in University Café. Patty had called Lisa after the conversation with Marvin, requesting they get together, and Lisa had agreed to meet here ASAP.

"Well, I guess it all started out okay." Lisa pulled back in her chair and looked down at her mug. "I mean, I was the last one there, but I swear I was on time."

"He didn't say anything about you being late, so I think you're fine there," Patty encouraged.

"And then he poured me a glass of wine, which surprised me a little because I guess I was in work mode. But everyone else was drinking, so I figured that was a normal part of the thing." She looked up for more encouragement. Patty nodded.

"But then . . ." She paused. "I don't know, Patty—they weren't asking about fashion at all. Or about anything, really. They were just pouring more wine, and each man was kind of paired off with one girl and the man with me was—" She paused again and shook her head, as if trying to forget. "I don't know. I just got a really bad feeling."

Patty felt her teeth clench at the implication that her sessions could be unpleasant. "So then what?" she asked.

"So then I went to the bathroom and all of a sudden felt really nauseous. I couldn't shake the feeling that something was off and—and so I left." She finally looked up at Patty and shrugged her shoulders.

"And you didn't feel the need to call me to tell me?" Patty felt her voice betray her irritation. "Not only did you not have the courtesy to go back to tell your hosts that you were leaving, you didn't have the manners to tell me what you'd done?"

"I'm sorry, Patty—I just didn't know—"

"I'm running a business here, Lisa," Patty snapped, suddenly finding Lisa's weakness irritating and pathetic, not empathy-inspiring. "I can't be caught off guard by angry clients calling because one of my employees was rude."

"I was not rude," Lisa said sternly.

"What would you call it, then?"

"I reacted normally to an awkward situation."

"What are you implying?"

"What you sent me to was not a focus group for young women's fashion, Patty."

"Then what was it?"

"I didn't care to stay long enough to find out." Lisa glared at her friend.

"How dare you suggest—"

"Are all of them like this?"

"Like what?"

"Girls meeting men at the Rosewood, after dark, with wine?"

"No; this one was special and I made a special effort to get you a spot on it."

"Well, you should have saved yourself the trouble."

"Apparently so."

The two girls sat in silence for a moment. Patty's mind was whirring: How could Lisa be so stupid? How could she be so uptight and dramatic? Had she watched so many bad made-for-TV movies that she thought any man offering a younger woman a glass of wine was somehow inappropriate?

"Have you ever done one?" Lisa finally asked.

Patty started to say "Of course," but then remembered that she actually hadn't. "Well, no," she answered, "not myself. But this is the first time anyone—client or Focus Girl—has ever said anything like what you're saying."

"Maybe I'm crazy," Lisa said quietly, "but I think you should go on one. Just to judge for yourself."

"I will," Patty said defiantly. "Just to prove to you that you're wrong."

Lisa nodded. "Good. I hope you do."

"In the meantime, though," Patty said, feeling she still needed to exercise her managerial power, "I'm afraid I can't compensate you for the evening."

"I assure you"—Lisa had power of her own—"I wouldn't take it if you did."

Patty ignored the sting. "We're settled, then."

Lisa nodded and sipped her coffee, then said quietly, "I look forward to hearing what you think after your date."

Patty glared at the word and lifted her hand to get the check.

36

Exit, Stage Left

"This is amazing." Amelia looked down at the chocolate milk shake on the other end of her straw in genuine astonishment. "How do they make it taste so good?"

"Don't ask," T-Bag said, sipping his own strawberry-banana concoction, "just enjoy."

They were at Peninsula Creamery, where T-Bag had dragged Amelia immediately upon learning she'd never heard of it, claiming it was an insult to one of Palo Alto's finest institutions that she'd never experienced their milk shake. It had been a long day in the computer lab, and Amelia happily accepted the study break, even though it meant braving the rain to get downtown in T-Bag's car.

"So, Amelia." He crossed his hands seriously on the table. "There's a conversation we can no longer avoid."

Amelia felt her lip tremble. Ever since the night of Roger's funeral, T-Bag had become the closest thing to a best friend she'd ever known other than Adam, and she often felt like she was waiting for the shoe to drop. For him to follow a statement like this with "This has been fun but it's all done: You're a total loser destined to have no friends."

"What is it?" she said quietly, dropping her eyes back to her milk shake.

"T. J. Bristol."

Amelia's head snapped up. "What about him?" she said, unable to hide the quiver in her voice.

T-Bag sat back in his chair and crossed his arms. "Really?" he said in an are-you-kidding-me tone.

"What?" she asked as innocently as she could.

T-Bag leaned forward again. "Listen, Amélie." She loved it when he used her new nickname. "It's fairly obvious that you like him."

"That's not—"

"Shhhh." He put a finger up to interrupt her. "You would be insane not to: He's hot and manly and successful and older." He paused. "However, liking him also makes you a giant cliché: The nerdy computer scientist who never had a boyfriend goes for the hunky frat boy, clearing her schedule to tutor him in dumbed-down Comp Sci assignments in the hopes of a single dribble of testosterone-fueled attention."

Amelia swallowed, thinking back on the tutorial at Gates. "That's a bit harsh."

"It's not the point."

"But I *don't* like him," she protested. "Really, I don't. Not like that."

T-Bag tilted his head and made a face. "Whatever. Still not the point."

"What is the point, then?" Amelia asked, starting to get annoyed.

"T.J. likes you."

Amelia froze. She felt her skin tingling with the feeling of T.J.'s touch at the computer lab as she let herself believe it had been intentional. T-Bag laughed and reached across the table to punch her arm. "See! You do like him! Otherwise you never would have reacted that way."

"What way?" she squeaked.

"Paralyzed! You're totally lovesick."

Amelia swallowed, irritated. "Oh, I see. So saying he likes me was just to see my reaction? Just to test whether I have a crush on him? You are such a jerk." She shook her head in disbelief, embarrassed that she'd fallen for his trick.

"No! I'm serious! He clearly has feelings for you, Amelia. I mean, did you see his drool during ZOSTRA?"

Amelia felt like her heart had been opened. She'd felt it, too: the way he leaned in a little closer than he used to and told her she was pretty and stayed around to play some stupid computer game. But she couldn't possibly allow herself to admit it. He was a jerk. He used women and she knew that. Then again, he'd loved Riley. Maybe he was a jerk the same way she was a loser, and it was just a matter of finding the right other person to bring you around.

"And you know what, Amélie? He's not as much of a douche bag as I thought he was. He's got a spectacular inner nerd. And he's been super nice to me, too, even though I wrote him off as a dumb homophobe."

"You don't think he's a douche bag?"

"I think he's in the douche bag closet. Trust me—I know a double life when I see one. Deep down he's more like you than the frat boy façade he presents. I also think that's why he's falling for you—he realizes he can be happy by being his true self."

Amelia shook her head. "I don't know. Even if by some absurd, ridiculous chance you were right, and even if by some even more absurd chance he actually did something, I couldn't date him. Not with all that's happened with Doreye."

Her shoulders collapsed forward as she said it, along with the fleeting hope that her love life could be such a fairy tale.

"You really miss it, don't you?"

"More than anything," she mumbled without looking up.

T-Bag frowned: Talking about boys was easy, but this was fragile territory he wasn't sure how to tread on.

Luckily, Amelia continued without coaxing. T-Bag had opened a valve and she couldn't help letting out her long-suppressed sadness.

"Doreye was like . . . everything to me. My time and my identity and the center of everything that made my life better. And now that it's gone . . . it feels even worse than if I'd never had it at all."

"But look at all you learned," T-Bag insisted. "That's what this place is all about: trying things and seeing how they go, and then trying again."

"All that I learned?" Amelia looked at him with a twisted brow. "I learned that the only thing that matters is money, and that people—even my brother—are totally selfish jerks."

Her voice quivered on the last line.

T-Bag sighed. He'd never met Adam and they'd never mentioned him before, but he obviously knew the story from the gossip mill.

"It can't be that bad," T-Bag coaxed. "Don't you still own Doreye?"

"We split the equity between us, but it vested over four years. So since I was only there for a year, I own less than ten percent. Even though I *built* the thing."

"Have you talked to him since?"

"Adam? Not since Roger's funeral. He texted but I ignored him. I can't face him."

"What are you going to do?"

"I don't know. I just feel so suffocated. Everything about campus and this town reminds me of Doreye and Roger and Adam and all these things I've lost."

"Why don't you take a break from it all?" T-Bag sat up straight with an idea. "What are you doing for spring break?"

"I was—" Amelia started but stopped herself, remembering she had no plans. Despite the final projects and looming deadlines, she hadn't allowed the reality to sink in. "I don't have any plans, I guess."

"Come to Tahoe with me!" T-Bag said with enthusiastic encouragement. "Do you ski?"

Amelia let out a choked laugh. "Me? Ski? Are you kidding? Do you think Indiana foster homes have competitive ski teams?"

T-Bag waved it off. "Whatever, you don't have to know how. Half the people there won't. Oh, Amelia, you have to come, it'll be so good for you to get away."

"Who are you going with?"

T-Bag took a deep breath and looked seriously at Amelia. "Can you keep a secret?"

Amelia looked around her and wanted to say, "Whom am I going to tell?" But she just nodded.

"It's super super secret, so please, please don't ever say a word." T-Bag's eyes were serious.

"Of course not." Amelia met his concerned tone and leaned forward.

"I've got a sort-of boyfriend in the business school. The trip is with a bunch of his business-school friends."

"Ohhhh," Amelia said, smiling. "I can't wait to meet him."

"The thing is, he's not totally out."

"Out of what?"

"The closet. I mean, not everyone knows he's gay. I mean, he hasn't really told anyone."

Amelia looked quizzically at him. "So how do you?—"

"We're telling people I'm his cousin."

"His cousin?"

T-Bag shrugged and laughed helplessly. "It seemed like the easiest thing to say."

"Okay, then." Amelia smiled back. "I would love to join you and your cousin on your business-school trip to Tahoe."

"Really?" T-Bag's eyes lit up. "Perfect! Oh, this'll be so much fun. Classes end on Wednesday and we're leaving Thursday at noon."

"Perfect." Amelia sipped the remaining chocolate from her glass and felt a sensation she hadn't felt in a long time: She had something to look forward to.

37

Mourning After

It was afternoon, but T.J. was still in his pajamas, slumped in a chair at the kitchen table with his legs stretched out and his arms crossed, staring into space while a bowl of Frosted Flakes got soggy in the bowl in front of him. He wore a bathrobe over old flannel pajamas and hadn't bothered to turn on the light. His mind was in too much of a twist from what had happened last night to deal with normal human routines.

And yet the discovery that his father had had an affair—had probably had lots of affairs—did not make him sad. It actually made him feel better: like he'd found a missing puzzle piece that confirmed the instinct he'd always had that his father was not a good man.

As he sat at the kitchen table, his mind raced, slotting the new reality of his dishonest father into all the gaps from his childhood.

The soccer games he missed when T.J. was in high school: *click.*

The fights with Mrs. Bristol in the kitchen: *click.*

The I'm-working-late-on-an-important-deal excuses for missing family movie night: *click.*

His trust fund: T.J. paused. His eyes snapped up. What about his trust fund?

T.J. bolted out of the chair and into his father's office. Without hesitation he started rifling through files, looking for the ones containing his trust fund documents. With each manila folder T.J. continued to get increasingly anxious. He thought back on how Ted had brought up the trust at Roger's funeral, how he insisted that T.J. sign the papers immediately, and how weird his insistence had seemed. *Was there a lie behind this, too?* T.J. had signed the papers without hesitation and even willingly transferred his Doreye Inc. equity into his own trust.

T.J. looked up the number for Johan, the family attorney.

He called Johan's line, but an associate who introduced himself as Ryan picked up. "Johan's in a meeting; is there something I can help you with?"

"Yes," T.J. said calmly, "I'm trying to find documentation on my trust, but I can't seem to locate it."

"No problem. Let me just pull it up and find out who has privileges; if you're listed, I can send it to you directly." He clicked his tongue as he searched his database on the other end. "Is there a particular reason you wanted to see it?"

"In fact, there is," T.J. said, working hard to keep his voice steady. "I want to find out about taking control of the trust. What it would require, that sort of thing." Then, thinking on his toes for a reasonable explanation: "You see, I'm part owner in a company called Doreye and recently transferred my shares of the company into the trust for estate planning purposes. My company's lawyers"—T.J. prayed his lie made sense—"just asked me to verify that I still control the shares because of an upcoming liquidity event."

"Got it," Associate Ryan said. "Just found your docs. Let's see . . ." He mumbled as he read through: "Looks like you're not allowed to take control until you turn forty." Ryan paused. "Wait, hold on." He read silently on the other end of the line. "I'm so sorry, but I'm actually not allowed to discuss the details of your trust with you. Actually, I really wasn't allowed to tell you the other piece. Can you please not tell? I've been here all night and I—"

"What?" T.J. interrupted. He really didn't care about Ryan's long hours.

"You're not authorized."

"What? But it's my trust!"

"Afraid I can't let out any information without the trustees'—your parents'—consent."

T.J. let his head fall back in frustration. Of course his father would have imposed such limits.

"So let's just talk in general terms," he tried, thinking fast. "What happens when someone moves their shares of a company into a trust like this?"

"Well, now the trust owns your shares, not you."

"And what does that mean, practically?"

"It means the shares of the company are now controlled—like for buying and selling purposes—by the trustee."

"My father?"

"And your mother, technically."

"Can I get my shares back out of the trust?"

"I suppose if you plead duress and speak with the company's other shareholders," Ryan said, "which you know will be a pill given it's Doreye."

"What do you mean?"

"I mean, it's going to be difficult to get proper sign-off of Doreye's shareholders when no one knows who Doreye's shareholders are," Ryan said as if this was the most obvious thing in the world.

"What are you talking about?"

Ryan laughed. "You know, the whole Doreye ownership debacle."

"What debacle?" T.J. demanded.

Ryan was quiet. "Seriously?"

"Yes, seriously."

"We've been working on it for, like, the past month with Ross Brown over at PKC. They screwed up—big-time. The money they put up to invest in Doreye was mostly from a silent partner. PKC is really only managing the money. Apparently they didn't do their homework, and now they can't figure out who the silent partner actually *is*—it's just a circuit of shell companies—and they're freaking out. They hired us to figure out who's behind it, but . . . we're at a total loss."

T.J. was silent.

"Did you seriously not know?"

"No," he said softly, his mind spinning. "Shouldn't PKC have told me? I'm the goddamn CEO."

"Legally they're not obligated. Under Code 31 of Section 509A—"

"Yeah, fine," T.J. interrupted. He didn't need this kid's legal jargon right now. As he felt the whole world crashing down on him, he caught a glimmer of hope. "Does it really matter, though? I mean, for my purposes? PKC only owns forty percent of the company, right? So it's not like they're majority shareholders."

"Well," Ryan said, sighing, "when they invested, they owned forty-two point six percent of the company. But then your cofounder left, right? That girl? When she was fired, over three hundred thousand of her shares hadn't yet vested."

"So," T.J. said, stunned, "when Amelia left everyone's relative ownership increased?"

"Yep. So PKC—or rather, this mystery investor—now owns over half—fifty-one point four percent to be precise—of the company. That's why they're freaking out." A phone rang in the background. "Listen, I gotta hop on that other line. Sorry I can't be more help on the trust—you should probably just talk to your dad. He's the trustee, so as long as I've got his approval I can give you whatever you want."

"Thanks, Ryan. You've been unbelievably helpful."

When he hung up the phone, T.J. let the silence of the empty, ransacked office consume him.

Could anything else go wrong? His father was a cheater, his perfect Atherton family was a farce, Riley didn't have feelings for him at all, and the vapid women he'd tried to replace her with suddenly made him nauseous. He'd been so distracted by his personal drama that he'd let Amelia get fired. And now, not only did he no longer control his stake in Doreye, but the company itself was controlled by a mysterious invisible entity. It's not that he wasn't in control of the things that affected him; it's that the things that affected him were uncontrollable.

T.J. carefully put away the mess he'd created in the office. When everything was in its place he sat in silence and felt empty. He needed to take back control, but of what? The company? His life? Where could he even start?

38

Head in the Clouds

Adam had already been at the office for four hours when T.J. arrived at nine.

"Hey." He nodded as T.J. walked into the conference room. "Just a sec." He finished a diagram he was drawing in red marker on the floor-to-ceiling dry-erase-board wall, which was at present covered from corner to corner in Adam's handwriting.

"What are you doing?" T.J.'s voice was stunned.

"Hold on," Adam said, finishing the diagram and standing back, arms crossed over his chest, to reflect on what he'd just mapped out. He nodded to himself and reached for a Philz coffee cup, his third of the day, as he turned to T.J.

"This," he said, indicating with his eyebrows his wall handiwork, "is how we're going to save Doreye."

T.J.'s face was cautious, unsure how to process this version of Adam, whose caffeinated energy seemed to fill the whole room. Adam was cleanly shaven and standing with perfect poise, and his eyes were bright with a sense of purpose and direction he hadn't had since the fateful day with Amelia.

T.J. stayed cautious, putting the conversation he'd planned to have with him on hold as he peered at Adam, moving closer to the whiteboard wall and reading what was there.

Adam sat patiently back as his cofounder read, nodding occasionally.

T.J. finally turned to him, hopeful for the first time since he'd gotten off the phone with Ryan. "This could work."

Adam raised his eyebrows as he grinned and nodded, exhilarated by his problem solving.

"But it's incredibly risky. I mean, to refocus our attention right now . . . if it doesn't work, we're—"

"It's going to work," Adam interrupted, not with arrogance but with manic belief.

"Have you told the engineers?"

"They'll be in at ten. I think we should tell them together."

T.J. cocked his head. Adam had never shared credit for anything, especially things that were uniquely his own, not that T.J. could remember that ever happening.

"You know"—Adam shrugged, picking up on T.J.'s confusion—"present a united front."

"What happened to you?" T.J. studied Adam's face. "Did you get laid?"

Adam laughed but deflected. If only he'd gotten laid! Instead he'd gotten thrown in jail with some rambling drunks and a kindhearted police officer.

But something about that night had cleared his thoughts. It's not that he wasn't thinking about Lisa or about Amelia or about wanting to go have a drink, he just wasn't doing it *right now*. Right now, and until it was finished, he was fixing Doreye.

When the engineers had all arrived, Adam called a group meeting in the living room–turned-lounge.

"As you all know," Adam started, "we've run into some problems with Doreye. The app itself is too advanced for the devices currently available to users. One solution is for us to wait a few years for Apple and Samsung to catch up. But there may be another solution. One that, if we all work together, won't be as difficult as we may have previously thought."

The team of eight all looked at Adam and then looked at T.J. for his reaction, but T.J. kept his eyes forward to hear Adam out.

"I've divvied up all of Doreye's functions between three teams. These teams will be led by T.J., Arjun, and me. If the smartphone hardware that Doreye runs on isn't advanced enough, then we simply won't use the smartphones. We'll use the cloud." Adam looked out across his engineers to let it sink in. "For the next week, we are going to research the processes that other companies, like Oracle and Hewlett-Packard, are using to accomplish similar tasks. By outsourcing these functions I think we can reduce the overload that's making the devices crash when they load Doreye. We can do this without increasing the size of the app. Does this make sense?"

Now Adam turned to Arjun, who had been increasingly skeptical since taking over as head engineer from Amelia, and everyone else's eyes followed.

Arjun was standing next to the couch, arms crossed over his chest. He breathed in through his nose and clicked his tongue, thinking.

Finally, he responded. "To do this quickly we need to find an off-the-shelf solution that is somehow compatible, which means we'd either need to license an expensive patent or spend eight months re-creating everything from scratch."

"At the very least, it's worth taking some time to know what else is out there," T.J. stepped in and said. "Plus we've got funding to make acquisitions and could do it quietly if it came to that. We need to at least try."

"What we need"—Arjun shook his head and said under his breath, but with the clear intention of being heard—"is Amelia."

"Sorry?" Adam asked pointedly. "If you're going to say something, say it."

Arjun looked straight at him, the frustration he'd been suppressing for weeks mounting in his voice. "I said, what we need is Amelia. It's time to stop dicking around and get her back. She was everything in this company and you screwed it up. That's the problem that needs to be fixed."

Adam nodded in patient acknowledgment; he knew Arjun felt Amelia was the only solution. He also knew that Arjun was afraid to say anything since Adam had snapped at him. This time Adam took a different approach and said quietly, "You're right: I messed things up. And I admit it, and I'm sorry all of you had to see it and suffer because of it." He looked around the room at the faces of each of his employees. "But I'm going to fix it. Maybe not the way that you want, but I will fix it and bring this company back up to the standard you deserve."

Adam looked back at Arjun. "And don't worry about the patents. If you can take a chance and trust me one last time on this, I promise you I'll take care of making sure we can execute."

Pretty Woman

Patty felt her heart racing with anticipation as she walked toward the Rosewood bar, but she was careful to take confident, measured steps: not too hurried, not too desperate. She was wearing her Stuart Weitzman boots with a short purple Alice & Olivia silk sheath dress. She'd done her full ninety-minute prep routine for tonight's meeting: shaved her legs, scrubbed her skin with an exfoliator before applying lightly perfumed lotion, plucked her eyebrows, flossed, blown out and curled her hair, and touched up her manicure. She'd even taken time in the shower to deep clean her belly button and the insides of her ears.

Over the past month, one-on-one focus groups had been requested at an increasing rate. Patty rationalized that it was easier for executives to zero in on the reactions of their target demographic without the social pressure of having other girls around.

When this request came in, Patty decided to take the one-on-one herself; she was determined to prove to Lisa that women could look great and help men understand their needs without being moral sellouts.

The man she was meeting had requested someone "interested in fashion" for a consulting project he was doing for a "boutique retailer in France looking to expand into the United States market." He'd requested to meet with a girl who had studied in Paris and considered herself up on the latest fashion trends. He suggested they meet at the bar at Rosewood for a two-hour one-on-one focus group.

"Trey?" Patty asked a man seated at a small cocktail table with a notebook in front of him. He had olive skin and dark silky hair, and was quite literally the most attractive man Patty had ever seen. She felt butterflies in her stomach with simultaneous hope and fear that this was the man she was meeting.

He looked up. "Patty Hawkins?"

"That's me." She blushed, ecstatic.

He stood up and they shook hands. His grip was firm around her hand and her mind wandered to his fingers in her hair. "Thanks so much for taking time to do this," he said as he pulled out her chair and lifted a hand to the waitress. "Can I get you a drink?"

"Sure." Patty instinctively batted her eyelashes. "I'll have a glass of Chardonnay, please."

"Sure," he said as the waitress took the order. "Just a Coke for me." He smiled at her.

Patty felt her heart sink: a Coke? Should she not have ordered alcohol? *Just drink it slowly,* she told herself, remembering that he was paying for her opinion because she was fashionable and of French persuasion.

"So how much time have you spent in France?" Trey asked.

"I've been several times, actually," Patty explained. "I spent a summer in Paris when I was in high school as part of an exchange program, and my family took a long trip to the Côte d'Azur when I was in middle school. I'm heading back for fall quarter next year; I'm hoping to study at the Sorbonne, coincidentally where my sister is a resident. I'm still trying to figure out what classes I can get into and still get credit at Stanford."

"I see." Trey wrote her answers down.

"Are you from France?" she asked, detecting an accent. She crossed her legs and shifted her weight onto one hip to move herself closer to him.

"Oh, me?" He looked surprised. "No, no, no. I'm Italian. Milanese, actually, but have been in America a long time. So what are your favorite brands?"

Patty thought it strange that he spoke so little about himself, but she went on: "I love Alice & Olivia—that's what this dress is." She pushed back in her chair and opened her arms so he could see.

"It's nice." He nodded neutrally. Or did he look at her chest? Her insides tingled.

"And I wear a lot of Rachel Zoe's stuff and of course Citizens and Paige for jeans. And Rebecca Taylor."

He nodded without looking up from his notepad.

"And for special occasions, I love Hervé Léger, but who doesn't, right?" She leaned across the table and tapped his tanned arm affectionately.

"Indeed. Beautiful pieces. Where do you mostly shop?"

Patty felt a pang of insecurity twist in her gut when she realized his eyes were looking down at his notepad—not at her. What if Lisa had been right, and he had thought this was a date, but he'd gotten here and taken one look at her and decided she wasn't worth it? Of course that was it, her brain started to settle: He'd been expecting a hot, skinny Parisian fashionista. And she, even after ninety minutes of prepping, was a big and bulky and lately-gone-up-a-dress-size nobody.

She took a big gulp of wine and said softly, "I like Neiman Marcus."

"Anywhere else?" He looked up, confused by her change in tone.

"And obviously I shop on Gilt Groupe and Bloomspot and Piperlime."

"Oh, you do? Do you prefer online shopping to in-store?"

This was so humiliating. She was the head of the company and she couldn't do the work. She was the ugly madame who collected money while the pretty girls got to have all the fun.

"It depends. I like both. Obviously there's always a place for going to the mall with friends or whatever, but it's nice having the option of online."

"Okay; just a few more questions."

This sucks, Patty thought to herself, finishing the wine and gesturing to the waitress for another without asking his permission. She answered a few more questions until, after a mere forty-five minutes of their two-hour session, Trey said he thought he'd gotten what he needed.

"Okay," Patty said, standing up. The two glasses of wine had made her more confident, or more reckless, and she turned to him in a last-ditch attempt. "Are you staying here tonight?"

"I am." He nodded. "Flying back to New York tomorrow, but here for the evening."

"Is the room nice?" she asked. "I've never seen the rooms here."

"It is," Trey said casually, studying her eyes carefully.

"Could I see yours?"

"I think we could arrange that," Trey said while looking into her eyes, and she felt her heart melt. *Boldness does pay,* she thought to herself.

As she followed him back to his room, Patty came to understand a new view of the situation: He was intimidated. He was a good guy; he'd never done this before and was nervous about how it worked. She felt her affection for him grow: handsome and timid, like the boy next door who doesn't know he's prom king.

He held the door open and she proceeded in, pretending to admire the decor.

"What do you think?" he asked, his firm eye contact making her skin tingle.

She walked close to him and put her hand on his well-defined arm. "I think a lot of things."

"What do you mean?"

"I mean, I think you're really hot, and I think I'm in your hotel room, and I think I'd like to know what you want."

The left corner of Trey's mouth curled up into a smile and he stared into Patty's eyes for several beats, studying her and what she'd just said.

Finally he stepped back and pulled something out of his pocket.

"What's that?" Patty asked flirtatiously.

Trey held the object up and let it flip open so she could see.

"A police badge," he said.

Patty felt the blood in her face drain, not sure how to process this information. But he didn't give her time to speculate.

"We've gotten several tips that Focus Girls is running a questionable operation. I met with you to try to decipher whether what you're doing qualifies as prostitution."

Patty felt like he had punched her in the gut. *Prostitution?* It was one thing for Lisa to think it was sketchy, but her friends weren't prostitutes. Her legs were weak, and she sat on the corner of the bed, her hands on her knees.

"What do you have to say?"

Patty opened her mouth but couldn't find words and just shook her head at Trey before looking back at the carpet. This couldn't possibly be happening. Her brain flashed back to the man who she'd thought was insulting her ability to run a company. *You don't seem like the type,* he'd said. Did he know? Did everyone know, except her?

She felt her stomach lurch and looked up at the cop, terrified, before bolting to the bathroom and vomiting into the toilet bowl.

She emerged a half hour later. Trey was sitting in a chair, reading from a file.

"I'm sorry," Patty mumbled.

"It's okay; I'll have someone come clean it up."

"Are you going to arrest me?" Patty squeaked, looking down at her feet.

"No," Trey said. "I'm just trying to understand what's going on with your company."

Patty nodded silently like a child who knows she deserves punishment.

"Here's what I think we should do," Trey said. "You take a cab home and get some sleep, then come to the station tomorrow and we'll talk through what's going on and where it might have gotten out of control."

She looked up hopefully. "So you mean I won't be in trouble?"

"I didn't say that. But prostitution rings tend to have many constituents doing questionable things, which means you've got a lot of room to cooperate."

Patty nodded rapidly. "Yes. I understand. I will."

"Okay." Trey let out a sigh and handed her his card. "Get home. But *do not drive*. I'll call you tomorrow to set up a time for you to come in."

Patty turned to leave.

"And Patty?" Trey said. "As a man, not as a police officer, can I just say you're way too beautiful a woman to wear so much makeup and such a short dress."

40

Shabby Chic

A streetlamp orange-illuminated a steady drizzle that pattered against the glistening pavement in front of a bus stop on Hanover Street in midtown Palo Alto. Two homeless men took shelter under the bus stop's cover, one laid out sleeping on the bench and the other sitting upright with his head curled down, huddled into himself for warmth.

The headlights of a slow-moving Hewlett-Packard security car illuminated the men before rolling on to patrol the other areas of the technology giant's campus. The homeless man who was seated watched the car turn a corner as he pulled his jacket hood forward and dashed out into the rain, across a dark lawn that in the day was a perfectly manicured entryway to HP's headquarters.

The man stopped at the corner of a building and pressed his back against the brick exterior in an attempt to make himself very flat as he watched a security camera in the corner move; as soon as the lens passed the alleyway he proceeded to cross.

He sprinted silently to the end of the alleyway and stopped at a large square Dumpster secured by a thick rectangular lock. He felt along the backside of the lock for a button he seemed to know was there. He pressed the button to open the top of the lockbox, where he entered a code, waited for another click, and pushed back the heavy Dumpster lid.

The man lifted one leg, then the other, to climb into the Dumpster, where the rain fell on waist-high piles of shredded paper, disks, drives, and discarded plastic casings. He pulled a stopwatch out of his pocket and set it for twenty minutes before digging through the Dumpster's contents, stuffing various items into the pockets of his shabby canvas coat.

When the stopwatch went off, he cursed under his breath, reaching for a pile of folders and jamming them up under his coat. He pushed himself out of the Dumpster and reached to pull back the lid. His hands shook as he replaced the lock in its proper position, and he ducked down behind the Dumpster just in time to miss the beam of a flashlight surveying the alleyway.

The man breathed heavily but silently from his perch, waiting for the darkness to return. When all was quiet, he took a deep breath, checked the security of his loaded-down coat, and dashed back across the lawn to the street.

A light caught him midway and he heard a security guard yell. He paid no heed, singularly focused on reaching the street.

"Stop! You there! I said stop!" the voice called. A whistle blew and a bright fluorescent light snapped on from overhead. He sprinted across the lawn and leapt into the passenger seat of a BMW convertible that sped up Page Mill Road toward the highway as the security guard chased helplessly on foot.

"Get what you needed?" Violet asked as Adam pushed the hood off his hair and turned to check the security guard's progress.

"Do you think he got your plates?" Adam panted, ignoring her question.

"Doesn't matter. I put the fake plates on just in case."

Adam nodded appreciably, not thinking to ask why Violet had fake plates in the first place. He let his head fall back on the seat and breathed greedily to settle his pounding heart.

"So did you get the patent applications?" Violet repeated her initial question calmly, not at all rattled by what had just happened.

"I think so," Adam said. "I wish I'd had just five more minutes, but they've got to be somewhere in this pile." He moved forward in his seat to take off his coat and started rifling through the drives and files he'd collected from the Dumpster.

"Nice work," Violet said, glancing over from the driver's seat as she exited on University Avenue, reaching her hand over to rub Adam's neck. He blushed at her touch.

"Yeah, this is going to be good," he said as he flipped through the pages, nodding excitedly. He wanted to make out with Violet but he forced himself to concentrate. "Can you take me to the office? I want to get going on this." Adam looked at his watch: 3:45 A.M. He'd hardly slept the last three nights but wasn't at all tired.

"Sure thing," Violet said, "but I'm going to sleep there if it's okay—have an eight o'clock meeting on campus."

God, she made staying focused hard. "Nap room's all yours," Adam said, referring to the bedroom they'd installed with four twin beds to accommodate late nights and midafternoon naps.

The two were quiet the rest of the ride, but as Violet pulled into the Doreye office drive and shut off the engine, she broke the silence: "So how'd you do it?"

Adam looked up. "What do you mean?"

"How'd you know where to look? And how'd you find out the code?"

Adam cocked an eyebrow slyly. "You wouldn't believe me if I told you."

Violet studied his face and, concluding that he really wasn't going to give it up, opened the door and went inside to bed, swinging her hips from side to side as she went.

Adam waited fifteen minutes from the time she went upstairs and then dialed Jeremy Jacobs, the rambling lunatic from his night in jail, whose contact information Officer Anthony Rodrigues had been kind enough to supply. Jeremy picked up on the second ring.

"Did you get it?" he asked anxiously.

"I don't know. I think so. Can you talk me through it?" Adam whispered into the phone.

"Okay, did you get the black drive labeled 'PHOENIX'?"

"Got it." Adam pulled the drive out and waited for further instruction.

"Plug it into your computer and open the file that says . . ."

Adam spent the rest of the night and morning on the phone walking through the top-secret information he'd collected from HP's Dumpster. Jeremy, the former chief engineer for Hewlett-Packard who had been fired when the firm's management changed hands, was all too happy to give Adam his Hewlett-Packard research on how to efficiently outsource data storage and logic functions to the cloud. "I gave them ten years of my best work, Adam," he'd said remorsefully on the phone. "They said all that work, all my ideas, belonged to them; I barely had time to throw everything away before they escorted me out of the building."

When Adam was done copying the code and notes from Jeremy, following his instructions for what to change in order to avoid patent infringement, he put all the evidence in a box with a mail label addressed to his former cellmate. Inside he included a note: "Here's ten years of your best work. Looking forward to whatever comes next . . ."

41

Riding Shotgun

Amelia squished her mouth to one side as she looked at the open drawer before her. What in her wardrobe could she possibly wear on a ski trip in Tahoe? She hadn't been in sub-fifty-degree temperatures since she'd come to college, much less seen snow.

She shut the drawer and bent down on hands and knees, peering back under her bed for an oversize canvas bag she'd zipped up for the last time two years ago. She struggled to pull it out into the center of the room and mentally braced herself as she opened it to reveal the contents of her Indiana existence.

She pulled out a pair of thick gloves and her old winter socks. She dug for the white long johns she'd worn under jeans on particularly bitter January mornings. She found her snow pants and a bright red Columbia jacket she'd bought in a secondhand store and worn every day the winter of her senior year in high school.

Nestled under the jacket, jammed in the corner of the bag, was a cloth satchel with something in it. She distinctly remembered jamming it there two years ago after the rest of the bag was full in a last-minute resolution that she ought not to let it go. She took the bag out and sat back on her heels, resting it on her lap and slowly undoing the tie as if pretending to herself she didn't know what was inside.

She pulled out a floppy, worn rag doll and held it familiarly beneath the arms, slowly running her finger around the plastic eyes and down the blue-buttoned dress. She let her brain open the part of itself that remembered holding this doll as a little girl on the school bus, as a middle schooler when she and Adam were briefly sent to separate group homes, as a teenager when she was in jail and the guard had let her sneak it into her room even though wards weren't allowed to have any personal possessions. She always believed it was from her mother, though she didn't remember if anyone told her that or if she'd invented it to feel like she was a regular kid.

She'd tried to throw it away every time she'd moved, but the past two years were as close as she'd come to letting it go, and holding it here now, she was glad she hadn't.

A knock at the door interrupted her nostalgia. "It's open," she called, and quickly stuffed the doll back into its bag and the bag into the larger one.

"Hi." T.J. stuck his head in and Amelia blushed with surprise.

"Oh," she said, standing up from her seat on the floor, trying not to let T-Bag's words, *he likes you,* creep into her brain. "Hi, T.J., I didn't—"

"Don't get up. I didn't mean to interrupt," he said.

"Oh, you're not. Come in." She pulled her legs around in front of her and clasped her hands at the knees. *Don't think about it. Don't think about how he feels about you.*

He took a seat at her desk chair. He was wearing black gym shorts and a tight white t-shirt, and Amelia tried not to stare at his perfectly defined calves, now at her eye level. Where had she seen calves like that? Oh, yes, on statues of Greek gods.

"Sorry for being so informal—I'm meeting a buddy at the gym."

"Stop apologizing," she said, smiling. "It's nice to see you." She hoped that didn't sound too forward or too hyper-self-conscious-of-being-too-forward.

"Well, I wanted to swing by because I remembered you saying you were going to Tahoe—"

"Yeah. I'm leaving this afternoon, actually."

"Oh." T.J. noticed the clothes strewn on her floor and pieced together what the effort was for. "I'm glad I caught you, then."

She wasn't sure how to respond so she didn't.

"Anyway, I figured I'd stop by and tell you to have a good trip. And be careful, you know." He leaned his elbows forward onto his knees. His right heel tapped, causing his calf muscle to flex. *Stop looking.* She'd never looked at boys before; why was she doing it now? "I mean, skiing but also driving around. The roads are icy and people drink a lot up there and then drive when they shouldn't and—" He paused and finally sighed, looking up at her. "I don't know, Amelia. When you said you were going to Tahoe I got this really weird feeling."

Amelia's heart stopped: He got a feeling? About her? "What do you mean?" she said as casually as she could.

"I don't know. I don't know what I'm saying. It's probably nothing, but I got this weird feeling that . . ." He paused and said quietly, as if testing the words, "That I wouldn't see you again." He paused and stared at her, his blue eyes sparkling. "And so . . . I guess I just wanted to see you, to tell you good-bye."

"Is everything okay?" Amelia breathed. "I mean, is something else going on?"

T.J.'s shoulder lifted and he opened his right hand as if presenting something and nodded. "Well, actually, Doreye's . . . it's in trouble. We're in trouble."

Amelia's disappointment hit her like a bucket of cold water; of course he came because there was a problem with Doreye. Just like he stayed at ZOSTRA because he was trying not to fail CS 101. T-Bag was wrong: T.J. didn't *like* her, he needed her brain. That was it. "What's going on?" she asked, not caring whether her disappointment showed.

"It's the same problem you left us with. The app keeps crashing. Adam convinced himself he can fix it, but . . ." T.J. shrugged. "I don't know whether his new energy is good or whether he's just gone crazy."

Amelia laughed gently, thinking about her brother's habit of semidelusional enthusiasm, and wondered with jealousy if he was returning to his old self. "Don't worry," she said, rolling her eyes. "If Adam's got a plan, he'll figure it out."

T.J. cocked one eyebrow. "He's no you."

Amelia shook her head, looking back at her bag and stuffing another pair of socks in it. "No. In a lot of ways he's better. He gets distracted, but at his core he's"—she looked back up at T.J. and shrugged—"at his core he's really good."

Amelia was surprised by her own honesty, even after what Adam had done. He'd hurt her, but he was real; unlike her imaginary relationship with T.J.

"There's something else," T.J. said, looking seriously at Amelia. Her heart beat with hope and she pushed it away. "Something your brother doesn't know. Something I just found out and haven't told anyone."

"What is it?" Amelia asked, bracing herself.

T.J. took a deep breath and looked down at the floor. "It's the company's investors. We don't actually know who they are."

"What do you mean?" She squinted. "The investor is PKC."

"Something bad happened. The fund PKC used to invest in Doreye is owned by someone else—some silent partner wrapped in a shell company—and after you left and your unvested shares left the company, this mystery investor's ownership went from forty-three percent to fifty-one percent. Which is enough to have final say about everything. And nobody knows who's behind it."

Amelia's jaw dropped as she tried to comprehend. She didn't understand the mechanics of investment, but she understood that shell companies masked the puppet masters pulling the strings, and she understood fifty-one percent meant majority voting rights. "How could that have happened?"

"Adam was in such a hurry to close the round, and PKC was offering us so much more than anyone else." T.J. half laughed and shook his head. "It almost feels like . . . like this was all on purpose."

Amelia's phone rang. She saw it was T-Bag, who had told her he'd call when they were on their way over to pick her up.

"We never had Roger look at the terms," T.J. went on, placing his hand on Amelia's, ignoring the ringing phone and running his thumb along her hand absentmindedly. "He was so sick I didn't want to bother him, but now . . . I don't know who else—"

"I've got to go." Amelia stood up, dropping T.J.'s hand a bit too forcefully. She couldn't deal with this, couldn't get sucked into solving this because T.J. was stroking her hand *just so*. She finished throwing her things in her suitcase and stood up to open the door.

His perfect calves pushed him up from the chair and he intercepted, grabbing her shoulders to stop her. "Stop," he said. "Amelia, wait."

His hands were so strong on her shoulders she couldn't move, and she didn't want to. She could feel the heat of his chest three inches from her own, but taller and wider, as though it could shield her whole body from whatever lay outside the door. He was staring into her eyes, so close she could see the specks of dark blue in his light blue irises, revealing the details of the complexity that made them so addictive.

"I have to go," she whispered, her voice cracking.

"What are you going to do?" he asked, not moving his grip or his stance.

"What can I do?" She pulled her shoulders away from him. "I was fired," she said bluntly. "I have no power."

"You underestimate your own power, Amelia," he said.

A car honked outside and Amelia picked up her bag. "I've got to go."

"I'll walk you out," T.J. said, grabbing the bag to carry it for her.

"It's okay," she said.

"No"—he gripped her wrist, his wide hand easily enveloping it—"I want to."

When they reached the door to the parking lot, Amelia paused and turned back to him. "The other day," she started, "why did you stay at Gates? I mean, why did you stay to play ZOSTRA?"

T.J. laughed. "Honestly?"

"Yes," Amelia said, hoping helplessly he would say it was to be with her. "Was it just to get extra credit with T-Bag?"

"No." T.J. grimaced. "Is that really what you thought?"

"What was the real reason, then?"

"Well," T.J. said, sighing, "I'm kind of a closet video-game addict. I mean, I didn't just *used* to play Dungeons & Dragons . . . I was a *tournament-level* Dungeon Master. My bedroom at home is still full of twenty-sided dice and trophies of wizards. The two games have a lot of similarities." His eyes sparkled at the confession.

Amelia felt her heart drop again. *For real, Amelia, let it go.* She looked at T.J., though, and thought of another question. "So what do you do when your character is Lawful Good and your opponent is Lawful Evil?"

"You lose the game, is what happens."

"Come on," she said, scratching her earlobe nervously, "what's the way out?"

T.J. thought for a moment. "You'd have to team up with a Chaotic Neutral character. You know, a trickster leprechaun, a pirate or a con man. You'd have to ally with this person and use their disregard for order to your advantage."

Amelia's lower lip curled under and she nodded, the wheels in her head spinning. "Okay," she said, pushing the door open.

"And Amelia?"

T-Bag jumped out of the car and took her bag from T.J., putting it in the backseat. "You get shotgun. Privilege of being the only girl in the car," he said cheerily. "Oh, hey, T.J."

"What is it?" Amelia asked, addressing T.J.'s earlier question.

"Never mind," he said. "Have a good trip."

"Yeah, I will," she said. "Thanks for coming by."

He leaned forward and wrapped his arms around her in a tight hug. She lifted onto her tiptoes to meet his embrace. She could feel her whole body disappear in his arms, and she tried to engrave the feeling of his hands tightly gripping the sides of her waist at the same time she tried to let the feeling of wanting it to never slip away.

"Take care of yourself," he said softly into her ear.

"I will," she whispered into his.

Amelia avoided looking at him as she opened the passenger door to the SUV and climbed inside.

The driver was on the phone but waved and mouthed an enthusiastic "Hi!" as he lifted a finger to indicate he'd be done in a second so they could catch up. Amelia studied his face, her mind racing to remember where she'd seen it, and felt her jaw drop as she pieced it together: She was about to spend the next six hours in a car to Tahoe with T-Bag, his secret business-school boyfriend, and *Chad Bronson*—Patty's sister's former fiancé and Patty's former secret lover.

42

The Donner Pass

"This part of the drive always gives me creeps!" Jason, T-Bag's secret boyfriend and fake cousin, said from the backseat.

The foursome was three hours into their ride to Tahoe and they'd been chatting ceaselessly since leaving campus, mostly about start-ups. Jason and Chad would come up with an idea they thought was brilliant, and Amelia and T-Bag would explain all the reasons it wouldn't work technologically. Then Amelia and T-Bag would come up with an idea that Jason and Chad would pick apart for being unfeasible from a business perspective. So far they'd come up with one idea they all agreed would work: a delivery service that served healthy meals marketed toward body-conscious frat boys who were too ashamed to shop at Whole Foods. T-Bag had suggested they call it "T.J.'s."

Chad was so unawkward that Amelia decided he must not remember she was Patty's roommate and definitely didn't know she knew about their hooking up, and she was grateful for it and happily ignored it, too.

"Where are we?" Amelia turned to ask. She liked Jason, and was happy to see T-Bag so happy with him.

"The sadistically named Donner Pass. It's where the Donner party became *the Donner party.*"

Amelia gave Jason a blank stare, to which he responded with shock: "You don't know about the Donner family?"

Amelia shook her head no.

"So basically this group of explorers was trying to cross the mountains right over there. They got stuck in a snowstorm and ended up eating each other for survival."

"Wait, wait, wait," Chad interrupted. "It wasn't quite that dramatic. They were snowed in and ran out of food. They tried eating tree bark first—you can still see strips of bark removed from the tree trunks. Well, turns out you can't survive on tree bark, so after a few members of the party died, the ones who were still living ate the dead bodies."

"Ewww," T-Bag moaned. "That is so, so gross."

"What else were they going to do?" Chad asked defensively. "There was no point in everyone starving. And humans have meat just like any cow or pig."

"Did they survive?" Amelia asked, wanting to get off the subject of eating human flesh.

"Yeah," Chad said, "a lot of them did. Which is why we know how."

"I could never eat someone I'd previously had a conversation with," Jason insisted. "I mean, can you imagine?"

"I don't think you can judge people's actions when they're in that desperate a situation. I mean, have you ever been that close to death? I think our survival instinct can lead us to extraordinary behavior," Chad continued to defend the legend.

"Ugh," Jason said, "which is why I try to avoid situations that call upon my unfiltered biological tendencies."

"No comment," T-Bag said wryly.

"Which is also why," Jason continued, "I am going to take a nap before we get to the house. So that my biological tendency to be a grump when I'm sleepy doesn't cause poor behavior at tonight's party."

"There's a party tonight?" Amelia asked.

"Just people playing beer pong and cooking dinner at the house. Nothing major," Chad explained.

A few minutes later Amelia heard Jason and T-Bag's quiet snoring in the backseat. She turned and smiled at her friend.

"How long have you known Theo?"

It took a minute to register that Chad meant T-Bag, who had sent her a text earlier that day warning her he went by a different iteration of his name with this crowd.

"Since last year. Computer Science geek circuit," she explained.

The silence resumed.

"I really like Jason," she said to fill it. "I mean, I like them together. He seems really good for . . . Theo."

Chad looked at her with a lifted eyebrow. "What do you mean?"

Amelia suddenly realized her faux pas. Surely Chad knew? T-Bag told her Jason wasn't out of the closet, but they were practically cuddling in the backseat, and Chad was Jason's roommate. Was he really not in on the secret?

Before she could think of a way to backpedal, Chad whispered, "Wait—are they a couple?"

Amelia shook her head frantically. This was it—she'd finally blown her one friendship, given up the first and only secret T-Bag had ever trusted her with. "I—I—I don't know."

"I knew it!" Chad whispered excitedly, grinning from ear to ear.

"No!" Amelia hissed. "I don't know. Oh my God, I just assumed . . ."

"He told me they were cousins. Ha. That asshole." He smiled in the rearview back at his sleeping friend.

"You can *not* tell," Amelia pleaded. "Please please please don't tell. He's my only friend. I can't—"

"Don't worry," Chad said. "I always suspected. I mean, I don't care, but I'm his roommate, so even if I said something to him it would be totally plausible that I figured it out on my own."

Amelia was staring at him with pleading eyes, unsatisfied.

"What?" Chad lifted his eyebrows. "It's not like you don't have anything on me."

So he did remember. Amelia looked straight ahead at the road and said resolutely, "It's not my place to judge what you do."

"The fact that it's not your place does not preclude you from doing so," Chad said with a smile. Then, "Regardless, I appreciate your keeping what happened between Patty and me quiet."

Amelia didn't say anything.

"I guess I got what I deserved, though, in the end."

Still, Amelia kept quiet.

"I mean, it didn't make the whole thing any less humiliating. Being stood up at the altar and having your fiancée pick up with some other guy when you were supposed to be on your honeymoon is awfully humbling," Chad mused. "But I guess it was all more bearable thinking of it as deserved punishment."

"Did you love her?" Amelia finally said. She was thinking of T.J., wondering how people knew.

"Honestly?" Chad asked, with genuine reflection. "I loved them both." He paused, and then said, as if he was trying the phrase out for the first time: "But I didn't love either of them completely."

Amelia nodded, not because she understood, but because she didn't know what else to do. And felt a pang thinking maybe that was T.J.'s feeling toward her: He cared about her a little bit, but not completely.

"I mean, I think if you love someone completely, you're not capable of doing what I did. And I guess I live in this world where I love certain people for certain things. But when I find a woman who I really love for everything, even the things about her that drive me crazy . . . well, then I guess I'll know I've found the one."

He turned and smiled a sad smile at Amelia that made her want to give him a hug.

"How about you?"

"What?"

"Are you seeing anyone?"

Amelia instinctively laughed. "Are you kidding?"

"What?"

"Look at me." She gestured to herself, suddenly feeling again how ridiculous the whole T.J. fantasy was. "I'm a computer dork. I don't date."

"That's ridiculous."

"Please don't tell me I'm not that bad; that just makes it worse."

"No, I'm sure you are just as dorky as you think. But *I* think there's someone out there for everyone, and that the only way you find them is by being your full self."

Chad looked in the rearview mirror again, at the couple sleeping in the back. "Can you imagine how difficult it is?"

"What?"

"Being Jason. I mean, feeling like you can't tell your friends about the people you're attracted to. Thinking they won't accept you if they know who you really are."

"People are cruel," Amelia said softly. "They don't understand."

"The people who matter understand," Chad argued, "and anyone who doesn't understand? Screw 'em."

Amelia felt the words settle in the air. How could he say that so casually?

"So do you ski?"

"No."

"You going to try?"

"I wouldn't know where to start."

"Want me to teach you?"

Amelia felt herself blush and was grateful for the darkness. "Sure," she heard herself say.

"It's a date," he said, and leaned forward to turn on music from his iPhone. "Grateful Dead okay?"

43

Under Par

Ted Bristol spiraled his torso right and left, stretching out his spine, then swung his arms to loosen up his chest before reaching for his driver.

He squinted to see the pin and mentally calculated the angle at which to align his stroke with the golf ball. He took a few practice swings, appreciating the gentle *swoosh* as the club hit the top of the ground *just so,* and he knew today was going to be a good golf day. The rain had kept him off the course for the past three weeks, but the clouds had finally cleared to hand him a perfect, crisp, sunny day and an eleven-o'clock tee time.

He moved forward to address the ball, carefully lining the front of his club with the tee. He shifted his weight from foot to foot and gently bounced in his knees to get his balance just right. Ted paused, exhaled, and pulled his driver back and through, making perfect contact with the ball and sending it soaring, straight down the fairway. He followed it with his eyes and let his face curve into a smile as he saw it land right where he wanted it to, thinking to himself for the millionth time that golf really is the perfect sport.

"Nice shot," a woman's voice said from behind him.

He turned to find Violet wearing a short white golf skirt and navy collared shirt whose top three buttons were all undone. Her hair was back in a curled ponytail and she had a white glove on one hand. Golf was also a great game for a sexy woman in the right outfit, and Violet was definitely a sexy woman in the right outfit. That she saw his perfect drive made it even better.

"All in a day's work." He grinned flirtatiously. "You're right on time. Walk with me?"

"Yep," she said, picking up her clubs.

"How was your game?" he asked, knowing from having checked the member sign-in sheet that she'd had an 8:30 A.M. tee time with someone named Austin, which made him irrationally jealous.

"Great," she said, unsurprised that he knew. "Shot seventy-two. Not bad for me."

"Well done," Ted said, struggling to hide his astonishment. The best he'd ever shot on this course was a seventy-five, and that was ten years ago. Suddenly his drive didn't feel so perfect.

They headed down the cart path toward Ted's ball. When they were out of sight of the clubhouse Ted reached into the pocket of his bag and pulled out a thin envelope, which he handed to Violet.

She opened it and read the number on the check, which was branded by a bank in the Cayman Islands. "More than we agreed," she commented, looking up at him skeptically.

"I threw in a bonus for your work with Adam Dory. I'd never have convinced him to fire Amelia on my own."

Violet took her iPhone out of her pocket and logged in to her Chase online banking app, snapping a picture of the check to deposit it to her account. "Can I be sure this check's going to clear? You know I'd have preferred cash."

Ted's voice betrayed his irritation. He hated when attractive women tried to be tough businessmen. She should be grateful for the bonus. "You have my guarantee the check will clear."

She watched the phone to see that the transaction had been processed, then put it and the check in her bag. She said calmly, "It's just I know your cash situation isn't quite what it used to be, since the Gibly deal."

"Just because Gibly didn't sell for two point three billion doesn't mean it didn't sell for a lot," Ted answered, his voice loaded like a spring. "Our investors still made money."

"Some made money. But not you." She stared fearlessly into Ted's eyes, the slightest hint of a smile at the corner of her dark pink lips.

Ted studied her face, wanting at once to hit and to fiercely kiss her. "What do you know?" he demanded in a low voice.

She lifted an eyebrow. "Well," she started, turning her gaze to a nearby tree. "Hours before the deal was first announced you secretly loaded all of your net worth into the company, expecting to make an impressive—albeit not public—return. But"—she turned back to face him—"of course you can't say anything since it wasn't exactly a legal move to begin with; your American government doesn't take kindly to transactions made off of insider knowledge."

The British accent he'd found so irresistible when he hired her now grated on his last nerve. "So what," he said. "I lost my money. Shit, Violet, I lost a lot of it. But I'll recover."

"Kind of throws a kink in the plan to destroy Amelia Dory, though, doesn't it?"

"What are you talking about?"

"You hired me to help you hurt Amelia, to get back at her for ruining your Gibly deal."

"Yes."

"But now you need money. And you're not getting it from that stupid social music iPhone app. So Doreye's looking like your best investment."

"What are you talking about?"

"PKC would pay me a lot more than you just did—even with that very generous bonus; thank you, by the way—to show them that the infamous Ted Bristol is Doreye's secret investor."

Ted didn't move a muscle as he locked eyes with Violet, trying to decipher whether she was bluffing or had information.

"But Doreye is on the rocks, Ted. It won't succeed without Amelia." Violet finally broke the stare with a giggle. "Aren't these little ironies just delicious? Your only chance to reclaim your wealth is for Doreye to work, but now you're starting to realize that to make it work you need help from the girl you set out to destroy in the first place."

Ted's palms were sweating inside his white golf gloves. Of course the dilemma had occurred to him, but he still had T.J. and Adam in the company and was holding out for them to turn Doreye around without *that girl*. If Violet were a man, he would have punched her.

"Don't be so nervous," she said, giggling and lifting a finger to scratch the corner of her glossed lip. "I won't tell."

"You don't know what you're talking about."

"But I do." Violet shifted her finger from her lip and pressed it into the center of Ted's chest. "That's the thing. I *do* know about your secret investment in Doreye and I *do* know how you did it and I *do* know other things, too."

"Like what?"

"Nuh-uh-uh." Violet shook her head, then pinched her fingers and playfully zipped her lips.

"I think you should leave," Ted said abruptly. "Your work with Doreye and Adam Dory is done."

"No; *your* work with Adam is done. Mine is just beginning."

44

When Instinct Takes Over

"Amelia, wake up." Amelia heard a whisper and felt a hand gently shake her shoulder. She opened her eyes and blinked several times to remember where she was—next to an MBA girl in a bedroom where two other girls were sleeping on air mattresses on the floor.

Chad was standing over her in boxer shorts and no shirt. His chest was almost as perfect as T.J.'s; not that she had ever seen T.J. shirtless, but she'd imagined it a lot. "Can you be ready in ten? I want to beat the crowds. We'll pick up a breakfast on the way."

Amelia nodded, pulling her legs from under the covers and making her way to the bathroom.

She slurped water greedily from the faucet, desperately thirsty from the altitude and the—three? four? five? six?—drinks she'd had the night before. When their car had arrived at a massive eight-bedroom ski house in North Lake Tahoe, a dozen MBA students were seated at a table eating heaping plates of spaghetti and pizza. Three trash cans full of empty wine bottles and beer cans betrayed an aggressive predinner happy hour, and the table was in excellent spirits. The girls all squealed when Chad and Jason entered, and they'd all welcomed their friends Amelia and Theo. One girl handed Amelia a vodka-and-cranberry and said, "You look like a vodka-cran girl. Are you Shandi?" to which Amelia had blushed and tried to explain, but the girl had already drunkenly skipped away to hug Jason.

Amelia looked up at her face in the mirror, trying to make her eyes adjust to the light as she reluctantly put her contacts in.

When she finally came upstairs, Chad handed her ski goggles, a helmet, and poles. "Good news—Leslie's too hungover to ski today and said you could use her stuff so you don't have to rent. Skis are in the car. Let's go."

Amelia followed Chad to the car, trying to process how he had so much energy after such a late night. "What time is it?" was all she could find to say.

"Seven-thirty. Late!" he chirped.

They stopped at a café and picked up breakfast burritos and coffee to have in the car. By the time they got to the slopes Amelia was feeling ready to take on the new challenge.

For the next two hours, Chad guided Amelia onto her skis and down the bunny slopes, carefully avoiding packs of children in ski school. By midmorning, Amelia was starting to get the hang of it and was actually going respectably quickly down the hill.

"You're a natural!" Chad patted her on the back, his cheeks ruddy with the cold.

"You're a good teacher," she insisted humbly. She'd never been a natural at anything other than programming.

"Let's try a blue."

Amelia followed Chad to the chairlift and, slowly but steadily, down a harder ski slope. They stopped for lunch with some of Chad's classmates at noon. Amelia was exhausted and cold and not sure she'd ever tasted anything so wonderful as the bowl of chili before her.

"Little more?" Chad asked when she was finished. "I think you should see backcountry."

Amelia's thighs were screaming from all the work, but she

didn't want today to be over. "Sure," she said, and they replaced their helmets and bid farewell to their lunch companions.

Chad led Amelia to a ski lift, then to another, and when they got off they were on the ridge of a mountain looking down on Lake Tahoe. The wind hissed and blew sharp snow in her face, but Amelia didn't care: The lake thousands of feet below was crystal blue, accentuated by the brightness of the snow on the shores around it. She thought it might be the most beautiful thing she'd ever seen. It made all the problems back on campus feel totally manageable—small, even, like the trees barely visible along the lake edge.

"Pretty, huh?" Chad smiled at her, seeming genuinely happy to introduce Amelia to this new world.

Amelia was panting from the exercise and the cold, but smiled openmouthed and nodded.

"Let's go," Chad said, pushing into his poles and whizzing off down the hill. Amelia took a deep breath and followed, carefully gliding her skis right and left through the powder.

When they got to the bottom of the mountain, Chad gestured to a cabin. "Want to grab a drink? This place is the whole reason to do that run."

She nodded. Everything else Chad had suggested had been great; why stop now?

They unclipped their skis and entered a large room with low ceilings and wooden walls. Two fireplaces blazed on the side wall and a long wooden table stretched through the center of the room, which was filling up with exhausted but exhilarated skiers like them.

"Find a table. I'll get us some drinks," Chad said, moving toward the bar.

Amelia unbuckled her boots so it was easier to walk and plodded close to the fireplace, where a couple was leaving a small two-top table.

Chad returned with a beer and a mug of mulled wine. "Try this. I think you'll like it." He handed her the mug.

She sipped the hot sugared wine and felt the liquid heat spread through her blood. It was delicious.

They made small talk for a while and ordered another round. Amelia liked Chad, but she didn't feel the same desire for him that she had felt for Sundeep or—she'd admit it now that she'd had two glasses of wine—for T.J.

"So I have to make a confession," Chad said. "I decided last night I needed to be nice to you for two reasons: The first was that I think you're going to be a big deal, and I want to be a venture capitalist, and I'm hoping if you like me, you'll pick me as your next investor. And, secondly, I really, really, really need to make sure you'll never say anything about me and Patty."

Amelia's heart dropped. Why did attractive men always have an ulterior motive for paying attention to her?

"And I'm telling you this because I realize I sound like a scumbag, as if I was only nice to you because I needed something. But I've had a really amazing time today and I think you're a really good person and I feel like I owe you that honesty. And that really is honest. I mean, I'm not just saying it."

Amelia swallowed. "It's okay. People like you only ever talk to me if they need something."

"No!" Chad exclaimed. "I mean, yes, I did that, but it was a mistake."

Amelia shook her head, looking down at her lap.

"I mean, if people do that, that's their problem, not yours. You are so much more than a good programmer. Or a good skier. You're really, really cool and fun to be around. Don't let people pigeonhole you."

Amelia looked into his eyes and somehow she knew he wasn't lying. "Do you mean that?"

"Yes! Really!" He nodded rapidly to make the point.

She laughed at his enthusiasm. "I know you're not a bad guy."

"Really?"

"Yes, really." She smiled in agreement.

"Because ever since the wedding, I've really wondered."

She grimaced. "You don't seem like the guy who questions your actions."

"I fundamentally reject regrets," he said, "but looking back on it, part of me wishes I'd tried to do something. I wish I hadn't just stood there, paralyzed, and let Shandi leave. She may not have been what I ultimately wanted, but I didn't try to figure out what had happened."

"Why?"

"I don't know. But I think—well, when it happened, there was this real fight-or-flight instinct. And I realized that people, when they're confronted with that kind of shock, they either fight to get to the bottom of it or they just run away. And maybe I didn't fight because I wasn't sure it was what I wanted, but maybe I didn't fight because I'm just . . ."—he shrugged—"the kind of guy who flees."

Amelia felt a pinch in her stomach. Did he know about Doreye? Was he talking about her?

Amelia spun her empty mug in a circle on the table. "Do you think I should fight for my company? Should I fight for Doreye?" she said softly.

"That depends on what kind of a person *you* are," Chad answered unhesitatingly, and Amelia got the sense telling her this had been the point all along.

"What if I fight and lose it anyway?"

"What if you flee but could have gotten it back?"

Amelia nodded without looking up. "I can't," she said.

"Why not?" he challenged.

"I mean, I can't stay here. I have to leave, Chad. Can you take me to the bus station tonight?"

Chad nodded, his lips curling into a smile. "There's one in Reno. It will take us an hour."

"Great." She nodded, piecing everything together in her brain.

"Where are you going to go?"

"Home," she said. "To Indiana."

45

99 Problems but a Glitch Ain't One

"It's been a while since we met, and I wanted to check in to update you on our progress this quarter," Adam said, smiling coyly at Ross and the hyenas. His heart sank realizing Lucy wasn't coming—her internship had ended last week—but just as well: better to focus on the good news he had about Doreye.

Ross frowned; he wasn't deaf to the rumors that had been flying about Doreye.

Adam stood at the head of the room, a clicker for the slide show in one hand and the other jammed in the pocket of a new pair of designer jeans he'd purchased for this occasion.

"I won't try to hide from you that we were slowed down by Amelia's departure. But it was short-term pain for a good long-term decision: We're on a better track now than we've ever been."

He clicked to the next slide.

"As you can see from this timeline, over one month ago the app kept crashing. The CPU required to control multiple devices or find multiple objects was too large. This made the app dead in the water."

Next slide.

"At first we tried to simply increase the memory usage, but as you can see, this led to a significant increase in the size of the app, which would make it impossible to download and would never be approved by Apple."

Next slide.

"So instead we took a hiatus to study the iPhone and learn how competitors keep memory usage low for complicated tasks."

Next slide.

"We discovered most of them don't. It turns out Doreye is the most advanced software out there, but unfortunately, software as advanced as ours simply can't run on the current generation of smartphones. Rather than dumb down our product, we used this huge problem as an inspiration for our next big innovation."

Next slide.

"It got us thinking outside the box and collaborating as a team." Adam beamed because it was true. Over the last few weeks, the full team had had seven all-nighters, not because Adam had demanded it but because they had all wanted to stay to work out the problem. They'd ordered stacks of pizza and consumed gallons of Red Bull, but every moment had been filled with the adrenaline-laden excitement of being on to something.

"And we discovered that we can be the forefront of a movement. We can be a leader in a whole new field. We can innovate the next big thing."

Next slide.

"The cloud," Adam said, looking at the screen, where he'd inserted a picture of a fluffy white cloud with the text "DOREYE" in the middle. "It's not just for uploading pictures and sharing files. We can use the cloud for much, much more."

He looked at the hyenas, who were looking at Ross glaring at him, unsure whether to applaud or kick him out for being delusional.

"We've discovered a way to outsource our processing, our algorithm, and our database to the cloud. Now, the app will not only do everything we promise without crashing the phone, the Doreye software will actually run faster than it ever did before. We use our own servers and our own supercomputers to do the heavy lifting."

Ross Brown cleared his throat. "All due respect, Adam, but why hasn't Apple thought of this?"

"No demand," Adam explained. "If they had our level of technology, they would build a new iPhone to support it. They'll have a hard time catching up, too: We're too advanced for the next several generations of the iPhone."

"Don't you have to have some kind of contract with a cloud provider to pull this off?" Ross began his inquisition. "And won't that provider charge a precious fee when they discover they're integral to your system?"

"We've actually got a contractor lined up, a British company who's eager to partner."

Adam grinned. The Hewlett-Packard innovation his drunken cellmate Jeremy had been working on was the patented code required to outsource all the data and processes to the cloud. The PHOENIX drive gave him the code he needed, but Ross was right: It was worthless without a supplier with supercomputers.

Adam had thought he was finished, but then he struck gold again.

When he had complained to Violet about his latest dilemma, she laughed: Didn't Adam know that the holding company she worked for in London had a cloud-computing company, and that the whole reason she was in Silicon Valley was to find California partners? It was almost too good to be true.

"Moreover," Adam went on, "the British partnership will be a great way to get us an entry point into the UK market, which we expect will be the next after our U.S. launch."

"Which will be when?" Ross Brown asked with a cocked eyebrow.

"We are submitting to Apple next week. We should be good to go live two weeks from today." Adam grinned. It was a full two months ahead of schedule.

"You're sure you're ready?" Ross asked.

"I've never been so sure of anything in my life."

46

Run://Program

A city bus dirty with the grimy gray muck of salt-treated snowy roads stopped at a run-down street corner and deposited Amelia Dory, weighed down by her canvas duffel, onto the sidewalk.

It was early morning and the streets were quiet. She took a deep breath, her exhale blowing white in the cold winter air, and took in the formerly familiar surroundings before adjusting her bag on her shoulder and beginning her walk.

When she arrived at the front door, she let her bag fall to the ground and closed her eyes before she reached out for the doorbell.

There was no answer, and Amelia felt part of her try to convince the other part of her that this was a sign: Going back to Indiana was a mistake.

She heard footsteps inside and braced herself for the opening door.

Michael Dawson's face was plastered with surprise at the sight of his visitor, his mouth trying but failing to find words. Amelia stood patiently, not saying anything until the color returned to his face and he let out a laugh. "The famous Amelia Dory. Well, well, well."

"Hello, Mr. Dawson," she said shortly. "May I come in?"

He turned his broad, fatherly frame to allow her to pass into the home where she and Adam had spent the years before she went to prison. Amelia walked in, pulling her bag behind her, immediately taken with the familiar smell of the house, a mix of bacon and carpet cleaner and cinnamon-scented candles that flooded her brain with memories.

She tried to ignore the old images and feelings flashing through her brain. She hadn't made the trip from California back to Indiana to rehash old problems; she'd made it to solve new ones.

For the very same reasons she hated her con-artist foster father, Amelia needed him now. He was the partner she required to defeat whoever or whatever was controlling Doreye and take the company back.

Amelia knew she couldn't do it alone. She was too good to see the truth; she needed someone more ethically . . . flexible.

She paused in the foyer and looked around. Nothing had changed: The same woven afghan was thrown over the same brown couch; the same beige carpet lined the stairs; the same mirror hung above the same side table where Dawson's car keys were familiarly thrown.

Amelia walked without being invited to the kitchen. Michael Dawson followed and they sat across from each other at the table, his eyebrows scrunched. She didn't take off her coat. He didn't offer her anything and she didn't ask.

"I need you to come to Silicon Valley," she said bluntly.

He smiled sardonically. "What? No pleasantries?"

She didn't say anything, just stared at him, her hands folded in front of her on the table.

"Although I would love a little sunshine, I can't." His face lost its laugh. "I'm on parole, remember? From when you sent me to jail?"

"How often does your parole officer check in with you?" She ignored the jab.

"Once a month."

"When was the last time he came?"

"Two days ago."

"Good. We've got twenty-eight days, then. It won't take longer than that."

Dawson looked suspiciously at her. He had changed these past three years: His thick hair had begun to gray above the ears and his skin looked worn. But his crisp brown eyes still had the same smoothness of selfish ambition.

"What are we doing?" he asked after a moment, then quickly corrected, "That is, if I decide to join you?"

"We're getting my company back."

"From who?"

"That's what I need you to help me figure out."

"Why me?"

"You're chaotic and selfish and don't follow the rules. You see things I can't."

Dawson pursed his lips, and smiled wryly at her deliberate rudeness.

"I'll give you equity in the company," she offered.

Dawson studied her. "How much?"

"Two percent."

"On what condition?"

"That we get the company back."

He considered for a moment. "That all?"

She rolled her eyes. "That's it." Amelia knew her old foster father well enough to understand what pushed his buttons; Dawson didn't care as much about the cash as he did about the hunt. He wanted a challenge, and her hunt in California was far more interesting than any mischief he could find in Indiana.

He knew this, too. "When do we leave?"

"Tomorrow. There's an eight A.M. bus. It'll take two days to get there, but I'll use the time to explain everything."

He nodded and let out a laugh. "Who'd ever have thought it, eh? Michael Dawson and Amelia Dory, forming a team."

Amelia reached her hand out to finalize the transaction, ignoring the statement. "So we have a deal?"

Dawson accepted her hand and shook it firmly. "You've got yourself a partner. Let's go get your company back."

Part III

Reboot

47

Keg Stand for Principle

"One hundred thousand!" Arjun's arms were victoriously thrown up in the air and everyone in the room cheered him on. A bottle of champagne popped as the number on the computer monitor climbed to 100,001 . . . 100,002 . . . a steady clip of twelve unique downloads every second.

Just over two hours had passed since the Doreye app launched, but it was already a massive success. If this momentum continued, they would average one million downloads per day. The release team at Apple called T.J. and Adam to tell them they were the number one trending app, the fastest to achieve such status in Apple's history. The downtown Palo Alto office of Doreye Inc. was alive with employees, reporters, investors, and friends who had come for the party that started at 8:03, the minute Doreye went live, chosen in honor of Adam and Amelia's August 3rd birthday.

The last two weeks had been a flurry of press campaigns to hype up the launch; everyone had expected a massive rush of subscribers this morning, but one hundred thousand users in fewer than three hours was beyond anyone's expectations. And the new users weren't just from Silicon Valley. The engineers used the real-time Doreye data and Google Maps to project a map of the United States onto a flatscreen in the office living room, and a yellow dot appeared for every new log-in: The map was speckled in yellow from California to Florida.

"Kansas loves Doreye!" an engineer's girlfriend shouted from the monitor, clearly tipsy from too much champagne as she said cheers to no one in particular and took a big gulp.

"We're up to fourteen downloads a second!" Arjun announced with an enthusiastically hoarse voice.

"Taco truck is here!" T.J. called from the front door, sparking another round of hoorays as revelers left their perches at the craft-beer kegs and headed outside for freshly prepared carnitas from the food truck hired specially for the occasion.

"Get you one?" Bruce, one of the hyenas from PKC, put a hand on Adam's shoulder.

"No thanks." Adam forced a close-lipped smile. "But you better go get one before they're gone."

Bruce agreed and eagerly moved past. Adam stuffed a hand in his pocket and took a sip of Gatorade from his post in the corner, watching the line of jubilant taco-eaters speaking over one another about the massive success of the company of which he was COO.

This was the day they'd been building toward for a full year, the moment Adam had been imagining and dreaming about since he'd seen the first e-mail Roger Fenway sent his sister; for a year he allowed himself to think the world he'd witnessed at T. J. Bristol's graduation party could be his.

So why didn't he feel better about this?

Maybe it was because he hadn't had a good night's sleep in the past month—he'd been at the office nonstop, occasionally leaving to get a change of clothes or do some laundry on campus, even less frequently leaving to go to his spring quarter classes. The cot in the nap room upstairs had become his permanent bed, and he'd seen the delivery guys from respective pizza, Chinese, and Indian restaurants on University Avenue more than he'd seen anyone outside of Doreye.

But it wasn't just that he was tired; it was that Amelia wasn't here. And he knew that was the real reason, even if he didn't want to admit it.

He couldn't celebrate. Not without Amelia here, and especially not without knowing where she was. Every time he thought about her, or about trying to accept the congratulations he was receiving, he felt a pang of unresolved guilt, like he was a little kid who broke the cookie jar and was now waiting for a time-out. Except in this case, everyone knew he broke the cookie jar but no one was willing to give him his punishment.

Amelia wanted Doreye to be free. As the number of downloads increased and the investors clinked their plastic champagne flutes, he knew they were calculating the company's value and how their portion of the success would affect next year's family budget. The downloads didn't feel like success to Adam, they felt like one hundred thousand little jabs reminding him that when the kegs were rolled out and the party was cleaned up, he'd be expected to deliver real revenue. Charging for Doreye or selling user data or any responsible revenue strategy would go against everything Amelia stood for.

He wondered what she'd think now: whether she'd be able to celebrate all these people loving the thing she'd created if she knew he was going to start making money off of it soon.

He'd worked up the courage three weeks ago to ask T.J. to invite Amelia to the launch party. T.J.'s response was short, admitting that he didn't know Amelia's whereabouts. There was anxiety and loss in T.J.'s voice as he confessed that he was starting to get worried. Adam was surprised, but he wasn't concerned for Amelia's safety; he didn't believe in telepathy, but he'd always been able to sense when something was wrong with his twin sister, and he didn't have that sense now. Weirdly, he had the sense she was doing really well, wherever she was. As for himself, though, he couldn't shake the feeling that he was on the verge of doing another very bad thing.

"Hey mister." Violet suddenly appeared by his side, knocking her hip flirtatiously into his. She was bright and smiley and full of energy, the way people are when they're excited about something new or have had too much Red Bull.

"Hey." He smiled and returned her kiss on the cheek, a European habit she'd maintained and which he no longer misinterpreted as sexual. "You're in a good mood."

"I've got an idea," she said, and bit her glossed lip mischievously. Adam hoped the idea was sex—that she would take him back into the office crash pad and finally hook up with him, an up-until-now nonoccurrence that was starting to make him insecure. She'd been so aggressively forward when they'd met—or rather, remet—in San Francisco, but she'd never actually acted on any of her flirtations, only ever going *just so far*.

"What is it?"

"Well . . ." She nodded her head in a dramatic pause. "You know how you have to turn all of these downloads into dollars?"

Adam's heart sank. Not only was he not having sex, but it was not yet three hours after launch and he was already confronted with the revenue conversation. "Can we at least wait until the party's over to talk about that?"

She lifted an eyebrow and smiled sarcastically. "What? Because you're enjoying this party so much?"

He shrugged.

"Listen," she said, punching his shoulder. "I found a buyer. For your user data."

"Excuse me?" Adam shifted uncomfortably.

"You can't start charging clients for your service; it'll turn a lot of them off, and you'll have to get involved in all sorts of payment nonsense that'll eat into company funds and take focus away from the product. This eliminates all that. Just sell the data you've already got. You don't even have to format it: Just give a buyer access to your database."

Adam turned his face away from her. "I don't want to talk about revenue right now."

"Your investors sure do." Violet gestured toward the PKC hyenas scarfing down tacos.

"So your idea is—what?—the path of least resistance?"

"I called in a lot of favors to find you this buyer, Adam. And lucky you; they are willing to pay so much money that you'll never have to think about revenue again. And you can continue with business as usual: acquiring users."

Adam turned to look into Violet's eyes. They were bright above her smile, filled with genuine excitement and belief. He could tell she was proud of the deal she'd sourced and that it made perfect sense to her for Doreye.

He let out a breath and turned his face back toward the room. "Amelia wouldn't like it."

He didn't look up but could feel her smile disappear.

"I think it's time to stop thinking about her," Violet snapped in a low voice. "She's gone, Adam. You can't make decisions around her anymore. Not that you ever should have; she almost destroyed the company."

"That's my sister you're talking about," he snapped back.

"You're the one who fired her."

"And whose idea was that, initially?" He glared at her.

"Forgive me for saving your company. And trying to save your ass now, too."

"Can we please just not talk about it right now?" Adam conceded.

She looked at her iPhone. "Fine. I've got to go anyway."

She lifted her head proudly as she turned to leave, brushing past T.J., who was standing next to the keg with a group of engineers, slowly sipping his beer and looking curiously at Adam, now standing alone.

48

The Best Laid Schemes of Mice and Men

A mouse scampered up the wall next to her and Amelia jumped, startled, almost dropping her laptop. She shook her head, trying not to think about it and to focus instead on her computer screen. The room was dark except for her computer's faint blue glow. She tried to ignore the sound of the mouse lightly scratching, and instead turned her attention to the buzzing of the processor and the overhead ceiling light.

Michael Dawson was sleeping in the next room. He'd offered the room to her, but Amelia preferred to crash on the couch, near the computer, even if it meant being closer to the mice.

They'd been lucky to find a place at all: Even East Palo Alto, the downtrodden other-side-of-the-tracks neighborhood near the illustrious downtown "artery of Silicon Valley" had gotten expensive with the recent boom of IPOs. But Amelia and Dawson had cobbled together a $1,000 living budget, which afforded them a month's rent in this basement one-bedroom apartment in East Palo Alto. They now had fifteen days before Dawson had to head back to Indiana to meet with his parole officer, and they were still far from figuring it out.

She no longer overthought her partnership with Dawson: She needed his help, and that was clear. She was too naïve, too trusting; in order to get Doreye back she needed a partner unafraid to pretend in public. Amelia could do the hacking to find out who was behind taking Doreye away from her, but she needed Dawson to track them down and bring them in.

In Tahoe, it had dawned on her that Adam wasn't to blame for her being fired. He was the one who had pulled the trigger, yes, and that wasn't nice or good, but whereas cheating was in Dawson's nature, cruelty wasn't in Adam's. She suspected he'd done what he thought was right, only he'd made that determination using wrong information. That realization lifted the fog that had been clouding her: She could forgive Adam and focus on what and who had caused him to think it was the right thing to do. Once she figured that out, she could get back both the company and her brother.

She decided to start where it all began—with Gibly. She'd always found it peculiar that the Gibly deal had gone through after all, even if it was at a much-discounted price. One year ago she had exposed layers upon layers of shady dealings: Gibly's secret database full of user information, the unbelievable price tag from the Aleister Corporation, and the secret payments to Aleister from a mysterious entity called VIPER.

Retracing her steps a year later and under very different circumstances, Amelia once again daisy-chained into the basic security of the Aleister Corporation. She searched through the finance portal and found that the payments from VIPER stopped one year ago, right at the time her anonymous TechCrunch exposé was published.

Now she sat at her computer screen and cross-referenced the VIPER account number to see what other types of companies it was associated with. The round icon on her computer twirled, thinking, before revealing another checking account located in the United States.

Her heart froze, and she clicked to open it.

"Ugh!" she silently moaned. It was, of course, restricted. "How do I figure out who they're paying now?" she asked the computer.

She sat back in her chair again and stared at the screen. She chewed her gum, which had long ago lost its flavor, and thought. Finally she sat up, placed her fingers across her keyboard, and began furiously coding.

Three hours later the morning light was starting to creep in and Amelia had deciphered that the bank coded individual accounts differently than entity accounts. The restricted account, 4XX-XX-XXXX, was an individual, not a company. A little more searching revealed a call record from a 650 area code: That was the Bay Area. She tried tracing the number: unlisted.

"How's it coming?" Dawson's sleepy voice startled her.

"Good," she said, keeping her eyes on the screen and her fingers typing rapidly. "I got a phone number."

"For what?"

"The person receiving payments from VIPER."

"What's VIPER?"

"A shell company that used to pay Aleister for the user data from Gibly."

"What's Gibly?"

"The company that got sold to Aleister."

Dawson grunted, realizing he wasn't going to follow this rabbit hole. "So what's the point?"

"I need to figure out whose phone number this is. They're the ones receiving payments from VIPER."

"Can you tell where they're located?"

"Somewhere in the Bay Area. But all the names are coded. There isn't a yellow pages for this type of thing."

"Why don't you use Doreye?"

"What?" She was only half listening as she typed, annoyed with his questions.

"You've got the phone number, right? So why don't you program that fancy app of yours to locate the cell phone associated with that number?"

Amelia turned in her chair, her brow scrunched as she processed what Dawson had proposed. Finally, she nodded. "Right. Yes, that's exactly right."

Dawson shrugged arrogantly at her previous annoyance. "I do what I can."

"And then we can take it around town, I mean, like a metal detector, and find who it is," Amelia said, turning back to her laptop.

"Bingo."

Amelia launched the code for Doreye for the first time in two months and got started.

49

Not Just Ones and Zeroes

"I owe you an apology." Patty was looking down at her hands, which were folded in her lap under the table at Woodside Bakery.

Lisa said softly, "What happened?" She glanced at the waiter and shook her head so he wouldn't come over to take their order. It had been weeks since the girls had seen each other, since Lisa recounted what happened at her first Focus Girls session and since Patty went on her Focus Girls one-on-one to prove Lisa wrong.

"You were right," Patty said quietly. She knew that Lisa had heard rumors about the cop at Rosewood and the subsequent hold she'd placed on Focus Girls, but she'd finally mustered the courage to ask her to brunch and apologize in person. She twisted her hands in her lap and watched herself do so, too embarrassed to lift her eyes to Lisa. "I still can't believe it; I mean, I can't believe how stupid I was to think—"

"Stop it." Lisa reached her hand under the table to grab Patty's.

Patty felt ridiculous for lots of reasons, but particularly because Lisa had been the one to finally tell her what was going on. It wasn't that she didn't like Lisa a lot, but she'd always seen herself as older and wiser, even if their birthdays were less than a year apart, and there was something about having a freshman expose Patty's blind spot that was particularly humiliating.

"Look at me," Lisa softly demanded, and Patty obeyed. "This is not your fault."

"Yes it is." Patty felt her voice crack. "I started the company! And I let the whole thing go on without even noticing—without even thinking. It's entirely my fault: How could it be anyone else's?"

"You had a great idea," Lisa insisted. "You *have* a great idea. And you never had the intention of it becoming what it did."

"But I should have seen what was happening. I should have realized—"

"When?" Lisa cut her off. "When would you have had time to notice? You were running a rapidly growing enterprise and you were going to school and you were having a life."

"I wouldn't be so certain about that having-a-life part." Patty shrugged, suddenly feeling incredibly sad about all the parties and brunches she'd missed while working on a company that had come to nothing . . . worse than nothing.

"All you can do is move forward," Lisa counseled. Patty looked at her, eyes brimming with tears, and felt even worse. Not only had younger Lisa seen what Patty naïvely could not, but now she was turning Patty's attempt at an apology brunch into a make-Patty-feel-better session. On the other hand, it was nice to have the empathy. "What ended up happening with the cops?"

Patty shrugged. "I wasn't technically doing anything illegal, so they couldn't press charges. But you should have heard what this cop said to me. When they brought me down to the station he said my behavior was 'unbecoming of someone with my up-bringing' and that he questioned a future where people 'of my morals' were able to start companies. I mean, he basically called me a terrible human being."

"Oh, Patty, I'm so sorry." Lisa turned her lips into each other. "But you know you can't listen to that—he was just trying to get to you."

Patty shook her head. "No, that's the thing. He was right. I mean, I'm a bad person. Like, *really* a bad person."

"Stop it." Lisa shook her head and looked at her menu. "I'm not listening to that. Let's order."

"No, you don't understand," Patty insisted.

"What?" Lisa looked up. "Patty, you are *not* a bad person. You made a mistake, that's all. Everyone makes mistakes. You'll learn from this mistake and you'll be fine."

"I kissed Chad," Patty blurted.

Lisa's face went white and her jaw loosened. "What?"

"I kissed Chad. Well, we did other stuff, too," Patty admitted. "Chad cheated on my sister . . . with me."

"When?"

"It started at T.J.'s graduation party."

"Is that why they—"

"I don't know. I haven't spoken to Chad since December. Shandi's never said anything, and I feel like she would have if that had been the reason, but I don't know."

"Wow." Lisa's eyes were wide.

"See?" Patty insisted. "I'm a terrible person."

Lisa shook her head. "No, you're still not." She paused. "Or if you are, I'm much worse."

Patty snorted. "Please. You're perfect. Literally."

Lisa shook her head before admitting: "I was in love with Adam Dory. Like, really in love."

Patty scrunched her face. "What are you talking about? How do you even know him?"

"We were together, Patty. Since you introduced us at T.J.'s graduation party last year. He and I just . . . clicked. But even though I felt like it was love at first sight, I never stopped dating Sundeep."

Patty sat back in her chair, trying to process a world in which Lisa Bristol—perfect, angelic Lisa Bristol—cheated on her boyfriend Sundeep with a loser like Adam Dory. "What happened?"

"He found out," Lisa said, and sniffed. "I mean, Adam found out about Sundeep." Then she said quickly, "As soon as I met Adam I was going to break it off with Sundeep—I really, really was—but then his family disowned him, and every time I tried to tell Adam, he said something or did something and I just couldn't bring myself to do it."

"But what about now? Sundeep's gone, why can't you legit date Adam?" Then she made a face and added, "Though God knows why you'd want to."

Lisa ignored the jab. "He wouldn't do it. He hates me."

"Whatever. You're the best he'll ever do by like a thousand. I'm sure he's still totally in love with you."

"No. He's changed."

"Do you still love him?"

"I still love the old him. Not the new him."

"You mean the successful, TechCrunch-covered entrepreneur? It must have all gone to his head."

"No; he changed before the company launched. It's hard to even be happy for him after what he did to Amelia."

"Seriously." Patty took a sip of water, her tone getting serious. "I've been trying to track her down for weeks. I was hoping Amelia would be able to help extinguish the Focus Girls Web site in case the cops change their minds about wanting to press charges."

"I haven't seen her all quarter, either. I e-mailed her about getting coffee but never heard back. I figured she was avoiding me because of all that happened. I wish she knew that I'm on her side with the whole Adam thing."

Patty cocked her head. "You don't think she's in trouble, do you?"

Lisa's face showed concern. "I don't know."

Patty felt her heart start to race thinking about Amelia being in trouble and no one knowing. She was the kind of person who could disappear for days without talking to anyone. Suddenly, Patty's desire to track down Amelia was no longer a selfish one to use her friend's computer skills, but a genuine concern for Amelia's safety.

"We have to find her," Patty blurted.

Lisa sat up in her chair, and Patty could tell her mind was similarly racing. "T-Bag."

"What?"

"T-Bag. He's Amelia's Comp Sci friend. He must know."

"Do you have his number?"

"No, but T.J. does."

"What?" Patty's face wrinkled. Why did T.J. have a CS friend of Amelia's number?

Lisa was already pressing the phone against her ear to call her brother. "They've been playing some video game together like, all the time." She lifted her eyebrow in agreement with Patty's shock. "He'll know."

"Feel better?" Mrs. Hawkins asked as Patty entered the kitchen.

"Yeah," Patty said, opening the fridge and taking a long sip of coconut water. Apologizing to Lisa directly had been her mom's idea. As usual, her mother had been right: It did make Patty feel better.

"Hand me that spatula?" Her mother pointed to the utensil on the counter as she tended to the mixer. The counter was covered with flour and eggs and cake-baking paraphernalia.

Patty handed her the spatula. "What are you making?"

"An apple cake for Maria Simons. Poor thing just had knee surgery. She's not going to be able to play tennis for *eight weeks*."

Patty thought about Mrs. Simons, a hard-body country club friend of her mother's who worked out three hours a day and was notoriously obsessed with her zero-body-fat, wrinkle-free physique. "Is she not freaking out she's going to get fat?"

"Of course she is."

"So why are you making her a cake?"

"She's the only thing between me and the Atherton tennis

championship title." Mrs. Hawkins looked at her daughter and smiled. "I'm not above competitive tactics."

Patty rolled her eyes and laughed, imagining Maria's fake gratitude and her mother's fake well wishes when she delivered her completely irresistible and calorie-laden dessert.

"So what's next?" Mrs. Hawkins went on.

"I don't know. I don't feel resolved about everything." Mrs. Hawkins had been surprisingly unfazed by her daughter's brush with the law. She wasn't pleased, of course, but she calmly swung into action to ensure it didn't seep into the community gossip mill. After the Shandi wedding fiasco, Mrs. Hawkins was a pro at gossip spin.

Patty was flustered by the ordeal, but her mother helped her pick up the pieces. "I mean," Patty went on, "I do feel relieved, like I've dug myself out of a hole, but I still want . . . I guess I want some good to come out of this"—she waved her hand in the air searching for the word—"this whole endeavor."

Mrs. Hawkins put down her spatula and turned toward her daughter. "Good will come out of this, Patty," she said. "It might take a long time, but one day something will happen and you'll understand that everything—even this—happens for a reason."

She turned back to the whirring mixer.

Patty sighed. "I guess I just wish it would happen soon."

"Patience, my dear," her mother said. "Just keep your eyes open for an opportunity so you don't miss it."

50

What Are You Driving At?

"Nice swing," Ted Bristol encouraged from next to Adam, whacking his own ball about two hundred yards past the one Adam had just hit.

Ted had bought Adam a set of golf clubs as a congratulatory gift for the Doreye launch. He'd gotten beat by a woman, Ted had explained to Adam, and he needed to start having their mentor-mentee meetings on the driving range so Ted could improve his swing.

Adam wanted to be good at the sport, which he associated with wealth and success, but he felt desperately uncomfortable here, where men lined up at their individual tees with buckets of golf balls, slicing them all out into the long field ahead. The driving range was to them, it seemed to Adam, totally natural, a familiar routine they'd developed over tens of thousands of swings. Whereas Adam constantly missed contact with his ball altogether, looking around sheepishly when he did.

"So how are things going post-launch?" Ted asked, guiding a ball to the center of the tee box with his five iron.

Adam kept his eyes on the ball below him, adjusting his stance as Ted had shown him, glad Ted couldn't see his face. "Fine," he said simply.

Ted smirked, sending another ball soaring in a perfect arc. "That all I get?"

"You know how it goes," Adam responded.

"You mean you need to find revenue now?"

"Yes."

"Well, you've got lots of options."

Adam's swing clipped the top of his ball and sent it rolling on the ground. Adam blushed looking at it sitting so close to the tee, a glaring marker of his amateurism.

"None that fit the mission."

"What mission?"

Adam hesitated. "Amelia's mission."

"You've got investors, Adam. It's their mission that matters now."

Adam didn't say anything.

Ted hit another ball before continuing, "And their mission is to make a return on their investment in you. Which means your mission is to make money. That's it. It's that simple."

"It's not, though," Adam said instinctively, turning to look over his shoulder for some semblance of empathy. "You know it's not."

Ted kept his head down, but lifted his eyes to his mentee. "You need to take your emotions out of this. You'll get nowhere—*nowhere*—in business if you can't learn to keep your emotions out of your decisions."

Adam swallowed and turned back to his ball.

"Leave Amelia out of it, Adam. Sell the data. It's the right thing to do for the company and your employees and your shareholders and yourself."

Adam lifted his club behind him, forcing Amelia out of his brain and keeping his head down and his eye on the ball. He swung hard, knocking the ball to the left, but grateful that it at least traveled a respectable distance in the air.

"Hold your follow-through," Ted coached, his voice cracking with surprise force, "I've told you that."

Adam tensed at the reprimand. He already felt like he was on the rocks with Violet lately; he couldn't afford to lose Ted, too. He took a deep breath as he walked to his bag and pulled out the large, heavy-ended driver. As he reached for another ball a thought hit him: How did Ted know about the option to sell the data? He turned around and looked at Ted, who was preparing for another perfect drive. Adam shrugged off the question. Of course Ted knew selling data was a hypothetical option. It had been a hypothetical option long before Violet's offer. *Hypothetical*: That's what Ted meant.

"You have time for a Scotch after this?" Ted asked, trying to make up for his earlier snipe. "You seem like you could use one."

Adam smiled at the cordiality. *Quit being so paranoid,* he chided himself. He hadn't had a drink in two weeks, and he wasn't going to solve Doreye's problems tonight anyway. "Yes, that sounds really great. Thank you."

51

Scar Tissue

T.J. looked at the three-sentence e-mail he'd spent the last forty-eight minutes drafting. The cursor blinked above the send button. He read it again:

> Riley—I'm sure you won't even respond to this, but are you around this week? Can I buy you a drink? I need to talk to you about something.

He shook his head and replaced the last line.

> Riley—I'm sure you won't even respond to this, but are you around this week? Can I buy you a drink? I could really use your advice on something. I know you don't owe me anything, but

No, it all sounded too desperate. He tried again.

> Riley—Are you around this week? Can I buy you a drink? I could really use your advice on something. It would mean a lot to me. T.

He read it one last time, held his breath and hit "Send." He stared at his computer screen: *Was that a huge mistake?*

Whatever. He wanted to see her. She was the only one he could talk to about this. A g-chat message popped up in the corner of the screen: *Tonight?*

It was Riley. T.J. felt his heart drop. He could see she was still typing and held his breath.

Riley: Red-eye to New York but can meet before
I go to airport. 7 at Wine Room?

T.J.'s hands hovered above the keyboard. It was almost four o'clock. He wanted to see her, but was three hours enough time to prepare? He still needed to think about how to recover from their last terrible encounter at the Rosewood.

Perfect, he watched himself type. Then, quickly, *Thanks.*

Riley: See you soon x

T.J. looked up. He was really having drinks with Riley tonight. In three hours. He had to go to the gym.

After an aggressive ninety-minute workout, shower, shave, and debate over whether his favorite button-down made it look like he was trying too hard (he decided it didn't), T.J. arrived at the Wine Room. Riley was already seated at the bar, her leather jacket thrown over a small black suitcase on the floor next to her. She was wearing boots over tight jeans and her legs were crossed as she tapped away at her iPhone.

"Hi," he said as he approached her chair. His heart was beating quickly, waiting for her to yell at him or . . .

"Oh, hi, hi." She jumped up cheerily. "Sorry, I'm just finishing this e-mail to my boss. Hold on a sec." She finished tapping and hit "Send" before putting the phone in her purse and turning her shoulders to face T.J. She smiled warmly at him, as though their last encounter had never happened, then paused to study his face. "Everything okay?" she asked, her eyebrows pinching together in that way she always did when she went into empathic mode.

"Yeah," he said, nodding. "Sorry I'm overdressed." He was wishing he hadn't worn the shirt after all. "I have a dinner up in the city after this," he lied.

"Oh, you do? Could you drop me at the airport on your way up?" she asked. "Cabs from here are so absurd."

"Yes, of course," he agreed, cursing himself for the lie, but also flattered that she'd asked. She didn't seem to hate him after all, and he felt himself starting to relax.

"Great. Here"—she pulled out the seat next to her—"sit down."

They ordered two glasses of Merlot and after some more pleasantries about the weather and her *Forbes* assignment she looked at her watch and pushed her mouth to one side. "So what's up?"

T.J. cracked his knuckles and sighed, ready. "I needed someone to talk to. Someone who would be honest with me. And I know you will be."

Riley lifted her eyebrows and acknowledged the truth of his point, taking a sip of wine.

"And I trust your opinion," he continued, afraid he'd caused offense. "I mean, I don't always agree with it or like it, but I . . . respect it."

"Thank you," she accepted the compliment.

"Though I guess I'm surprised you were so willing to meet. I figured after how I acted at the Rosewood you would try to avoid me at all costs." T.J. couldn't shake his bewilderment over the fact that she wasn't angry.

"I would have thought the same," Riley retorted. She took a sip of her wine and went on when she realized he was waiting for her to say more. "I mean, what I said to you wasn't easy to hear; I didn't think you'd listen, much less ask for more."

"But weren't you mad?"

"I was annoyed, sure. You were a total jerk. But I was also . . . relieved."

"What?" He instinctively leaned in to her. He could smell her perfume.

"Well, first I realized you did have some emotion left for me. And that was a relief, because what we had in college was incredibly special. I mean"—she laughed and her cheeks tinted in a nervous blush—"we were young and stupid, but we were really in love, and I guess I hoped we would always keep some special feelings for each other." She turned and looked at him seriously. "To feel like someone is totally neutral toward you, even after having known you so well, that is just like a knife, you know?"

T.J. did know. It's how he felt about her. He felt a warmth spread from his chest down to his arms and had to stop his hand from lifting to brush her cheek.

"And second, I was relieved because it reminded me why I broke up with you, and that I'm glad I did." It was an icicle skewer that eviscerated the warmth. T.J. buried his nose in his wineglass to avoid having to look at her.

"Sorry," she said, "was that too harsh?"

T.J. nodded honestly, keeping his focus on the mirror behind the bar instead of turning to face her. "Yes. I mean, Jesus," he scoffed. "But no." He finally turned to her, sighing. "I know. I guess that's part of why I'm here. I really messed up, Riley."

Riley's face got pale and he could sense she was nervous about what was coming next. Did she think he was referencing their relationship?

"Don't worry," he assured her quickly, "I'm not asking you out."

She laughed nervously; he wasn't sure whether it was nervous relief or nervous disappointment.

He continued: "I messed up this company."

"What do you mean?" She sat up in her chair, shifting into advice mode.

"I guess I always had this grand dream of entrepreneurship. Of starting my own thing and being super successful at it," he admitted, knowing she knew this from the hours and hours of conversations they'd had about it in college.

"Haven't you done that?"

"No." He shook his head at his first vocal admission of his own failure. "I latched on to two kids. One had talent and the other was reckless enough to do anything I wanted." He looked up and shrugged. "I feel like I took advantage of them . . . and I didn't add any value myself, you know?"

"What do you mean?" She grimaced as though she didn't buy it.

T.J. insisted, "Exactly that: I didn't add any value. I haven't. I don't have engineering talent. I got a *C* in CS 101, Riley," he said seriously. "And I was trying *really hard*."

"Not everyone's brain is built to program," she consoled.

"Still, that's not the only issue," he went on. "I also don't have this blind, stop-at-nothing ambition. Adam might not be the smartest, but he's got that. And now I've got this opportunity to have my name in lights, and all I can think is that I don't want it because I'm afraid I'll be uncovered as a fraud. As some rich kid who doesn't have that extra . . . oomph."

Riley moved her eyes away and didn't say anything. T.J. cringed at the validation of what he'd hoped was a dramatic over-statement.

"Please say something."

Riley lifted her left shoulder and tilted her ear toward it. "I mean, that's exactly what you used to say about your dad."

T.J. shook his head. "This isn't about my dad; it's about me."

She shifted her elbow onto the bar and leaned forward, rest-ing her chin on her hand and looking at him gently. "No. It's about you both. You're still so angry with him, and with the part of you that's like him, that you can't move past it. You use up all your energy either fighting behavior like his or giving up and defaulting to it."

T.J. sat back and let this sink in. She was right: Sometimes when he was nice to people, it was because he was trying to be different from his father; but when he got tired and frustrated, he became arrogant and selfish and used people like it was okay.

"But what if I'm really not talented," he pushed back. "What if I just don't have the entrepreneur thing in me?"

"Then you'll find something else to do," Riley answered simply. "Everyone's good at something. Most people just waste a lot of time working at things for the wrong reasons."

"Is that why you decided to be a photographer?"

"I don't know. I don't know what I'm supposed to do." Riley's face took on a consternation that made T.J. realize she was struggling with something herself. For a moment she looked vulnerable, like she didn't have the answer. It was the most beautiful she'd ever been. T.J. realized he hadn't even bothered to ask why she was going to New York. "But"—she turned and looked at him and the doubt vanished—"I think once you get over your daddy issues you'll find that you *do* have a huge amount to offer."

T.J. rolled his eyes and turned back to his wine, the moment finished. "Daddy issues?"

"Sorry," she said playfully, "but it's true."

"I know." He paused and smiled at her candid feedback, then: "Do you think I can do it?"

"You responded to my telling you the truth at Rosewood by asking for more: I'd say you already are."

He laughed and took another sip of wine. Maybe there was more to come in their story.

"What's in New York?" he tried.

Riley laughed. "A guy."

T.J. felt his heart sink but stayed composed. "That's great. You like him?"

She nodded and smiled a childish smile. "I do."

T.J. stood up and picked up her suitcase. "We should get going," he said before she could elaborate.

"Are you seeing anyone?" she asked.

"Nah. No time."

"I still think you should go out with Amelia, if she ever resurfaces," Riley said casually as she climbed off her stool and went to the door.

T.J. felt his face burn as he stood, dumbfounded by her comment.

Riley turned around and laughed. "What? You know you two are perfect for each other."

52

Dealmakers

Violet sat at a dark, back table at Tamarind, an upscale Vietnamese fusion restaurant on University Avenue. As good as the Empire rice was, Tamarind was mostly the place people came when they didn't want to be seen.

She leaned on one elbow, balancing her chin on her left fingers while her right fingers rapped the table impatiently. She checked her phone for the third time and ordered a martini and spring rolls from the waiter, continuing to keep her irritated eye on the door.

Finally, Ted Bristol appeared and came toward her unurgently. She put her hand out to greet him but didn't stand up.

"I went ahead and ordered spring rolls," she said as he sat down.

"Good." He looked at the waiter. "Scotch, please. Neat."

She looked at him, not trying to hide her annoyance.

"Sorry I'm late," he finally conceded. "Happy?"

"I'll be better after this," she said, taking a sip of her martini. Violet knew that her temperament was difficult to track: Sometimes she was cool and easygoing, but other times, like right now, others' tardiness made her irrationally angry. For the longest time, Ted Bristol had been playing right into her hands. As she expected, after their conversation on the golf course when Violet teased him with her knowledge of his ownership of Doreye, he predictably gave her another assignment. Also as she expected, this time the assignment came with a bigger paycheck. But as she'd sat waiting for a tardy Ted Bristol, she became anxious that she'd overplayed her hand. She worried that she'd admitted to knowing too much, and now Ted was taking her for granted. She resented the implications of his showing up twenty-five minutes late to an appointment he himself had scheduled and wondered whether she should ditch him and their arrangement altogether.

"Well, I didn't have the best day, either."

Violet took a breath and tried to muster an ounce of caring. "Why is that?"

"I got my first distribution from the Gibly sale."

"Why is that bad?"

"It's insulting to have to see the number."

"It's your own fault." She was sick of his constant moaning about Gibly.

"What?" he snapped back at her brusqueness.

She met it with equal authority. She'd long since forgotten she was almost thirty years his junior. "You mishandled Amelia. You shouldn't have let her leak what she knew about Gibly's security."

"How would you know I mishandled her?"

"Because I understand people." Her voice oozed passive-aggressiveness.

Ted scoffed, "I should have offered her more."

Violet shook her head. "Jesus, you don't get it at all. Our generation isn't like that."

"Everyone can be bought, even your over-idealizing, social media–bred generation."

"Maybe. But not with money. That was your mistake. You used the wrong currency with Amelia."

Ted huffed a sigh. "I didn't come here to talk about this. How's Adam?"

"Didn't you just play golf with him?"

"Yes. How did you know that?"

She lifted her eyebrows and sipped her drink triumphantly, relishing that she didn't actually have to say "I know everything."

"Whatever." Ted rolled his eyes at Violet's confidence. "I told him he had to start making money. And should sell the data."

"You should have stuck to the first point; he's still conflicted on the latter."

"This has to work." Ted looked at her seriously.

"Don't get emotional." She met his gaze. "Our interests are aligned."

"So your backers are still on board?"

"Yes. But they don't know about you, and they can't: They still blame you for Gibly."

"Gibly was Amelia's fault."

"No," she said patiently. "As we've established, it was yours. But now you've got me to make sure things go smoothly. You'll get what you want out of this: Doreye will have a massive pop in value and you can sell and recoup your money. And I'll get what I want."

"You mean what your backers want?"

"Ted, I may be a hired hand, and you may think I only exist to do your bidding, but you don't know me at all if you think I don't have my own motives for this." She knew it was wise to keep Ted thinking she was a blind executor of his and his British counterpart's ideas, but it was starting to grate on her pride.

A camera flash from the corner of the room made Violet turn. A party had assembled at a large table in the corner and a group of overdressed men and women her age were laughing and snapping photos. She wondered sometimes, seeing crowds like this, whether she shouldn't have just gone to college and been a normal kid after all.

"So we're square on the new goal? We just need Adam to agree to it," Ted said, bringing her back.

"Yes."

"How is the other deal going? The cloud-computing thing?"

"Fine. It's working and he feels like a hero and he trusts me to make good deals."

"And Aleister is happy, too?"

"Of course. This'll make the other piece that much easier with them."

"Very good." Ted smiled.

"I have to go to the restroom," she said abruptly, sliding out of her chair and straightening her skirt as she walked to the back of the restaurant.

A ruggedly handsome man with olive skin and slicked hair, dressed in jeans and a fitted tweed blazer, held back the curtain that blocked the hallway to the restrooms from the rest of the restaurant. His deep brown eye caught hers and he nodded his head politely as she passed. She felt herself blush instinctively at the attention, and as she exited the bathroom a few minutes later she found herself hoping he'd still be there.

"I've unfortunately got to go." Ted was tapping at his iPhone and stood up as he saw Violet return.

"It's fine," she said, taking a last sip of her martini and reaching for her coat. "I think we were finished anyway."

"Keep up the good work," Ted said, leaning over to kiss her cheek casually.

She pulled back but accepted the gesture.

"I think we make a good team, you know," Ted said. "Always have."

She squinted and studied his face. The waitress approached the table. "He's got it," Violet told the waitress, indicating the check, as she headed to the door.

As she walked back to her car, Violet saw the man from the restaurant, sitting on a bench on the opposite side of the street reading a newspaper. It was chilly out and he wore a gray overcoat, but looked untroubled by the wind as he sat cross-legged reading the paper. She stood for a moment to see if he'd look up, and then thought for a second maybe she should just go over, but then thought better of it and walked on.

53

Mind Over Body

Adam was lying on his back on the floor of his office, his hands folded gently across his abdomen. He'd pulled the blinds so that the room was dark, save for the sunlight creeping in around the corner of the curtain. He stared up at the white ceiling made blue by the dark. He was thinking.

On the one hand, Amelia had always been the person he trusted the most, and she would never sell user data. On the other hand, Amelia was gone and replaced by Ted and Violet, two people who believed in him and valued his contributions. They both thought he should sell data, and Violet had even found a buyer. Moreover, he hadn't talked to Amelia since Roger Fenway's funeral. She hadn't wanted to sell the data last year, but if she knew what he knew, maybe she would have come around?

He sat up. Yes, exactly. He couldn't make this big of a decision based on what he *thought* Amelia *probably* wanted. Just look at how much his views had changed in the past year as he'd learned more about business: Surely hers had similarly evolved—or would have if she'd approached the world with as open a mind as he had.

It felt very clear all of a sudden. He needed to sell the data. Violet was right; it was best for the company. And it was wrong for him to make any decision based on Amelia. It was irrational and emotional and not even grounded in reality, as he didn't have any factual basis for knowing what she wanted.

He stood up and walked back out into the light of the hallway toward T.J.'s desk.

"I've made a decision."

T.J. looked up from his laptop. "What's that?"

"I found a buyer for our data. We're going to go into contract with them before the end of the quarter. I'll have the team write an app update that links user data to their database. We'll start with the iPhone app and then move to Droid."

T.J. tilted his chin down and peered up at Adam. "You want to sell user data?"

"It's the best thing for the company, and for users. It'll quickly generate revenue without forcing us to charge our users or run ads."

"It's unethical," T.J. said shortly, his inner voice screaming, *It's something my father would do.*

"That's an archaic way of thinking. You don't have any way to prove that it's bad for users."

"You don't have any way to prove it's *not* bad for them."

"But I can absolutely prove it will generate revenue, and that will help the company develop more products, and those products will benefit them."

"You can't do this."

"Doing the update won't hurt." Adam went into charming negotiator mode. "And we're not committing to anything by having the conversation with potential buyers."

T.J.'s face didn't move, he just stared at Adam, studying him.

"What about Amelia?" he finally said. "What about what she wanted?"

"How do I know what Amelia would want? I haven't spoken to her in months."

T.J. scoffed, "Don't be a fool."

"I'm not," he insisted genuinely. "She left. And if she'd stayed her opinions on the matter might very well have evolved, as mine have."

"Are you listening to yourself?" T.J. blurted. "Are you delusional?"

Adam kept his face calm, insisting on his previous argument. "There's no way of knowing."

T.J. ignored it. "So you haven't heard from her?"

Adam swallowed and shook his head silently. "Have you?"

"I found out she went to Indiana, but T-Bag hasn't heard from her since."

"Well, I guess there's nothing we can do but move forward," Adam heard himself say, his heart jumping. *Why did she go to Indiana?*

T.J.'s jaw dropped. He stood up and pushed past Adam. "Go to hell."

T.J. hurried down the stairs of the office, suddenly desperate to get out into the fresh air. It was all too much: needing to get revenue and Amelia being gone and Adam being a douche bag and Riley having a boyfriend and all of it overlaid with this new lens that he had daddy issues.

He walked to University Café and headed straight for the back counter to order a coffee, his eye catching a pretty girl typing away at her laptop in the front corner. *No*, he thought. *No more women. Not right now.*

Maybe Adam was right. It was the best thing for the company and for investors. And three months ago he wouldn't have even hesitated. But now, now his whole foundation for what was right or wrong felt shaky.

He paid for his latte and went around the bar to wait for it. He took a deep breath and looked at the tables of chatting diners and furiously typing nerds at their laptops. His senses suddenly flashed back to a year ago and his meeting here—at that table right there—with Roger Fenway. He replayed the encounter, the salad he'd ordered and how Roger had been distracted and then gone and talked to that girl who was sitting at the table in the front corner. That girl had ended up being Amelia Dory, the girl who had changed everything in his life.

T.J.'s brain jumped to a moment earlier. That pretty girl when he'd walked in—could it have been Amelia? Or was his brain just trying to bring the memory of her back to life? To go back to before all this started? He slowly crossed the café, secretly praying it was true, but when he arrived at the table again, she was gone.

54

The World Wide Spider Web

"Not here. Meet @ City Hall parking garage instead."

Amelia texted Dawson as she scurried out of University Café with her head down, her whole body tense with the expectation that someone was about to call out her name. She should have known better than to agree to meet Dawson in such a public place. She'd hardly been waiting for ten minutes before T.J. had come in for a coffee.

Her heart fell when she saw him. She knew her fear of being seen and having to explain what she was doing put her on edge, but there was something else troubling her. As soon as Amelia saw T.J., all the feelings she'd tried to push out—the feelings of longing for and missing him—came flooding back and she help-lessly indulged the memory of his hands on her waist as he hugged her good-bye and felt his breath on her neck when they sat close at Gates. But he hadn't even looked when he came into the Café. Whatever was there—if there had been anything there—he'd probably let it go by now.

He'd e-mailed her eleven times since she'd left for Tahoe, the first few asking where she was; then he shifted, giving her up-dates while insisting he respected her silence and that he didn't expect a reply. The last e-mail had just said he hoped she was okay. That was eight days ago.

T-Bag and Riley and Patty and even Lisa had e-mailed, too. (Adam hadn't.) It was the e-mails from T.J., though, that made Amelia's breath stop when she saw them in her inbox, and which she found herself reopening late at night, rolling the words around in her head, thinking about what T.J. had been thinking about when he wrote them, and landing on the conclusion that made her heart melt: He'd been thinking about *her*. She wanted so badly to talk to T.J., especially when she started doubting her theory, thinking it really had been as simple as Adam wanting her off the team. At those moments she'd come so close to sending a reply. *Yes. Let's meet. Thank you, really.*

But in the end she hadn't.

She had to focus, she told herself. She'd never, ever been distracted by boys, and now was not the time to start.

The late-afternoon sun was fading into evening and taking what warmth it offered with it; Amelia jammed her hands into her pockets and walked quickly across the street, ducking into the parking garage below City Hall and following the ramp down to the bottom level, where a few cars were parked but most employees had already left for the day.

"You're going to love me." Dawson's voice startled her as she turned to meet him. He unbuttoned his overcoat and pulled his iPhone from the inside breast pocket of the tweed blazer he wore as he approached.

"Don't get ahead of yourself," Amelia answered, but felt her heart racing with nervous excitement for what he might have found.

"I did like you showed me and used your little app to track the phone of the person who's receiving the mysterious payments, and"—he held out the phone and offered a picture—"she's quite the looker."

Amelia snatched the phone, her palms sweating nervously. The photo was dark and showed a woman sitting in a beige upholstered chair at a table with a white cloth, daintily fingering a martini. Amelia pulled the phone up toward her glasses to get a better look: Could it really be? "Violet," she heard herself breathe.

"You know her?" Dawson asked.

Amelia's head was spinning. A year ago, VIPER was paying the Aleister Corporation in London for its Gibly data—now they were paying Violet in Palo Alto? The same Violet who had posed as a reporter to reveal Amelia's past, the same Violet who feigned a company called RemoteX to steal Doreye's thunder, the same Violet who'd shown up at the *Forbes* photo shoot and been hanging on her brother ever since?

"What is she doing?" Amelia asked the air.

"Keep scrolling," Dawson urged, watching Amelia's face with a satisfied smirk. "She's got a companion."

Amelia swiped her finger across the screen to the next photo. Violet stood up to greet someone. A man's back entered the frame. The next image showed the two talking intently, but Amelia couldn't make out his face.

"I can't tell who it is." Amelia lifted her eyes to Dawson for help.

"Keep going. I got one with a flash. Almost got me caught, but you can make him out in it."

Amelia kept scrolling until she got to one where both their faces were crystal clear. "Ted," she said firmly, her jaw instinctively setting.

Amelia's weight dropped back into her heels and she looked up, mouth agape. She started to nod as she put the pieces together. Ted was linked to Violet. Did that mean that Ted had a role in her other dealings—as a reporter and with RemoteX and . . . with Adam?

Amelia was still angry with Ted. It went deeper than being insulted that he'd thought he could pay her off way back when they first met at University Café to discuss what Amelia uncovered about Gibly. She was angry with him because he'd ruined her illusions about Silicon Valley: It wasn't a clear, clean place where innovation happened for innovation's sake. It was full of manipulation and greed, and Ted Bristol embodied all of it.

She swallowed with effort and finally lifted her head to Dawson. "This man. This is Ted Bristol. This girl . . . her name is Violet."

"How do you know them?"

Amelia started to explain but changed her mind when she looked at Dawson. His eyes had a glimmer, a hunger for information that she still didn't trust. She gestured toward the time on her iPhone to indicate the urgency of getting to the bottom of this new revelation. "It's a long story; I'll explain later."

"No hints?"

"Better you're not swayed by my suspicions." Her brain felt clear now, and she had a new energy that her instincts were right. *See?* she said to herself. *No need to call T.J.—you're fine on your own.*

"Fair. What do we do now?"

"I need to figure out how they're connected. Give me a few minutes." Amelia opened her laptop and perched herself on the trunk of a nearby Audi. She connected to the building's Wi-Fi and was quickly sorting through encrypted FedEx shipping records from last December. It took her a minute to find the RemoteX delivery records. In another forty seconds, she found the credit card that paid for the delivery. And twenty seconds later, she found the address associated with the credit card, which Google Maps showed to be a mansion in Atherton. Ted Bristol's, in fact.

So Ted was the puppet master behind RemoteX. Amelia remembered how he first tried to get revenge on her by taking her and Adam's scholarships away. When that didn't work and Roger bailed them out, he must have set up RemoteX to get revenge on Amelia through embarrassment. But that didn't work out, either. What else would this man resort to? What had he done next? She couldn't shake the feeling that Ted was the mystery investor. But how? And what was he plotting to do if he was?

"Is everything all right?" Michael Dawson's patience was

running thin; not because he was annoyed, but because he wanted to help.

"Everything is fine. We're a lot closer than we were yesterday."

"So should we head home and relax?" he asked sardonically.

She shook her head and smiled. "Not time to celebrate yet. But I do have another project for you."

55

Please Allow Me to Introduce Myself

"Whiskey soda," Dawson said, leaning his elbow against the bar and smiling at the buxom bartender. He turned his torso to face the man sitting two seats down; it was the same person from the photo at Tamarind. Dawson tapped his foot while waiting for the woman to return with his cocktail, trying to figure out his next move.

"Man, have I missed California women," he casually mused.

Ted Bristol looked up from his iPhone at the speaker, then at the woman he referenced, then back at the stranger. He smiled and lifted his eyebrows in agreement. "Bay Area's no L.A., but this is a good spot to find the best of the neighborhood."

Ted Bristol went back to reading something on his iPhone.

"I'd say," Dawson responded, undeterred. He slid out of his tweed blazer and unbuttoned the top button of his shirt, loosening his collar as the bartender returned.

"Tough day?" She smiled as she placed the drink in front of him.

"Honey, you don't know the half of it." His brown eyes smiled as he pulled his lips quizzically to one side, offering his best draw-you-in grin. His broad jaw was bristled with stubble. He was handsome, to be sure, but he had a confidence that made him seem much more so.

The bartender's heavily-mascaraed eyes darted up and down the bar, presumably to see if any other patrons were waiting for drinks, but really to see if her supervisor was watching or if a momentary flirtation would be allowed. Dawson laughed in his head. *Women are so predictable.*

"Want to tell me about it?" She moved her shoulders parallel with his and put her hands on the bar, straightening her arms so that her cleavage jutted out of her tight-bodiced dress. Out of the corner of his eye, Dawson saw Ted's head lift as he tuned in to the conversation.

"Oh, I don't want to bore you," Dawson flirted. But she moved closer and tilted her head, her long brown hair falling over her shoulder, indicating nothing he said could bore her.

He laughed in false humility, loudly enough for Ted to hear. "Really: I'm a corporate accountant. I spend my day looking at balance sheets. You know what's worse than that? I live in the Midwest! Trust me, all my stories are boring." Then, for good measure, Dawson ended with: "Especially compared to the kind of fun a beautiful brunette in California must have."

She blushed and grinned at the Midwesterner, speechless.

"Miss?" a man at the other end of the bar called for her attention. Dawson lifted his head to indicate she should go do her job. She obeyed, and Dawson took a sip of his whiskey, waiting for Ted to say something, which he shortly did. Men were predictable, too.

"You're an accountant, huh?" Ted said.

Dawson pretended to be surprised by his question: "I'm sorry?"

"I overheard you." Ted indicated the space where the bartender had just been. "Did you say you're a corporate accountant?"

"I am." Dawson puffed himself up as he nodded assuredly. He then recited the lines that Amelia drilled into him before sending him on this mission. "My specialty is preventing equity investments from losing their financial value; you know, antidilution provisions and all that."

"Oh?" Ted raised his eyebrow. "And you live . . . well, you don't live here?"

"Nope." Dawson shook his head. "I gave up the big lights. Live in the middle of nowhere in Indiana."

"That must be lonely," Ted empathized, trying to reconcile how someone with Dawson's looks, charm, and obvious penchant for gorgeous women survived in a small town in the Midwest.

"After my wife died, I adopted a couple kids—they're teenagers now"—he shook his head in reflection—"hard to believe. Anyhow, they keep me company."

He turned his head to Ted and smiled. "You got any kids?"

"Two," Ted answered, clearly thinking about something else. "Our youngest, Lisa, is actually adopted, too."

"No way," Dawson said. "She turn out okay?"

"She's an angel," Ted admitted. "Probably better than my own genes ever could have managed."

"Mine too," Dawson agreed, lifting his glass to clink Ted's. "To picking 'em good."

Ted laughed and accepted the cheers.

"So what brings you to California?"

"I have clients with some business out here. A few Chicago-based VC firms watching out to make sure they don't get taken."

"Oh, yeah? Who are you working for? Madison Dearborn? Apex?"

"Sorry," Dawson said, smiling, "accountant-client privileges and all that."

"Must be quite a project to send an accountant all the way out here."

"It was some tricky stuff that needed first-person attention."

"What kind of tricky stuff?" Ted moved closer.

"Eh, I shouldn't talk about it." Dawson lifted a hand and shook his head. "I pride myself on confidentiality."

Ted nodded. "As you should."

The two men sat in silence for a moment before Ted stood up and moved to sit on the empty stool between them.

"You know, I probably could have used a guy like you about a year ago." Ted stopped and peered at his glass. "I had equity in a company that was being acquired for *a lot* of money. But because of some bad press the deal fell apart and the value crashed to one-tenth of the original offer. I got screwed." He said it with the air of someone trying to be lighthearted but feeling the opposite.

"Brutal. Sorry, man." Dawson shook his head in commiseration.

"There's a new company that I just got control over, though. I think they've got real potential to bring me back."

"What is it?"

Ted looked at him, evaluating whether he was trustworthy, and deciding that he was. "You've never heard of it. It's an app that lets your phone see other electronic devices, like an eye. More importantly, collects user data."

"Until that company hits it big, you know you can write your investment losses off, right? Who's your business manager?"

"I can? My who?" Ted asked.

Shit, Dawson thought, *wrong word choice.* "You know, the guy managing your accounts." He took a sip of his drink.

"Oh, Stuart?" Ted tilted his head. "He's smart and all but super old-school. I'm a private man and he's kind of an expert at setting up shell companies. He's totally OCD—you should see his home office," Ted said, chuckling. "Anyway, he's not cutting-edge, but I trust him. He's loyal."

"That's good," Dawson said, nodding. "You want OCD in an accountant." Then he thought to add quickly, "Not Stuart Kipling, is it?"

"No. Chen. Never heard of Stuart Kipling. Is he local?"

Dawson stored "Stuart Chen" away in his brain. "No. Just a guy I went to school with who's a total slime. Knew it was a long shot but thought I'd check in case."

"Good of you." Ted clinked his glass again. "Very OCD yourself." He smiled and after a pause offered his hand. "I'm Ted."

"Randall," Dawson said, accepting the handshake, "Randall Jameson."

"Any relation?" Ted jovially noted the whiskey in his glass.

"I wish!" Dawson conceded. "Wouldn't have to slave away so hard if I'd gotten that inheritance." He took the chance to look at his watch. "On that note, I ought to get going. Big day tomorrow."

"Indeed." Ted stood up and moved out of his way. "Have you got a card? In case I ever need a nonlocal accountant?"

"Ahh," Dawson said, patting his pockets to feel for business cards he knew weren't there, "unfortunately not. Give me one of yours and I'll shoot you my info?"

"Sure thing." Ted pulled a crisp, heavy-stock card from his wallet and handed it to Dawson. "Pleasure meeting you; enjoy the rest of your stay."

"Pleasure's been all mine." Dawson's left dimple curled into a smile and he held Ted's hand a moment longer than necessary before turning merrily out of the bar.

56

Kryptonite Firewall

The door opened and Amelia jumped in her chair. She stood from the computer and pulled a blanket around her shoulders as Dawson entered the room.

"Hey," he greeted her as he threw his jacket on the sofa and headed for the minifridge in the corner, where he pulled out a beer and took a long swig.

Amelia wiggled her toes to keep warm as she waited for him to report on the rest of his evening.

Dawson let out a long, satisfied sigh, his eyes closed, appreciating the taste of the beer he'd half finished.

"So?" Amelia finally prompted. "Did you find him?"

Dawson opened his eyes and looked at her in mock surprise, pulling Ted's card out of his pocket and tossing it onto the table in front of her as he went into the bedroom to change out of his "Randall Jameson" costume.

"Where'd you get this?" she called from the front room. "Did you meet him?" Her voice was eager. Dawson was quiet, getting back at her for being so guarded in the parking lot.

"No, I found it on the street," Dawson called back.

Amelia's shoulders dropped in disappointment. He popped his head back through the doorframe. "I'm kidding. Of course I met him."

She perked up again and sat back in the chair, tapping her foot and tugging at her earlobe anxiously while she waited for him to return.

He reentered the room in sweatpants and a white under-shirt, tossing the empty beer can in the garbage as he pulled out another.

"What have you been working on?" he asked innocently.

"I'll tell you later." Amelia was annoyed by the pleasure he took in stringing this out, and the fact that she hadn't uncov-ered anything new about VIPER. "Come on," she pleaded, "what did you find out? Did you talk to Ted about Violet?"

"Nope."

"What?" Amelia snapped. "Why not? That was the point."

"I did you one better." Dawson smiled. "Ted's your mystery owner."

"What are you talking about?" She felt her heart drop. She thought it was true, but she hadn't prepared herself for confir-mation.

"He's doing it all through a shell company; doesn't want any-one to know."

Amelia sank back in her chair. "Ted Bristol owns Doreye." She let herself say it out loud.

Dawson waited, not sure what to do.

"But why?" She twisted her mouth, looking at Dawson for an answer. "Doesn't he want to bring the whole thing down? Doesn't he want to punish me?"

"Amelia, you're sitting in a mouse-infested basement and your only ally is me, a man you threw in jail. I would call this rock bottom."

"But . . ." It was the first time Amelia realized what had be-come of her. He was right. Before her emotions took over she shook her head. *Don't think about that right now.*

"But what's his angle? I mean, what is he trying to do?"

"He wants to make money, I presume."

"But Ted lost all his money in Gibly. Where did he get twenty million to invest in Doreye?"

"Maybe he got it from somewhere else?"

"Okay." Amelia's voice was annoyed at the obvious statement. "So how do we find that out?"

"Easy," Dawson said, smiling. "Stuart Chen."

"Who?" she grumbled.

"Ted Bristol's accountant."

Amelia lifted her head, and her eyes shined with a new hope before she turned back to her computer and googled his name.

"Doubt you'll find anything," Dawson interjected. "Ted said he's old-school. Has a home office, though."

"So what do you suggest we do?"

Dawson finished his beer. "That's enough for me today. I'm hitting the hay."

"But—" Amelia protested.

"And I suggest, young lady, that you do the same," Dawson lectured, then said more tenderly: "You look exhausted. And we made a lot of progress today. Get some sleep—the next step will be clear tomorrow."

Amelia's eyelids fell with admission that she was exhausted, and that he was right.

"Thank you," she whispered from her chair, but he'd already turned back to the bedroom.

Virtual Reality Bites

"What a treat," T-Bag exclaimed with equal parts mockery and earnestness. "Delta Gamma brunch? This is every gay man's dream. Are there a lot of cute boys here?"

Patty laughed as she opened the door for him to come in through the kitchen, wondering uncomfortably whether his flamboyance might be a greater cause for concern than the Comp Sci geekery she'd initially been hesitant about.

"I'm kidding," he said in a normal voice. "I promise I won't embarrass you in front of your friends."

Patty blushed at being called out and felt a pang of shame at her own shallowness.

"Can I get you coffee?" she asked to redeem herself, leading the way through the kitchen, where two chefs were busy flipping pancakes and cooking eggs, and into the dining room, where girls and guys were filing in for brunch.

Delta Gamma's chef served brunch every Friday, replete with bacon, pancakes, and made-to-order omelets. It was the perfect antidote to the inevitable hangovers following Sigma Chi's Thursday-night Penthouse parties, and was so popular that each girl was only allowed one guest. The result was that the Delta Gamma brunch became notorious across campus;

invites were coveted, and the meal took on an exclusive allure.

Patty knew this, of course, and thought using this week's invitation for T-Bag would be a powerful message of how much she appreciated his help finding Amelia.

"Coffee would be great," T-Bag answered. "I assume you have nonfat soy milk and Splenda?"

"Of course." Patty found T-Bag's mockery of DG's girly dietary habits pleasantly disarming. She grinned. "And egg-white omelets cooked without oil."

"Perfection." He grinned behind his glasses. He had really great bone structure, she thought, and perfectly clear skin. His plaid shirt and dark-wash jeans were really well assembled. In short, she approved of his style and general demeanor, and applauded herself for being open-minded to someone from outside her normal clique.

The two piled food from the buffet onto their plates and took a seat in the corner, where they chitchatted about classes and Patty's plans for an internship and her dabbling with start-ups. They talked about relationships and commiserated over the selfishness of boys.

When they were finished with their food, T-Bag dabbed his mouth with a napkin. "But I know you didn't bring me here to discover the intricacies of my love life, so let's talk about Amelia."

Patty bit her lip. "What do you know?"

"I don't know where she physically is, but I think I know how to find her virtually."

Patty lifted an eyebrow.

"There's this video game we all play called ZOSTRA," he explained, "but Amelia has blocked T.J. and me from finding her. However, if you set up an account, you should be able to hunt her down. That is, assuming she's still playing. But I can't imagine she wouldn't be."

"I still can't believe T.J.'s a video-gamer loser." Patty rolled her eyes and laughed as she sipped her orange juice.

T-Bag glared at her.

"Sorry." She blushed again.

"T.J. plays, and you are about to. Come on, I'll set you up."

T-Bag followed Patty to her room and showed her how to log on to ZOSTRA, how to set up an account, how to navigate the virtual worlds. As they were choosing Patty's avatar's wardrobe, T-Bag's phone rang. He ignored it, but the caller tried back and T-Bag looked, concerned, at the caller ID.

"Is it the boy?" Patty asked.

"Yes, but I don't want to talk to him."

Patty rolled her eyes. "Stop being a girl." She shooed him out of the room. "Go! I think I've got it."

"You sure?" T-Bag asked.

"Yes." She stood up and hugged him without thinking, and held on until his surprised arms relaxed and returned the embrace. "This has been fun."

"Yeah," he said, "you're a good time, Patty Hawkins. I mean, for a sorority chick."

"You too, for a geek."

He smiled as he put on the messenger bag over his head and prepared to go. "Call me if you have any trouble. Oh, and I'd recommend starting in Paris. That's where Amelia used to hang when she was feeling down."

"You think she's sad?"

"Of course she's sad," T-Bag chirped as he exited the room, "she hasn't seen me in weeks!"

"Bye!" Patty said, rolling her eyes.

"*Ciao, bella.*"

Patty turned to her computer monitor, a bright pink Apple screen she'd begged for last Christmas, and finished assembling her avatar.

Virtual Patty was an artist. She was short and slim, with dark curly hair that bounced when she walked. She wore high black boots over leggings and Yoko Ono glasses. *Domicile?* The program asked her. "Brooklyn," she typed. *Super skill?* "Painting," she entered, thinking briefly on the art classes she'd taken as a child and wondering if it was too late to find one at Stanford this term, now that Focus Girls was done and she had more time.

The ZOSTRA screen asked whether she wanted to join a game, find a community, or explore on her own. She selected the last option and followed T-Bag's suggestion to head to Paris.

The digital map zoomed in on France, then dove in for the capital city, where the sun was disappearing over a gloomy winter afternoon. Patty scrolled familiarly down the Champs-Élysées, thinking back on her high-school summer there, to the tall monolith in the center of the Place de la Concorde. The game gave her the option of hiding other players, but so far she hadn't seen anyone else, and enjoyed having Paris all to herself. She directed her virtual self up rue du Faubourg Saint-Honoré and entered the Christian Louboutin store before remembering her mission and assuring herself that, even in a fantasy land, there was no chance she'd find Amelia shopping for shoes.

She wandered to the Louvre and stood before the glass pyramid looking for . . . what? She felt a pang of anxiety: What were the chances that Amelia was even logged on to the game right now, much less that she was in the same part of the virtual world as Patty?

Patty scrolled along the bottom of the screen for her options and found a "Post a Message" selection. She clicked the icon and selected "For anyone to read." Amelia had been avoiding everyone for months: What could Patty post that would make her come around? A plea for help? A threat?

Suddenly the opportunity her mother had told her to watch out for hit her: She finally knew how to use Focus Girls for good. *Yes!* She almost laughed it was so obvious. She scribbled a note she knew Amelia would answer: *Ameel, my company's in trouble. Need your help. You're the only one smart enough and the only one I trust. SOS. Patty.*

She posted the message on the entrance to the Louvre, then

went inside and perused the paintings. There was something cool about being alone with the *Venus de Milo*, even if it was in HD 3-D.

Suddenly a message popped up on Patty's screen.

AMealYeah:
Hey.

Patty laughed at Amelia's avatar photo; it looked exactly like the real thing, down to the glasses and the hoodie. Patty wrote back:

BrooklynBrush:
Hi!
AMealYeah:
How'd you find out about this?
BrooklynBrush:
I made a new friend. A nice compsci geek who shares my taste in men.
AMealYeah:
LOL. Is T-Bag doing okay?
BrooklynBrush:
I think so. We just had brunch.
AMealYeah:
Delta Gamma brunch?
BrooklynBrush:
Yes.
AMealYeah:
Oh. What's going on with Focus Girls?
BrooklynBrush:
It got shut down
AMealYeah:
What happened?
BrooklynBrush:
Turns out the men were using it to get dates, and

the girls were happily accepting pretty big tips
for their . . . affection.
AMealYeah:
WHAT?

Patty had said it so many times that she was no longer
shocked by the gravity of the situation.

BrooklynBrush:
Yeah. It's been an interesting couple of weeks.
AMealYeah:
Is everything okay? Are you in trouble?
BrooklynBrush:
Yeah, it'll be okay. The police know what it
turned into, but they're not pressing charges.
But I need someone to wipe the database, to
make sure none of the clients or girls' names
are anywhere on the Internet so no one can ever
incriminate them.

Patty watched the screen and then typed what she really
wanted to know.

BrooklynBrush:
When are you coming back?

There was a long pause and Patty held her breath, certain
she'd blown it and waiting to see Amelia's profile drop off the
screen. Virtual Amelia finally replied:

AMealYeah:
I am back.

Patty's first thought was that she meant "virtually," but then
typed skeptically:

BrooklynBrush:
For real? Where?
AMealYeah:
I can't tell you.
BrooklynBrush:
I understand
AMealYeah:
But we should meet and talk about it. I think you
can help me, too.

Patty's heart was beating fast and she wasn't sure whether it was because she'd managed to locate Amelia or because Amelia needed her help.

BrooklynBrush:
Tell me when and where.
AMealYeah:
Medieval history stacks of Green Library? In an
hour?
BrooklynBrush:
I'm on my way.

58

Tangents

"Ow!" Violet snapped, rubbing her arm in overreaction to the man who had just knocked into her, sending her phone skidding on the pavement. "Watch where you're going!"

"So sorry, miss." The old man pulled his briefcase close to him in apology and raced to pick up her phone, toying with the case before he handed it back to her. "Is this one of those new Apple phones?"

She snatched the device back. "An iPhone?" she asked in exasperated impatience. "Yes."

She hated being on campus. It made her think about her own lack of a degree. *You could have had it if you'd wanted it,* she reminded herself, *but instead you have four-hundred-dollar designer boots and a BMW, and they're wearing sweatpants and riding skateboards.* She turned to keep walking toward the Stanford bookstore, where she was going to pick up a book she'd ordered for Adam as part of her new woo-him-with-gifts strategy.

"Miss?" The old man was suddenly at her side, pulling her coat sleeve.

She instinctively pulled her arm away in disgust. The man's wool blazer had a moth hole in its sleeve and was pathetically worn at the lapel; his trousers were too short and accompanied by orthopedic walking shoes. His eyes darted, giving the sense he wasn't all there, and she concluded he must be either homeless or a professor.

"I'm so sorry, Miss," he continued in a surprisingly gruff voice, "I know I'm not the one to be making requests, but could you direct me to the post office?"

She looked at him for a moment, considering, then conceded: "It's right up this way"—she pointed in the same direction she was headed—"just past the bookstore."

"Thank you so much." He gave a little bow in appreciation. "Off to mail my latest article to *The New Yorker*. It's based off some very titillating research."

She studied his face—he looked somehow familiar, and she wondered whether he was one of the great Stanford professors one reads about from time to time in a magazine, half remembering their theories but inevitably forgetting their names. Regardless, her irritation began to melt as they kept in step together toward their respective destinations. *Calm down,* she told herself. *No need to take your anxieties out on this old man.*

"What is your research topic?" she asked.

"The prisoner's dilemma." He offered a sly grin, as if this was the universe's sexiest academic topic.

"Interesting," she said in a tone that said it wasn't, and stopped in front of the bookstore. "Post office is right up there," she said, encouraging him along.

"Thank you so very much, Miss—" He stuck out his hand and waited for her name.

"Weatherford," she said, accepting his grasp, "Violet Weatherford."

"Pleasure, Miss Weatherford. Perhaps I'll see you around sometime."

She retracted her hand from his grip and felt her sentiment shifting back to being creeped out. Nevertheless, she offered a polite smile. "Yes, perhaps." And she headed quickly up the stairs to the bookstore.

59

The Lonely Hearts Club

Stuart Chen checked his watch again. 6:48 P.M. Only two minutes had passed since he'd last checked, and the girl still wasn't late for their seven-o'clock date at The Cheesecake Factory. He needed to be ready for her arrival, though, and focused on how he wanted to look when she came in.

Casual, he thought, slouching in the booth. But doing so made his pleated khaki pants bunch in the waist, and he straightened back up in his chair, thinking about how he'd have to iron them when he got home.

Important, he thought. He needed to look important. He pulled out his BlackBerry, a three-year-old model, and prayed the red light in the corner would start blinking and deliver him something to read. His inbox was, of course, empty, all his e-mails in their respective folders, which he backed up, carefully filed, and erased every Friday at six o'clock before the weekend. Seeing as it was Saturday, he had nothing to look at, and stared instead at the blank Outlook folder.

A waitress startled him. "Can I get you something to drink while you wait?"

"No," he inadvertently snapped, "I won't be waiting much longer."

The waitress lifted her eyebrows and forced a smile, moving on to another table where a mother was trying to calm an unruly toddler throwing crayons at his brother.

Stuart's palms started sweating: Maybe booking this place had been a mistake? He never went out, except when clients took him to fancy restaurants where the absurdity of the prices made him squirm. Ted Bristol was the worst of them all, blowing fifty dollars on a piece of fish and some steamed vegetables. It was unacceptable for anyone, no matter how much money they had, but the irresponsibility was particularly appalling for a man on the verge of bankruptcy.

No, Stuart reassured himself, this was a good choice. There was always a long line out the door, so it must be popular, and it felt youthful, like the last girl he had met through Focus Girls.

6:54.

Of course, that meeting had been more than six weeks ago. He'd liked the girl. They'd met for coffee. But when he'd called the number back to make another appointment, the phone line had been disconnected. He'd tried and tried again and then convinced himself that the girl must have complained—he must have been blacklisted and blocked from making further appointments.

So when he'd gotten a call the other day from the company's founder saying he was one of their most valuable customers and asking him to schedule another appointment, he'd almost dropped the phone.

6:56.

But what if it had been a joke? What if it was a cruel prank? His face flushed with the embarrassment of his high-school self.

No, he told himself. It wasn't. She was supposed to be here at seven o'clock, and women liked to be a little late on top of that, so he still had at least until 7:05 before he needed to panic. It was possible she was already here, he realized; after all, he didn't even know what tonight's girl would look like, let alone her name.

Look important, he reminded himself.

The BlackBerry still wasn't flashing. He saw the game icon

and contemplated: He suddenly had an irresistible urge to play a round of Minesweeper. Yes, he thought, that would calm him down. But what if she caught him? Could he stand that judgment? On the other hand, how would she know what he was doing on his device? As long as he looked focused he'd look important. He opened the app and set up his game strategy.

"Hi," a girl's voice interrupted him. He glanced up at a vivacious blond girl with tanned skin and an athletic build. "Are you Stuart?" she asked confidently.

"Yes." He smiled in relief and joy and stood, shaking her hand and immediately wishing he'd kissed her cheek instead. She wasn't petite like the last girl, which was normally his taste, but she was still very pretty. And she was here, with him, which was the important thing.

"Mind if I sit?" she asked.

"Oh, yes, of course, please," he stammered. He was not doing well.

"Were you playing Minesweeper?" the girl asked, sliding to the middle of the booth across from him and indicating his phone.

Stuart blushed furiously. "Oh, yeah, I just got here a little early and I thought—"

"I love that game," she interrupted, smiling.

"Really?" He perked up in his seat. Maybe this wasn't so bad after all.

"Yeah. One time I clicked the wrong cell and I got so angry that I threw my phone across the room. After that I got into another game and stopped playing as much," she explained.

"That's awesome!" Stuart's face lit up. What luck that he'd found a girl who shared his interest in Minesweeper.

The waitress came back to the table to take their order. "Oh, sure," Stuart said, "I'll have a burger, I guess."

"Which one?" The waitress didn't look up from her pad.

"Oh, are there multiple choices?"

She looked up from the pad, evaluating whether or not he

could actually be serious, and directed him to page seven of twelve in the menu, where two dozen burgers were described.

Stuart's face flushed. "I'll have the Factory Burger, I guess."

"Anything to drink?"

"Oh, a beer, please." He hurried to look at that menu. "This one," he said, and pointed to the first on the list.

"For you?" She turned to the girl.

"I'll have the Maui Chicken Salad, please, and a glass of Chardonnay," the girl said, and he suddenly realized he'd forgotten to ask her name.

"What's your name?" he asked after the waitress left.

"Patricia," she said, smiling coyly.

"It's really nice to meet you, Patricia." He reached across the table to grab her hand, but she'd kept them folded in her lap so he awkwardly squeezed her shoulder instead. Where was that beer?

Stuart and Patricia made it through the dinner with pleasant conversation, mostly carried by her bubbly musings on random pop culture he pretended to know about. By the time the waitress asked if they wanted dessert, he still wasn't sure if he could get her to come home with him, but he didn't want this to end.

He turned to her, nervous about how to proceed. "I could use something sweet, could you?"

"I'd love that." She smiled at the waitress and said, "How about two slices of Oreo cheesecake to go?" Then she turned back to him. "Okay if we get out of here?"

Stuart cocked his eyebrow. "Back to my place?"

"Unless you've got a better idea?" Her flirtatious grin made his heart pound in his chest.

He turned triumphantly to the waitress. "You heard the lady."

"Sure thing," the waitress said, rolling her eyes as she turned.

"I really like you," Stuart said to Patricia.

"Yeah, you too," she answered, downing the rest of her wine.

He paid the check and they headed to the door. "I just live up the street on Hawthorne," he said. "Are you okay to walk?"

"Sure. What's the address?"

"Twenty-seven Hawthorne," he answered, wondering why she needed the address, but she asked so casually he decided it was nothing.

"Great," she said. "Do you mind if I send a super quick text to a friend? I was supposed to meet her a little later, but I'd rather stay with you."

Stuart blushed furiously. "Oh . . . yeah, of course." No woman had ever come on to him like this, and he liked it.

They got back to his apartment and Stuart fumbled to open the door.

"You sit," Patricia insisted, pushing him onto the couch. "I'll take care of the cheesecake. Do you have any booze?"

"There's vodka in the freezer." He got up to help her, but she shooed him back.

"I've got it," she said, taking the to-go bag to the kitchen and returning shortly with a plate of dessert and two glasses of vodka and orange juice. She handed him one and clinked his glass. "Drink up!" she said, smiling.

He took a long sip of the drink and reached to pull her close.

"Nu-unh." She shook her finger. "I need at least one drink to get up my courage."

He smiled: as if this girl needed courage. He drank his drink quickly to encourage her along. A few minutes later, he felt on top of the world.

"Do you dance?" he asked, standing up and grabbing her arm.

"Only after another drink," she answered. "But don't let that stop you."

And it didn't. He stood up and put on music and started swaying, then swaying more. And then the whole room started swaying and he wasn't sure whether it was moving or he was. The CD switched songs, and he gripped the sofa to steady himself. "I think I need to sit down."

Patricia stood up and guided him gently to the couch.

"I don't feel so good," he blurted, belching inadvertently.

"It's okay," she said calmly. "Just lie down."

"You're so calm," he said.

"It's okay, it happens to everyone," Patricia coaxed, guiding his head toward the pillow.

"You're so . . . beautiful." He clumsily brushed her face. "But I'm just so tired all of a sudden." His heavy eyelids fell and his neck relaxed into the throw pillow.

Patty steadily watched him breathing and waited five heavy exhales before she stood up and took a long exhale herself. She ran to the door and opened it for Amelia.

"What took you so long?" Amelia asked. "It's freezing out there."

"He wasn't drinking fast enough," Patty said. "Don't worry, we're good now. Here," she said, guiding her friend through the house. "The office is back here."

According to Dawson, they had two hours from the moment Stuart fell asleep until he'd be fully recovered. It wasn't a drug, she'd been assured, just a mixture of herbs that, when digested alongside alcohol, helped people go to sleep.

Patty couldn't believe it was actually working: that she'd managed to drug a Focus Girls client and that he was actually sleeping now, providing her friend Amelia with full access to his home office and the accounting information Stuart apparently had and Amelia desperately needed.

"Don't jinx it," Amelia said.

"Can I help?"

"Go keep an eye on him—I'll call you if I need you."

Amelia produced her laptop and opened it on Stuart's desk, plugging it into his hard drive, logging in to his computer and quickly hacking past security. His inbox was empty and his hard drive clear. *Weird,* she mouthed.

She looked up from the computer at his bookshelf, where locked boxes were neatly labeled and organized alphabetically.

She found one labeled "Bristol" and pulled it down from the shelf. But the lock was fully secure. She couldn't take the whole box, could she? Picking locks was not part of her security-breaching toolbox.

She scratched her head and wracked her brain for ideas. Where would Stuart keep the keys? Her eyes scanned around the office: Surely he wouldn't keep them in here. She went into the bedroom, equally meticulous in its organization. She pulled open drawers and perused shelves but to no avail.

She finally wondered whether he might keep them on his person and went back into the living room. Stuart was splayed on the couch, his right arm stretched down toward the floor and his mouth open wide. Patty looked at Amelia looking at him and the two girls giggled.

"I think he's got a key with him," she whispered.

Patty tiptoed to his side and reached carefully into his pocket, her right-hand fingers gripping his wallet while she used her left hand to pull the front of the pocket up and extract the billfold. He rustled but didn't wake. She unfolded the wallet. The cards were carefully inserted into their slots and the bills neatly folded. The bottom credit card slot was empty, though, and she felt down inside and discovered a small memory chip. She took it out triumphantly and handed it to Amelia. "This it?"

"Hope so!" Amelia went back into the office and inserted it into her computer.

An Excel file opened with a list of names in one column and combinations in the other. Ted Bristol's was 31-6-36.

What was that for? The box had a key lock, not a code. She looked at her watch. Only fifty minutes left. She had to figure this out fast.

She picked up the metal box labeled "Bristol" again and moved her fingers around it. At the back of the box, down in the corner, she felt a small metal door. She turned the box to get a better look, and slid the metal door open, revealing a combination lock. Of course. The traditional lock was a decoy.

She entered the code assigned to Bristol and the box's lid popped open, revealing a pile of compact discs and hard drives, organized quarterly and going back to the 1990s. She pulled them out and started inserting them into her laptop, starting with the most recent and downloading the data one disc at a time.

She watched the download timer and urged it along, keeping a careful eye on the clock. She had four CDs left when she heard a groan from the front room. Her clock told her she had six minutes left. She stuck in another disk and started putting the others back in place. She was going to have to go without the last three.

"Amelia, he's waking up." Patty was at the office door. "Did you get what you need?"

"Come on!" Amelia yelled at her computer. It finished uploading the disc's contents and she snapped it out and put it back into the box as Patty scrambled to the living room. Amelia closed her laptop and slid it back into her oversize purse, then pushed the Bristol box back into its place and hurried back out to the main room toward the front door.

Wait! She remembered the chip right as she was turning the latch to exit. She sat her laptop down and returned to the office, finding the chip on the desk where she left it. She tiptoed back to Stuart.

"What are you doing?" Patty whisper-yelled.

"The chip!" Amelia said, sliding it into place in his wallet. He groaned and slung his arm across his torso, almost knocking her down as he turned onto his side.

"Forget it," Patty snapped. "We have to go."

Amelia ignored her. "I'm not letting you get in trouble for this," she snapped back at her friend. Amelia waited a moment before going for his pocket, carefully opening it to make room for the wallet.

His eyes snapped open and he gripped her shoulders so tight she couldn't move her arms.

"Oh, you're a sneaky little thing, aren't you, Patricia?"

Her face went white with fear. She literally couldn't move under his grip.

"Wait for me to fall asleep so you can take off my pants?" He grinned greedily and pulled her head down to meet his lips.

She pushed away with all her strength before his open mouth touched hers. She scrambled off the couch and searched the floor for her shoes. Stuart grunted from the couch, grumbling something about how he couldn't get up.

Amelia picked up her bag and followed Patty out to the street, letting the door slam behind them as they ran up Hawthorne to the bus stop. Neither girl exhaled until the bus doors closed, and they looked at each other in shocked triumph.

Patty burst into laughter, her face exuberant. "Oh my God! We did it!"

Amelia laughed helplessly, too, and without thinking pulled Patty into a hug. "Thank you so much," she gasped.

"No," Patty said, "thank you—this made it all worth it."

They took a seat, ignoring the staring passengers. "Did you get what you need?" Patty asked.

Amelia glanced at her computer bag, which now had the information she needed to understand Ted Bristol's full involvement with Doreye, and how to get it back from him. "Yeah," she said. "We're good."

Guess Who's Coming to Dinner?

"Open it!" Violet encouraged from her side of the table. She was wearing a sleeveless purple sheath dress and a long silver necklace. She'd made up her face and pulled her hair back in a curled ponytail. Her pink lips shimmered in the candlelight, and Adam was having a hard time focusing on anything else.

Violet had been particularly affectionate and doting lately. They'd even finally made out, and it was awesome. She kissed like someone who really knew what she was doing, and Adam couldn't stop thinking about taking it to the next level.

Adam pulled the red ribbon to undo the bow on the gift she'd presented him after the waiter cleared their entrées.

Violet took another sip of wine and her lips smiled on the edge of the glass as she kept her eyes on Adam's reaction to her present.

"You really shouldn't have done this." Adam grinned back.

"Don't be silly." Violet shooed the thought away with her long, thin arm. "I'm thrilled to be the one that gets to celebrate with you."

They were celebrating the new Doreye update, which included a new array designed to capture and transmit user data in a simple form. Violet had supplied him with the code and the instructions, and, just like that, Adam's revenue-generation problem was solved. The update had been submitted to Apple for their final review before releasing through the App Store, but the guys at Apple had assured Adam that, as the most popular app in history, an approval for Doreye shouldn't take long.

"I wouldn't be here without you, you know." Adam paused his unwrapping and looked Violet square in the eye. She'd made her eyes look even bigger and brighter than normal, and he stared into them purposefully, trying to capture her full attention so that she would know how much he was starting—he thought—to really love her.

Her recent affection convinced him that her earlier withdrawing had been his doing. Last month when he felt like they weren't going anywhere—like it was all flirting and no action— that was all *his* fault. He'd been hanging on to Lisa, not giving himself fully to Violet, and she'd picked up on that. Now, though, he was done with Lisa Bristol. Violet Weatherford was the new thing. The right girlfriend for the COO of a profitable company. And she was *hot.*

"Come on," she said, reaching across the table and sliding her fingers up his arm, squeezing his bicep affectionately. "Open it!"

Adam laughed confidently and refocused his attention. "Okay, okay." He peeled back the paper with a hand sweating nervously from the sensation of her touch and what it implied for later.

"*Paths to Power,*" he read the title of the book, "by Jeffrey Pfeffer." He turned the book over to read its back jacket.

"He's a professor at Stanford's business school. His research is totally brilliant: all about how to create more power for yourself as you build your career."

Adam smiled at the book, letting the feeling of power accumulation settle and stir in his veins. He transferred the smile up to Violet and, without thinking, pushed himself across the table and kissed her lips. Her lips responded in kind.

"Is having a gorgeous girlfriend part of it?" he asked before he sat back.

"Yes," she said, "but you must listen to everything she says."

"Thank you," he said as he dropped back into his chair.

She smiled for a moment, then looked back down at the dessert menu on the table. "So should we order the chocolate soufflé?"

"Isn't it amazing?" Adam wasn't through reflecting. "To think that this time a year ago—it was just during spring quarter—Amelia and I had just lost our scholarships? That's why she agreed to join the incubator, you know—so she could stay at Stanford." He chuckled, thinking back on her pouting. "God, she didn't want to do it."

"Well, she shouldn't have sent that letter to TechCrunch. For that matter, she shouldn't have hacked into Gibly," Violet said without looking up from the menu. "Maybe we should have the panna cotta instead?"

Adam thought about that objectively: Maybe it was wrong of Amelia to have hacked into Gibly. He could understand Ted's frustration now, thinking about how upset he'd be if someone hacked into Doreye and jumped to conclusions about its business practices, and then used those presumptions to expose delicate information. He'd be as angry as Ted was at Amelia.

"Wait." Something in his brain clicked, and he looked at Violet. "How did you know about Amelia's letter to TechCrunch?" The whole thing had been anonymous: Amelia had made sure of it.

"Don't be ridiculous. Everyone knows," Violet answered without missing a beat. "Where is the waiter? Don't you have to give twenty minutes' notice for the soufflé?"

"Oh." Adam let that sink in. Everyone knew Amelia had written the article?

"Can we have the soufflé and the panna cotta?" Violet asked the waiter, smiling at Adam. "And two glasses of something sweet? We're celebrating."

The waiter nodded. "Of course, Mademoiselle," he said, and took the menu.

"Why didn't TechCrunch ever contact her, then?" Wouldn't Adam have heard if everyone knew?

"What?" Violet looked irritated. "Are we still talking about this?"

"I mean, it was all over *The Wall Street Journal*. If it was common knowledge, why didn't anyone contact Amelia?"

"Maybe they did and you just don't know. She had a habit of keeping secrets from you, didn't she?" Violet's voice was starting to lose its casual evenness.

Adam took a sip of his drink, realizing he was dangerously close to spoiling his chances of hooking up tonight.

"Not like you're talking to her these days," Violet muttered under her breath.

Adam couldn't help himself: "And whose fault is that?"

"Yours, Adam," Violet snapped, her voice on the edge of desperation and rage. The people at the next table looked up. "It's your fault," she hissed. "All of it's your fault."

Adam's mouth fell open, taken aback by her tone. She'd been sarcastic before, but never mean.

Her eyes suddenly looked panicked. She quickly pushed herself across the table and kissed his mouth, recovering her old tone. "I'm sorry, Adam," she tried. "Talking about your sister just . . . always seems to upset you, and . . . and I want this night to be perfect. For you."

Adam swallowed, pulling his jaw back into place. "Of course," he said softly.

The waiter arrived with their dessert and two cocktail concoctions, and Violet lifted hers in a toast: "To Adam, and Doreye, and your new revenue."

Adam clinked her glass and took a deep sip, willing the drink to return him to his previous state of blissful confidence.

As he put down his drink, though, he caught Violet looking over his shoulder.

"Oh, Mr. Dory, you have not been following the advice I gave you at our lunch," a gruff voice Adam recognized whispered into his ear. Adam, startled, turned to find an old man he quickly registered as Professor Marsh pulling a chair up to the table. Marsh took a seat between Violet and himself.

Violet looked quizzically at the man, studying his face. "From campus the other day," she whispered to herself. She looked nauseous.

She hurriedly grabbed her purse and pulled out her iPhone, lifting the cover off it and staring at a tiny sticker on the back. She glanced up at Marsh, serious. Her chest heaved with panic.

"As they say in the movies, we can do this the easy way or the hard way," Marsh said quietly but firmly.

Adam watched Violet's eyes dart, like a chess player deciding her next move. Finally she picked her chin up and looked at Marsh directly. "Sir, we are trying to have dinner, if you don't mind."

"Professor Marsh, what are you doing here?" Adam was beyond confused.

"There is a car waiting for you outside, Miss . . . Weatherford?" Marsh opened up his tweed jacket and removed a card from his wallet. Once he slid it across the table Adam could see that it had Marsh's photo and said in large letters CENTRAL INTELLI-GENCE AGENCY. He looked up at Marsh in shock: Were the rumors about him true?

"You have nothing," Violet said as if reading a line, the color only half returning to her cheeks. "Even with your stupid tracking chip." She gestured to the phone. "Kudos for the clever move, though." She lifted her cocktail.

"I thought so," Marsh said, grinning and chuckling softly. "But you're wrong: I do have something. We know you work for VIPER, and we have quite a few questions to ask you."

Adam's heart raced: Was Marsh a CIA agent spying on Violet? His brain searched for where he'd heard of VIPER. As if clicking through memories of the past year, Adam suddenly registered the name: VIPER was the company Amelia uncovered as making mystery payments for Gibly.

"VIPER," he repeated aloud.

"Mr. Dory," Marsh said, turning to Adam, "have you ever asked your friend here about her friends back in England? We have reason to believe that VIPER is engaged in activities that might be considered cyberterrorism."

Adam looked at Violet, horrified. "But Violet works for Aleister," he tried. "The company who Doreye just . . ." Was VIPER the data buyer she'd arranged?

She was paying him no attention, though, instead staring at Marsh with her jaw set, studying his face and weighing her options.

Finally she stood smoothly and calmly from her seat. She brushed the front of her dress and folded her napkin and lifted her jacket from the back of the chair around her shoulders.

"Well?" she said to Marsh, who rose to escort her. He held her elbow firmly but gently out the door.

It didn't occur to Adam to tell them to wait until they were already gone, and he sat, stunned, staring at the white tablecloth. He hadn't ever questioned Violet's code or her buyer. But if the buyer was VIPER, and Apple approved the updated app, then Doreye would be capable of doing exactly what Amelia risked everything to keep Gibly from doing. He had to stop his new app from being released. And fast.

"I'll take this whenever you're ready," the waitress whispered quietly, sliding a silver tray with the dinner bill next to his half-eaten soufflé.

61

The Shell Game

The door slammed and Amelia jumped. She was still on a nervous high from the evening with Stuart, and sitting here with Dawson, a paroled criminal, reading confidential financial statements she'd stolen from an accountant she drugged in his own home while her friend posed as a prostitute wasn't making her any less paranoid.

"Amelia?" Patty's voice called as her head popped through the door. "I hope sushi's okay." She entered the room with two bags of takeout in hand.

"This is Mr. Dawson," Amelia told Patty, indicating her foster father, who stood up to shake her hand.

"Patty Hawkins." She shook his hand. "Nice to meet you."

"Pleasure's all mine," he returned. "Do you really know this guy?" He tilted his forehead to the evidence he and Amelia were plowing through.

"Who? Ted Bristol? Yeah, we're old family friends. He coached my first-grade soccer team." Family relation or no, she couldn't resist a scandal: Her eyes got wide and she blurted excitedly, sitting down on the floor beside Amelia and adjusting her skirt, "What'd you find on him?"

Dawson crossed his arms and stroked his chin theatrically.

"Well, so far, insider trading and a lot of draft bankruptcy filings."

"Bankruptcy filings?" Patty's brow furrowed. "Ted's not bankrupt."

"You'd be surprised," Dawson mused, handing her a sheet of paper as he continued, "Turns out just before the Gibly sale was announced to the public, Ted Bristol spent all of his money—literally every last available cent—propping up the company."

"What? Why?"

"Well, according to this e-mail here"—Dawson pointed at another sheet of paper—"he confirmed the terms of the sale with the Aleister Corporation at 3:32 P.M.; he bought up the shares by 5:48 P.M.; the sale was announced to the public at 7:04 P.M."

"But isn't that . . ."

"Illegal? Yes. It's called insider trading. He was trying to get more bang for his buck." Dawson smiled at Patty. "Take it from me, it was a brilliant move. I would never have been able to pull off something like that. He would have gotten away with it, too, except—"

"Gibly fell apart, right? My dad lost a ton of money, too."

"But I bet your dad didn't lose everything." Mr. Dawson picked up a few printouts. "Look: Bristol is selling his homes to pay off his debts. He's living in the red. He took a huge gamble and failed because he didn't expect someone like Amelia Dory to come along." Dawson looked at Amelia with a glimmer of fatherly pride.

"There's something else, Patty." Amelia held up a piece of paper. "Ted is the owner of Doreye. Like, he owns fifty-one point four percent of the company."

When they'd gotten together in the stacks to discuss how to get to Stuart Chen, Amelia hadn't explained why she needed Ted Bristol's information, just that she did, and that Stuart, whom Amelia found to be an old Focus Girls client, had it.

"Nobody knows because he used a bunch of shell companies."

"But where did Ted find the money to invest in Doreye? I thought you said he was filing for bankruptcy?"

Dawson nodded. "Who knows—maybe he borrowed money to do it, or sold one of their houses or something?"

"I haven't found anything like that, though," Amelia said, disheartened.

"Amelia," Patty consoled, "take a break and eat your dinner." She turned to Dawson, holding out a platter of ornate sashimi. "Want some? I overordered."

"Sure," he said, pulling out his wallet.

"It's on me," Patty chirped, waving away his attempt to contribute.

Dawson smirked. "Where does a college girl get money to buy gourmet sushi?"

"Well," Patty said, grinning, "I was once the proud owner of a very lucrative escort service. But these days it all just comes from my trust fund."

Patty turned to Amelia to see if she laughed at the joke, but stopped when she saw her friend's face change.

Amelia sat up in her chair and her eyes darted back and forth as though she were looking at something hanging in the air. "That's it," she whispered. She turned back to the computer and hurriedly searched through Stuart Chen's files.

"Amelia, what is it?" Patty was suddenly at her side.

"The trust," Amelia said, only her lips moving. She clicked to open a file.

"What?"

"On the third disk I downloaded, remember how we couldn't figure out why T.J.'s trust instrument was in the documents?"

"You think he stole from his son's trust?"

"It wouldn't be stealing," Amelia reasoned. She opened up the file that contained megabytes of e-mail correspondence between Ted Bristol and Stuart Chen and used a PERL script she'd written to search for language that would answer their questions.

"Let me see." Dawson pulled the keyboard from Amelia. "I think you're right." He clicked through the files, nodding as he read the language aloud. "Jesus, that's good." He sat back with a satisfied grin.

"Did you figure it out? Does it say who owns Doreye?"

"T.J.'s trust fund owns Doreye," Mr. Dawson explained. "I tried this once but got caught. Of course, I didn't have the expertise to set up a shell company like your friend Ted Bristol." Dawson went on: "Being a trustee of his son's fund allows Ted to invest as he sees fit. So this guy Ted, he took money from T.J.'s trust fund and invested it in Doreye. This way, if or when Doreye has a pop in value—let's say it sells or something—he takes all the profits and filters them through the shell company, then puts the original amount back into the trust fund like none of it ever happened."

"But if it's T.J.'s trust that owns it, why doesn't T.J. just give Amelia back the company?" Patty demanded. "Problem solved?"

"I'm not an expert in these things," Dawson replied, "but it's not T.J.'s until the trust is activated. Until then the trustee controls it, who I have to imagine is solely Ted."

"So Ted is stealing from T.J.?" Patty couldn't believe it. Ted Bristol wasn't her favorite person, but he was her parents' friend and T.J. and Lisa's dad. "This isn't possible."

"Anything's possible when you're desperate." Amelia thought about her own situation, being connected yet again with Dawson. "You've got to talk to T.J.," she said, turning to Patty.

"What about Adam?" Patty asked. "Does he know any of this yet?"

Amelia looked uncomfortably at Dawson. "Adam's the worst part of all this," she told Patty. "You know that new girlfriend Adam has? Violet? She works for Ted."

"Hmph." Patty was silent for a moment. "And here I thought I was the only one pimping out girls in Palo Alto."

"I need you to talk to T.J., Patty. Find out the last time he looked at his trust. Maybe there's another explanation for this."

Patty put her jacket on and flung her arms around Amelia. "Don't worry," she whispered in her ear, "I'm on it."

62

Caged Animal

Violet pushed her face between the bars and pouted at the guard until he looked up from his desk.

"What is it, Miss Weatherford?" he sighed, looking back down at his paperwork.

"Can you get me something from my purse?" she said in a baby voice. "Pretty, pretty please?"

"You know I'm not allowed to do that." The guard didn't look up, but she could see him blush.

"I just need my nail polish," she said. "How am I going to cause any trouble with nail polish?"

"You're about to be extradited to Britain, where you will probably spend many years in jail. Maybe you should be thinking about that instead?"

"I am thinking about that, but," she said, jutting her hands through the bars and flipping her hands up so he could see her fingernails, "they're going to put me in the papers first, and I can't bear for my last public image to be a girl with chipped nails."

The guard couldn't resist a chuckle, and she smiled at her accomplishment. He sighed and pushed himself up from his chair, removing the polish from her handbag and passing it into the cell. "Be quick about it, though; Roy's back in an hour and he won't like it."

"I could kiss you." She tossed him an air-kiss and went back to the bench to apply the bright red lacquer. She hummed as she did so, admiring her handiwork.

The guard shook his head, confused by her good mood. He tried to do his paperwork, but he wasn't used to having beautiful women under his watch. He looked for something to say: "You know you get a phone call, right?"

She nodded from her perch, and then looked up. "Oh, yes! That reminds me." She stood up and came back to the bars, careful not to mess up her fingernails. She'd unzipped the orange jumpsuit as far as it could go and tied a piece of string around the waist to accentuate her curves. And it worked: She actually made the jail uniform sexy. "Can you look up the number for Spruce?"

"What?"

"It's a restaurant, in San Francisco. I need to call them."

"Your one call is to a restaurant?"

"It's near impossible to get a reservation at any reasonable hour unless you call right when they open their books three weeks before the date. So I need to call." She glanced at the clock. "*Now*," she emphasized, "if I'm going to get in."

"In three weeks you'll be in England," he pointed out. "In jail." She still didn't seem fazed. "For cyberterrorism," he reminded her, as if speaking to a child.

"No matter," Violet chirped.

He stared at her, not sure whether to find her carelessness sexy or unnerving.

"You can't tell me who I can or can't call, Larry." She pouted her lips again, and his heart welled helplessly hearing her say his name.

"I know." He handed her the phone and went back to his desk to look up the number for Spruce.

"Hello?" she said into the phone after she dialed. "Hello, yes. I'd like to make a dinner reservation for two, three weeks from today, at seven o'clock. The name? Dory: D-O-R-Y."

63

Trust Me

"T.J.!" Patty ran across the parking lot to catch him. It was raining softly and T.J. had pulled up the hood of his sweatshirt as he ducked from the gym back to his car. He turned when he heard his name.

"T.J.!" she repeated, putting her hand on his shoulder and leaning over to catch her breath, lifting the other finger to signal she needed a minute.

"Come on." He pulled his arm around her and led her to his car. "Get in out of the rain."

She opened the door to the passenger seat and sank into T.J.'s BMW, squinting her nose at the thick smell of spicy cologne.

"Do you wear cologne to the gym?" she blurted through her heavy breathing.

"No," he said, and looked at her defensively, then admitted, "the bottle spilled in the back."

She laughed, and he rolled his eyes. "I need to get it cleaned, I just haven't had time, okay?"

"Too busy playing video games?" She couldn't resist.

He punched her arm. "Owwww!" She kept giggling.

When she finally caught her breath, she said, "I need to talk to you."

"Evidently."

"It's about Amelia."

His brain clenched and he sat forward in the driver's seat. "Did you find her?" He didn't care whether his voice sounded desperate. Lately that's how he felt.

"Yes," she said, "but that's not the point. She broke—I mean, we—well, we've found something is up with Doreye."

T.J. shook his head. "Tell me something I don't know." Doreye was all T.J. had been thinking about . . . except, of course, Amelia. "Wait, Amelia knows?"

"Yeah." Patty nodded anxiously. "And she figured out who the mystery investor is. She knows who owns Doreye."

"Who?" His heart was beating faster than it had been when he was working out.

"Your father."

"What?" He could feel his head starting to spin.

"Your father."

"I heard what you said," T.J. snapped, "but how is that possible?"

Patty shrugged. "You tell me."

"But why would he want to own Doreye? He hates Amelia." A million questions suddenly flooded his mind. "And why would he go to so much trouble to keep it a secret?"

"Because of where he got the money."

"What do you mean? He has the money."

"He's bankrupt, T.J. After Gibly he filed for bankruptcy."

T.J. gripped the wheel in silence, bracing himself for the next question but already knowing the answer. "So where did he get the money?"

"He used your trust fund, T.J.," she said quietly. "When was the last time you looked at it?"

T.J. shook his head, unable to believe he'd signed those papers. He still didn't understand the trap his father set, but he knew now he'd walked right into it. "I don't have permission to see or do anything with my trust until I'm forty," T.J. answered. "Believe me, I've tried."

"Well, your trust owns fifty-one percent of Doreye, so if you got control of it, you could give it back to Amelia."

"Well, I can't do that, Patty," he said angrily. "So long as my parents are alive."

Patty wasn't fazed by his meanness. "There's one more thing," she continued. "That girl Adam is always with—Violet? Amelia thinks she works for your dad. And that someone's paying her to manipulate Adam."

"What?" T.J. turned toward her. "I can believe my father is shady and desperate and conniving . . . but he wouldn't seriously hire someone to . . ."

"When was the last time Amelia was wrong about something like this?"

T.J. stopped. Violet was a constant presence at the Doreye headquarters. She was always at Adam's side. Some of the engineers had started calling her "Lady MacDory." And she was even the one who . . . T.J. could feel sweat collect on his forehead. It was all so clear: She was the one who had connected Doreye with the cloud-computing company, and she was the one who had found a buyer for Doreye's user data. A move that made sense if you wanted to turn a quick profit and then . . .

"Oh my God," T.J. croaked. "I have to call Adam." T.J.'s hands fumbled as he picked up his phone and pressed Adam's contact number. He connected his phone to his car's hands-free system. The call was answered on the second ring. "Adam?"

"T.J.? What, uh—" Adam's voice was already shaking as it filled the car. It sounded like Adam was on edge. "Sorry, I've been tied up and haven't gotten to . . ."

"We need to talk about Violet."

Patty and T.J. heard breathing on the other end of the line.

"What did you hear?" Adam finally replied, and then more aggressively, desperately, "Tell me what you heard about Violet."

"Adam, I don't think her intentions are what you think they are."

"No shit they aren't, T.J.!" Adam snapped. "Is that some kind of a touchy-feely way of telling me that she's a fucking terrorist?"

Patty's eyes widened and she stared at T.J. "Is he crazy?" she whispered.

T.J.'s brow squinted but he spoke calmly into the receiver. "Hey, Adam. Maybe you should take a moment to calm down. We can talk about this another time." He looked to Patty for reassurance that was the right thing to say. "Why don't I come in and—"

"We don't have any more time, T.J." Adam sounded like he was going to cry. "It's going to happen, and I can't stop it."

"What's going to happen, Adam?"

"The code! The app update! What they couldn't do with Gibly, they're going to do with Doreye."

"What are you talking about?" T.J. insisted as patiently as he could.

"You don't know?" Adam's tone changed immediately. "Why did you call me to talk about Violet?"

"She works for my father, Adam. I think he hired her to . . ." He hesitated to tell Adam given his state. "To manipulate you."

"What?" Adam's voice got soft. "Ted's in on this, too?"

"Adam," T.J. said quietly, "what happened?"

"I was at dinner with Violet last night. And Marsh—you know Professor Marsh? He arrested her. All those rumors on campus about him are true: He works for the CIA. I saw his badge. He shows up at dinner, flashes it, and then takes her away."

"What do you mean? Why would she be arrested?"

"I thought she was a successful consultant." Adam sounded like he was hyperventilating. "But she's . . ." He struggled to say it. "She's somehow connected to an organization called VIPER. It's the same company Amelia uncovered with—"

"With Gibly," T.J. interrupted, remembering the TechCrunch article from a year ago and the fallout that ensued.

"Marsh said that VIPER might be some kind of a cyberterrorist organization. Well, Violet's code is in the Doreye app, and as soon as it's approved it's going to expose tens of millions of people to *whatever* VIPER is."

"Calm down," T.J. counseled. "I think I know what to do. Go get some breakfast and chill. I'll call you back in an hour."

T.J. hung up the phone and turned to Patty. "Where's Amelia?"

Patty hesitated. "I can't tell you."

T.J. slammed his hand into the steering wheel and his voice intensified, saying, "I'm not messing around, Patty. Where's Amelia?"

"I'll show you," she conceded softly as he turned on the ignition. Then she added more firmly, "But, T.J., do *not* screw this up. She cares about you."

"And I care about her," he snapped, feeling the full force of his admission. "Now call her and tell her what's going on. She's got to hack into Apple's approval hub and scramble the new code. We haven't got much time."

"What are you going to do?"

"I need to call an attorney. I think I know how to give Doreye back to Amelia."

64

Old Habits

"How's it coming?" Patty asked as she entered the house.

"You're going to have to give me time," Amelia snapped without looking up from the computer, her voice flustered.

"Sorry," Patty mouthed silently, looking to Dawson, who shrugged his shoulders. The two were helpless: It was up to Amelia to hack into Apple and fix the code. All they could do was watch and bring her coffee she didn't drink and hope she was the computer-science phenomenon they all believed she was.

Amelia stared at the screen, but her thoughts were on Adam. The reality of all that had happened was starting to sink in. For the past year she'd seen her brother change, and she always feared that his ambition would cause him to do something wrong. Amelia shuddered to realize how correct those fears were. She'd never not listen to her instincts again.

From what she could learn about VIPER, if the app update went through, then Doreye would become a vehicle for an event unlike any the world had seen. Tens of millions of phones would be compromised: bank accounts, credit cards, address books, locations . . . everything personal and private would be available to VIPER. The entire country could become paralyzed—or worse.

Amelia blamed herself. She felt it was her responsibility to convince her brother to be more careful and to not rush into things. They were supposed to complement each other; she was supposed to be the yin to his yang. They were a team. They were the Dorii. She should have fought harder to keep them together.

Her fingers hadn't moved in several minutes, and she was clenching her jaw to hold back tears.

"You okay?" Dawson noticed the quiet from the keyboard.

She shook her head silently without turning around.

"Oh, Amelia, what's wrong?" Patty was at her side.

"It's all my fault." Amelia's voice cracked.

"What's your fault?" Patty's voice was an impression of her mother's soothing her after a time-out. She sat on the desk to face Amelia.

"Adam. I should have stopped him."

"From what?" Patty coaxed.

"From spending time with Violet. From getting to know her. From being influenced by her."

Patty rubbed Amelia's arm. "Honey, Adam was going to do whatever he was going to do. You couldn't have done anything to prevent it." Patty waited a second, then kneeled down next to Amelia so they were both facing the computer screen. "But this," she said, pointing at the computer, "this is something you can control."

Amelia swallowed and nodded. "You're right." Her chest heaved one last time, and she shook her head rapidly as if to shake out any remaining sadness and distraction.

Patty left her side as Amelia began typing again. Dawson gave her a silent thumbs-up, and Patty matched it with a silent "Whew!"

Two hours later, Amelia had figured out a way to daisy-chain into Apple's complicated security infrastructure and access their application update approval hub. She found the Doreye application and searched for its status.

"Did T.J. say how many approval steps there are?" Amelia asked out loud.

Patty jumped in her chair, where she was reading a *Vanity Fair* article on her iPad in an attempt to pass the time calmly. "I'll call him." She jumped at the opportunity to be useful.

"Never mind," Amelia said, finding the answer.

"What'd you find?"

"The new app is currently under review by a team in Mumbai. It's on step four of six in the Apple system. It looks like most apps have gotten through the last two approval steps in less than a day."

"Does it matter?" Dawson pointed out. "You should focus on fixing the code, not on the timer. It's irrelevant. You either fix it in time or you don't."

Amelia said softly, "Not exactly."

"What do you mean?"

"There are two ways to fix the code. But one takes longer than the other."

"Do the faster one," Dawson exclaimed, dumbfounded.

"The faster way is to put a lethal corruption on top of the bad code, so that it doesn't work at all."

"So do that," he said, and then added, "Am I missing something? I don't understand the problem."

"If that happens, Apple will reject it, flag it, and then put Doreye under review. The company could lose its status as an app publisher, and Apple may freeze every Doreye app from every smartphone," she explained. "The company will be finished, and Adam will get blamed."

"You can't seriously be trying to protect Adam right now." Dawson's jaw dropped.

Patty's face was pale and she glanced from Amelia to Dawson, trying to find a way to help. "What's the alternative?" she asked Amelia.

"To go back and undo the new code. And add something simple so Apple can justify the update submission."

"I'm sorry, wasn't your entire point in all this to get control of Doreye again?" Dawson couldn't let the first point go. "And wouldn't the fact that Doreye released bad code under Adam's direction give investors a perfectly valid reason to fire him and reinstate you?"

Amelia shook her head. "That's cheating. That's not how I want to play."

Dawson stood up from his chair. "You have got to be kidding me!" he shouted. "Are you seriously going to be self-righteous *now*? After everything you've found? Look at where being a good guy has gotten you, Amelia." He gestured around the musty house. "Quit being so naïve."

Amelia's head didn't move, but her lower eyelids tightened into a squint at Dawson. She studied him and her mind raced through her childhood and the past year and who he was and who she wanted to be.

"Patty." She finally spoke, turning to her friend. "You speak French, right?"

Patty nodded. "Why?"

"The next person to approve is a man named Laurent Solanet, based in Paris." Amelia wrote it down on a piece of scrap paper and handed it to Patty. "Think you can distract him? I need at least a day to undo the bad code. If there's a way to keep him from getting to it today, we should be okay."

"I'm on it." Patty took the paper and went into the next room.

Amelia turned back to her computer.

"This is unbelievable." Dawson couldn't let up. "Do I need to remind you that if this app goes out, it's an act of terrorism? That's worse shit than I ever did! You don't pull this off, your precious little company is going to be destroyed, right after the man who's spent the past year trying to screw you over runs away with all the profit?"

"No."

"No what?"

"No, you don't need to remind me," she said simply.

"Listen, Amelia." He'd stood from his chair and was at her side, towering over her, his jaw set. "I came all the way out here to help you. I broke my parole and did a lot of illegal things. Not to mention all the illegal things you've done. And now you've got an easy fix and you're risking it for both of us to save the brother that betrayed you?"

"What do you want?" Amelia asked without emotion.

"My job here is done, Amelia. I didn't come out here with you because I wanted whatever percent of your company you promised me. I came out here because after a few years in jail it sounded like real excitement. And, while we're being honest"—Dawson's voice kept rising—"because after my actions landed you in juvie, maybe I felt like I owed you something. Maybe I thought I could be a good person and help the girl that was supposed to be my daughter."

"I know," Amelia coolly replied. "I know that's why you came."

She could see his face flush at the admission and her validation of it.

"But now if this blows up and I don't get back to Indiana to meet with my parole officer . . . I go back to jail."

"You aren't going back to jail," she said. "And your parole officer isn't checking up on you anymore."

"What are you talking about?"

Amelia turned to her computer and pulled up the U.S. Correctional Facility database. She typed in Dawson's Social Security number and a screen appeared with a simple phrase:

No criminal offenses.
No misdemeanor offenses other than minor traffic violations.

"I cleared your record," she answered. "I'm letting you start your life again. Although I left your parking tickets on file. It didn't seem totally credible otherwise."

Dawson stared at the screen and then at Amelia, his brows lifted in disbelief. "You did?"

"You deserve another chance," she said. "I guess I think everyone does."

Dawson swallowed and stuck out his hand to shake hers. "Thank you," he said with meaning, his eyes glassy.

"You're welcome," Amelia answered. "You would have been a really good dad, you know," she said, meaning it. "Now will you please let me get back to programming?"

Dawson laughed and nodded.

Amelia turned back to her computer and started typing furiously, her mind entering the trance of programming she loved most.

65

Full Circle

"Hey," Arjun's voice said through the phone.

"What's up?" Adam asked, trying to sound casual and wondering whether he shouldn't have picked up on the first ring and if that was the tone he was aiming for.

"Good news." Arjun's voice was cheerful. "Apple approved the update!"

Adam's heart sank into his stomach and his forehead dropped to his desk with a thud. He stared at the carpet, noticing a loop of wool that had pulled up from the others. The contemplation of anything beyond that carpet suddenly felt beyond his grasp.

"Hello? Adam?" the voice said in the phone.

"Yeah," Adam's voice answered in a daze, "I'm here."

"Dude, are you okay?"

"Hmph," Adam grunted, immobile, his stomach churning with nausea. The app had been approved. Should he face the feds directly or try to run?

"Are you sure? Because there's something else," Adam heard Arjun say.

He pushed himself up and leaned forward on his elbows, supporting his heavy head in his hand, clicking the phone to speaker and throwing it on the desk. "What is it?" He braced himself, hot tears pushing under his eyeballs.

"Well, it's the code."

Adam winced.

"I was looking through the report from Apple, and all their comments were about the addition of code that lets you opt into a friend-finding tracker. It didn't say anything about the new line that saves information for the database."

Adam wasn't listening to Arjun's words, thinking instead about how much user data was currently being tracked and stored and probably already milled by crazy bad guys.

"At first I thought maybe they'd sent us the wrong report, but then I called this guy in France in charge of the approval, and he showed me what he was looking at, and"—he hesitated—"Adam, it's not the same code we submitted."

He was thinking about jail and about his name on the front of magazines as the villain of Internet security, the one who had started the unraveling of the world's trust in Silicon Valley. Would he end up in white-collar prison or go to Gitmo?

"Did you hear me?" Arjun asked. "Adam, what Apple approved isn't what we submitted."

"What?" Adam finally registered the statement and sat up in his chair, lifting the phone back up to his ear. "What do you mean?"

"I don't know what I mean, just that what I'm looking at has nothing to do with preserving user data. The database is completely gone. All the code we've been working on . . . the code you gave us to follow from Violet . . . It simply isn't here."

Adam felt the blood rush back to his face. "You mean Apple didn't approve the code that tracked user data?"

"I mean they never even got it *to* approve. All they approved is this new opt-in GPS friend finder. The same thing you've got on your iPhone now, just a lot faster and easier to use. It's actually really gorgeous code—I wish I could claim that I'd done it."

Adam felt a lump drop through his throat and into his stomach. "Arjun, I gotta go."

"But I want to figure out—"

"Yeah, we'll figure it out. Just take the weekend off, okay? You deserve it."

Adam hung up the iPhone and laid it flat in front of him. He tapped his contacts folder and slowly, deliberately, scrolled to Amelia's number.

He took a deep breath and composed a text message, but he couldn't bring himself to send it. He sat up and let his heart return to its regular rhythm. He needed to get some air.

Adam's right knee ached. It felt like bone was rubbing against bone in the joint socket, but he didn't care. He kept running, starting his second loop of campus drive.

He was relieved, of course, that the code had been fixed before Doreye became a party to whomever it was Violet arranged on the other end of the deal. There was a little voice in his head that, half-convincingly, pointed out that he didn't necessarily know the buyer was VIPER. Even if Violet was a criminal—which was yet to be proven—it didn't necessarily mean *this* deal was criminal.

But even Adam knew better than to be defensive at a time like this, and forced the voice out of his mind.

What he could not force out of his mind, and what he chose instead to try to figure out by running, was an undeniable frustration that it had been Amelia who had, again, bailed him out.

He didn't know the details, but he knew enough: Amelia figured out Violet's sketchy past and hacked into Apple to save the day. She'd disappeared and dropped out of the spring quarter only to return to save him, and hadn't even bothered to call to let him know.

Not that he would have answered.

And that, really, was what made it all so bad, wasn't it? That he'd bought so much into his own hype, gotten so caught up in his obsession to succeed without his sister, Amelia, that he couldn't see the obvious mistakes in front of him, or hear the voices of reason trying to get through.

The sun was setting and the road was dark as he jogged past the driving range and turned onto Junipero Serra Boulevard. Cars passed, blinding him with their headlights. *What if one of these cars hit me?* his inner voice whispered. *Would anyone notice? Would the world be any worse off?*

He ran faster to get past the stretch with the cars and back onto campus. He came up to the SAE house but didn't stop: There was more to think about.

"Mind if I join you?" a man in a gray sweatsuit appeared at his side.

Adam jumped in surprise and made a face he hoped the man didn't see. "Sure," he mumbled, not sure how to say no despite how much he wanted to be alone.

"Great night for a jog, huh?"

"Uh-huh," Adam said curtly.

"California's great for that. Don't get much weather like this in Indiana."

Adam's feet skidded to a stop. He knew that voice. The man stopped, too, and faced him, pushing the hood of his sweatshirt back with a grin.

"Hope I didn't scare you too bad. It was always a secret hope of mine we'd be able to run together. You know, father-and-son like."

"What are you doing here?" Adam demanded, panting to catch his breath while his adrenaline pumped at the sight of Michael Dawson.

"I was helping Amelia with a few things," Dawson explained. "But that's not important now. Point is, I couldn't leave California without saying hello to you, too."

"I assure you, it wasn't necessary." Adam's face searched Dawson's in the dark: Was he serious? Had he really been working with Amelia?

"Still, it didn't seem fair to help one twin without helping the other." He pulled a brown manila envelope from behind his back, where he'd had it tucked into the band of his shorts. "Sorry it's a bit sweaty: You run faster than I expected."

Adam looked at the envelope but made no move to accept it.

"Oh, come on. Take the damn thing," his former foster father urged, grabbing his hand and putting the envelope into it. "I owe it to you."

"Amelia'd never use what's in here. But men find more relief in revenge than kindness."

Adam didn't know how to respond, so he didn't.

"Good luck to you, son." Dawson reached out his hand, but when Adam left it hanging, he gripped his shoulder affectionately before jogging off.

Adam looked at the envelope in his hand for a solid minute before turning and walking back to SAE. He put the envelope on his desk and went to dinner. He came back to his room and logged in to his Netflix account and watched three episodes of *Arrested Development*, intermittently glancing at the envelope as if to see if it had moved.

He opened his history textbook and looked at the syllabus and closed it again when he discovered how far behind he was.

He logged in to Facebook and opened his friend requests and deleted the spam requests from people whose names were in non-Roman-alphabet languages. Except the ones from hot women, which he accepted. Just because he couldn't read their names didn't mean he couldn't appreciate their beauty. Especially now that Violet was gone. Or had never really been there.

Finally, at 12:32 A.M., Adam picked up the envelope and brought it to his bed. What was he so afraid of? It was probably all stuff he knew already.

He opened the seal and pulled out a thin stack of papers. On top was a photo of Violet and Ted, in a restaurant. Adam's chest burned. He put down the stack and went into his roommate's room, where he found a bottle of vodka and poured himself a generous glass before returning to his bed.

He read through years of legal documents and receipts, covered with Post-it notes and highlighted by Michael Dawson to indicate what was important for Adam to know. The first documents, from two years earlier, were about Gibly. Adam couldn't make sense of why Dawson gave him this information until he saw that a contract regarding Gibly's user data was signed by Ted Bristol and countersigned by Violet Weatherford. Soon it all came into focus: It was Violet who had Ted create the secret Gibly database for VIPER. It was Violet who convinced Ted Bristol to do so by promising a highly priced acquisition of Gibly that would solidify Ted Bristol's reputation in Silicon Valley lore.

And then, shortly after the Gibly deal fell apart, the Gibly documents stopped and Adam found e-mails between Ted, Violet, and Ted's accountant, Stuart Chen.

Adam felt like throwing up—not from the vodka he was liberally drinking but from the reality of what his life had become. Ted hired Violet as a consultant to help him with "new acquisitions" and "business development" involving Doreye. This was last summer, before Hawaii, before RemoteX, and before Adam and Violet's "relationship." They'd been manipulating Adam all along. Adam going to PKC for funding, Adam firing Amelia, Adam falling for Violet, Adam selling the data—it was all part of Ted's plan.

Why did Dawson give me this? Adam wondered as he continued through the folder. It felt like cruel flagellation, nothing else. And it didn't accomplish anything except confirming for the thousandth time that Adam was more of a loser than he'd ever thought humanly possible.

He flipped through the remaining pages. E-mail after e-mail exchange about "Adam Dory" that made him more and more sick. He could take some cold comfort in the fact that Violet was in jail, but Ted? Ted was getting off, and it made Adam furious.

He shook his head in disgust and reached for the envelope to put the papers back. But when he did, a smaller envelope fell out of the larger one. He slowly opened it. There were three sheets of paper, showing Ted Bristol's holdings in Gibly, an increase in those holdings with a different date, and a note outlining how Ted used all his assets to purchase shares from his venture partners before the announcement of a major event.

"This is called <u>insider trading</u>," was scribbled across a Post-it note found on the last page, in Dawson's handwriting.

Adam held the papers in his hand and looked out the window, where the setting moon was suspended above a palm tree, silhouetted by the dawn light.

The warm sensation of real, rightful purpose spread through his veins. He pulled his MacBook onto his lap and did a Google search for the Securities and Exchange Commission. He found a link titled "Report suspicious activity," and clicked to open a blank e-mail. He scanned the evidence Dawson gave him into his computer. His hands were shaking as he typed out Ted Bristol's illegal maneuvers and prepared to hit "Send."

His cursor hovered over the button, but his brain focused on Lisa. If he did this—if he sent this report and she found out—it was over. Really, really, no-going-back-to-the-way-things-were over.

He moved his cursor to shut the browser, closed his laptop, and turned out the light, slamming his face into the pillow. So what if he didn't have his sister's courage? Maybe relationships were more important than always being right.

He turned on his iPhone and opened the message app to the text he had previously composed to Amelia.

He took a deep breath and hit "Send."

"Thank you," it said.

66

Final Contract

It was early in the morning and Amelia's phone lit up from its spot next to her laptop on the table at University Café. Her heart swelled as she read Adam's name. *"Thank you,"* it said simply, and that was just enough.

"(-:" she typed back, wondering if an emoticon had ever carried so much weight before.

The recoding had worked in the end. Patty had called Laurent in Paris and pretended to be a radio-show host, claiming he was the winner of a sweepstakes but that to collect the prize he had to come to the station's studio across town immediately. Patty grinned with pride when she recounted the conversation to Amelia and the two giggled imagining poor Laurent's face when he showed up at the address Patty had given him, an old stocking factory buried in Montmartre.

Dawson had packed his bags and left Palo Alto. He and Amelia exchanged a meaningful hug before he boarded the bus, the first time she could ever remember hugging him. She still didn't trust Dawson, but her heart felt lighter somehow, like the whole sequence of events had freed some part of her soul.

And it felt good to be back in the real world, no longer sneaking around and hiding and pretending she wasn't there. She'd e-mailed T-Bag and they planned to meet up for drinks and ZOS-TRA tonight in the LAIR. She was trying not to get her hopes up, but suspected he was corralling a group of her friends for a surprise party and was secretly giddy with excitement. She also hoped, desperately, that T.J. would be there.

It was too late to reenroll in classes this term, but she'd go by the registrar's office on Monday to see what her options were for summer classes.

As for Doreye: She still had to figure out how to get ownership away from Ted Bristol, but for now her worst fears about what he would do with the company were appeased. Violet had been extradited, and Amelia knew Adam wouldn't try to sell user data again. The other piece could wait until next week.

For now, she was back in University Café working on a new array she'd dreamed about last night during a fifteen-hour nap in Patty's parents' pool house, where she was recovering from two weeks of perpetual all-nighters.

A gust of cold tickled her bare toes as the door to the café opened.

"Amelia." T.J. appeared in the seat opposite her. His eyes were bright and he leaned so far across the table she could smell his spearmint breath and the spice of his cologne. "Amelia," he said, folding her laptop and putting it to the side, reaching across the table to take her hands in his.

"T.J.—" she started, feeling her heart push up into her throat and her hands start shaking in his. They'd talked about Doreye during the whole meltdown, but she hadn't seen him since the day she left for Tahoe, even if the thought of his face had been hung like a picture frame in her brain the whole time. His rugged jawline was covered in stubble and his blue eyes sparkled. The muscles around his eyes tensed and released as he spoke, looking straight at her with his speckled eyes. Everything in her body tingled.

"Amelia," he said, smiling helplessly, "Amelia, marry me."

She opened her mouth but nothing came out. Was she dreaming? Yes, she must be: Everything about this felt significantly less real than anything about T.J. she'd allowed herself to imagine. "What?" she finally croaked.

"Marry me." He said it again. "Be my . . . wife."

She shook her head in confusion, and he gripped her hands more tightly. "T.J., I—"

"Amelia, I know it sounds crazy but . . ." He laughed. His voice was giddy with excitement to the point where she thought he might be unstable. "If you marry me, you get Doreye back."

She let out a sob. *No no no,* she screamed inside. *Why do you let yourself think it's something else when it's always, always about Doreye? That is the only thing he sees you for.*

She swallowed and tried to wind back her emotions, saying as calmly as she could, "What are you talking about?"

"You were right. My dad used my trust fund to buy Doreye. *My* trust owns fifty-one percent of *your* company. But I don't get control of the trust, and therefore control of Doreye, until I turn forty or . . ."

"Or what?"

"I get married," he said as though it were obvious. She stared, not comprehending. "My mother," he said, laughing, "my crazy mother put it in because she was afraid I'd need it before I turned forty—if I had kids or whatever—but they couldn't change the age, so they put this clause in that says if I'm legally married I get to take control. I guess that makes me responsible or something." He laughed again, as though it were totally unserious.

"T.J., you can't just . . ."

"Stop it, Amelia." He put his finger on her lip, sending a chill down her spine. "We've got to get married," T.J. repeated calmly. He'd clearly already thought this whole thing through and nothing about it seemed odd anymore.

Amelia adjusted her glasses and peered at him. Were his eyes bright because he was on drugs? "T.J., getting married is a really big deal." The word made her head flood with all the images she associated with her wedding day. Not that she was the kind of girl who read wedding magazines and plotted out all the details, but she couldn't help imagining being swept off her feet, wearing a white dress and a ring that reminded her someone loved her.

"It *is* a big deal," T.J. chirped happily, moving from the chair to kneel on one knee before her on the floor. "That's why it's lucky for me you're the most amazing person I know."

T.J. pulled a ring box out of his pocket. A flash from someone's camera phone went off behind him and Amelia realized everyone in the café was staring.

He opened the ring box to reveal a small round-cut diamond, then paused, wanting to say the next words perfectly. "Amelia Dory, will you marry me?"

Amelia was dumbfounded. She looked at him with mouth agape. Someone at the coffee bar shouted, "Aw, don't leave the guy hanging."

"Please get up," she whispered.

"Not until you agree to be my wife."

"I can't . . . I mean . . ." She pinched her earlobe. He was so beautiful, and so smart, and so considerate and so . . . "Marriage is a really big deal," she repeated.

"I know that." T.J. nodded. "But I also know I care about you and I respect you and I . . ." He paused. "And you respect me," he said instead, "at least I hope you do. I know we started off on a strange foot a year ago, but now we've been through so much together—I think we can get through *anything* together."

Amelia pulled her hand from him and turned to start collecting her things. She couldn't handle this. Not now.

"Amelia, wait," he said. "This is the first thing I've ever done that actually feels right. Let me do right by you. I'll give you the company back and I'll . . . I'll take care of you."

She shook her head. "What about all your other girlfriends?"

"I don't need—I don't *want* them anymore," he said. "It only has to be a year," he said, his voice sounding more guarded, "for me to be able to transfer everything to you. I mean, you only have to stay married to me for a year if that's what you're worried about."

"A year?" Amelia pinched her earlobe again.

"Yeah, but—"

"But what?"

"But I . . ." He shook his head as if he couldn't believe he was saying it. "I guess I wouldn't mind if it's longer than that."

Her heart shot back into her throat. "You wouldn't?" she tried.

He shook his head and grinned helplessly, as if the words were a relief to finally admit. Sensing the beating of her heart, he stood up and lifted Amelia out of her chair, taking her face in his hands. His lips weren't even two inches from her own.

"Say something," he pleaded.

Amelia felt buoyant tears brim on her eyelids. She thought about Roger telling her not to let them see her cry—when the reporters harassed her about her past, when Adam fired her, when the whole company seemed doomed—but these tears, she knew, were okay. These were tears of happiness, and she felt her whole heart sing with thanks and joy and love and the feeling that everything was going to be okay. Amelia looked into T.J.'s eyes, opened her mouth, and heard her voice enter the room.

"Yes."